# THE WORKS

## OF

# JAMES FENIMORE COOPER

## HOMEWARD BOUND

### OR

## THE CHASE

G. P. PUTNAM'S SONS

NEW YORK
27 WEST TWENTY THIRD STREET

LONDON
24 BEDFORD STREET, STRAND

The Knickerbocker Press
1896

# PREFACE.

IN one respect, this book is a parallel to Franklin's well-known apologue of the hatter and his sign. It was commenced with a sole view to exhibit the present state of society in the United States, through the agency, in part, of a set of characters with different peculiarities, who had freshly arrived from Europe, and to whom the distinctive features of the country would be apt to present themselves with greater force, than to those who had never lived beyond the influence of the things portrayed. By the original plan, the work was to open at the threshold of the country, or with the arrival of the travellers at Sandy Hook, from which point the tale was to have been carried regularly forward to its conclusion. But a consultation with others has left little more of this plan than the hatter's friends left of his sign. As a vessel was introduced in the first chapter, the cry was for "more ship," until the work has become "all ship"; it actually closing at, or near, the spot where it was originally intended it should commence. Owing to this diversion from the author's design—a design that lay at the bottom of all his projects—a necessity has been created of running the tale through two separate works, or of making a hurried and insufficient conclusion. The former scheme has, consequently, been adopted.

It is hoped that the interest of the narrative will not be essentially diminished by this arrangement.

There will be, very likely, certain imaginative persons, who will feel disposed to deny that every minute event mentioned in these volumes ever befell one and the same ship, though ready enough to admit that they may very well have occurred to several different ships ; a mode of commenting that is much in favor with your small critic. To this objection, we shall make but a single answer. The cavalier, if any there should prove to be, is challenged to produce the log-book of the Montauk London packet, and if it should be found to contain a single sentence to controvert any one of our statements or facts, a frank recantation shall be made. Captain Truck is quite as well known in New York as in London or Portsmouth, and to him also we refer with confidence, for a confirmation of all we have said, with the exception, perhaps, of the little occasional touches of character that may allude directly to himself. In relation to the latter, Mr. Leach, and particularly Mr. Saunders, are both invoked as unimpeachable witnesses.

Most of our readers will probably know that all which appears in a New York journal is not necessarily as true as the gospel. As some slight deviations from the facts accidentally occur, though doubtless at very long intervals, it should not be surprising that they sometimes omit circumstances that are quite as veracious as anything they do actually utter to the world. No argument, therefore, can justly be urged against the incidents of this story, on account of the circumstance of their not being embodied in the regular marine news of the day.

Another serious objection on the part of the American reader to this work is foreseen. The author has endeavored to interest his readers in occurrences of a date as antiquated as two years can make them, when he is quite aware, that, in order to keep pace with a state of society in which there was no yesterday, it would have been much safer to anticipate things, by laying his scene two years in advance. It is hoped, however, that the public sentiment will not be outraged by this glimpse at antiquity, and this the more so, as the sequel of the tale will bring down events within a year of the present moment.

Previously to the appearance of that sequel, however, it may be well to say a few words concerning the fortunes of some of our characters, as it might be *en attendant.*

To commence with the most important: the Montauk herself, once deemed so "splendid" and convenient, is already supplanted in the public favor by a new ship; the reign of a popular packet, a popular preacher, or a popular anything else, in America, being limited, by a national *esprit de corps*, to a time materially shorter than that of a lustre. This, however, is no more than just; rotation in favor being as evidently a matter of constitutional necessity, as rotation in office.

Captain Truck, for a novelty, continues popular, a circumstance that he himself ascribes to the fact of his being still a bachelor.

Toast is promoted, figuring at the head of a pantry quite equal to that of his great master, who regards his improvement with some such eyes as Charles the Twelfth of Sweden regarded that of his great rival Peter, after the affair of Pultowa.

Mr. Leach now smokes his own cigar, and issues his own orders from a monkey rail, his place in the line being supplied by his former "Dickey." He already speaks of his great model, as of one a little antiquated, it is true, but as a man who had merit in his time, though it was not the particular merit that is in fashion to-day.

Notwithstanding these little changes, which are perhaps inseparable from the events of a period so long as two years in a country so energetic as America, and in which nothing seems to be stationary but the ages of Tontine nominees and three-life leases, a cordial esteem was created among the principal actors in the events of this book, which is likely to outlast the passage, and which will not fail to bring most of them together again in the sequel.

*April,* 1838.

# HOMEWARD BOUND.

## CHAPTER I.

"An inner room I have,
Where thou shalt rest and some refreshment take,
And then we will more fully talk of this."

ORRA.

THE coast of England, though infinitely finer than our own, is more remarkable for its verdure, and for a general appearance of civilization, than for its natural beauties. The chalky cliffs may seem bold and noble to the American, though compared to the granite piles that buttress the Mediterranean they are but mole-hills; and the travelled eye seeks beauties instead, in the retiring vales, the leafy hedges, and the clustering towns that dot the teeming island. Neither is Portsmouth a very favorable specimen of a British port, considered solely in reference to the picturesque. A town situated on a humble point, and fortified after the manner of the Low Countries, with an excellent haven, suggests more images of the useful than of the pleasing; while a background of modest receding hills offers little beyond the verdant swales of the country. In this respect England itself has the fresh beauty of youth, rather than the mellowed hues of a more advanced period of life; or it might be better to say, it has the young freshness and retiring sweetness that distinguish her females, as compared with the warmer tints of Spain and Italy, and which, women and landscape alike, need the near view to be appreciated.

Some such thoughts as these passed through the mind of the traveller who stood on the deck of the packet Montauk, resting an elbow on the quarter-deck rail, as he contemplated the view of the coast that stretched before him, east and west, for leagues. The manner in which this gentleman, whose temples were sprinkled with gray hairs, regarded the scene, denoted more of the thoughtfulness of experience, and of tastes improved by observation, than it is usual to meet amid the bustling and commonplace characters that compose the majority in almost every situation of life. The calmness of his exterior, an air removed equally from the admiration of the novice, and the superciliousness of the tyro, had, indeed, so strongly distinguished him from the moment he embarked in London to that in which he was now seen in the position mentioned, that several of the seamen swore he was a man-of-war's-man in disguise. The fair-haired, lovely, blue-eyed girl at his side, too, seemed a softened reflection of all his sentiment, intelligence, knowledge, tastes, and cultivation, united to the artlessness and simplicity that became her sex and years.

"We have seen nobler coasts, Eve," said the gentleman, pressing the arm that leaned on his own ; "but, after all, England will always be fair to American eyes."

"More particularly so if those eyes first opened to the light in the eighteenth century, father."

"You, at least, my child, have been educated beyond the reach of national foibles, whatever may have been my own evil fortune ; and still, I think even you have seen a great deal to admire in this country, as well as in this coast."

Eve Effingham glanced a moment towards the eye of her father, and perceiving that he spoke in playfulness, without suffering a cloud to shadow a countenance that usually varied with her emotions, she continued the discourse, which had, in fact, only been resumed by the remark first mentioned.

"I have been educated, as it is termed, in so many different places and countries," returned Eve, smiling, "that I sometimes fancy I was born a woman, like my great predecessor and namesake, the mother of Abel. If a congress of nations, in the way of masters, can make one independent of prejudice, I may claim to possess the advantage. My greatest fear is, that in acquiring liberality, I have acquired nothing else."

Mr. Effingham turned a look of parental fondness, in which parental pride was clearly mingled, on the face of his daughter, and said with his eyes, though his tongue did not second the expression, "This is a fear, sweet one, that none besides thyself would feel."

"A congress of nations, truly!" muttered another male voice near the father and daughter. "You have been taught music in general, by seven masters of as many different states, besides the touch of the guitar by a Spaniard; Greek by a German; the living tongues by the European powers; and philosophy by seeing the world: and now, with a brain full of learning, fingers full of touches, eyes full of tints, and a person full of grace, your father is taking you back to America, to 'waste your sweetness on the desert air.'"

"Poetically expressed, if not justly imagined, cousin Jack," returned the laughing Eve; "but you have forgot to add, 'and a heart full of feeling for the land of my birth.'"

"We shall see, in the end."

"In the end, as in the beginning, now and forevermore."

"All love is eternal in the commencement."

"Do you make no allowance for the constancy of woman? Think you that a girl of twenty can forget the country of her birth, the land of her forefathers or, as you call it yourself when in a good humor, the land of liberty?"

"A pretty specimen you will have of its liberty!" returned the cousin, sarcastically. "After having passed a girlhood of wholesome restraint in the rational society of Europe, you are about to return home to the slavery of American female life, just as you are about to be married!"

"Married! Mr. Effingham?"

"I suppose the catastrophe will arrive, sooner or later; and it is more likely to occur to a girl of twenty than to a girl of ten."

"Mr. John Effingham never lost an argument for the

want of a convenient fact, my love," the father observed, by
way of bringing the brief discussion to a close. "But here
are the boats approaching ; let us withdraw a little, and
examine the chance medley of faces with which we are to
become familiar by the intercourse of a month."

"You will be much more likely to agree on a verdict of
murder," muttered the kinsman.

Mr. Effingham led his daughter into the hurricane-house
—or, as the packet-men quaintly term it, the coach-house,
where they stood watching the movements on the quarter-
deck for the next half-hour ; an interval of which we shall
take advantage to touch in a few of the stronger lights of
our picture, leaving the softer tints and the shadows to be
discovered by the manner in which the artist "tells the
story."

Edward and John Effingham were brothers' children ;
were born on the same day ; had passionately loved the
same woman, who had preferred the first-named, and died
soon after Eve was born ; had, notwithstanding this collision
in feeling, remained sincere friends, and this the more so,
probably, from a mutual and natural sympathy in their
common loss ; had lived much together at home, and
travelled much together abroad, and were now about to
return in company to the land of their birth, after what
might be termed an absence of twelve years ; though both
had visited America for short periods in the intervals,—
John not less than five times.

There was a strong family likeness between the cousins,
their persons and even features being almost identical ;
though it was scarcely possible for two human beings to
leave more opposite impressions on mere casual spectators
when seen separately. Both were tall, of commanding
presence, and handsome ; while one was winning in appearance, and the other, if not positively forbidding, at least
distant and repulsive. The noble outline of face in Edward
Effingham had got to be cold severity in that of John ; the
aquiline nose of the latter, seeming to possess an eagle-like
and hostile curvature,—his compressed lip, sarcastic and
cold expression, and the fine classical chin, a feature in

which so many of the Saxon race fail, a haughty scorn that caused strangers usually to avoid him. Eve drew with great facility and truth; and she had an eye, as her cousin had rightly said, "full of tints." Often and often had she sketched both of these loved faces, and never without wondering wherein that strong difference existed in nature which she had never been able to impart to her drawings. The truth is, that the subtle character of John Effingham's face would have puzzled the skill of one who had made the art his study for a life, and it utterly set the graceful but scarcely profound knowledge of the beautiful young painter at defiance. All the points of character that rendered her father so amiable and so winning, and which were rather felt than perceived, in his cousin were salient and bold, and, if it may be thus expressed, had become indurated by mental suffering and disappointment.

The cousins were both rich, though in ways as opposite as their dispositions and habits of thought. Edward Effingham possessed a large hereditary property, that brought a good income, and which attached him to this world of ours by kindly feelings toward its land and water; while John, much the wealthier of the two, having inherited a large commercial fortune, did not own ground enough to bury him. As he sometimes deridingly said, he "kept his gold in corporations, that were as soulless as himself."

Still, John Effingham was a man of cultivated mind, of extensive intercourse with the world, and of manners that varied with the occasion: or perhaps it were better to say, with his humors. In all these particulars but the latter the cousins were alike; Edward Effingham's deportment being as equal as his temper, though he was also distinguished for a knowledge of society.

These gentlemen had embarked at London, on their fiftieth birthday, in the packet of the 1st of October, bound to New York; the lands and family residence of the proprietor lying in the State of that name, of which all of the parties were natives. It is not usual for the cabin passengers of the London packets to embark in the docks; but Mr. Effingham,—as we shall call the father in general, to distinguish him from the bachelor, John—as an old and experienced traveller, had determined to make his daughter familiar with the peculiar odors of the vessel in smooth water, as a protection against seasickness ; a malady, however, from which she proved to be singularly exempt in the end. They had, accordingly, been on board three days, when the ship came to an anchor off Portsmouth, the point where the remainder of the passengers were to join her on that particular day when the scene of this tale commences.

At this precise moment, then, the Montauk was lying at a single anchor, not less than a league from the land, in a flat calm, with her three topsails loose, the courses in the brails, and with all those signs of preparation about her that are so bewildering to landsmen, but which seamen comprehend as clearly as words. The captain had no other business there than to take on board the wayfarers, and to renew his supply of fresh meat and vegetables ; things of so familiar import on shore as to be seldom thought of until missed, but which swell into importance during a passage of a month's duration. Eve had employed her three days of probation quite usefully, having, with the exception of the two gentlemen, the officers of the vessel, and one other person, been in quiet possession of all the ample, not to say luxurious, cabins. It is true, she had a female attendant ; but to her she had been accustomed from childhood, and Nanny Sidley, as her quondam nurse and actual lady's-maid was termed, appeared so much a part of herself, that, while her absence would be missed almost as greatly as that of a limb, her presence was as much a matter of course as a hand or foot. Nor will a passing word concerning this excellent and faithful domestic be thrown away, in the brief preliminary explanations we are making.

Ann Sidley was one of those excellent creatures who, it is the custom with the European travellers to say, do not exist at all in America, and who, while they are certainly less numerous than could be wished, have no superiors in the world, in their way. She had been born a servant, lived a servant, and was quite content to die a servant,—

and this, too, in one and the same family. We shall not
enter into a philosophical examination of the reasons that
had induced old Ann to feel certain she was in the precise
situation to render her more happy than any other that to
her was attainable; but feel it she did, as John Effingham
used to express it, " from the crown of her head to the sole
of her foot." She had passed through infancy, childhood,
girlhood, up to womanhood, *pari passu* with the mother of
Eve, having been the daughter of a gardener, who died in
the service of the family, and had heart enough to feel that
the mixed relations of civilized society, when properly understood and appreciated, are more pregnant of happiness than
the vulgar scramble and heart burnings that, in the *mêlée* of
a migrating and unsettled population, are so injurious to
the grace and principles of American life. At the death
of Eve's mother, she had transferred her affections to the
child ; and twenty years of assiduity and care had brought
her to feel as much tenderness for her lovely young charge
as if she had been her natural parent. But Nanny Sidley
was better fitted to care for the body than the mind of
Eve; and when, at the age of ten, the latter was placed
under the control of an accomplished governess, the good
woman had meekly and quietly sunk the duties of the nurse
in those of the maid.

One of the severest trials—or "crosses," as she herself
termed it—that poor Nanny had ever experienced, was
endured when Eve began to speak in a language she could
not herself comprehend ; for, in despite of the best intentions
in the world, and twelve years of use, the good woman could
never make anything of the foreign tongues her young
charge was so rapidly acquiring. One day, when Eve had
been maintaining an animated and laughing discourse in
Italian with her instructress, Nanny, unable to command
herself, had actually caught the child to her bosom, and,
bursting into tears, implored her not to estrange herself
entirely from her poor old nurse. The caresses and solicitations of Eve soon brought the good woman to a sense of her
weakness ; but the natural feeling was so strong, that it
required years of close observation to reconcile her to the

thousand excellent qualities of Mademoiselle Viefville, the lady to whose superintendence the education of Miss Effingham had been finally confided.

This Mademoiselle Viefville was also among the passengers, and was the one other person who now occupied the cabins in common with Eve and her friends. She was the daughter of a French officer who had fallen in Napoleon's campaigns, had been educated at one of those most admirable establishments which form points of relief in the ruthless history of the conqueror, and had now lived long enough to have educated two young persons, the last of whom was Eve Effingham. Twelve years of close communion with her *élève* had created sufficient attachment to cause her to yield to the solicitations of the father to accompany his daughter to America, and to continue with her during the first year of her probation, in a state of society that the latter felt must be altogether novel to a young woman educated as his own child had been.

So much has been written and said of French governesses, that we shall not anticipate the subject, but leave this lady to speak and act for herself in the course of the narrative. Neither is it our intention to be very minute in these introductory remarks concerning any of our characters; but having thus traced their outlines, we shall return again to the incidents as they occurred, trusting to make the reader better acquainted with all the parties as we proceed.

# CHAPTER II.

"Lord Cram and Lord Vultur,
Sir Brandish O'Cultur,
With Marshall Carouzer,
And old Lady Mouser."

*Bath Guide.*

THE assembling of the passengers of a packet-ship is at all times a matter of interest to the parties concerned. During the western passage in particular, which can never safely be set down at less than a month, there is the prospect of being shut up for the whole of that period, within the narrow compass of a ship, with those whom chance has brought together, influenced by all the accidents and caprices of personal character, and a difference of nations, conditions in life, and education. The quarter-deck, it is true, forms a sort of local distinction, and the poor creatures in the steerage seem the rejected of Providence for the time being ; but all who know life will readily comprehend that the *pêle-mêle* of the cabins can seldom offer anything very enticing to people of refinement and taste. Against this evil, however, there is one particular source of relief ; most persons feeling a disposition to yield to the circumstances in which they are placed, with the laudable and convenient desire to render others comfortable, in order that they may be made comfortable themselves.

A man of the world and a gentleman, Mr. Effingham had looked forward to this passage with a good deal of concern, on account of his daughter, while he shrank with the sensitiveness of his habits from the necessity of exposing one of her delicacy and plastic simplicity to the intercourse of a

ship. Accompanied by Mademoiselle Viefville, watched
over by Nanny, and guarded by himself and his kinsman,
he had lost some of his apprehensions on the subject during
the three probationary days, and now took his stand in the
centre of his own party to observe the new arrivals, with
something of the security of a man who is intrenched in his
own doorway.

The place they occupied, at a window of the hurricane-
house, did not admit of a view of the water; but it was
sufficiently evident from the preparations in the gangway
next the land, that boats were so near as to render that
unnecessary.

"*Genus*, cockney; *species*, bagman," muttered John
Effingham, as the first arrival touched the deck. "That
worthy has merely exchanged the basket of a coach for the
deck of a packet; we may now learn the price of buttons."

It did not require a naturalist to detect the species of the
stranger, in truth; though John Effingham had been a little
more minute in his description than was warranted by the
fact. The person in question was one of those mercantile
agents that England scatters so profusely over the world,
some of whom have all the most sterling qualities of their
nation, though a majority, perhaps, are a little disposed to
mistake the value of other people as well as their own.
This was the *genus*, as John Effingham had expressed it;
but the *species* will best appear on dissection. The master
of the ship saluted this person cordially, and as an old
acquaintance, by the name of Monday.

"A *mousquetaire* resuscitated," said Mademoiselle Viefville, in her broken English, as one who had come in the
same boat as the first-named thrust his whiskered and mus-
tached visage above the rail of the gangway.

"More probably a barber, who has converted his own
head into a wig-block," growled John Effingham.

"It cannot, surely, be Wellington in disguise!" added
Mr. Effingham, with a sarcasm of manner that was quite
unusual for him.

"Or a peer of the realm in his robes!" whispered Eve,
who was much amused with the elaborate toilet of the sub-

ject of their remarks, who descended the ladder supported
by a sailor, and, after speaking to the master, was formally
presented to his late boat-companion, as Sir George Templemore. The two bustled together about the quarter-deck
for a few minutes, using eye-glasses, which led them into
several scrapes by causing them to hit their legs against
sundry objects they might otherwise have avoided, though
both were much too high-bred to betray feelings—or fancied
they were, which answered the same purpose.

After these flourishes, the new-comers descended to the
cabin in company, not without pausing to survey the party
in the hurricane-house, more especially Eve, who, to old
Ann's great scandal, was the subject of their manifest and
almost avowed admiration and observation.

"One is rather glad to have such a relief against the
tediousness of a sea-passage," said Sir George, as they went
down the ladder. "No doubt you are used to this sort of
thing, Mr. Monday; but with me, it is voyage the first,—
that is, if I except the Channel and the seas one encounters
in making the usual run on the Continent."

"O, dear me! I go and come as regularly as the equinoxes, Sir George, which you know is quite, in rule, once a
year. I call my passages the equinoxes, too, for I religiously make it a practice to pass just twelve hours out of
the twenty-four in my berth."

This was the last the party on deck heard of the opinions
of the two worthies, for the time being; nor would they
have been favored with all this, had not Mr. Monday what
he thought a rattling way with him, which caused him
usually to speak in an octave above everyone else. Although their voices were nearly mute, or rather lost to those
above, they were heard knocking about in their state-rooms;
and Sir George, in particular, as frequently called out for
the steward, by the name of "Saunders," as Mr. Monday
made similar appeals to the steward's assistant for succor,
by the appropriate appellation of "Toast."

"I think we may safely claim this person, at least, for a
countryman," said John Effingham: "he is what I have
heard termed an American in a European mask."

"The character is more ambitiously conceived than skilfully maintained," replied Eve, who had need of all her *retenue* of manner to abstain from laughing outright. "Were I to hazard a conjecture, it would be to describe the gentleman as a collector of costumes, who had taken a fancy to exhibit an assortment of his riches on his own person. Mademoiselle Viefville, you who so well understand costumes, may tell us from what countries the separate parts of that attire have been collected?"

"I can answer for the shop in Berlin where the travelling cap was purchased," returned the amused governess; "in no other part of the world can a parallel be found."

"I should think, ma'am," put in Nanny, with the quiet simplicity of her nature as well as of her habits, "that the gentleman must have bought his boots in Paris, for they seem to pinch his feet, and all the Paris boots and shoes pinch one's feet,—at least, all mine did."

"The watch-guard is stamped 'Geneva,'" continued Eve. "The coat comes from Frankfort: *c'est une équivoque.*" "And the pipe from Dresden, Mademoiselle Viefville."

"The *conchiglia* savors of Rome, and the little chain annexed bespeaks the Rialto, while the *moustaches* are anything but *indigènes*; and the *tout ensemble*, the world: the man is travelled, at least."

Eve's eyes sparkled with humor as she said this: while the new passenger, who had been addressed as Mr. Dodge, and as an old acquaintance also, by the captain, came so near them as to admit of no further comments. A short conversation between the two soon let the listeners into the secret that the traveller had come from America in the spring, whither, after having made the tour of Europe, he was about to return in the autumn.

"Seen enough, ha!" added the captain, with a friendly nod of the head, when the other had finished a brief summary of his proceedings in the eastern hemisphere. "All eyes, and no leisure or inclination for more?"

"I've seen as much as I *warnt* to see," returned the traveller, with an emphasis on, and a pronunciation of, the word we have italicized, that cannot be committed to paper

but which were eloquence itself on the subject of self-satisfaction and self-knowledge.

"Well, that is the main point. When a man has got
all he wants of a thing, any addition is like over-ballast.
Whenever I can get fifteen knots out of the ship, I make it a
point to be satisfied, especially under close-reefed topsails and
on a taut bowline."

The traveller and the master nodded their heads at each
other, like men who understood more than they expressed ;
when the former, after inquiring with marked interest if
his room-mate, Sir George Templemore, had arrived, went
below. An intercourse of three days had established something like an acquaintance between the latter and the passengers he had brought from the River, and turning his red,
quizzical face towards the ladies, he observed with inimitable
gravity,

"There is nothing like understanding when one has
enough, even if it be of knowledge. I never yet met with
the navigator who found two ' noons ' in the same day, that
he was not in danger of shipwreck. Now I dare say, Mr.
Dodge there, who has just gone below, has, as he says, seen
all he *warnts* to see, and it is quite likely he knows more
already than he can cleverly get along with. Let the people be getting the booms on the yards, Mr. Leach ; we shall
be *warnting* to spread our wings before the end of the passage."

As Captain Truck, though he often swore, seldom
laughed, his mate gave the necessary order with a gravity
equal to that with which it had been delivered to him ; and
even the sailors went aloft to execute it with greater alacrity
for an indulgence of humor that was peculiar to their trade,
and which, as few understood it so well, none enjoyed so
much as themselves. As the homeward-bound crew was the
same as the outward-bound, and Mr. Dodge had come abroad
quite as green as he was now going home ripe, this traveller
of six months' finish did not escape divers commentaries
that literally cut him up " from clew to ear-ring," and
which flew about in the rigging much as active birds flutter
from branch to branch in a tree. The subject of all this wit,

however, remained profoundly, not to say happily, ignorant
of the sensation he had produced, being occupied in disposing of the Dresden pipe, the Venetian chain, and the Roman
*conchiglia* in his state-room, and in "instituting an acquaintance," as he expressed it, with his room-mate, Sir George
Templemore.

"We must surely have something better than this," observed Mr. Effingham, "for I observed that two of the
staterooms in the main cabin are taken singly."

In order that the general reader may understand this, it
may be well to explain that the packet-ships have usually
two berths in each state-room, but they who can afford to pay
an extra charge are permitted to occupy the little apartment
singly. It is scarcely necessary to add, that persons of gentlemanly feeling, when circumstances will at all permit, prefer
economizing in other things in order to live by themselves
for the month usually consumed in the passage, since in
nothing is refinement more plainly exhibited than in the
reserve of personal habits.

"There is no lack of vulgar fools stirring with full pockets," rejoined John Effingham : "the two rooms you mention may have been taken by some 'yearling' travellers,
who are little better than the semi-annual *savant* who has
passed us."

"It is at least something, cousin Jack, to have the wishes
of a gentleman."

"It is something, Eve, though it end in wishes, or even
in caricature."

"What are the names?" pleasantly asked Mademoiselle
Viefville ; "the names may be a clue to the characters."

"The papers pinned to the bed-curtains bear the anti-
thetical titles of Mr. Sharp and Mr. Blunt ; though it is
quite probable the first is wanting of a letter or two by
accident, and the last is merely a synonym of the old *nom
de guerre*, 'Cash.' "

"Do persons, then, actually travel with borrowed names, in
our days?" asked Eve, with a little of the curiosity of the
common mother whose name she bore.

"That do they, and with borrowed money too, as well as

in other days.  I dare say, however, these two co-voyagers
of ours will come just as they are, in truth, Sharp enough,
and Blunt enough."

" Are they Americans, think you?"

" They ought to be ; both the qualities being thoroughly
*indigènes*, as Mademoiselle Viefville would say."

" Nay, cousin John, I will bandy words with you no longer ;
for the last twelve months you have done little else than try
to lessen the joyful anticipations with which I return to the
home of my childhood."

"Sweet one, I would not willingly lessen one of thy
young and generous pleasures by any of the alloy of my
own bitterness; but what wilt thou?  A little preparation
for that which is as certain to follow as that the sun succeeds
the dawn, will rather soften the disappointment thou art
doomed to feel."

Eve had only time to cast a look of affectionate gratitude
towards him,  for whilst he spoke tauntingly. he spoke with
a feeling that her experience from childhood had taught her
to appreciate,  ere the arrival of another boat drew the common attention to the gangway.  A call from the officer in at-
tendance had brought the captain to the rail ; and his order
to " Pass in the luggage of Mr. Sharp and Mr. Blunt," was
heard by all near.

" Now for *l s indigèn s*," whispered Mademoiselle Viefville,
with the nervous excitement that is a little apt to betray a
lively expectation in the gentler sex.

Eve smiled ; for there are situations in which trifles help to
awaken interest, and the little that had just passed served to
excite curiosity in the whole party.  Mr. Effingham thought
it a favorable symptom that the master. who had had inter-
views with all his passengers in London, walked to the gangway to receive the new-comers ; for a boat-load of the quarter-
deck *oi polloi* had come on board a moment before without
any other notice on his part than a general bow, with the
usual order to receive their effects.

"The delay denotes Englishmen," the caustic John had
time to throw in, before the silent arrangement of the gangway was interrupted by the appearance of the passengers.

The quiet smile of Mademoiselle Viefville, as the two travellers appeared on deck, denoted approbation, for her practised eye detected at a glance that both were certainly gentlemen. Women are more purely creatures of convention in their way than men, their education inculcating nicer distinctions and discriminations than that of the other sex ; and Eve, who would have studied Sir George Templemore and Mr. Dodge as she would have studied the animals of a caravan, or as creatures with whom she had no affinities, after casting a sly look of curiosity at the two who now appeared on deck, unconsciously averted her eyes, like a well-bred young person in a drawing-room.

" They are indeed English," quietly remarked Mr. Effingham ; "but out of question, English gentlemen."

" The one nearest appears to me to be continental," answered Mademoiselle Viefville, who had not felt the same impulse to avert her look as Eve ; "he is *jamais Anglais !* "

Eve stole a glance in spite of herself, and with the intuitive penetration of a woman, intimated that she had come to the same conclusion. The two strangers were both tall, and decidedly gentleman-like young men, whose personal appearance would cause either to be remarked. The one whom the captain addressed as Mr. Sharp had the most youthful look, his complexion being florid, and his hair light ; though the other was altogether superior in outline of features as well as in expression : indeed, Mademoiselle Viefville fancied she never saw a sweeter smile than that he gave on returning the salute of the deck ; there was more than the common expression of suavity and of the usual play of features in it, for it struck her as being thoughtful, and almost melancholy. His companion was gracious in his manner, and perfectly well toned ; but his demeanor had less of the soul of the man about it, partaking more of the training of the social caste to which it belonged. These may seem to be nice distinctions for the circumstances ; but Mademoiselle Viefville had passed her life in good company, and under responsibilities that had rendered observation and judgment highly necessary, and particularly observations of the other sex.

Each of the strangers had a servant; and while their luggage was passed up from the boat, they walked aft nearer to the hurricane-house, accompanied by the captain. Every American, who is not very familiar with the world, appears to possess the mania of introducing. Captain Truck was no exception to the rule; for, while he was perfectly acquainted with a ship, and knew the etiquette of the quarter-deck to a hair, he got into blue water the moment he approached the finesse of deportment. He was exactly of that school of *élégants* who fancy drinking a glass of wine with another, and introducing, are touches of breeding; it being altogether beyond his comprehension that both have especial uses, and are only to be resorted to on especial occasions. Still, the worthy master, who had begun life on the forecastle, without any previous knowledge of usages, and who had imbibed the notion that "Manners make the man," taken in the narrow sense of the axiom, was a devotee of what he fancied to be good breeding, and one of his especial duties, as he imagined, in order to put his passengers at their ease, was to introduce them to each other; a proceeding which, it is hardly necessary to say, had just a contrary effect with the better class of them.

"You are acquainted, gentlemen?" he said, as the three approached the party in the hurricane-house.

The two travellers endeavored to look interested, while Mr. Sharp carelessly observed that they had met for the first time in the boat. This was delightful intelligence to Captain Truck, who did not lose a moment in turning it to account. Stopping short, he faced his companions, and with a solemn wave of the hand, he went through the ceremonial in which he most delighted, and in which he piqued himself at being an adept.

"Mr. Sharp, permit me to introduce you to Mr. Blunt; Mr. Blunt, let me make you acquainted with Mr. Sharp."

The gentlemen, though taken a little by surprise at the dignity and formality of the captain, touched their hats civilly to each other, and smiled. Eve, not a little amused at the scene, watched the whole procedure; and then she too detected the sweet melancholy of the one expression, and the marble-like irony of the other. It may have been this that caused her to start, though almost imperceptibly, and to color.

"Our turn will come next," muttered John Effingham; "get the grimaces ready."

His conjecture was right; for, hearing his voice without understanding the words, the captain followed up his advantage to his own infinite gratification.

"Gentlemen, Mr. Effingham, Mr. John Effingham,"—every one soon came to make this distinction in addressing the cousins,—"Miss Effingham, Mademoiselle Viefville: Mr. Sharp, Mr. Blunt, ladies; gentlemen, Mr. Blunt, Mr. Sharp."

The dignified bow of Mr. Effingham, as well as the faint and distant smile of Eve, would have repelled any undue familiarity in men of less tone than either of the strangers, both of whom received the unexpected honor like those who felt themselves to be intruders. As Mr. Sharp raised his hat to Eve, however, he held it suspended a moment above his head, and then dropping his arm to its full length, he bowed with profound respect, though distantly. Mr. Blunt was less elaborate in his salute, but as pointed as the circumstances at all required. Both gentlemen were a little struck with the distant hauteur of John Effingham, whose bow, while it fulfilled all the outward forms, was what Eve used laughingly to term "imperial." The bustle of preparation, and the certainty that there would be no want of opportunities to renew the intercourse, prevented more than the general salutations, and the new-comers descended to their state-rooms.

"Did you remark the manner in which those people took my introduction?" asked Captain Truck of his chief mate, whom he was training up in the ways of packet-politeness, as one in the road of preferment. "Now, to my notion, they might have shook hands at least. That's what I call *Vattel*."

"One sometimes falls in with what are *rum* chaps," returned the other, who, from following the London trade, had caught a few cockneyisms. "If a man chooses to keep

his hands in the beckets, why let him, say I ; but I take it
as a slight to the company to sheer out of the usual track in
such matters."

" I was thinking as much myself; but after all, what can
packet-masters do in such a case?  We can set luncheon
and dinner before the passengers, but we can't make them
eat.  Now, my rule is, when a gentleman introduces me, to
do the thing handsomely, and to return shake for shake, if
it is three times three ; but as for a touch of the beaver, it
is like setting a topgallant-sail in passing a ship at sea,
and means just nothing at all.  Who would know a vessel
because he has let run his halyards and swayed the yard
up again?  One would do as much to a Turk for manners'
sake.  No, no ! there is something in this, and d——n me,
just to make sure of it, the first good opportunity that
offers, I 'll—ay, I 'll just introduce them all over again !
Let the people ship their handspikes, Mr. Leach, and heave
in the slack of the chain.  Ay, ay !  I 'll take an opportunity when all hands are on deck, and introduce them,
ship-shape, one by one, as your greenhorns go through a
lubber's-hole, or we shall have no friendship during the
passage."

The mate nodded approbation, as if the other had hit
upon the right expedient, and then he proceeded to obey
the orders, while the cares of his vessel soon drove the
subject temporarily from the mind of his commander.

# CHAPTER III.

" By all description, this should be the place.
Who 's here? Speak, ho! No answer! What is this ? "
*Timon of Athens.*

A SHIP with her sails loosened and her ensign
abroad is always a beautiful object; and the
Montauk, a noble New York built vessel of seven
hundred tons' burden, was a first-class specimen
of the "kettle-bottom" school of naval architecture, wanting in nothing that the taste and experience of the day can
supply. The scene that was now acting before their eyes
therefore soon diverted the thoughts of Mademoiselle Viefville and Eve from the introductions of the captain, both
watching with intense interest the various movements of
the crew and passengers as they passed in review.

A crowd of well-dressed, but of an evidently humbler
class of persons than those farther aft, were thronging the
gangways, little dreaming of the physical suffering they
were to endure before they reached the land of promise,—
that distant America, towards which the poor and oppressed
of nearly all nations turn longing eyes in quest of a shelter.
Eve saw with wonder aged men and women among them ;
beings who were about to sever most of the ties of the
world, in order to obtain relief from the physical pains and
privations that had borne hard on them for more than
threescore years. A few had made sacrifices of themselves
in obedience to that mysterious instinct which man feels in
his offspring ; while others, again, went rejoicing, flushed
with the hope of their vigor and youth. Some, the victims
of their vices, had embarked in the idle expectation that a
change of scene, with increased means of indulgence, could

produce a healthful change of character. All had views
that the truth would have dimmed, and, perhaps, no single
adventurer among the emigrants collected in that ship entertained either sound or reasonable notions of the mode in
which his step was to be rewarded, though many may meet
with a success that will surpass their brightest picture of
the future. More, no doubt, were to be disappointed.

Reflections something like these passed through the mind
of Eve Effingham, as she examined the mixed crowd, in
which some were busy in receiving stores from boats;
others in holding party conferences with friends, in which a
few were weeping : here and there a group was drowning
reflection in the parting cup ; while wondering children
looked up with anxiety into the well-known faces, as if
fearful they might lose the countenances they loved, and
the charities on which they habitually relied, in such a
*mêlée*.

Although the stern discipline which separates the cabin
and steerage passengers into castes as distinct as those of
the Hindoos had not yet been established, Captain Truck
had too profound a sense of his duty to permit the quarter-
deck to be unceremoniously invaded. This part of the
ship, then, had partially escaped the confusion of the moment ; though trunks, boxes, hampers, and other similar
appliances of travelling, were scattered about in tolerable
affluence. Profiting by the space, of which there was still
sufficient for the purpose, most of the party left the hurricane-house to enjoy the short walk that a ship affords. At
that instant, another boat from the land reached the vessel's
side, and a grave-looking personage, who was not disposed
to lessen his dignity by levity or an omission of forms, appeared on deck, where he demanded to be shown the master. An introduction was unnecessary in this instance ;
for Captain Truck no sooner saw his visitor than he recognized the well-known features and solemn pomposity of a
civil officer of Portsmouth, who was often employed to
search the American packets, in pursuit of delinquents of
all degrees of crime and folly.

"I had just come to the opinion I was not to have the

pleasure of seeing you this passage, Mr. Grab," said the captain, shaking hands familiarly with the myrmidon of the law; "but the turn of the tide is not more regular than you gentlemen who come in the name of the king. Mr. Grab, Mr. Dodge; Mr. Dodge, Mr. Grab. And now, to what forgery, or bigamy, or elopement, or *scandalum magnatum* do I owe the honor of your company this time? Sir George Templemore, Mr. Grab; Mr. Grab, Sir George Templemore."

Sir George bowed with the dignified aversion an honest man might be supposed to feel for one of the other's employment; while Mr. Grab looked gravely and with a counter dignity at Sir George. The business of the officer, however, was with none in the cabin; but he had come in quest of a young woman who had married a suitor rejected by her uncle,—an arrangement that was likely to subject the latter to a settlement of accounts which he found inconvenient, and which he had thought it prudent to anticipate by bringing an action of debt against the bridegroom for advances, real or pretended, made to the wife during her nonage. A dozen eager ears caught an outline of this tale as it was communicated to the captain, and in an incredibly short space of time it was known throughout the ship, with not a few embellishments.

"I do not know the person of the husband," continued the officer, "nor indeed does the attorney who is with me in the boat; but his name is Robert Davis, and you can have no difficulty in pointing him out. We know him to be in the ship."

"I never introduce any steerage passengers, my dear sir; and there is no such person in the cabin, I give you my honor,—and that is a pledge that must pass between gentlemen like us. You are welcome to search, but the duty of the vessel must go on. Take your man—but do not detain the ship. Mr. Sharp, Mr. Grab; Mr. Grab, Mr. Sharp. Bear a hand there, Mr. Leach, and let us have the slack of the chain as soon as possible."

There appeared to be what the philosophers call the attraction of repulsion between the parties last introduced, for the tall, gentlemanly-looking Mr. Sharp eyed the officer

with a supercilious coldness, neither party deeming much
ceremony on the occasion necessary. Mr. Grab now summoned his assistant, the attorney, from the boat, and there
was a consultation between them as to their further proceedings. Fifty heads were grouped around them, and
curious eyes watched their smallest movements, one of the
crowd occasionally disappearing to report proceedings.

Man is certainly a clannish animal ; for without knowing
anything of the merits of the case, without pausing to
inquire into the right or the wrong of the matter, in the
pure spirit of partisanship, every man, woman, and child of
the steerage, which contained fully a hundred souls, took
sides against the law, and enlisted in the cause of the
defendant. All this was done quietly, however, for no one
menaced or dreamed of violence, crew and passengers usually taking their cues from the officers of the vessel on
such occasions, and those of the Montauk understood too
well the rights of the public agents to commit themselves
in the matter.

"Call Robert Davis," said the officer, resorting to a *ruse*,
by affecting an authority he had no right to assume.
"Robert Davis!" echoed twenty voices, among which was
that of the bridegroom himself, who was nigh to discover
his secret by an excess of zeal. It was easy to call, but no
one answered.

"Can you tell me which is Robert Davis, my little fellow?" the officer asked coaxingly, of a fine, flaxen-headed
boy, whose age did not exceed ten, and who was a curious
spectator of what passed. "Tell me which is Robert Davis,
and I will give you a sixpence."

The child knew, but professed ignorance.

"*C'est un esprit de corps admirable!*" exclaimed Mademoiselle Viefville ; for the interest of the scene had
brought nearly all on board, with the exception of those
employed in the duty of the vessel, near the gangway.
"*Ceci est délicieux*, and I could devour that boy!"

What rendered this more odd, or indeed absolutely ludicrous, was the circumstance that, by a species of legerdemain,
a whisper had passed among the spectators so stealthily,

and yet so soon, that the attorney and his companion were the only two on deck who remained ignorant of the person of the man they sought. Even the children caught the clue, though they had the art to indulge their natural curiosity by glances so sly as to escape detection.

Unfortunately, the attorney had sufficient knowledge of the family of the bride to recognize her by a general resemblance, rendered conspicuous as it was by a pallid face and an almost ungovernable nervous excitement. He pointed her out to the officer, who ordered her to approach him,—a command that caused her to burst into tears. The agitation and distress of his wife were near proving too much for the prudence of the young husband, who was making an impetuous movement towards her, when the strong grasp of a fellow-passenger checked him in time to prevent discovery. It is singular how much is understood by trifles when the mind has a clue to the subject, and how often signs, that are palpable as day, are overlooked when suspicion is not awakened, or when the thoughts have obtained a false direction. The attorney and the officer were the only two present who had not seen the indiscretion of the young man, and who did not believe him betrayed. His wife trembled to a degree that almost destroyed the ability to stand; but, casting an imploring look for self-command on her indiscreet partner, she controlled her own distress, and advanced towards the officer, in obedience to his order, with a power of endurance that the strong affections of a woman could alone enable her to assume.

"If the husband will not deliver himself up, I shall be compelled to order the wife to be carried ashore in his stead!" the attorney coldly remarked, while he applied a pinch of snuff to a nose that was already saffron-colored from the constant use of the weed.

A pause succeeded this ominous declaration, and the crowd of passengers betrayed dismay, for all believed there was now no hope for the pursued. The wife bowed her head to her knees, for she had sunk on a box as if to hide the sight of her husband's arrest. At this moment a voice spoke from among the group on the quarter-deck,—

"Is this an arrest for crime, or a demand for debt?" asked the young man who has been announced as Mr. Blunt.

There was a quiet authority in the speaker's manner that reassured the failing hopes of the passengers, while it caused the attorney and his companion to look round in surprise, and perhaps a little in resentment. A dozen eager voices assured "the gentleman" there was no crime in the matter at all—there was even no just debt, but it was a villainous scheme to compel a wronged ward to release a fraudulent guardian from his liabilities. Though all this was not very clearly explained, it was affirmed with so much zeal and energy as to awaken suspicion, and to increase the interest of the more intelligent portion of the spectators. The attorney surveyed the travelling dress, the appearance of fashion, and the youth of his interrogator, whose years could not exceed five-and-twenty. and his answer was given with an air of superiority.

"Debt or crime, it can matter nothing in the eye of the law."

"It matters much in the view of an honest man," returned the youth with spirit. "One might hesitate about interfering in behalf of a rogue, however ready to exert himself in favor of one who is innocent, perhaps, of everything but misfortune."

"This looks a little like an attempt at a rescue! I hope we are still in England, and under the protection of English laws?"

"No doubt at all of that, Mr. Seal," put in the captain, who having kept an eye on the officer from a distance, now thought it time to interfere, in order to protect the interests of his owners. "Yonder is England, and that is the Isle of Wight, and the Montauk has hold of an English bottom, and good anchorage it is; no one means to dispute your authority. Mr. Attorney, nor to call in question that of the king. Mr. Blunt merely throws out a suggestion, sir; or rather, a distinction between rogues and honest men; nothing more, depend on it, sir; Mr. Seal, Mr. Blunt; Mr. Blunt, Mr. Seal. And a thousand pities it is, that the distinction is not more commonly made."

The young man bowed slightly, and with a face flushed, partly with feeling, and partly at finding himself unexpectedly conspicuous among so many strangers, he advanced a little from the quarter-deck group, like one who feels he is required to maintain the ground he has assumed.

" No one can be disposed to question the supremacy of the English laws in this roadstead," he said, "and least of all myself; but you will permit me to doubt the legality of arresting, or in any manner detaining, a wife in virtue of a process issued against the husband."

" A briefless barrister!" muttered Seal to Grab. " I dare say a timely guinea would have silenced the fellow. What is now to be done?"

" The lady must go ashore, and all these matters can be arranged before a magistrate."

" Ay, ay! let her sue out a *habeas corpus* if she please," added the real attorney, whom a second survey caused to distrust his first inference. " Justice is blind in England as well as in other countries, and is liable to mistakes; but still she is just. If she does mistake sometimes, she is always ready to repair the wrong."

" Cannot *you* do something here?" Eve involuntarily half-whispered to Mr. Sharp, who stood at her elbow.

This person started on hearing her voice making this sudden appeal, and glancing a look of intelligence at her, he smiled and moved nearer to the principal parties.

" Really, Mr. Attorney," he commenced, " this appears to be rather irregular, I must confess,—quite out of the ordinary way, and it may lead to unpleasant consequences."

" In what manner, sir?" interrupted Seal, measuring the other's ignorance at a glance.

" Why, irregular in form, if not in principle. I am aware that the *habeas corpus* is all-essential, and that the law must have its way; but really this does seem a little irregular, not to describe it by any harsher term."

Mr. Seal treated this new appeal respectfully, in appearance at least, for he saw it was made by one greatly his superior, while he felt an utter contempt for it in essentials, as he perceived intuitively that this new intercession was made in a profound ignorance of the subject. As respects Mr. Blunt, however, he had an unpleasant distrust of the result, the quiet manner of that gentleman denoting more confidence in himself, and a greater practical knowledge of the laws. Still, to try the extent of the other's information, and the strength of his nerves, he rejoined, in a magisterial and menacing tone,—

"Yes, let the lady sue out a writ of *habeas corpus* if wrongfully arrested; and I should be glad to discover the foreigner who will dare to attempt a rescue in old England, and in defiance of English laws."

It is probable Paul Blunt would have relinquished his interference, from an apprehension that he might be ignorantly aiding the evil-doer, but for this threat; and even the threat might not have overcome his prudence, had not he caught the imploring look of the fine blue eyes of Eve.

"All are not necessarily foreigners who embark on board an American ship at an English port," he said steadily, "nor is justice denied those that are. The *hab. as corpus* is as well understood in other countries as in this, for, happily, we live in an age when neither liberty nor knowledge is exclusive. If an attorney, you must know yourself that you cannot legally arrest a wife for a husband, and that what you say of the *hab. as corpus* is little worthy of attention."

"We arrest, and whoever interferes with an officer in charge of a prisoner is guilty of a rescue. Mistakes must be rectified by the magistrates."

"True, provided the officer has warranty for what he does."

"Writs and warrants may contain errors, but an arrest is an arrest," growled Grab.

"Not the arrest of a woman for a man. In such a case there is design, and not a mistake. If this frightened wife will take counsel from me, she will refuse to accompany you."

"At her peril, let her dare to do so!"

"At *your* peril do you dare to attempt forcing her from the ship!"

"Gentlemen, gentlemen! let there be no misunderstanding, I pray you," interposed the captain. "Mr. Blunt, Mr. Grab ; Mr. Grab, Mr. Blunt. No warm words, gentlemen, I beg of you. But the tide is beginning to serve, Mr. Attorney, and 'time and tide,' you know—If we stay here much longer, the Montauk may be forced to sail on the 2d, instead of the 1st, as has been advertised in both hemi-spheres. I should be sorry to carry you to sea, gentlemen, without your small stores ; and as for the cabin, it is as full as a lawyer's conscience. No remedy but the steerage in such a case. Lay forward, men, and heave away. Some of you man the fore-topsail halyards. We are as regular as our chronometers ; the 1st, 10th, and 20th, without fail."

There was some truth, blended with a little poetry, in Captain Truck's account of the matter. The tide had indeed made in his favor, but the little wind there was blew directly into the roadstead ; and had not his feelings become warmed by the distress of a pretty and interesting young woman, it is more than probable the line would have incurred the disgrace of having a ship sail on a later day than had been advertised. As it was, however, he had the matter up in earnest, and he privately assured Sir George and Mr. Dodge, if the affair were not immediately disposed of, he should carry both the attorney and officer to sea with him, and that he did not feel himself bound to furnish either with water. "They may catch a little rain, by wringing their jackets," he added, with a wink ; "though October is a dryish month in the American seas."

The decision of Paul Blunt would have induced the attorney and his companion to relinquish their pursuit but for two circumstances. They had both undertaken the job as a speculation, or on the principle of " No play, no pay," and all their trouble would be lost without success. Then the very difficulty that occurred had been foreseen, and while the officer proceeded to the ship, the uncle had been busily search-ing for a son on shore, to send off to identify the husband, —a step that would have been earlier resorted to, could the young man have been found. This son was a rejected suitor, and he was now seen by the aid of a glass that Mr. Grab always carried, pulling towards the Montauk, in a two-

oared boat, with as much zeal as malignancy and disappointment could impart. His distance from the ship was still
considerable; but a peculiar hat, with the aid of the glass,
left no doubt of his identity. The attorney pointed out the
boat to the officer, and the latter, after a look through the
glass, gave a nod of approbation. Exultation overcame the
usual wariness of the attorney, for his pride, too, had got to
be enlisted in the success of his speculation, --men being so
strangely constituted as often to feel as much joy in the
accomplishment of schemes that are unjustifiable, as in the
accomplishment of those of which they may have reason to
be proud.

On the other hand, the passengers and people of the
packet seized something near the truth, with that sort of in-
stinctive readiness which seems to characterize bodies of
men in moments of excitement. That the solitary boat
which was pulling towards them in the dusk of the evening
contained some one who might aid the attorney and his myrmidon, all believed, though in what manner none could tell.

Between all seamen and the ministers of the law there is
a long-standing antipathy, for the visits of the latter are
usually so timed as to leave nothing between the alternatives of paying or of losing a voyage. It was soon apparent then, that Mr. Seal had little to expect from the apathy
of the crew, for never did men work with better will to get
a ship loosened from the bottom.

All this feeling manifested itself in a silent and intelligent
activity rather than in noise or bustle, for every man on
board exercised his best faculties, as well as his best good-
will and strength ; the clock-work ticks of the palls of the
windlass resembling those of a watch that had got the
start of time, while the chain came in with surges of half
a fathom at each heave.

" Lay hold of this rope, men," cried Mr. Leach, placing
the end of the main-topsail halyards in the hands of half-a-
dozen athletic steerage passengers, who had all the inclination in the world to be doing, though uncertain where to lay
their hands ; " lay hold, and run away with it."

The second mate performed the same feat forward, and as

the sheets had never been started, the broad folds of the Montauk's canvas began to open, even while the men were heaving at the anchor. These exertions quickened the blood in the veins of those who were not employed, until even the quarter-deck passengers began to experience the excitement of a chase, in addition to the feelings of compassion. Captain Truck was silent, but very active in preparations. Springing to the wheel, he made its spokes fly until he had forced the helm hard up, when he unceremoniously gave it to John Effingham to keep there. His next leap was to the foot of the mizzen-mast, where, after a few energetic efforts alone, he looked over his shoulder and beckoned for aid.

"Sir George Templemore, mizzen-topsail halyards; mizzen-topsail halyards, Sir George Templemore," muttered the eager master, scarce knowing what he said. "Mr. Dodge, now is the time to show that your name and nature are not identical."

In short, nearly all on board were busy, and, thanks to the hearty good-will of the officers, stewards, cooks, and a few of the hands that could be spared from the windlass, busy in a way to spread sail after sail with a rapidity little short of that seen on board of a vessel of war. The rattling of the clew-garnet blocks, as twenty lusty fellows ran forward with the tack of the mainsail, and hauling forward of braces, was the signal that the ship was clear of the ground, and coming under command.

A cross current had superseded the necessity of casting the vessel, but her sails took the light air nearly abeam; the captain understanding that motion was of much more importance just then than direction. No sooner did he perceive by the bubbles that floated past, or rather appeared to float past, that his ship was dividing the water forward, than he called a trusty man to the wheel, relieving John Effingham from his watch. The next instant, Mr. Leach reported the anchor catted and fished.

"Pilot, you will be responsible for this if my prisoners escape," said Mr. Grab, menacingly. "You know my errand, and it is your duty to aid the ministers of the law."

"Harkee, Mr. Grab," put in the master, who had warmed himself with the exercise; "we all know, and we all do our duties, on board the Montauk. It is your duty to take Robert Davis on shore if you can find him; and it is my duty to take the Montauk to America; now, if you will receive counsel from a well-wisher, I would advise you to see that you do not go in her. No one offers any impediment to your performing your office, and I'll thank you to offer me none in performing mine. Brace the yards farther forward, boys, and let the ship come up to the wind."

As there were logic, useful information, law, and seamanship united in this reply, the attorney began to betray uneasiness; for by this time the ship had gathered so much way as to render it exceedingly doubtful whether a two-oared boat would be able to come up with her, without the consent of those on board. It is probable, as evening had already closed, and the rays of the moon were beginning to quiver on the ripple of the water, that he would have abandoned his object, though with infinite reluctance, had not Sir George Templemore pointed out to the captain a six-oared boat, that was pulling towards them from a quarter that permitted it to be seen in the moonlight.

"That appears to be a man-of-war's cutter," observed the baronet uneasily, for by this time all on board felt a sort of personal interest in their escape.

"It does indeed, Captain Truck," added the pilot; "and if *she* makes a signal, it will become my duty to heave-to the Montauk."

"Then bundle out of her, my fine fellow, as fast as you can; for not a brace or a bowline shall be touched here, with my consent, for any such purpose. The ship is cleared —my hour is come—my passengers are on board—and America is my haven. Let them that want me, catch me. That is what I call *Vattel*."

The pilot and the master of the Montauk were excellent friends, and understood each other perfectly, even while the former was making the most serious professions of duty. The boat was hauled up, and, first whispering a few cautions about the shoals and the currents, the worthy marine guide leaped into it, and was soon seen floating astern—a cheering proof that the ship had got fairly in motion. As he fell out of hearing in the wake of the vessel, the honest fellow kept calling out "to tack in season."

"If you wish to try the speed of your boat against that of the pilot, Mr. Grab," called out the captain, "you will never have a better opportunity. It is a fine night for a regatta, and I will stand you a pound on Mr. Handlead's heels. For that matter, I would as soon trust his head, or his hands, in the bargain."

The officer continued obstinately on board, for he saw that the six-oared boat was coming up with the ship, and, as he well knew the importance to his client of compelling a settlement of the accounts, he fancied some succor might be expected in that quarter. In the meantime, this new movement on the part of their pursuers attracted general attention, and, as might be expected, the interest of this little incident increased the excitement that usually accompanies a departure for a long sea-voyage, fourfold. Men and women forgot their griefs and leave-takings in anxiety, and in that pleasure which usually attends agitation of the mind that does not proceed from actual misery of our own.

## CHAPTER IV.

"Whither away so fast?
                O God save you!
Even to the hall, to hear what shall become
Of the great Duke of Buckingham."

*Henry VIII.*

THE assembling of the passengers of the large packet-ship is necessarily an affair of coldness and distrust, especially with those who know the world, and more particularly still when the passage is from Europe to America. The greater sophistication of the old than of the new hemisphere, with its consequent shifts and vices, the knowledge that the tide of emigration sets westward, and that few abandon the home of their youth unless impelled by misfortune at least, with other obvious causes, unite to produce this distinction. Then come the fastidiousness of habits, the sentiments of social castes, the refinements of breeding, and the reserves of dignity of character, to be put in close collision with bustling egotism, ignorance of usages, an absence of training, and downright vulgarity of thought and practices. Although necessity soon brings these chaotic elements into something like order, the first week commonly passes in reconnoitring, cool civilities, and cautious concessions, to yield at length to the never-dying charities; unless, indeed, the latter may happen to be kept in abeyance by a downright quarrel, about midnight carousals, a squeaking fiddle, or some incorrigible snorer.

Happily, the party collected in the Montauk had the good fortune to abridge the usual probation in courtesies, by the stirring events of the night on which they sailed. Two

3

hours had scarcely elapsed since the last passenger crossed
the gangway, and yet the respective circles of the quarter-
deck and steerage felt more sympathy with each other than
the boasted human charities ordinarily quicken in days
of commonplace intercourse. They had already found out
each other's names, thanks to the assiduity of Captain
Truck, who had stolen time, in the midst of all his activity,
to make half-a-dozen more introductions, and the Americans
of the less trained class were already using them as freely
as if they were old acquaintances. We say Americans, for
the cabins of these ships usually contain a congress of
nations, though the people of England, and of her *ci-devant*
colonies, of course predominate in those of the London lines.
On the present occasion, the last two were nearly balanced
in numbers, so far as national character could be made out ;
opinion (which, as might be expected, had been busy the
while) being suspended in reference to Mr. Blunt, and one
or two others whom the captain called " foreigners," to
distinguish them from the Anglo-Saxon stock.

This equal distribution of forces might, under other circumstances, have led to a division in feeling ; for the con-
flicts between American and British opinions, coupled with
a difference in habits, are a prolific source of discontent in
the cabins of packets. The American is apt to fancy himself at home, under the flag of his country ; while his trans-
atlantic kinsman is strongly addicted to fancying that when
he has fairly paid his money, he has a right to embark all
his prejudices with his other luggage.

The affair of the attorney and the newly-married couple,
however, was kept quite distinct from all feelings of nationality ; the English apparently entertaining quite as lively a
wish that the latter might escape from the fangs of the law,
as any other portion of the passengers. The parties themselves were British, and although the authority evaded was
of the same origin, right or wrong, all on board had taken
up the impression that it was improperly exercised. Sir
George Templemore, the Englishman of highest rank, was
decidedly of this way of thinking—an opinion he was
rather warm in expressing—and the example of a baronet

had its weight, not only with most of his own countrymen,
but with not a few of the Americans also. The Effingham
party, together with Mr. Sharp and Mr. Blunt, were, indeed,
all who seemed to be entirely indifferent to Sir George's
sentiments; and, as men are intuitively quick in discovering who do and who do not defer to their suggestions, their
accidental independence might have been favored by this
fact, for the discourse of this gentleman was addressed in
the main to those who lent the most willing ears. Mr.
Dodge, in particular, was his constant and respectful listener
and profound admirer: —but then he was his room-mate, and
a democrat of a water so pure, that he was disposed to maintain no man had a right to any one of his senses, unless by
popular sufferance.

In the meanwhile, the night advanced, and the soft light
of the moon was playing on the waters, adding a semi-mys-
terious obscurity to the excitement of the scene. The two-
oared boat had evidently been overtaken by that carrying six
oars, and, after a short conference, the first had returned reluctantly towards the land, while the latter, profiting by its
position, had set two lug-sails, and was standing out into the
offing, on a course that would compel the Montauk to come
under its lee, when the shoals, as would soon be the case,
should force the ship to tack.

"England is most inconveniently placed," Captain Truck
dryly remarked, as he witnessed this manœuvre. "Were
this island only out of the way, now, we might stand on as
we head, and leave those man-of-war's-men to amuse themselves all night with backing and filling in the roads of
Portsmouth."

"I hope there is no danger of that little boat's overtaking
this large ship!" exclaimed Sir George, with a vivacity
that did great credit to his philanthropy, according to the
opinion of Mr. Dodge at least; the latter having imbibed a
singular bias in favor of persons of condition, from having
travelled in an *eilwagen* with a German baron, from whom
he had taken a model of the pipe he carried but never
smoked, and from having been thrown for two days and
nights into the society of a "Polish countess," as he uni-

formly termed her, in the *gondole* of a diligence between Lyons and Marseilles. In addition, Mr. Dodge, as has just been hinted, was an ultra-freeman at home—a circumstance that seems always to react, when the subject of the feeling gets into foreign countries.

"A feather running before a lady's sigh would outsail either of us in this air, which breathes on us in some such fashion as a whale snores, Sir George, by sudden puffs. I would give the price of a steerage passage, if Great Britain lay off the Cape of Good Hope for a week or ten days."

"Or Cape Hatteras!" rejoined the mate.

"Not I; I wish the old island no harm, nor a worse climate than it has got already; though it lies as much in our way, just at this moment, as the moon in an eclipse of the sun. I bear the old creature a great-grandson's love,—or a step or two farther off, if you will,—and come and go too often to forget the relationship. But, much as I love her, the affection is not strong enough to go ashore on her shoals, and so we will go about, Mr. Leach; at the same time, I wish from my heart that two-lugged rascal would go about his business."

The ship tacked slowly but gracefully, for she was in what her master termed "racing trim"; and as her bows fell off to the eastward, it became pretty evident to all who understood the subject, that the two little lug-sails that were "eating into the wind," as the sailors express it, would weather upon her track ere she could stretch over to the other shoal. Even the landsmen had some feverish suspicions of the truth, and the steerage passengers were already holding a secret conference on the possibility of hiding the pursued in some of the recesses of the ship. "Such things were often done," one whispered to another, "and it was as easy to perform it now as at any other time."

But Captain Truck viewed the matter differently: his vocation called him three times a year into the roads at Portsmouth, and he felt little disposition to embarrass his future intercourse with the place by setting its authorities at a too open defiance. He deliberated a good deal on the propriety of throwing his ship up into the wind, as she

slowly advanced towards the boat, and of inviting those in
the latter to board him.   Opposed to this was the pride of
profession, and Jack Truck was not a man to overlook or
forget the "yarns" that were spun among his fellows at
the New England Coffee-House, or among those farming
hamlets on the banks of the Connecticut, whence all the
packet-men are derived, and whither they repair for a shelter when their careers are run, as regularly as the fruit
decays where it falleth, or the grass that has not been har-
vested or cropped withers on its native stalk.

"There is no question, Sir George, that this fellow is a
man-of-war's-man," said the master to the baronet, who
stuck close to his side.   "Take a peep at the creeping rogue
through this night-glass, and you will see his crew seated at
their thwarts with their arms folded, like men who eat the
king's beef.   None but your regular public servant ever
gets that impudent air of idleness about him, either in England or America.   In this respect, human nature is the same
in both hemispheres, a man never falling in with luck, but
he fancies it is no more than his deserts."

"There seems to be a great many of them!   Can it be
their intention to carry the vessel by boarding?"

"If it is, they must take the will for the deed," returned
Mr. Truck a little coldly.   "I very much question if the
Montauk, with three cabin officers, as many stewards, two
cooks, and eighteen foremast-men, would exactly like the
notion of being 'carried,' as you style it, Sir George, by a
six-oared cutter's crew.   We are not as heavy as the planet
Jupiter, but have somewhat too much gravity to be 'carried'
as lightly as all that, too."

"You intend, then, to resist?" asked Sir George, whose
generous zeal in behalf of the pursued apparently led him
to take a stronger interest in their escape than any other
person on board.

Captain Truck, who had never an objection to sport,
pondered with himself a little, smiled, and then loudly
expressed a wish that he had a member of congress or a
member of parliament on board.

"Your desire is a little extraordinary for the circum-

stances," observed Mr. Sharp ; "will you have the goodness to explain why ? "

"This matter touches on international law, gentlemen,"
continued the master, rubbing his hands ; for, in addition to
having caught the art of introduction, the honest mariner
had taken it into his head he had become an adept in the
principles of Vattel, of whom he possessed a well-thumbed
copy, and for whose dogmas he entertained the deference
that they who begin to learn late usually feel for the particular master into whose hands they have accidentally fallen.
"Under what circumstances, or in what category, can a
public armed ship compel a neutral to submit to being
boarded—not 'carried,' Sir George, you will please to
remark ; for d——n me, if any man 'carries' the Montauk
that is not strong enough to 'carry' her crew and cargo
along with her !—but in what category, now, is a packet
like this I have the honor to command obliged, in comity,
to heave-to and to submit to an examination at all?   The
ship is aweigh, and has handsomely tacked under her canvas ;
and, gentlemen, I should be pleased to have your sentiments
on the occasion.   Just have the condescension to point out
the category."

Mr. Dodge came from a part of the country in which men
were accustomed to think, act, almost to eat and drink and
sleep, in common ; or, in other words, from one of those
regions in America, in which there was so much community,
that few had the moral courage, even when they possessed
the knowledge, and all the other necessary means, to cause
their individuality to be respected.   When the usual process
of conventions, sub-conventions, caucuses, and public meet-
ings did not supply the means of a "concentrated action,"
he and his neighbors had long been in the habit of having
recourse to societies, by way of obtaining "energetic means,"
as it was termed ; and from his tenth year up to his twenty-
fifth, this gentleman had been either a president, vice-presi-
dent, manager, or committee-man, of some philosophical,
political, or religious expedient to fortify human wisdom,
make men better, and resist error and despotism.   His
experience had rendered him expert in what may well

enough be termed the language of association. No man of
his years, in the twenty-six States, could more readily apply
the terms of "taking up"—"excitement"—"unqualified
hostility"—"public opinion"—"spreading before the public," or any other of those generic phrases that imply the
privileges of all, and the rights of none. Unfortunately, the
pronunciation of this person was not as pure as his motives,
and he misunderstood the captain when he spoke of comity,
as meaning a "committee"; and although it was not quite
obvious what the worthy mariner could intend by "obliged
in committee (comity) to heave-to," yet, as he had known
these bodies to do so many "energetic things," he did not
see why they might not perform this evolution as well as
another.

"It really does appear, Captain Truck," he remarked
accordingly, "that our situation approaches a crisis, and the
suggestion of a comity committee) strikes me as being
peculiarly proper and suitable to the circumstances, and in
strict conformity with republican usages. In order to save
time, and that the gentlemen who shall be appointed to serve
may have opportunity to report, therefore, I will at once
nominate Sir George Templemore as chairman, leaving it
for any other gentleman present to suggest the name of any
candidate he may deem proper. I will only add, that in my
poor judgment this comity committee) ought to consist of
at least three, and that it have power to send for persons
and papers."

"I would propose five, Captain Truck, by way of amendment," added another passenger of the same kidney as the
last speaker, gentlemen of their school making it a point to
differ a little from every proposition by way of showing their
independence.

It was fortunate for both the mover of the original motion,
and for the proposer of the amendment, that the master was
acquainted with the character of Mr. Dodge, or a proposition
that his ship was to be worked by a committee (or indeed
by comity) would have been very likely to meet with but
an indifferent reception; but, catching a glimpse of the
laughing eyes of Eve, as well as of the amused faces of Mr.

Sharp and Mr. Blunt, by the light of the moon, he very gravely signified his entire approbation of the chairman named, and his perfect readiness to listen to the report of the aforesaid committee as soon as it might be prepared to make it.

"And if your committee, or comity, gentlemen," he added, "can tell me what Vattel would say about the obligation to heave-to in a time of profound peace, and when the ship or boat in chase can have no belligerent rights, I shall be grateful to my dying day; for I have looked him through as closely as old women usually examine almanacs to tell which way the wind is about to blow, and I fear he has overlooked the subject altogether."

Mr. Dodge, and three or four more of the same community-propensity as himself, soon settled the names of the rest of the committee, when the nominees retired to another part of the deck to consult together; Sir George Templemore, to the surprise of all the Effingham party, consenting to serve with a willingness that rather disregarded forms.

"It might be convenient to refer other matters to this committee, captain," said Mr. Sharp, who had tact enough to see that nothing but her habitual *retenue* of deportment kept Eve, whose bright eyes were dancing with humor, from downright laughter; "there are the important points of reefing and furling, the courses to be steered, the sail to be carried, the times and seasons of calling all hands together, with sundry other customary duties, that no doubt would be well treated on in this forthcoming report."

"No doubt, sir; I perceive you have been at sea before, and I am sorry you were overlooked in naming the members of the comity; take my word for it, all that you have mentioned can be done on board the Montauk by a comity, as well as settling the question of heaving-to, or not, for yonder boat. By the way, Mr. Leach, the fellows have tacked, and are standing in this direction, thinking to cross our bows and speak us. Mr. Attorney, the tide is setting us off the land, and you may make it morning before you get into your nests, if you hold on much longer. I fear Mrs. Seal and Mrs. Grab will be unhappy women."

The bloodhounds of the law heard this warning with indifference, for they expected succor of some sort, though
they hardly knew of what sort, from the man-of-war's boat,
which, it was now plain enough, must weather on the ship.
After putting their heads together, Mr. Seal offered his companion a pinch of snuff, helping himself afterwards, like a
man indifferent to the result, and one patient in time of duty.
The sunburnt face of the captain, whose standing color was
that which cooks get when the fire burns the brightest, but
whose hues no fire or cold ever varied, was turned fully on
the two, and it is probable they would have received some
decided manifestation of his will, had not Sir George Templemore, with the four other committee-men, approached to
give in the result of their conference.

"We are of opinion, Captain Truck," said the baronet,
"that, as the ship is under way, and your voyage may be
fairly said to have commenced, it is quite inexpedient and
altogether unnecessary for you to anchor again ; but that it
is your duty—"

"I have no occasion for advice as to my duty, gentlemen.
If you can let me know what Vattel says, or ought to have
said, on the subject, or touching the category of the right of
search, except as a belligerent right, I will thank you ; if
not, we must e'en guess at it. I have not sailed a ship in
this trade these ten years to need any jogging of the memory about port-jurisdiction either, for these are matters in
which one gets to be expert by dint of use, as my old master
used to say when he called us from table with half a dinner.
Now, there was the case of the blacks in Charleston, in
which our government showed clearly it had not studied
Vattel, or it never would have given the answer it did.
Perhaps you never heard that case, Sir George, and as it
touches a delicate principle, I will just run over the category
lightly ; for it has its points, as well as a coast."

"Does not this matter press—may not the boat—"

"The boat will do nothing, gentlemen, without the permission of Jack Truck. You must know, the Carolinians
have a law that all niggers brought into their State by ships,
must be caged until the vessel sails again. This is to pre-

vent emancipation, as they call it, or abolition, I know not which.  An Englishman comes in from the islands with a crew of blacks, and, according to law, the authorities of Charleston house them all before night.  John Bull complains to his minister, and his minister sends a note to our secretary, and our secretary writes to the governor of Carolina, calling on him to respect the treaty, and so on.  Gentlemen, I need not tell you what a treaty is—it is a thing in itself to be obeyed ; but it is all-important to know what it commands.  Well, what was this said treaty ?  That John should come in and out of the ports, on the footing of the most favored nation ; on the *statu quo ante bellum* principle, as Vattel has it.  Now, the Carolinians treated John just as they treated Jonathan, and there was no more to be said.  All parties were bound to enter the port, subject to the municipals, as is set forth in Vattel.  That was a case soon settled, you perceive, though depending on a nicety.''

Sir George had listened with extreme impatience, but, fearful of offending, he listened to the end ; then, seizing the first pause in the captain's discourse, he resumed his remonstrances with an interest that did infinite credit to his humanity, at the same time that he overlooked none of the obligations of politeness.

" An exceedingly clear case, I protest,'' he answered, "and capitally put—I question if Lord Stowell could do it better —and exceedingly apt, that about the *ante bellum* ; but I confess my feelings have not been so much roused for a long time as they have been on account of these poor people.  There is something inexpressibly painful in being disappointed as one is setting out in the morning of life, as it were, in this cruel manner; and rather than see this state of things protracted, I would prefer paying a trifle out of my own pocket.  If this wretched attorney will consent, now, to take a hundred pounds and quit us, and carry back with him that annoying cutter with the lug-sails, I will give him the money most cheerfully—most cheerfully, I protest.''

There is something so essentially respectable in practical generosity, that, though Eve and all the curious auditors of what was passing felt an inclination to laugh at the whole

procedure up to this declaration, eye met eye in commenda-
tion of the liberality of the baronet. He had shown he had
a heart, in the opinion of most of those who heard him,
though his previous conversation had led several of the ob-
servers to distrust his having the usual *quantum* of head.

"Give yourself no trouble about the attorney, Sir George,"
returned the captain, shaking the other cordially by the
hand; "he shall not touch a pound of your money, nor do
I think he is likely to touch Robert Davis. We have caught
the tide on our lee bow, and the current is wheeling us up
to windward, like an opposition coach flying over Black-
heath. In a few minutes we shall be in blue water; and
then I'll give the rascal a touch of Vattel that will throw
him all aback, if it don't throw him overboard."

"But the cutter?"

"Why. if we drive the attorney and Grab out of the ship,
there will be no process in the hands of the others, by
which they can carry off the man, even admitting the jurisdiction. I know the scoundrels, and not a shilling shall
either of the knaves take from this vessel with my consent.
Harkee, Sir George, a word in your ear: two of as d——d
cockroaches as ever rummaged a ship's breadroom: I'll see
that they soon heave about, or I'll heave them both into
their boat, with my own fair hands."

The captain was about to turn away to examine the position of the cutter, when Mr. Dodge asked permission to
make a short report in behalf of the minority of the comity
(committee), the amount of which was, that they agreed in
all things with the majority, except on the point that, as it
might become expedient for the ship to anchor again in
some of the ports lower down the Channel, it would be wise
to keep that material circumstance in view, in making up
a final decision in the affair. This report on the part of
the minority, which, Mr. Dodge explained to the baronet,
partook rather of the character of a caution than of a protest, had quite as little influence on Captain Truck as the
opinion of the majority, for he was just one of those persons
who seldom took advice that did not conform with his own
previous decision; but he coolly continued to examine the

cutter, which, by this time, was standing on the same course
as the ship, a short distance to windward of her, and edging a little off the wind, so as to bring the two nearer to
each other, every yard they advanced.

The wind had freshened to a little breeze, and the captain
nodded his head with satisfaction when he heard, even
where he stood on the quarter-deck, the slapping of the
sluggish swell, as the huge bows of the ship parted the
water. At this moment those in the cutter saw the bubbles
glide swiftly past them, while to those in the Montauk the
motion was still slow and heavy; and yet, of the two, the
actual velocity was rather in favor of the latter, both having
about what is technically termed "four-knot way" on them.
The officer of the boat was quick to detect the change that
was acting against him, and by easing the sheets of his lug-
sails, and keeping the cutter as much off the wind as he
could, he was soon within a hundred feet of the ship, running along on her weather-beam. The bright, soft moonlight permitted the face of a young man in a man-of-war
cap, who wore the undress uniform of a sea lieutenant, to be
distinctly seen, as he rose in the stern-sheets, which contained also two other persons.

"I will thank you to heave-to the Montauk," said the
lieutenant, civilly, while he raised his cap, apparently in
compliment to the passengers who crowded the rail to see
and hear what passed. "I am sent on the duty of the
king, sir."

"I know your errand, sir," returned Captain Truck,
whose resolution to refuse to comply was a good deal shaken
by the gentlemanlike manner in which the request was
made; "and I wish you to bear witness, that if I do consent to your request, it is voluntarily; for, on the principles
laid down by Vattel and the other writers on international law, the right of search is a belligerent right, and
England being at peace, no ship belonging to one nation
can have a right to stop a vessel belonging to another."

"I cannot enter into these niceties, sir," returned the
lieutenant, sharply; "I have my orders, and you will excuse
me if I say, I intend to execute them."

" Execute them with all my heart, sir : if you are ordered
to heave-to my ship, all you have to do is to get on board,
if you can, and let us see the style in which you handle
yards. As to the people now stationed at the braces, the
trumpet that will make them stir is not to be spoken
through at the Admiralty. The fellow has spirit in him,
and I like his principles as an officer, but I cannot admit
his conclusions as a jurist. If he flatters himself with being
able to frighten us into a new category, now, that is likely
to impair national rights, the lad has just got himself into a
problem that will need all his logic, and a good deal of his
spirit, to get out of again."

" You will scarcely think of resisting a king's officer in
British waters !" said the young man, with that haughti-
ness that the meekest tempers soon learn to acquire under a
pennant.

"Resisting, my dear sir ! I resist nothing. The miscon-
ception is in supposing that you sail this ship instead
of John Truck. That is my name, sir ; John Truck. Do
your errand in welcome, but do not ask me to help you.
Come aboard, with all my heart ; nothing would give me
more pleasure than to take wine with you ; but I see no
necessity of stopping a packet, that is busy on a long road,
without an object, as we say on the other side of the big
waters."

There was a pause, and then the lieutenant, with the sort
of hesitation that a gentleman is apt to feel when he makes
a proposal that he knows ought not to be accepted, called
out that those in the boat with him would pay for the de-
tention of the ship. A more unfortunate proposition could
not be made to Captain Truck, who would have hove-to his
ship in a moment had the lieutenant proposed to discuss
Vattel with him on the quarter-deck, and who was only
holding out as a sort of salvo to his rights, with that disposition to resist aggression that the experience of the last
forty years has so deeply implanted in the bosom of every
American sailor, in cases connected with English naval
officers, and who had just made up his mind to let Robert
Davis take his chance, and to crack a bottle with the hand-

some young man who was still standing up in the boat. But Mr. Truck had been too often to London not to understand exactly the manner in which Englishmen appreciate American character ; and, among other things, he knew it was the general opinion in the island that money could do anything with Jonathan, or, as Christophe is said once to have sententiously expressed the same sentiment, "If there were a bag of coffee in h——l, a Yankee could be found to go and bring it out."

The master of the Montauk had a proper relish for his lawful gains as well as another, but he was vainglorious on the subject of his countrymen, principally because he found that the packets outsailed all other merchant ships, and fiercely proud of any quality that others were disposed to deny them.

At hearing this proposal, or intimation, therefore, instead of accepting it, Captain Truck raised his hat with formal civility and coolly wished the other "Good night." This was bringing the affair to a crisis at once ; for the helm of the cutter was borne up, and an attempt was made to run the boat alongside of the ship. But the breeze had been steadily increasing, the air had grown heavier as the night advanced, and the dampness of evening was thickening the canvas of the coarser sails in a way sensibly to increase the speed of the ship. When the conversation commenced the boat was abreast of the fore-rigging ; and by the time it ended, it was barely up with the mizzen. The lieutenant was quick to see the disadvantage he labored under, and he called out "Heave!" as he found the cutter was falling close under the counter of the ship, and would be in her wake in another minute. The bowman of the boat cast a light grapnel with so much precision, that it hooked in the mizzen rigging, and the line instantly tightened so as to tow the cutter. A seaman was passing along the outer edge of the hurricane-house at the moment, coming from the wheel, and with the decision of an old salt, he quietly passed his knife across the stretched cordage, and it snapped like pack-thread. The grapnel fell into the sea, and the boat was tossing in the wake of the ship, all as it might be while one could draw a breath. To furl the sails and ship the oars consumed but an instant, and then the cutter was ploughing the water under the vigorous strokes of her crew.

"Spirited! spirited and nimble!" observed Captain Truck, who stood coolly leaning against a shroud, in a position where he could command a view of all that was passing, improving the opportunity to shake the ashes from his cigar while he spoke; "a fine young fellow, and one who will make an admiral, or something better, I dare say, if he live; perhaps a cherub, in time. Now, if he pull much longer in the back-water of our wake, I shall have to give him up, Leach, as a little marinish: ah! there he sheers out of it like a sensible youth as he is! Well, there is something pleasant in the conceit of a six-oared boat's carrying a London liner by boarding, even admitting the lad could have got alongside."

So it would seem, thought Mr. Leach and the crew of the Montauk; for they were clearing the decks with as much philosophy as men ever discover when employed in an unthankful office.

This *sang-froid* of seamen is always matter of surprise to landsmen; but adventurers who have been rocked in the tempest for years, whose utmost security is a great hazard, and whose safety constantly depends on the command of the faculties, come in time to experience an apathy on the subject of all the minor terrors and excitements of life, that none can acquire unless by habit and similar risks. There was a low laugh among the people, and now and then a curious glance of the eye over the quarter, to ascertain the position of the struggling boat; but there the effect of the little incident ceased, so far as the seamen were concerned.

Not so with the passengers. The Americans exulted at the failure of the man-of-war's-man; and the English doubted. To them, deference to the crown was habitual, and they were displeased at seeing a stranger play a king's boat such a trick, in what they justly enough thought to be British waters. Although the law may not give a man any more right than another to the road before his own door, he comes in time to fancy it, in a certain degree, his particular road. Strictly speaking, the Montauk was perhaps still under the dominion of the English laws; though she had been a league from the land when lying at her anchor, and by this time the tide and her own velocity had swept her broad off into the offing quite as far again; indeed, she had now got to such a distance from the land, that Captain Truck thought it his "duty" to bring matters to a conclusion with the attorney.

"Well, Mr. Seal," he said, "I am grateful for the pleasure of your company thus far; but you will excuse me if I decline taking you and Mr. Grab quite to America. Half an hour hence you will hardly be able to find the island; for as soon as we have got to a proper distance from the cutter, I shall tack to the southwest, and you ought, moreover, to remember the anxiety of the ladies at home."

"This may turn out a serious matter, Captain Truck, on your return passage! The laws of England are not to be trifled with. Will you oblige me by ordering the steward to hand me a glass of water? Waiting for justice is dry duty, I find."

"Extremely sorry I cannot comply, gentlemen. Vattel has nothing on the subject of watering belligerents or neutrals, and the laws of Congress compel me to carry so many gallons to the man. If you will take it in the way of a night-cap, however, and drink success to our run to America, and your own to the shore, it shall be in champagne, if you happen to like that agreeable fluid."

The attorney was about to express his readiness to compromise on these terms, when a glass of the beverage for which he had first asked was put into his hand by the wife of Robert Davis. He took the water, drank it, and turned from the woman with the obduracy of one who never suffered feeling to divert him from the pursuit of gain. The wine was brought, and the captain filled the glasses with a seaman's heartiness.

"I drink to your safe return to Mrs. Seal, and the little gods and goddesses of justice,—Pan or Mercury, which is it? And as for you, Grab, look out for sharks as you pull in. If they hear of your being afloat, the souls of perse-cuted sailors will set them on you, as the devil chases male coquettes. Well, gentlemen, you are balked this time; but what matters it? It is but another man got safe out of a country that has too many in it; and I trust we shall meet good friends again, this day four months. Even man and wife must part, when the hour arrives."

"That will depend on how my client views your conduct on this occasion, Captain Truck; for he is not a man that it is always safe to thwart."

"That for your client, Mr. Seal!" returned the captain, snapping his fingers. "I am not to be frightened with an attorney's growl, or a bailiff's nod. You come off with a writ or a warrant, I care not which; I offer no resistance; you hunt for your man, like a terrier looking for a rat, and can't find him; I see the fine fellow, at this moment, on deck,- but I feel no obligation to tell you who or where he is; my ship is cleared and I sail, and you have no power to stop me; we are outside of all the headlands, good two leagues and a half off, and some writers say that a gunshot is the extent of your jurisdiction, once out of which, your authority is not worth half as much as that of my chief cook, who has power to make his mate clean the coppers. Well, sir, you stay here ten minutes longer and we shall be fully three leagues from your nearest land, and then you are in America, according to law, and a quick passage you will have made of it. Now, that is what I call a category."

As the captain made this last remark, his quick eye saw that the wind had hauled so far round to the westward, as to supersede the necessity of tacking, and that they were actually going eight knots in a direct line from Portsmouth. Casting an eye behind him, he perceived that the cutter had given up the chase, and was returning towards the distant roads. Under circumstances so discouraging, the attorney, who began to be alarmed for his boat, which was flying along on the water, towed by the ship, prepared to take his leave; for he was fully aware that he had no power to

4

compel the other to heave-to his ship, to enable him to get out of her. Luckily the water was still tolerably smooth, and with fear and trembling, Mr. Seal succeeded in blundering into the boat ; not, however, until the watermen had warned him of their intention to hold on no longer. Mr. Grab followed, with a good deal of difficulty, and just as a hand was about to let go the painter, the captain appeared at the gangway with the man they were in quest of, and said in his most winning manner,—

"Mr. Grab, Mr. Davis ; Mr. Davis, Mr. Grab : I seldom introduce steerage passengers, but to oblige two old friends I break the rule. That's what I call a category. My compliments to Mrs. Grab. Let go the painter."

The words were no sooner uttered than the boat was tossing and whirling in the caldron left by the passing ship.

## CHAPTER V.

" ' What country, friends, is this? '
      ' Illyria, lady.' "

*Twelfth Night.*

CAPTAIN TRUCK cast an eye aloft to see if everything drew, as coolly as if nothing out of the usual course had happened; he and his crew having seemingly regarded the attempt to board them as men regard the natural phenomena of the planets, or in other words, as if the ship, of which they were merely parts, had escaped by her own instinct or volition. This habit of considering the machine as the governing principle is rather general among seamen, who, while they ease a brace, or drag a bowline, as the coachman checks a rein, appear to think it is only permitting the creature to work her own will a little more freely. It is true all know better, but none talk, or indeed would seem to feel, as if they thought otherwise.

"Did you observe how the old barky jumped out of the way of those rovers in the cutter?" said the captain complacently to the quarter-deck group, when his survey aloft had taken sufficient heed that his own nautical skill should correct the instinct of the ship. "A skittish horse, or a whale with the irons in him, or, for that matter, one of the funniest of your theatricals, would not have given a prettier aside than this poor old hulk, which is certainly just the clumsiest craft that sails the ocean. I wish King William would take it into his royal head, now, to send one of his light-heeled cruisers out to prove it, by way of resenting the cantaverous trick the Montauk played his boat!"

The dull report of a gun, as the sound came short and deadened up against the breeze, checked the raillery of Mr. Truck. On looking to leeward, there was sufficient light to see the symmetrical sails of the corvette they had left at anchor, trimmed close by the wind, and the vessel itself standing out under a press of canvas, apparently in chase. The gun had evidently been fired as a signal of recall to the cutter, blue lights being burnt on board of both the ship and its boat, in proof that they were communicating.

The passengers now looked gravely at each other, for the matter, in their eyes, began to be serious. Some suggested the possibility that the offence of Davis might be other than debt, but this was disproved by the process and the account of the bailiff himself; while most concluded that a determination to resent the slight done the authorities had caused the cruiser to follow them out, with the intention of carrying them back again. The English passengers, in particular, began now to reason in favor of the authority of the crown, while those who were known to be Americans grew warm in maintaining the rights of their flag. Both the Effinghams, however, were moderate in the expression of their opinions; for education, years, and experience, had taught them to discriminate justly.

"As respects the course of Captain Truck, in refusing to permit the cutter to board him, he is probably a better judge than any of us," Mr. Effingham observed with gentlemanly reserve; "for he must better understand the precise position of his ship at the time; but concerning the want of right in a foreign vessel of war to carry this ship into port in a time of profound peace, when sailing on the high seas, as will soon be the case with the Montauk,—admitting that she is not there at present,—I should think there can be no reasonable doubt. The dispute, if there is to be any, has now to become matter of negotiation; or redress must be sought through the general agents of the two nations, and not taken by the inferior officers of either party. The instant the Montauk reaches the public highway of nations, she is within the exclusive jurisdiction of the country under whose flag she legally sails."

"Vattel, to the backbone!" said the captain, giving a nod of approbation, again clearing the end of his cigar.

Now, John Effingham was a man of strong feelings, which is often but another word for a man of strong prejudices; and he had been educated between thirty and forty years before, which is saying virtually, that he was educated under the influence of the British opinions that then weighed (and many of which still weigh) like an incubus on the national interests of America. It is true, Mr. Effingham was in all senses the contemporary, as he had been the school-fellow, of his cousin; that they loved each other as brothers, had the utmost reliance on each other's principles in the main, thought alike in a thousand things, and yet, in the particular of English domination, it was scarcely possible for one man to resemble another less than the widowed kinsman resembled the bachelor.

Edward Effingham was a singularly just-minded man, and having succeeded at an early age to his estate, he had lived many years in that intellectual retirement which, by withdrawing him from the strifes of the world, had left a cultivated sagacity to act freely on a natural disposition. At the period when the entire republic was, in substance, exhibiting the disgraceful picture of a nation torn by adverse factions, that had their origin in interests alien to its own; when most were either Englishmen or Frenchmen, he had remained what nature, the laws, and reason intended him to be, an American. Enjoying the *otium cum dignitate* on his hereditary estate, and in his hereditary abode, Edward Effingham, with little pretensions to greatness, and with many claims to goodness, had hit the line of truth which so many of the "godlikes" of the republic, under the influence of their passions, and stimulated by the transient and fluctuating interests of the day, entirely overlooked, or which, if seeing, they recklessly disregarded. A less impracticable subject for excitement,—the *primum mobile* of all American patriotism and activity, if we are to believe the theories of the times,—could not be found, than this gentleman. Independence of situation had induced independence of thought; study and investigation rendered him original and just, by simply exempting him from the influence of the passions ; and while hundreds were keener, abler in the exposition of subleties, or more imposing with the mass, few were as often right, and none of less selfishness, than this simple-minded and upright gentleman. He loved his native land, while he saw and regretted its weaknessess ; was its firm and consistent advocate abroad, without becoming its interested or mawkish flatterer at home ; and at all times, and in all situations, manifested that his heart was where it ought to be.

In many essentials, John Effingham was the converse of all this. Of an intellect much more acute and vigorous than that of his cousin, he also possessed passions less under control, a will more stubborn, and prejudices that often neutralized his reason. His father had inherited most of the personal property of the family, and with this he had plunged into the vortex of moneyed speculation that succeeded the adoption of the new constitution, and verified the truth of the sacred saying, that "where treasure is, there will the heart be also," he had entered warmly and blindly into all the factious and irreconcilable principles of party, if such a word can properly be applied to rules of conduct that vary with the interests of the day, and had adopted the current errors with which faction unavoidably poisons the mind.

America was then much too young in her independence, and too insignificant in all eyes but her own, to reason and act for herself, except on points that pressed too obviously on her immediate concerns to be overlooked ; but the great social principles,—or it might be better to say, the great social interests,—that then distracted Europe, produced quite as much sensation in that distant country, as at all comported with a state of things that had so little practical connection with the result. The Effingham family had started Federalists, in the true meaning of the term ; for their education, native sense, and principles, had a leaning to order, good government, and the dignity of the country ; but as factions became fiercer, and names got to be confounded and contradictory, the landed branch settled down into what they thought were American, and the commercial branch into what might properly be termed English Federalists. We do not mean that the father of John intended to be untrue to his native land; but by following up the dogmas of party he had reasoned himself into a set of maxims which, if they meant anything, meant everything but what had been solemnly adopted as the governing principles of his own country, and many of which were diametrically opposed to both its interests and its honor.

John Effingham had insensibly imbibed the sentiments of his particular sect, though the large fortune inherited from his father had left him too independent to pursue the sinuous policy of trade. He had permitted temperament to act on prejudice to such an extent that he vindicated the right of England to force men from under the American flag, a doctrine that his cousin was too simple-minded and clear-headed ever to entertain for an instant : and he was singularly ingenious in discovering blunders in all the acts of the republic, when they conflicted with the policy of Great Britain. In short, his talents were necessary, perhaps, to reconcile so much sophistry, or to render that reasonably plausible that was so fundamentally false. After the peace of 1815, John Effingham went abroad for the second time, and he hurried through England with the eagerness of strong affection ; an affection that owed its existence even more to opposition than to settled notions of truth, or to natural ties. The result was disappointment, as happens nineteen times in twenty, and this solely because, in the zeal of a partisan, he had fancied theories, and imagined results. Like the English radical, who rushes into America with a mind unsettled by impracticable dogmas, he experienced a reaction, and this chiefly because he found that men were not superior to nature, and discovered so late in the day what he might have known at starting, that particular causes must produce particular effects. From this time, John Effingham became a wiser and a more moderate man ; though, as the shock had not been sufficiently violent to throw him backward on truth, or rather upon the opposing prejudices of another sect, the remains of the old notions were still to be discovered

lingering in his opinions, and throwing a species of twilight
shading over his mind; as, in nature, the hues of evening
and the shadows of the morning follow, or precede the
light of the sun.

Under the influence of these latent prejudices, then, John
Effingham replied to the remarks of his cousin, and the
discourse soon partook of the discursive character of all
arguments, in which the parties are not singularly clear-
headed, and free from any other bias than that of truth.
Nearly all joined in it, and half an hour was soon passed
in settling the law of nations, and the particular merits or
demerits of the instance before them.

It was a lovely night, and Mademoiselle Viefville and
Eve walked the deck for exercise, the smoothness of the
water rendering the moment every way favorable. As has
been already said, the common feeling in the escape of the
new-married couple had broken the ice, and less restraint
existed between the passengers, at the moment when Mr.
Grab left the ship, than would have been the case at the
end of a week, under ordinary circumstances. Eve Effingham had passed her time since her eleventh year principally
on the Continent of Europe, and in the mixed intercourse
that is common to strangers in that part of the world; or,
in other words, equally without the severe restraint that is
usually imposed there on the young of her own sex, or
without the extreme license that is granted to them at
home. She came of a family too well toned to run into
the extravagant freedoms that sometimes pass for easy
manners in America, had she never quitted her father's
house even; but her associations abroad had unavoidably
imparted greater reserve to her ordinary deportment than
the simplicity of cis-Atlantic usages would have rendered
indispensable in the most fastidious circles. With the usual
womanly reserves, she was natural and unembarrassed in her
intercourse with the world, and she had been allowed to
see so many different nations, that she had obtained a self-
confidence that did her no injury, under the influence of an
exemplary education, and great natural dignity of mind.
Still, Mademoiselle Viefville, notwithstanding she had lost

some of her own peculiar notions on the subject, by having
passed so many years in an American family, was a little
surprised at observing that Eve received the respectful
advances of Mr. Sharp and Mr. Blunt with less reserve than
it was usual to her to manifest to entire strangers.  Instead of remaining a mere listener, she answered several
remarks of the first, and once or twice she even laughed
with him openly at some absurdity of the committee of
five.  The cautious governess wondered, but half disposed
to fancy that there was no more than the necessary freedom of a ship in it all,—for, like a true Frenchwoman,
Mademoiselle Viefville had very vague notions of the secrets of the mighty deep,—she permitted it to pass, confid-
ing in the long-tried taste and discretion of her charge.
While Mr. Sharp discoursed with Eve, who held her arm
the while, she herself had fallen into an animated conversation with Mr. Blunt, who walked at her side, and who
spoke her own language so well, that she at first set him
down as a countryman, travelling under an English appellation, as a *nom de guerre.*  While this dialogue was at its
height of interest—for Paul Blunt discoursed with his
companion of Paris and its excellences with a skill that
soon absorbed all her attention, " *Paris, a magnifique
Paris,*" having almost as much influence on the happiness
of the governess, as it was said to have had on that of
Madame de Staël, Eve's companion dropped his voice to a
tone that was rather confidential for a stranger, although it
was perfectly respectful, and said, -

"I have flattered myself, perhaps through the influence
of self-love alone, that Miss Effingham has not so far forgotten all whom she has met in her travels, as to think me
an utter stranger."

"Certainly not," returned Eve, with perfect simplicity
and composure; "else would one of my faculties, that of
memory, be perfectly useless.  I knew you at a glance, and
consider the worthy captain's introduction as so much finesse
of breeding utterly thrown away."

"I am equally gratified and vexed at all this ; gratified
and infinitely flattered to find that I have not passed before

your eyes like the common herd, who leave no traces of
even their features behind them ; and vexed at finding
myself in a situation that, I fear, you fancy excessively
ridiculous !''

"Oh ! one hardly dare to attach such consequences to
acts of young men, or young women either, in an age as
original as our own.  I saw nothing particularly absurd but
the introduction ; and so many absurder have since passed,
that this is almost forgotten.''

"And the name—''

"It is certainly a keen one.  If I am not mistaken, when
we were in Italy, you were content to let your servant bear
it ; but, venturing among a people so noted for sagacity as
the Yankees, I suppose you have fancied it was necessary
to go armed *cap-à-pié*.''

Both laughed lightly, as if they equally enjoyed the
pleasantry, and then he resumed,—

"But I sincerely hope you do not impute improper motives to the incognito ? ''

"I impute it to that which makes many young men run
from Rome to Vienna, or from Vienna to Paris ; which
causes you to sell the *vis-à-vis* to buy a *dormeuse* ; to know
your friends to-day, and to forget them to-morrow ; or, in
short, to do a hundred other things that can be accounted
for on no other motive.''

"And this motive—''

"Is simply caprice.''

"I wish I could persuade you to ascribe some better reason to all my conduct.  Can you think of nothing, in the
present instance, less discreditable?''

"Perhaps I can,'' Eve answered, after a moment of
thought ; then laughing lightly again, she added, quickly,
"but I fear, in exonerating you from the charge of unmitigated caprice, I shall ascribe a reason that does even less
credit to your knowledge.''

"This will appear in the end.  Does Mademoiselle Viefville remember me, do you fancy?''

"It is impossible ; she was ill, you will remember, the
three months we saw so much of you.''

"And your father, Miss Effingham ; am I really forgotten by him ?"

"I am quite certain you are not. He never forgets a face, whatever in this instance may have befallen the name."

"He received me so coldly, and so much like a total stranger !"

"He is too well-bred to recognize a man who wishes to be unknown, or to indulge in exclamations of surprise, or in dramatic starts. He is more stable than a girl, moreover, and may feel less indulgence to caprice."

"I feel obliged to his reserve ; for exposure would be ridiculous, and so long as you and he alone know me I shall feel less awkward in the ship. I am certain neither will betray me."

"Betray !"

"Betray, discover, annihilate me if you will. Anything is preferable to ridicule."

"This touches a little on the caprice ; but you flatter yourself with too much security ; you are known to one more besides my father, myself, and the honest man whom you have robbed of all his astuteness, which I believe was in his name."

"For pity's sake, who can it be ?"

"The worthy Nanny Sidley, my whilom nurse, and actual _femme de chambre_. No ogre was ever more vigilant on his ward than the faithful Nanny, and it is vain to suppose she does not recall your features."

"But ogres sometimes sleep ; recollect how many have been overcome in that situation."

Eve smiled, but shook her head. She was about to assure Mr. Sharp of the vanity of his belief, when an exclamation from her governess diverted the attention of both, and before either had time to speak again, Mademoiselle turned to them, and said rapidly in French,—

"I assure you, _ma chère_, I should have mistaken Monsieur for a _compatriote_, by his language, were it not for a single heinous fault that he has just committed."

"Which fault you will suffer me to inquire into, that I may hasten to correct it ?" asked Mr. Blunt.

" *Mais*, Monsieur, you speak too perfectly, too grammatically, for a native. You do not take the liberties with the language that one who feels he owns it thinks he has a right to do. It is the fault of too much correctness."

"And a fault it easily becomes. I thank you for the hint, Mademoiselle; but as I am now going where little French will be heard, it is probable it will soon be lost in greater mistakes."

The two then turned away again, and continued the dialogue that had been interrupted by this trifling.

"There may also be one more to whom you are known," continued Eve, as soon as the vivacity of the discourse of the others satisfied her the remark would not be heard.

"Surely, you cannot mean him?"

"Surely, I do mean him. Are you quite certain that 'Mr. Sharp, Mr. Blunt; Mr. Blunt, Mr. Sharp,' never saw each other before?"

"I think not until the moment we entered the boat in company. He is a gentlemanly young man; he seems even to be more, and one would not be apt to forget him. He is altogether superior to the rest of the set; do you not agree with me?"

Eve made no answer, probably because she thought her companion was not sufficiently intimate to interrogate her on the subject of her opinions of others. Mr. Sharp had too much knowledge of the world not to perceive the little mistake he had made, and after begging the young lady, with a ludicrous deprecation of her mercy, not to betray him, he changed the conversation with the tact of a man who saw that the discourse could not be continued without assuming a confidential character that Eve was indisposed to permit. Luckily, a pause in the discourse between the governess and her colloquist permitted a happy turn to the conversation.

"I believe you are an American, Mr. Blunt," he remarked; "and as I am an Englishman, we may be fairly pitted against each other on this important question of international law, and about which I hear our worthy captain flourishing extracts from Vattel as familiarly as household terms. I hope, at least, you agree with me in thinking that when the sloop-of-war comes up with us, it will be very silly on our part to make any objections to being boarded by her?"

"I do not know that it is at all necessary I should be an American to give an opinion on such a point," returned the young man he addressed, courteously, though he smiled to himself as he answered, "for what is right, is right, quite independent of nationality. It really does appear to me that a public armed vessel ought, in war or peace, to have a right to ascertain the character of all merchant ships, at least on the coast of the country to which the cruisers belong. Without this power, it is not easy to see in what manner they can seize smugglers, capture pirates, or otherwise enforce the objects for which such vessels are usually sent to sea, in the absence of positive hostilities."

"I am happy to find you agreeing with me, then, in the legality of the doctrine of the right of search."

Paul Blunt again smiled, and Eve, as she caught a glimpse of his fine countenance in turning in their short walk, fancied there was a concealed pride of reason in the expression. Still he answered as mildly and quietly as before,—

"The right of search, certainly, to attain these ends, but to attain no more. If nations denounce piracy, for instance, and employ especial agents to detect and overcome the freebooters, there is reason in according to these agents all the rights that are requisite to the discharge of the duties; but, in conceding this much, I do not see that any authority is acquired beyond that which immediately belongs to the particular service to be performed. If we give a man permission to enter our house to look for thieves, it does not follow that, because so admitted, he has a right to exercise any other function. I do believe that the ship in chase of us, as a public cruiser, ought to be allowed to board this vessel; but finding nothing contrary to the laws of nations about her, that she will have no power to detain or otherwise molest her. Even the right I concede ought to be exercised in good faith, and without vexatious abuses."

"But, surely, you must think that in carrying off a refugee from justice we have placed ourselves in the wrong, and cannot object, as a principle, to the poor man's being taken back again into the country from which he has escaped, however much we may pity the hardships of the particular case?"

"I much question if Captain Truck will be disposed to reason so vaguely. In the first place, he will be apt to say that his ship was regularly cleared, and he had authority to sail; that in permitting the officer to search his vessel, while in British waters, he did all that could be required of him, the law not compelling him to be either a bailiff or an informer; that the process issued was to take Davis, and not to detain the Montauk; that once out of British waters, American law governs, and the English functionary became an intruder, of whom he had every right to rid himself, and that the process by which he got his power to act at all became impotent the instant it was without the jurisdiction under which it was granted."

"I think you will find the captain of yonder cruiser indisposed to admit this doctrine."

"That is not impossible; men often preferring abuses to being thwarted in their wishes. But the captain of yonder cruiser might as well go on board a foreign vessel of war, and pretend to a right to command her, in virtue of the commission by which he commands his own ship, as to pretend to find reason or law in doing what you seem to predict."

"I rejoice to hear that the poor man cannot now be torn from his wife," exclaimed Eve.

"You then incline to the doctrine of Mr. Blunt, Miss Effingham?" observed the other controversialist a little reproachfully. "I fear you make it a national question."

"Perhaps I have done what all seem to have done, permitted sympathy to get the better of reason. And yet it would require strong proof to persuade me that villainous-looking attorney was engaged in a good cause, and that meek and warm-hearted wife in a bad one!"

Both the gentlemen smiled, and both turned to the fair

speaker, as if inviting her to proceed. But Eve checked
herself, having already said more than became her in her
own opinion.

"I had hoped to find an ally in you, Mr. Blunt, to sustain the claim of England to seize her own seamen when
found on board of vessels of another nation," resumed Mr.
Sharp, when a respectful pause had shown both the young
men that they need expect nothing more from their fair
companion ; "but I fear I must set you down as belonging
to those who wish to see the power of England reduced
*coûte qui coûte*."

This was received as it was meant, or as a real opinion
veiled under pleasantry.

"I certainly do not wish to see her power maintained,
*coûte qui coûte*," returned the other. laughing ; "and in this
opinion, I believe, I may claim both these ladies as allies."

"*Certainement!*" exclaimed Mademoiselle Viefville, who
was a living proof that the feelings created by centuries of
animosity are not to be subdued by a few flourishes of the
pen.

"As for me, Mr. Sharp," added Eve, "you may suppose,
being an American girl I cannot subscribe to the right of
any country to do us injustice ; but I beg you will not include me among those who wish to see the land of my
ancestors wronged in aught that she may rightfully claim as
her due."

"This is powerful support, and I shall rally to the rescue.
Seriously, then, will you allow me to inquire, sir, if you
think the right of England to the services of her seamen can
be denied?"

"Seriously then. Mr. Sharp, you must permit me to ask
if you mean by force, or by reason?"

"By the latter, certainly."

"I think you have taken the weak side of the English
argument ; the nature of the service that the subject, or the
citizen, as it is now the fashion to say at Paris, Mademoiselle—"

"*Tant pis*," muttered the governess.

"Owes his government," continued the young man,

slightly glancing at Eve, at the interruption, "is purely a point of internal regulation. In England there is compulsory service for seamen without restriction, or what is much the same, without an equal protection; in France, it is compulsory service on a general plan; in America, as respects seamen, the service is still voluntary."

"Your pardon—will the institutions of America permit impressment at all?"

"I should think not indiscriminate impressment; though I do not see why laws might not be enacted to compel drafts for the ships of war, as well as for the army; but this is a point that some of the professional gentlemen on board, if there be any such, might better answer than myself."

"The skill with which you have touched on these subjects to-night, had made me hope to have found such a one in you; for to a traveller, it is always desirable to enter a country with a little preparation, and a ship might offer as much temptation to teach as to learn."

"If you suppose me an *American lawyer*, you give me credit for more than I can lay claim to."

As he hesitated, Eve wondered whether the slight emphasis he had laid on the two words we have italicized, was heaviest on that which denoted the country, or on that which denoted the profession.

"I have been much in America, and have paid a little attention to the institutions, but should be sorry to mislead you into the belief that I am at all infallible on such points," Mr. Blunt continued.

"You were about to touch on impressment."

"Simply to say that it is a municipal national power; one in no degree dependent on general principles, and that it can properly be exercised in no situation in which the exercise of municipal or national powers is forbidden. I can believe that this power may be exercised on board American ships in British waters—or at least that it is a more plausible right in such situations; but I cannot think it can be rightfully exercised anywhere else. I do not think England would submit to such a practice an hour, reversing the case, and admitting her present strength ; and an appeal of this sort is a pretty good test of principle."

"Ay, ay, what is sauce for the goose is sauce for the gander, as Vattel says," interrupted Captain Truck, who had overheard the last speech or two ; "not that he says this in so many words, but then, he has the sentiment at large scattered throughout his writings. For that matter, there is little that can be said on a subject that he does not put before his readers as plainly as Beachy Head lies before the navigator of the British Channel. With Bowditch and Vattel, a man might sail round the globe, and little fear of a bad landfall, or a mistake in principles. My present object is to tell you, ladies, that the steward has reported the supper in waiting for the honor of your presence."

Before quitting the deck, the party inquired into the state of the chase, and the probable intentions of the sloop-of-war.

"We are now on the great highway of nations," returned Mr. Truck, "and it is my intention to travel it without jostling, or being jostled. As for the sloop, she is standing out under a press of canvas, and we are standing from her in nearly a straight line, in like circumstances. She is some eight or ten miles astern of us ; and there is an old saying among seaman that 'A stern chase is a long chase.' I do not think our case is about to make an exception to the rule. I shall not pretend to say what will be the upshot of the matter ; but there is not the ship in the British navy that can gain ten miles on the Montauk, in her present trim, and with this breeze, in as many hours ; so we are quit of her for the present."

The last words were uttered just as Eve put her foot on the step to descend into the cabin.

5

# CHAPTER VI.

> " *Trin.* Stephano,—
> *Steph.* Doth thy other mouth call me? Mercy! Mercy!"
>
> *Tempest.*

THE life of a packet steward is one of incessant mixing and washing, of interrogations and compoundings, all in a space of about twelve feet square. These functionaries, usually clever mulattoes who have caught the civilization of the kitchen, are busy from morning till night in their cabins, preparing dishes, issuing orders, regulating courses, starting corks, and answering questions. Apathy is the great requisite for the station; for woe betide the wretch who fancies any modicum of zeal, or good-nature, can alone fit him for the occupation. From the moment the ship sails until that in which a range of the cable is overhauled, or the chain is rowsed up in readiness to anchor, no smile illumines his face, no tone issues from his voice while on duty, but that of dogged routine—of submission to those above, or of snarling authority to those beneath him. As the hour for the "drink gelt," or "buona mana," approaches, however, he becomes gracious and smiling. On his first appearance in the pantry of a morning, he has a regular series of questions to answer, and for which, like the dutiful Zeluco, who wrote all his letters to his mother on the same day, varying the dates to suit the progress of time, he not unfrequently has a regular set of answers cut and dried, in his gastronomical mind. "How's the wind?" "How's the weather?" "How's her head?" all addressed to this standing almanac, are mere matters of course, for which he is quite prepared, though it is by no means unusual to hear him ordering a subordinate to go on deck, after the answer is given, with a view to ascertain the facts.   It is only when the voice of the captain is heard from his state-room, that he conceives himself bound to be very particular, though such is the tact of all connected with ships, that they instinctively detect the "know-nothings," who are uniformly treated with an indifference suited to their culpable ignorance.   Even the "old salt" on the forecastle has an instinct for a brother tar, though a passenger, and a due respect is paid to Neptune in answering his inquiries, while half the time the maiden traveller meets with a grave equivoque, a marvel, or a downright mystification.

On the first morning out, the steward of the Montauk commenced the dispensation of his news ; for no sooner was he heard rattling the glasses, and shuffling plates in the pantry, than the attack was begun by Mr. Dodge, in whom "a laudable thirst after knowledge," as exemplified in putting questions, was rather a besetting principle.   This gentleman had come out in the ship, as has been mentioned, and unfortunately for the interest of his propensity, not only the steward, but all on board, had, as it is expressed in slang language, early taken the measure of his foot. The result of his present application was the following brief dialogue.

"Steward," called out Mr. Dodge, through the blinds of his state-room, "whereabouts are we?"

"In the British Channel, sir."

"I might have guessed that myself."

"So I s'pose, sir ; nobody is better at guessing and divining than Mr. Dodge."

"But in what part of the Channel are we, Saunders?"

"About the middle, sir."

"How far have we come to-night?"

"From Portsmouth Roads to this place, sir."

Mr Dodge was satisfied, and the steward, who would not have dared to be so explicit with any other cabin passenger, continued coolly to mix an omelette.   The next attack was made from the same room, by Sir George Temple-more.

"Steward, my good fellow, do you happen to know whereabouts we are?"

"Certainly, sir; the land is still werry obwious."

"Are we getting on cleverly?"

"*Nicely*, sir;" with a mincing emphasis on the first word, that betrayed there was a little waggery about the grave-looking mulatto.

"And the sloop-of-war, steward?"

"Nicely too, sir."

There was a shuffling in the state-room, followed by a silence. The door of Mr. Sharp's room was now opened an inch or two, and the following questions issued through the crevice :—

"Is the wind favorable, steward?"

"Just her character, sir."

"Do you mean that the wind is favorable?"

"For the Montauk, sir; she's a persuader in this breeze."

"But is she going in the direction we wish?"

"If the gentleman wishes to perambulate America, it is probable he will get there with a little patience."

Mr. Sharp pulled-to his door, and ten minutes passed without further questions ; the steward beginning to hope the morning catechism was over, though he grumbled a wish that gentlemen would "turn out" and take a look for themselves. Now, up to this moment, Saunders knew no more than those who had just been questioning him, of the particular situation of the ship, in which he floated as indifferent to the whereabouts and the winds, as men sail in the earth along its orbit, without bethinking them of parallaxes, nodes, ecliptics, and solstices. Aware that it was about time for the captain to be heard, he sent a subordinate on deck, with a view to be ready to meet the usual questions from his commander. A couple of minutes were sufficient to put him *au courant* of the real state of things. The next door that opened was that of Paul Blunt, however, who thrust his head into the cabin, with all his dark curls in the confusion of a night scene.

"Steward!"

"Sir."

" How 's the wind ? "

" Quite exhilarating, sir."

" From what quarter ? "

" About south, sir."

" Is there much of it ? "

" A prewailing breeze, sir."

" And the sloop ? "

" She 's to leeward, sir, operating along as fast as she can."

" Steward ! "

" Sir," stepping hurriedly out of his pantry, in order to hear more distinctly.

" Under what sail are we ? "

" Topgallant-sails, sir."

" How 's her head ? "

" West-southwest, sir."

" Delicious !  Any news of the rover ? "

" Hull down to leeward, sir, and on our quarter."

" Staggering along. eh ? "

" Quite like a disguised person, sir."

" Better still.  Hurry along that breakfast of yours, sir ; I am as hungry as a Troglodyte."

The honest captain had caught this word from a recent treatise against agrarianism, and having an acquired taste for orders in one sense, at least, he flattered himself with being what is called a Conservative ; in other words, he had a strong relish for that maxim of the Scotch freebooter, which is rendered into English by the comely aphorism of " Keep what you 've got, and get what you can."

A cessation of the interrogatories took place, and soon after the passengers began to appear in the cabin, one by one.  As the first step is almost invariably to go on deck, especially in good weather, in a few minutes nearly all of the last night's party were again assembled in the open air, a balm that none can appreciate but those who have experienced the pent atmosphere of a crowded vessel.  The steward had rendered a faithful account of the state of the weather to the captain, who was now seen standing in the main-rigging, looking at the clouds to windward, and at the sloop-of-war to leeward, in the knowing manner of one who was making comparisons materially to the disadvantage of the latter.

The day was fine, and the Montauk, bearing her canvas nobly, was, to use the steward's language, also staggering along, under everything that would draw, from her topgallant-sails down, with the wind near two points forward of the beam, or on an easy bowline. As there was but little sea, her rate was quite nine knots, though varying with the force of the wind. The cruiser had certainly followed them thus far, though doubts began to be entertained whether she was in chase, or merely bound like themselves to the westward; a course common to all vessels that wish to clear the Channel, even when it is intended to go south, as the rocks and tides of the French coast are inconvenient neighbors in long nights.

"Who knows, after all, that the cutter which tried to board us," asked the captain aloud, "belongs to the ship to leeward?"

"I know the boat, sir," answered the second mate; "and the ship is the Foam."

"Let her foam away, then, if she wishes to speak us. Has any one tried her bearings since daylight?"

"We set her by the compass at six o'clock, sir, and she has not varied her bearing, as far as from one belaying pin to another, in three hours; but her hull rises fast: you can now make out her ports, and at daylight the bottom of her courses dipped."

"Ay, ay, she is a light-going Foam, then? If that is the case, she will be alongside of us by night."

"In which event, captain, you will be obliged to give him a broadside of Vattel," threw in John Effingham, in his cool manner.

"If that will answer his errand, he is welcome to as much as he can carry. I begin to doubt, gentlemen, whether this fellow be not in earnest: in which case you may have an opportunity of witnessing how ships are handled, when seamen have their management. I have no objection to setting the experience of a poor come-and-go sort of a fellow, like myself, in opposition to the geometry and Hamilton Moore of a young man-of-war's-man. I dare say, now, yonder chap is a lord, or a lord's progeny, while poor Jack Truck is just as you see him."

"Do you not think half an hour of compliance on our part might bring the matter to an amicable conclusion at once?" said Paul Blunt. "Were we to run down to him, the object of his pursuit could be determined in a few minutes."

"What! and abandon poor Davis to the rapacity of that rascally attorney?" generously exclaimed Sir George Templemore. "I would prefer paying the port-charges myself, run into the handiest French port, and let the honest fellow escape!"

"There is no probability that a cruiser would attempt to take a mere debtor from a foreign vessel on the open sea."

"If there were no tobacco in the world, Mr. Blunt, I might feel disposed to waive the categories, and show the gentleman that courtesy," returned the captain, who was preparing another cigar. "But while the cruiser might not feel authorized to take an absconding debtor from this vessel, he might feel otherwise on the subject of tobacco, provided there has been an information for smuggling."

Captain Truck then explained, that the subordinates of the packets frequently got their ships into trouble, by taking adventures of the forbidden weed clandestinely into European ports, and that his ship, in such circumstances, would lose her place in the line, and derange all the plans of the company to which she belonged. He did the English government the justice to say, that it had always manifested a liberal disposition not to punish the innocent for the guilty ; but were any such complaints actually in the wind, he thought he could settle it with much less loss to himself on his return, than on the day of sailing. While this explanation was delivered, a group had clustered round the speaker, leaving Eve and her party on the opposite side of the deck.

"This last speech of Mr. Blunt's quite unsettles my opinion of his national character, as Vattel and our worthy captain would say," remarked Mr. Sharp. "Last night, I set him down as a right loyal American ; but I think it would not be natural for a thorough-going countryman of yours, Miss Effingham, to propose this act of courtesy to a cruiser of King William.''

"How far any countrymen of mine, thorough-going or not, have reason to manifest extreme courtesy to any of your cruisers," Eve laughingly replied, "I shall leave Captain Truck to say. But, with you, I have long been at a loss to determine whether Mr. Blunt is an Englishman or an American, or indeed, whether he be either."

"Long, Miss Effingham ! He then has the honor of being well known to you ? "

Eve answered steadily, though the color mounted to her brow ; but whether from the impetuous exclamation of her companion, or from any feeling connected with the subject of their conversation, the young man was at a loss to discover.

"Long, as girls of twenty count time—some four or five years ; but you may judge how well, when I tell you I am ignorant of his country even."

"And may I venture to ask which do you, yourself, give him credit for being, an American or an Englishman ? "

Eve's bright eyes laughed, as she answered," You have put the question with so much finesse, and with a politeness so well managed, that I should indeed be churlish to refuse an answer—nay, do not interrupt me, and spoil all the good you have done by unnecessary protestations of sincerity."

" All I wish to say is, to ask an explanation of a finesse, of which I am quite as innocent as of any wish to draw down upon myself the visitations of your displeasure."

" Do you, then, really conceive it a credit to be an American ? "

" Nobody of less modesty than yourself, Miss Effingham, under all the circumstances, would dream of asking the question."

" I thank you for the civility, which must be taken as it is offered, I presume, quite as a thing *en règle* ; but to leave our fine opinions of each other, as well as our prejudices, out of the question—"

"You will excuse me if I object to this, for I feel my good sense implicated. You can hardly attribute to me opinions so utterly unreasonable, so unworthy of a gentleman—so unfounded, in short! Am I not incurring all the risks and hardships of a long sea-voyage, expressly to visit your great country, and, I trust, to improve by its example and society?"

"Since you appear to wish it, Mr. Sharp,"—Eve glanced her playful eye up at him as she pronounced the name.—"I will be as credulous as a believer in animal magnetism; and that, I fancy, is pushing credulity to the verge of reason. It is now settled between us, that you do conceive it an honor to be an American, born, educated, and by extraction."

"All of which being the case with Miss Effingham."

"All but the second; indeed, they write me fearful things concerning this European education of mine: some even go so far as to assure me I shall be quite unfitted to live in the society to which I properly belong!"

"Europe will be rejoiced to receive you back again, in that case; and no European more so than myself."

The beautiful color deepened a little on the cheek of Eve, but she made no immediate reply.

"To return to our subject," she at length said, "were I required to say, I should not be able to decide on the country of Mr. Blunt; nor have I ever met with any one who appeared to know. I saw him first in Germany, where he circulated in the best company; though no one seemed acquainted with his history, even there. He made a good figure; was quite at his ease; speaks several languages almost as well as the natives of the different countries themselves; and, altogether, was a subject of curiosity with those who had leisure to think of anything but their own dissipation and folly."

Mr. Sharp listened with obvious gravity to the fair speaker, and had not her own eyes been fastened on the deck, she might have detected the lively interest betrayed in his. Perhaps the feeling which was at the bottom of all this, to a slight degree, influenced his answer.

"Quite an Admirable Crichton!"

"I do not say that, though certainly expert in tongues. My own rambling life has made me acquainted with a few languages, and I do assure you, this gentleman speaks three or four with almost equal readiness, and with no perceptible accent. I remember, at Vienna, many even believed him to be a German."

"What! with the name of Blunt?"

Eve smiled, and her companion, who silently watched every expression of her varying countenance, as if to read her thoughts, noted it.

"Names signify little in these migratory times," returned the young lady. "You have but to imagine a *von* before it, and it would pass at Dresden, or at Berlin. Von Blunt, *der Edelgeborne Graf Von Blunt, Hofrath*—or if you like it better, *Geheimer Rath mit Excellenz und eure Gnaden*."

"Or, *Baw-Berg-Veg-Inspector-Substitut!*" added Mr. Sharp, laughing. "No, no! this will hardly pass. Blunt is a good old English name; but it has not finesse enough for Italian, German, Spanish, or anything else but John Bull and his family."

"I see no necessity, for my part, for all this Bluntishness; the gentleman may think frankness a good travelling quality."

"Surely, he has not concealed his real name!"

"Mr. Sharp, Mr. Blunt; Mr. Blunt, Mr. Sharp," rejoined Eve, laughing until her bright eyes danced with pleasure. "There would be something ridiculous, indeed, in seeing so much of the finesse of a master of ceremonies subjected to so profound a mystification! I have been told that passing introductions amount to little among you men, and this would be a case in point."

"I would I dared ask if it be really so."

"Were I to be guilty of indiscretion in another's case, you would not fail to distrust me in your own. I am, moreover, a Protestant, and objure auricular confessions."

"You will not frown if I inquire whether the rest of your party remember him?"

"My father, Mademoiselle Viefville, and the excellent Nanny Sidley, again; but, I think, none other of the ser-

vants, as he never visited us. Mr. John Effingham was
travelling in Egypt at the time, and did not see him at all,
and we only met in general society; Nanny's acquaintance
was merely that of seeing him check his horse in the Prater,
to speak to us of a morning."

"Poor fellow, I pity him; he has, at least, never had the
happiness of strolling on the shores of Como and the islands
of Laggo Maggiore in your company, or of studying the
wonders of the Pitti and the Vatican."

"If I must confess all, he journeyed with us on foot and in
boats an entire month, among the wonders of the Oberland,
and across the Wallenstadt. This was at a time when we
had no one with us but the regular guides and the German
courier who was discharged in London."

"Were it not for the impropriety of tampering with a
servant, I would cross the deck and question your good
Nanny, this moment!" said Mr. Sharp with playful menace.
"Of all torture, that of suspense is the hardest to be borne."

"I grant you full permission and acquit you of all sins,
whether of disrespect, meanness, impertinence, ungentleman-
like practices, or any other vice that may be thought to
attend and characterize the act."

"This formidable array of qualities would check the curiosity of a village gossip!"

"It has an effect I did not intend, then; I wish you to
put your threat in execution."

"Not seriously, surely?"

"Never more so. Take a favorable moment to speak to
the good soul, as an old acquaintance: she remembers you
well, and by a little of that interrogating management you
possess, a favorable opportunity may occur to bring in the
other subject. In the meantime, I will glance over the
pages of this book."

As Eve began to read, Mr. Sharp perceived she was in
earnest; and hesitating a moment, in doubt of the propriety
of the act, he yielded to her expressed desire, and strolled
carelessly towards the faithful old domestic. He addressed
her indifferently at first, until believing he might go further,
he smilingly observed that he believed he had seen her in

Italy. To this Nanny quietly assented; and when he indirectly added that it was under another name, she smiled, but merely intimated her consciousness of the fact, by a quick glance of the eye.

"You know that travellers assume names for the sake of avoiding curiosity," he added, "and I hope you will not betray me."

"You need not fear me, sir; I meddle with little besides my own duty, and so long as Miss Eve appears to think there is no harm in it, I will venture to say it is no more than a gentleman's caprice."

"Why, that is the very word she applied to it herself! You have caught the term from Miss Effingham."

"Well, sir, and if I have, it is caught from one who deals little harm to any."

"I believe I am not the only one on board who travels under a false name, if the truth were known?"

Nanny looked first at the deck, then at her interrogator's face, next towards Mr. Blunt, withdrawing her eye again, as if guilty of an indiscretion, and finally at the sails. Perceiving her embarrassment respecting her discretion, and ashamed of the task he had undertaken, Mr. Sharp said a few civil things suited to the condition of the woman, and sauntering about the deck for a short time, to avoid suspicion, soon found himself once more alongside of Eve. The latter inquired with her eyes, a little exultingly, perhaps, concerning his success.

"I have failed," he said; "but something must be ascribed to my own awkward diffidence; for there is so much meanness in tampering with a servant, that I had not the heart to push my questions, even while I am devoured by curiosity."

"Your fastidiousness is not a disease with which all on board are afflicted, for there is at least one grand inquisitor among us, by what I can learn; so take heed to your sins, and above all, be very guarded of old letters, marks, and other tell-tales that usually expose impostors."

"To all that, I believe, sufficient care has already been had, by that other Dromio, my own man."

"And in what way do you share the name between you? Is it Dromio of Syracuse, and Dromio of Ephesus? or does John call himself Fitz-Edward, or Mortimer, or De Courcy?"

"He has complaisance enough to make the passage with nothing but a Christian name, I believe. In truth, it was by a mere accident that I turned usurper in this way. He took the state-room for me, and being required to give a name, he gave his own, as usual. When I went to the docks to look at the ship, I was saluted as Mr. Sharp, and then the conceit took me of trying how it would wear for a month or six weeks. I would give the world to know if the *Geheimer Rath* got his cognomen in the same honest manner."

"I think not, as his man goes by the pungent title of Pepper. Unless poor John should have occasion for two names during the passage, you are reasonably safe. And still, I think," continued Eve, biting her lips, like one who deliberated, "if it were any longer polite to bet, Mr. John Effingham would hazard all the French gloves in his trunks, against all the English finery in yours, that the inquisitor just hinted at gets at your secret before we arrive. Perhaps I ought rather to say, ascertains that you are not Mr. Sharp, and that Mr. Blunt is."

Her companion entreated her to point out the person to whom she had given the *sobriquet* she mentioned.

"Accuse me of giving nicknames to no one. The man has this title from Mademoiselle Viefville, and his own great deeds. It is a certain Mr. Steadfast Dodge, who, it seems, knows something of us, from the circumstance of living in the same county, and who, from knowing a little in this comprehensive manner, is desirous of knowing a great deal more."

"The natural result of all useful knowledge."

"Mr. John Effingham, who is apt to fling sarcasms at all lands, his native country included, affirms that this gentleman is but a fair specimen of many more it will be our fortune to meet in America. If so, we shall not long be strangers; for, according to Mademoiselle Viefville and my good

Nanny, he has already communicated to them a thousand interesting particulars of himself, in exchange for which he asks no more than the reasonable compensation of having all his questions concerning us truly answered."

"This is certainly alarming intelligence, and I shall take heed accordingly."

"If he discover that John is without a surname, I am far from certain he will not prepare to have him arraigned for some high crime or misdemeanor; for Mr. John Effingham maintains that the besetting propensity of all this class is to divine the worst, the moment their imaginations cease to be fed with facts. All is false with them, and it is flattery or accusation."

The approach of Mr. Blunt caused a cessation of the discourse, Eve betraying a slight degree of sensitiveness about admitting him to share in these little asides, a circumstance that her companion observed, not without satisfaction. The discourse now became general, the person who joined them amusing the others with an account of several proposals already made by Mr. Dodge, which, as he expressed it, in making the relation, manifested the strong community-characteristics of an American. The first proposition was to take a vote to ascertain whether Mr. Van Buren or Mr. Harrison was the greatest favorite of the passengers; and, on this being defeated, owing to the total ignorance of so many on board of both the parties he had named, he had suggested the expediency of establishing a society to ascertain, daily, the precise position of the ship. Captain Truck had thrown cold water on the last proposal, however, by adding to it what, among legislators, is called a "ridor"; he having dryly suggested that one of the duties of the said society should be to ascertain also the practicability of wading across the Atlantic.

# CHAPTER VII.

"When clouds are seen, wise men put on their cloaks;
When go at leaves fall, the winter is at hand;
When the sun sets, who doth not look for night?
Untimely storms make men expect a dearth:
All may be well; but if God sort it so,
'T is more than we deserve, or I expect."

*Richard III.*

THESE conversations, however, were mere episodes of the great business of the passage. Throughout the morning, the master was busy in rating his mates, giving sharp reprimands to the stewards and cooks, overhauling the log-line, introducing the passengers, seeing to the stowage of the anchors, in getting down the signal-pole, throwing in touches of Vattel, and otherwise superintending duty. and dispensing opinions. All this time, the cat in the grass does not watch the bird that hops along the ground with keener vigilance than he kept his eye on the Foam. To an ordinary observer, the two ships presented the familiar spectacle of vessels sailing in the same direction, with a very equal rate of speed; and as the course was that necessary to clear the Channel, most of the passengers, and, indeed, the greater part of the crew, began to think the cruiser, like themselves, was merely bound to the westward. Mr. Truck, on the contrary, judging by signs and movements that more naturally suggested themselves to one accustomed to direct the evolutions of a ship, and to reason on their objects, than to the mere subjects of his will, thought differently. To him, the motive of the smallest change on board the sloop-of-war was as intelligible as if it had been explained in words, and he even foresaw many that were about to take place. Before noon, the Foam had got fairly abeam, and Mr. Leach, pointing out the circumstance, observed, that if her wish was to overhaul them, she ought then to tack; it being a rule among seamen, that the pursuing vessel should turn to windward as often as she found herself nearest to her chase. But the experience of Captain Truck taught him better; the tide was setting into the Channel on the flood, and the wind enabled both ships to take the current on their lee-bows, a power that forced them up to windward; whereas, by tacking, the Foam would receive the force of the stream on her weather broadside, or so nearly so, as to sweep her farther astern than her difference in speed could easily repair.

"She has the heels of us, and she weathers on us, as it is," grumbled the master; "and that might satisfy a man less modest. I have led the gentleman such a tramp already, that he will be in none of the best humors when he comes alongside, and we may make up our minds on seeing Portsmouth again before we see New York, unless a slant of wind, or the night, serve us a good turn. I trust, Leach, you have not been destroying your prospects in life by looking too wistfully at a tobacco-field?"

"Not I, sir; and if you will give me leave to say it, Captain Truck, I do not think a plug has been landed from the ship, which did not go ashore in a *bona fide* tobacco-box, that might appear in any court in England. The people will swear, to a man, that this is true."

"Ay, ay! and the Barons of the Exchequer would be the greatest fools in England not to believe them. If there has been no defrauding the revenue, why does a cruiser follow this ship, a regular packet, to sea?"

"This affair of the steerage passenger, Davis, sir, is probably the cause. The man may be heavily in debt, or possibly a defaulter; for these rogues, when they break down, often fall lower than the 'twixt decks of a ship like this."

"This will do to put the quarter-deck and cabin in good humor at sailing, and give them something to open an acquaintance with; but it is sawdust to none but your new beginners. I have known that Seal this many a year, and the rogue never yet had a case that touched the quarterdeck. It is as the man and his wife say, and I 'll not give them up, out here in blue water, for as much foam as lies on Jersey beach after an easterly blow. It will not be any of the family of Davis that will satisfy yonder wind-eater; but he will lay his hand on the whole family of the Montauk, leaving them the agreeable alternative of going back to Portsmouth in his pleasant society, or getting out here in mid-channel, and wading ashore as best they can. D—— n me! if I believe, Leach, that Vattel will bear the fellow out in it, even if there has been a whole hogshead of the leaves trundled into his island without a permit!"

To this Mr. Leach had no encouraging answer to make, for, like most of his class, he held practical force in much greater respect than the abstraction of books. He deemed it prudent, therefore, to be silent, though greatly doubting the efficacy of a quotation from any authority on board, when fairly put in opposition to a written order from the admiral at Portsmouth, or even to a signal sent down from the Admiralty at London.

The day wore away, making a gradual change in the relative positions of the two ships, though so slowly, as to give Captain Truck strong hopes of being able to dodge his pursuer in the coming night, which promised to be dark and squally. To return to Portsmouth was his full intention, but not until he had first delivered his freight and passengers in New York; for, like all men bound up body and soul in the performance of an especial duty, he looked on a frustration of his immediate object as a much greater calamity than even a double amount of more remote evil. Besides, he felt a strong reliance on the liberality of the English authorities in the end, and had little doubt of being able to extricate himself and his ship from any penalties to which the indiscretion or cupidity of his subordinates might have rendered him liable.

Just as the sun dipped into the watery track of the Montauk, most of the cabin passengers again appeared on deck, to take a look at the situation of the two vessels, and to form their own conjectures as to the probable result of the adventure. By this time the Foam had tacked twice, once to weather upon the wake of her chase, and again to resume her line of pursuit. The packet was too good a ship to be easily overtaken, and the cruiser was now nearly hull-down astern, but evidently coming up at a rate that would bring her alongside before morning. The wind blew in squalls, a circumstance that always aids a vessel of war, as the greater number of her hands enables them to make and shorten sail with ease and rapidity.

"This unsettled weather is as much as a mile an hour against us," observed Captain Truck, who was far from pleased at the fact of his being outsailed by anything that floated ; "and, if truth must be said, I think that fellow has somewhere about half a knot the best of it, in the way of foot, on a bowline and with this breeze. But he has no cargo in, and they trim their boats like steelyards. Give us more wind, or a freer, and I would leave him to digest his orders, as a shark digests a marline-spike or a ring-bolt, notwithstanding all his advantages; for little good would it then do him to be trying to run into the wind's eye, like a steam-tug. As it is, we must submit. We are certainly in a category, and be d——d to it ! "

It was one of those wild-looking sunsets that are so frequent in the autumn, in which appearances are worse, perhaps, than the reality. The ships were now so near the Chops of the Channel that no land was visible, and the entire horizon presented that chill and wintry aspect that belongs to gloomy and driving clouds, to which streaks of dull light serve more to give an appearance of infinite space than any of the relief of brightness. It was a dreary nightfall to a landsman's eye, though they who better understood the signs of the heavens, as they are exhibited on the ocean, saw little more than the promise of obscurity, and the usual hazards of darkness in a much-frequented sea.

"This will be a dirty night," observed John Effingham, "and we may have occasion to bring in some of the flaunting vanity of the ship, ere another morning returns."

"The vessel appears to be in good hands," returned Mr.

Effingham: "I have watched them narrowly; for, I know not why, I have felt more anxiety on the occasion of this passage than on any of the nine I have already made."

As he spoke, the tender father unconsciously bent his eyes on Eve, who leaned affectionately on his arm, steadying her light form against the pitching of the vessel. She understood his feelings better than he did himself, possibly, since, accustomed to his fondest care from childhood, she well knew that he seldom thought of others, or even of himself, while her own wants or safety appealed to his unwearying love.

"Father," she said, smiling in his wistful face, "we have seen more troubled waters than these, far, and in a much frailer vessel. Do you not remember the Wallenstadt and its miserable skiff? where I have heard you say there was really danger, though we escaped from it all with a little fright."

"Perfectly well do I recollect it, love; nor have I forgotten our brave companion, and his good service, at that critical moment. But for his stout arm and timely succor we might not, as you say, have been quit for the fright."

Although Mr. Effingham looked only at his daughter, while speaking, Mr. Sharp, who listened with interest, saw the quick, retreating glance of Eve at Paul Blunt, and felt something like a chill in his blood as he perceived that her own cheeks seemed to reflect the glow which appeared on that of the young man. He alone observed this secret evidence of common interest in some event in which both had evidently been actors, those around them being too much occupied in the arrangements of the ship, and too little suspicious, to heed the trifling circumstance. Capain Truck had ordered all hands called, to make sail, to the surprise of even the crew. The vessel, at the moment, was staggering along under as much canvas as she could apparently bear, and the mates looked aloft with inquiring eyes, as if to ask what more could be done.

The master soon removed all doubts. With a rapidity that is not common in merchant ships, but which is usual enough in the packets, the lower studding-sails, and two topmast studding-sails were prepared, and made ready for hoisting. As soon as the words "All ready" were uttered, the helm was put up, the sails were set, and the Montauk was running with a free wind towards the narrow passage between the Scilly Islands and the Land's End. Captain Truck was an expert Channel pilot, from long practice, and keeping the run of the tides in his head, he had loosely calculated that his vessel had so much offing as, with a free wind, and the great progress she had made in the last twenty-four hours, would enable him to lay through the pass.

"'T is a ticklish hole to run into in a dirty night, with a staggering breeze," he said, rubbing his hands as if the hazard increased his satisfaction, "and we will now see if this Foam has mettle enough to follow."

"The chap has a quick eye, and good glasses, even though he should want nerve for the Scilly rocks," cried the mate, who was looking out from the mizzen rigging. "There go his stunsails already, and a plenty of them!"

Sure enough, the cruiser threw out her studding-sails, had them full and drawing in five minutes, and altered her course so as to follow the Montauk. There was now no longer any doubt concerning her object; for it was hardly possible two vessels should adopt so bold a step as this, just at dark, and on such a night, unless the movements of one were regulated by the movements of the other.

In the meantime, anxious faces began to appear on the quarter-deck, and Mr. Dodge was soon seen moving stealthily about among the passengers, whispering here, cornering there, and seemingly much occupied in canvassing opinions on the subject of the propriety of the step that the master had just taken; though, if the truth must be told, he rather stimulated opposition than found others prepared to meet his wishes. When he thought, however, he had collected a sufficient number of suffrages to venture on an experiment, that nothing but an inherent aversion to shipwreck and a watery grave could embolden him to make, he politely invited the captain to a private conference in the state-room occupied by himself and Sir George Templemore. Changing the *venue*, as the lawyers term it, to his own little apartment,—no master of a packet willingly consenting to transact business in any other place,—Captain Truck, who was out of cigars at the moment, very willingly assented.

When the two were seated, and the door of the room was closed, Mr. Dodge carefully snuffed the candle, looked about him to make sure there was no eavesdropper in a room eight feet by seven, and then commenced his subject, with what he conceived to be a commendable delicacy and discretion.

"Captain Truck," he said, in a sort of low, confidential tone that denotes equally concern and mystery. "I think by this time you must have set me down as one of your warm and true friends and supporters. I came out in your ship, and, please God we escape the perils of the sea, it is my hope and intention to return home in her."

"If not, friend Dodge," returned the master, observing that the other paused to note the effect of his peroration, and using a familiarity in his address that the acquaintance of the former passage had taught him was not misapplied, "if not, friend Dodge, you have made a capital mistake in getting on board of her, as it is by no means probable an occasion will offer to get out of her, until we fall in with a news-boat, or a pilot-boat, at least somewhere in the latitude and longitude of Sandy Hook. You smoke, I believe, sir."

"I ask no better," returned Steadfast, declining the offer; "I have told every one on the Continent,"—Mr. Dodge had been to Paris, Geneva, along the Rhine, and through Belgium and Holland, and in his eyes this was the Continent,—"that no better ship or captain sails the ocean; and you know, captain, I have a way with me, when I please, that causes what I say to be remembered. Why, my dear sir, I had an article extolling the whole line in the most appropriate terms, and this ship in particular, put into the journal at Rotterdam. It was so well done, that not a soul suspected it came from a personal friend of yours."

The captain was rolling the small end of a cigar in his mouth to prepare it for smoking, the regulations of the ship forbidding any further indulgence below ; but when he received this assurance, he withdrew the tobacco with the sort of mystifying simplicity that gets to be a second nature with a regular votary of Neptune, and answered with a coolness of manner that was in ridiculous contrast to the affected astonishment of the words,—

"The devil you did ! Was it in good Dutch ? "

"I do not understand much of the language," said Mr. Dodge, hesitatingly ; for all he knew, in truth, was *yaw* and *nein*, and neither of these particularly well, "but it looked to be uncommonly well expressed. I could do no more than pay a man to translate it. But to return to this affair of running in among the Scilly Islands such a night as this."

"Return, my good fellow ! this is the first syllable you have said about the matter ! "

"Concern on your account has caused me to forget myself. To be frank with you, Captain Truck, and if I weren't your very best friend I should be silent, there is considerable excitement getting up about this matter."

"Excitement ! what is that like ? A sort of moral head-sea, do you mean ? "

"Precisely : and I must tell you the truth, though I had rather a thousand times not ; but this change in the ship's course is monstrous unpopular ! "

"That is bad news, with a vengeance, Mr. Dodge ; I shall rely on you, as an old friend, to get up an opposition."

"My dear captain, I have done all I could in that way already ; but I never met with people so bent on a thing as most of the passengers. The Effinghams are very decided, though so purse-proud and grand ; Sir George Templemore declares it is quite extraordinary, and even the French lady is furious. To be as sincere as the crisis demands, public opinion is setting so strong against you, that I expect an explosion."

"Well, so long as the tide sets in my favor, I must endeavor to bear it. Stemming a current, in or out of water, is up-hill work ; but with a good bottom, clean copper, and plenty of wind, it may be done."

"It would not surprise me were the gentlemen to appeal

to the general sentiment against you when we arrive, and
make a handle of it against your line!"

"It may be so indeed; but what can be done? If we
return, the Englishman will certainly catch us, and, in that
case, my own opinion would be dead against me!"

"Well, well, captain; I thought as a friend I would
speak my mind. If this thing should really get into the
papers in America, it would spread like fire in the prairies.
You know what the papers are. I trust, Captain Truck?"

"I rather think I do, Mr. Dodge, with many thanks for
your hints, and I believe I know what the Scilly Islands
are, too. The elections will be nearly or quite over by the
time we get in, and, thank God, they'll not be apt to make
a party question of it, this fall at least. In the meantime
rely on my keeping a good lookout for the shoals of popularity, and the quicksands of excitement. You smoke
sometimes, I know, and I can recommend this cigar as fit to
regale the nose of that chap of Strasbourg—you read your
Bible, I know, Mr. Dodge, and need not be told whom I
mean. The steward will be happy to give you a light on
deck, sir."

In this manner, Captain Truck, with the *sang froid* of
an old tar, and the tact of a packet-master, got rid of his
troublesome visitor, who departed, half suspecting that he
had been quizzed, but still ruminating on the expediency of
getting up a committee, or at least a public meeting in the
cabin, to follow up the blow. By the aid of the latter,
could he but persuade Mr. Effingham to take the chair, and
Sir George Templemore to act as secretary, he thought he
might escape a sleepless night, and, what was of quite as
much importance, make a figure in a paragraph on reaching
home.

Mr. Dodge, whose Christian name, thanks to a pious an-
cestry, was Steadfast, partook of the qualities that his two
appellations not inaptly expressed. There was a singular
profession of steadiness of purpose, and of high principle
about him, all of which vanished in Dodge at the close. A
great stickler for the rights of the people, he never considered that this people was composed of many integral parts,

but he viewed all things as gravitating towards the great aggregation. Majorities were his hobbies, and though singularly timid as an individual, or when in the minority, put him on the strongest side and he was ready to face the devil. In short, Mr. Dodge was a people's man, because his strongest desire, his "ambition and his pride," as he often expressed it, was to be a man of the people. In his particular neighborhood, at home, sentiment ran in veins, like gold in the mines, or in streaks of public opinion ; and though there might be three or four of these public sentiments, so long as each had its party, no one was afraid to avow it ; but as for maintaining a notion that was not thus upheld, there was a savor of aristocracy about it that would damn even a mathematical proposition, though regularly solved and proved. So much and so long had Mr. Dodge respired a moral atmosphere of this community-character, and gregarious propensity, that he had, in many things, lost all sense of his individuality; as much so, in fact, as if he breathed with a pair of county lungs, ate with a common mouth, drank from the town-pump, and slept in the open air.

Such a man was not very likely to make an impression on Captain Truck, one accustomed to rely on himself alone, in the face of warring elements, and who knew that a ship could not safely have more than a single will, and that the will of her master.

The accidents of life could scarcely form extremes of character more remote than that of Steadfast Dodge and that of John Truck. The first never did anything beyond acts of the most ordinary kind, without first weighing its probable effect in the neighborhood ; its popularity or unpopularity ; how it might tally with the different public opinions that were whiffling through the county ; in what manner it would influence the next election, and whether it would be likely to elevate him or depress him in the public mind. No Asiatic slave stood more in terror of a vindictive master than Mr. Dodge stood in fear and trembling before the reproof, comments, censures, frowns, cavillings, and remarks of every man in his county, who happened to belong to the political party that just at that moment was in power. As

to the minority, he was as brave as a lion, could snap his
fingers at them, and was foremost in deriding and scoffing
at all they said and did. This, however, was in connection
with politics only ; for, the instant party-drill ceased to be
of value, Steadfast's valor oozed out of his composition, and
in all other things he dutifully consulted every public opinion of the neighborhood. This estimable man had his weak
points as well as another, and what is more, he was quite
sensible of them, as was proved by a most jealous watchfulness of his besetting sins, in the way of exposure if not
of indulgence. In a word, Steadfast Dodge was a man that
wished to meddle with and control all things, without possessing precisely the spirit that was necessary to leave him
master of himself ; he had a rabid desire for the good opinion of everything human, without always taking the means
necessary to preserve his own ; was a stout declaimer for
the rights of the community, while forgetting that the community itself is but a means set up for the accomplishment
of a given end ; and felt an inward and profound respect for
everything that was beyond his reach, which manifested
itself, not in manly efforts to attain the forbidden fruit, but
rather in a spirit of opposition and detraction, that only betrayed, through its jealousy, the existence of the feeling,
which jealousy, however, he affected to conceal under an
intense regard for popular rights, since he was apt to aver
it was quite intolerable that any man should possess anything, even to qualities, in which his neighbors might not
properly participate. All these, moreover, and many similar traits, Mr. Dodge encouraged in the spirit of liberty !

On the other hand, John Truck sailed his own ship ; was
civil to his passengers from habit as well as policy ; knew
that every vessel must have a captain ; believed mankind to
be little better than asses ; took his own observations, and
cared not a straw for those of his mates ; was never more
bent on following his own views than when all hands grumbled and opposed him ; was daring by nature, decided from
use and long self-reliance, and was every way a man fitted
to steer his bark through the trackless ways of life, as well
as those of the ocean. It was fortunate for one in his par-

ticular position, that nature had made the possessor of so much self-will and temporary authority, cool and sarcastic rather than hot-headed and violent; and for this circumstance Mr. Dodge in particular had frequent occasions for felicitation.

## CHAPTER VIII.

"But then we are in order, when we are
Most out of order."

*Jack Cade.*

DISAPPOINTED in his private appeal to the captain's dread of popular disapprobation, Mr. Dodge returned to his secret work on deck; for like a true freeman of the exclusive school, this person never presumed to work openly, unless sustained by a clear majority; canvassing all around him, and striving hard to create a public opinion, as he termed it, on his sid · of the question, by persuading his hearers that every one was of his particular way of thinking already; a method of exciting a feeling much practised by partisans of his school. In the interval, Captain Truck was working up his day's reckoning by himself, in his own state-room, thinking little, and caring less, about anything but the results of his figures, which soon convinced him, that by standing a few hours longer on his present course, he should "plump his ship ashore" somewhere between Falmouth and the Lizard.

This discovery annoyed the worthy master so much the more, on account of the suggestions of his late visitor; for nothing could be less to his taste than to have the appearance of altering his determination under a menace. Still something must be done before midnight, for he plainly perceived that thirty or forty miles, at the farthest, would fetch up the Montauk on her present course. The passengers had left the deck to escape the night air, and he heard the Effinghams inviting Mr. Sharp and Mr. Blunt into the ladies' cabin, which had been taken expressly for their party, while the others were calling upon the stewards for the usual allowance of hot drinks, at the dining-table without. The talking and noise disturbed him ; his own state-room became too confined, and he went on deck to come to his decision, in view of the angry-looking skies and the watery waste, over which he was called to prevail. Here we shall leave him, pacing the quarter-deck, in moody silence alone, too much disturbed to smoke even, while the mate of the watch sat in the mizzen-rigging, like a monkey, keeping a lookout to windward and ahead. In the meantime, we will return to the cabin of the Effinghams.

The Montauk was one of the noblest of those surpassingly beautiful and yacht-like ships that now ply between the two hemispheres in such numbers, and which in luxury and the fitting conveniences seem to vie with each other for the mastery. The cabins were lined with satin-wood and bird's-eye maple ; small marble columns separated the glittering panels of polished wood, and rich carpets covered the floors. The main cabin had the great table, as a fixture, in the centre, but that of Eve, somewhat shorter, but of equal width, was free from all encumbrance of the sort. It had its sofas, cushions, mirrors, stools, tables, and an upright piano. The doors of the state-rooms and other conveniences, opened on its sides and ends. In short, it presented, at that hour, the resemblance of a tasteful boudoir, rather than that of an apartment in a cramped and vulgar ship.

Here, then, all who properly belonged to the place were assembled, with Mr. Sharp and Mr. Blunt as guests, when a tap at the door announced another visitor. It was Mr. Dodge, begging to be admitted on a matter of business. Eve smiled, as she bowed assent to old Nanny, who acted as her groom of the chambers, and hastily expressed a belief that her guest must have come with a proposal to form a Dorcas society.

Although Mr. Dodge was as bold as Cæsar in expressing his contempt for anything but popular sway, he never came into the presence of the quiet and well-bred without a feeling of distrust and uneasiness, that had its rise in the simple circumstance of his not being used to their company. Indeed, there is nothing more appalling, in general, to the vulgar and pretending, than the simplicity and natural ease of the refined. Their own notions of elegance lie so much on the surface, that they seem at first to suspect an ambush, and it is probable that, finding so much repose where, agreeably to their preconceived opinions, all ought to be fuss and pretension, they imagine themselves to be regarded as intruders.

Mr. Effingham gave their visitor a polite reception, and one that was marked with a little more than the usual formality, by way of letting it be understood that the apartment was private; a precaution that he knew was very necessary in associating with tempers like those of Steadfast. All this was thrown away on Mr. Dodge, notwithstanding every other person present admired the tact with which the host kept his guest at a distance, by extreme attention, for the latter fancied so much ceremony was but a homage to his claims. It had the effect to put him on his own good behavior, however, and of suspending the brusque manner in which he had intended to broach his subject. As everybody waited in calm silence, as if expecting an explanation of the cause of his visit, Mr. Dodge soon felt himself constrained to say something, though it might not be quite as clearly as he could wish.

"We have had a considerable pleasant time, Miss Effingham, since we sailed from Portsmouth," he observed familiarly.

Eve bowed her assent, determined not to take to herself a visit that did violence to all her habits and notions of propriety. But Mr. Dodge was too obtuse to feel the hint conveyed in mere reserve of manner.

"It would have been more agreeable, I allow, had not this man-of-war taken it into her head to follow us in this unprecedented manner." Mr. Dodge was as fond of his dictionary as the steward, though he belonged to the political, while Saunders merely adorned the polite school of talkers. "Sir George calls it a most 'uncomfortable procedure.' You know Sir George Templemore, without doubt, Miss Effingham?"

"I am aware there is a person of that name on board,

sir," returned Eve, who recoiled from this familiarity with the sensitiveness with which a well-educated female distinguishes between one who appreciates her character and one who does not, "but have never had the honor of his acquaintance."

Mr. Dodge thought all this extraordinary, for he had witnessed Captain Truck's introduction, and did not understand how people who had sailed twenty-four hours in the same ship, and had been fairly introduced, should not be intimate. As for himself, he fancied he was, what he termed, "well acquainted" with the Effinghams, from having talked of them a great deal ignorantly, and not a little maliciously; a liberty he felt himself fully entitled to take, from the circumstance of residing in the same county, although he had never spoken to one of the family, until accident placed him in their company on board the same vessel.

"Sir George is a gentleman of great accomplishments, Miss Effingham, I assure you; a man of unqualified merit. We have the same state-room, for I like company, and prefer chatting a little in my berth, to being always asleep. He is a baronet, I suppose you know,—not that I care anything for titles, all men being equal in truth, though—though—"

"Unequal in reality, sir, you probably meant to add," observed John Effingham, who was lolling on Eve's workstand, his eagle-shaped face fairly curling with the contempt he felt, and which he hardly cared to conceal.

"Surely not, sir!" exclaimed the terrified Steadfast, looking furtively about, lest some active enemy might be at hand to quote this unhappy remark to his prejudice. "Surely not! men are every way equal, and no one can pretend to be better than another. No, no,—it is nothing to me that Sir George is a baronet; though one would prefer having a gentleman in the same state-room to having a coarse fellow. Sir George thinks, sir, that the ship is running into great danger by steering for the land in so dark a night, and in such 'dirty' weather. He has many out-of-the-way expressions, Sir George, I must admit, for

one of his rank : he calls the weather 'dirty,' and the proceedings 'uncomfortable'; modes of expression, gentlemen,
to which I give an unqualified disapprobation.''

"Probably Sir George would attach more importance to
a qualified disapprobation," retorted John Effingham.

"Quite likely," returned Mr. Dodge innocently, though
the two other visitors, Eve, and Mademoiselle Viefville, permitted slight muscular movements about the lips to be seen :
"Sir George is quite an original in his way.   We have few
originals in our part of the country, you know, Mr. John
Effingham ; for to say the truth, it is rather unpopular to
differ from the neighborhood, in this or any other respect.
Yes, sir, the people will rule, and ought to rule.   Still, I
think Sir George may get along well enough as a stranger,
for it is not quite as unpopular in a stranger to be original,
as in a native.   I think you will agree with me, sir, in believing it excessively presuming in an American to pretend
to be different from his fellow-citizens ? ''

"No one, sir, could entertain such presumption, I am persuaded, in your case.''

"No, sir, I do not speak from personal motives ;   but on
the great general principles, that are to be maintained for
the good of mankind.   I do not know that any man has a
right to be peculiar in a free country.   It is aristocratic, and
has an air of thinking one man is better than another.   I
am sure Mr. Effingham cannot approve of it?"

"Perhaps not.   Freedom has many arbitrary laws that
it will not do to violate.''

"Certainly, sir, or where would be its supremacy ?   If
the people cannot control and look down peculiarity, or
anything they dislike, one might as well live in a despotism
at once.''

"As I have resided much abroad, of late years, Mr.
Dodge," inquired Eve, who was fearful her kinsman would
give some cut that would prove to be past bearing, as she
saw his eye was menacing, and who felt a disposition to be
amused at the other's philosophy, that overcame the attraction of repulsion she had at first experienced towards him,
"will you favor me with some of those great principles of

liberty of which I hear so much, but which, I fear, have been overlooked by my European instructors?"

Mademoiselle Viefville looked grave ; Messrs. Sharp and Blunt delighted ; Mr. Dodge, himself, mystified.

"I should feel myself little able to instruct Miss Effingham on such a subject," the latter modestly replied, "as no doubt she has seen too much misery in the nations she has visited, not to appreciate justly all the advantages of that happy country which has the honor of claiming her for one of its fair daughters."

Eve was terrified at her own temerity, for she was far from anticipating so high a flight of eloquence in return for her own simple request, but it was too late to retreat.

"None of the many illustrious and godlike men that our own beloved land has produced can pretend to more zeal in its behalf than myself, but I fear my abilities to do it justice will fall short of the subject," he continued. "Liberty, as you know, Miss Effingham, as you well know, gentlemen, is a boon that merits our unqualified gratitude, and which calls for our daily and hourly thanks to the gallant spirits who, in the days that tried men's souls, were foremost in the tented field, and in the councils of the nation."

John Effingham turned a glance at Eve, that seemed to tell her how unequal she was to the task she had undertaken, and which promised a rescue, with her consent ; a condition that the young lady most gladly complied with in the same silent but expressive manner.

"Of all this my young kinswoman is properly sensible, Mr. Dodge," he said by way of diversion ; "but she, and, I confess, myself, have some little perplexity on the subject of what this liberty is, about which so much has been said and written in our time. Permit me to inquire, if you understand by it a perfect independence of thought, action, and rights?"

"Equal laws, equal rights, equality in all respects, and pure, abstract, unqualified liberty, beyond all question, sir."

"What, a power in the strong man to beat the little man, and to take away his dinner?"

"By no means, sir ; Heaven forbid that I should main-

tain any such doctrine ! It means entire liberty : no kings,
no aristocrats, no exclusive privileges ; but one man as
good as another ! ''

" Do you understand, then, that one man is as good as
another, under our system, Mr. Dodge ? "

" Unqualifiedly so, sir ; I am amused that such a question
should be put by a gentleman of your information, in an
age like this ! "

" If one man is as good as another," said Mr. Blunt, who
perceived that John Effingham was biting his lips, a sign
that something more biting would follow, " will you do me
the favor to inform me, why the country puts itself to the
trouble and expense of the annual elections ? "

" Elections, sir ! In what manner could free institutions
flourish or be maintained, without constantly appealing to
the people, the only true sources of power ? "

" To this I make no objections, Mr. Dodge," returned the
young man, smiling ; " but why an election ? If one man
is as good as another, a lottery would be cheaper, easier, and
sooner settled. Why an election, or even a lottery at all ?
why not choose the President as the Persians choose their
king, by the neighing of a horse ? "

" This would be indeed an extraordinary mode of proceeding for an intelligent and virtuous people, Mr. Blunt ;
and I must take the liberty of saying that I suspect you
of pleasantry. If you wish an answer, I will say at once, by
such a process we might get a knave, or a fool, or a traitor."

" How, Mr. Dodge ! I did not expect this character of
the country from you ! Are the Americans, then, all fools,
or knaves, or traitors ? "

" If you intend to travel much in our country, sir, I
would advise great caution in throwing out such an insinuation, for it would be apt to meet with a very general and
unqualified disapprobation. Americans are enlightened and
free, and as far from deserving these epithets as any people
on earth."

" And yet the fact follows from your own theory. If one
man is as good as another, and any one of them is a fool, or
a knave, or a traitor,—all are knaves, or fools, or traitors !

7

The insinuation is not mine, but it follows, I think, inevitably, as a consequence of your own proposition."

In the pause that succeeded, Mr. Sharp said in a low voice to Eve, " He is an Englishman, after all ! "

" Mr. Dodge does not mean that one man is as good as another in that particular sense," Mr. Effingham kindly interposed, in his quality of host; " his views are less general, I fancy, than his words would give us, at first, reason to suppose."

" Very true, Mr. Effingham, very true, sir ; one man is not as good as another in that particular sense, or in the sense of elections, but in all other senses. Yes, sir," turning towards Mr. Blunt again, as one renews the attack on an antagonist, who has given a fall, after taking breath ; " in all other senses, one man is unqualifiedly as good as another. One man has the same rights as another."

" The slave as the freeman ? "

" The slaves are exceptions, sir. But in the free States, except in the case of elections, one man is as good as another in all things. That is our meaning, and any other principle would be unqualifiedly unpopular."

" Can one man make a shoe as well as another ? "

" Of rights, sir,—I stick to the rights, you will remember."

" Has the minor the same rights as the man of full age ; the apprentice as the master ; the vagabond as the resident ; the man who cannot pay as the man who can ? "

" No, sir, not in that sense either. You do not understand me, sir, I fear. All that I mean is, that in particular things, one man is as good as another in America. This is American doctrine, though it may not happen to be English, and I flatter myself it will stand the test of the strictest investigation."

" And you will allow me to inquire where this is not the case, in particular things? If you mean to say that there are fewer privileges accorded to the accidents of birth, or to fortune and station, in America, than is usual in other countries, we shall agree ; but I think it will hardly do to say there are none ! "

" Privileges accorded to birth in America, sir ! The idea
would be odious to her people ! "

" Does not the child inherit the property of the father ? "

" Most assuredly ; but this can hardly be termed a privilege."

" That may depend a good deal on taste. I should account it a greater privilege than to inherit a title without
the fortune."

" I perceive, gentlemen, that we do not perfectly understand each other, and I must postpone the discussion to a
more favorable opportunity ; for I confess great uneasiness
at this decision of the captain's, about steering in among the
rocks of Sylla." (Mr. Dodge was not as clear-headed as
common, in consequence of the controversy that had just
occurred.) " I challenge you to renew the subject another
time, gentlemen. I only happened in " (another peculiarity
of diction in this gentleman) " to make a first call, for I suppose there is no exclusion in an American ship ? "

" None whatever, sir," Mr. John Effingham coldly answered. " All the state-rooms are in common, and I propose to seize an early occasion to return this compliment,
by making myself at home in the apartment which has the
honor to lodge Mr. Dodge and Sir George Templemore."

Here Mr. Dodge beat a retreat, without touching at all on
his real errand. Instead of even following up the matter
with the other passengers, he got into a corner, with one or
two congenial spirits, who had taken great offence that the
Effinghams should presume to retire into their cabin, and
particularly that they should have the extreme aristocratical
audacity to shut the door, where he continued pouring into
the greedy ears of his companions his own history of the
recent dialogue, in which, according to his own account
of the matter, he had completely gotten the better of that
" young upstart, Blunt," a man of whom he knew positively nothing, divers anecdotes of the Effingham family,
that came of the lowest and most idle gossip of rustic malignancy, and his own vague and confused notions of the
rights of persons and of things. Very different was the conversation that ensued in the ladies' cabin, after the welcome

disappearance of the uninvited guest. Not a remark of any sort was made on his intrusion, or on his folly ; even John Effingham, little addicted in common to forbearance, being too proud to waste his breath on so low game, and too well taught to open upon a man the moment his back was turned. But the subject was continued, and in a manner better suited to the education, intelligence, and views of the several speakers.

Eve said but little, though she ventured to ask a question now and then ; Mr. Sharp and Mr. Blunt being the principal supporters of the discourse, with an occasional quiet, discreet remark from the young lady's father, and a sarcasm, now and then, from John Effingham. Mr. Blunt, though advancing his opinions with diffidence, and with a proper deference for the greater experience of the two elder gentlemen, soon made his superiority apparent, the subject proving to be one on which he had evidently thought a great deal, and that too with a discrimination and originality that are far from common.

He pointed out the errors that are usually made on the subject of the institutions of the American Union, by confounding the effects of the general government with those of the separate States ; and he clearly demonstrated that the confederation itself had, in reality, no distinctive character of its own, even for or against liberty. It was a confederation, and got its character from the characters of its several parts, which of themselves were independent in all things, on the important point of distinctive principles, with the exception of the vague general provision that they must be republics ; a provision that meant anything, or nothing, so far as true liberty was concerned, as each State might decide for itself.

"The character of the American government is to be sought in the characters of the State governments," he concluded, "which vary with their respective policies. It is in this way that communities that hold one half of their numbers in domestic bondage are found tied up in the same political *fasces* with other communities of the most democratic institutions. The general government assures neither liberty of speech, liberty of conscience, action, nor of anything else, except as against itself; a provision that is quite unnecessary, as it is purely a government of delegated powers, and has no authority to act at all on those particular interests."

"This is very different from the general impression in Europe," observed Mr. Sharp; "and as I perceive I have the good fortune to be thrown into the society of an American, if not an American lawyer, able to enlighten my ignorance on these interesting topics, I hope to be permitted, during some of the idle moments, of which we are likely to have many, to profit by it."

The other colored, bowed to the compliment, but appeared to hesitate before he answered.

"'T is not absolutely necessary to be an American by birth," he said, "as I have already had occasion to observe, in order to understand the institutions of the country, and I might possibly mislead you, were you to fancy that a native was your instructor. I have often been in the country, however, if not born in it, and few young men, on this side of the Atlantic, have had their attention pointed, with so much earnestness, to all that affects it, as myself."

"I was in hopes we had the honor of including you among our countrymen," observed John Effingham, with evident disappointment. "So many young men come abroad disposed to quarrel with foreign excellences, of which they know nothing, or to concede so many of our own, in the true spirit of serviles, that I was flattering myself I had at last found an exception."

Eve also felt regret, though she hardly avowed to herself the reason.

"He is then an Englishman, after all!" said Mr. Sharp, in another aside.

"Why not a German—or a Swiss—or even a Russian?"

"His English is perfect; no continental could speak so fluently, with such a choice of words, so totally without an accent, without an effort. As Mademoiselle Viefville says, he does not speak well enough for a foreigner."

Eve was silent, for she was thinking of the singular

manner in which a conversation so oddly commenced, had brought about an explanation on a point that had often given her many doubts. Twenty times had she decided in her own mind that this young man, whom she could properly call neither stranger nor acquaintance, was a countryman, and as often had she been led to change her opinion. He had now been explicit, she thought, and she felt compelled to set him down as an European, though not disposed, still, to believe he was an Englishman. For this latter notion she had reasons it might not have done to give to a native of the island they had just left, as she knew to be the fact with Mr. Sharp.

Music succeeded this conversation, Eve having taken the precaution to have the piano tuned before quitting port, an expedient we would recommend to all who have a regard for the instrument that extends beyond its outside, or even for their own ears. John Effingham executed brilliantly on the violin; and, as it appeared on inquiry, the two younger gentlemen performed respectably on the flute, flageolet, and one or two other wind instruments. We shall leave them doing great justice to Beethoven, Rossini, and Meyerbeer, whose compositions Mr. Dodge did not fail to sneer at in the outer cabin, as affected and altogether unworthy of attention, and return on deck to the company of the anxious master.

Captain Truck had continued to pace the deck moodily and alone during the whole evening, and he only seemed to come to a recollection of himself when the relief passed him on his way to the wheel, at eight bells. Inquiring the hour, he got into the mizzen-rigging, with a night-glass, and swept the horizon in search of the Foam. Nothing could be made out, the darkness having settled upon the water in a way to circumscribe the visible horizon to very narrow limits.

"This may do," he muttered to himself, as he swung off by a rope, and alighted again on the planks of the deck. Mr. Leach was summoned, and an order was passed for the relieved watch to remain on deck for duty.

When all was ready, the first mate went through the

ship, seeing that all the candles were extinguished, or that
the hoods were drawn over the sky-lights, in such a way
as to conceal any rays that might gleam upwards from the
cabin. At the same time attention was paid to the bin-
nacle-lamp. This precaution observed, the people went to
work to reduce the sail, and in the course of twenty minutes they had got in the studding-sails, and all the standing
canvas to the topsails, the fore-course, and a forward staysail. The three topsails were then reefed, with sundry
urgent commands to the crew to be active, for " the Englishman was coming up like a horse, all this time, no
doubt."

This much effected, the hands returned on deck, as much
amazed at the several arrangements as if the order had
been to cut away the masts.

" If we had a few guns, and were a little stronger-handed,"
growled an old salt to the second mate, as he hitched up his
trousers and rolled over his quid, " I should think the hard
one, aft, had been stripping for a fight ; but as it is, we have
nothing to carry on the war with, unless we throw sea-
biscuits into the enemy ! "

"Stand by to *veer* ! " called out the captain, from the
quarter-deck : or, as he pronounced it, "*wear*."

The men sprang to the braces, and the bows of the ship
fell off gradually, as the yards yielded slowly to the drag.
In a minute the Montauk was rolling dead before it, and
her broadside came sweeping up to the wind with the ship's
head to the eastward. This new direction in the course
had the double effect of hauling off the land, and of diverging at more than right angles from the line of sailing
of the Foam, if that ship still continued in pursuit. The
seamen nodded their heads at each other in approbation, for
all now as well understood the meaning of the change as if
it had been explained to them verbally.

The revolution on deck produced as sudden a revolution
below. The ship was no longer running easily on an even
keel, but was pitching violently into a head-beating sea,
and the wind, which, a few minutes before, was scarcely felt
to blow, was now whistling its hundred strains among the

cordage. Some sought their berths, among whom were Mr. Sharp and Mr. Dodge; some hurried up the stairs to learn the reason, and all broke up their avocations for the night.

Captain Truck had the usual number of questions to answer, which he did in the following succinct and graphic manner, a reply that we hope will prove as satisfactory to the reader, as it was made to be, perforce, satisfactory to the curious on board.

" Had we stood on an hour longer, gentlemen, we should have been lost on the coast of Cornwall ! " he said, pithily ; " had we stopped where we were, the sloop-of-war would have been down upon us in twenty minutes : by changing the course, in the way you have seen, he may get to leeward of us; if he find it out, he may change his own course, in the dark, being as likely to go wrong as to go right ; or he may stand in, and set up the ribs of his majesty's ship Foam to dry among the rocks of the Lizard, where I hope all her people will get safely ashore, dry-shod."

After waiting the result anxiously for an hour, the passengers retired to their rooms one by one; but Captain Truck did not quit the deck until the middle watch was set. Paul Blunt heard him enter his state-room, which was next to his own, and putting out his head, he inquired the news above. The worthy master had discovered something about this young man which created a respect for his nautical information, for he never misapplied a term, and he invariably answered all his questions promptly, and with respect.

" Dirtier, and dirtier," he said, in defiance of Mr. Dodge's opinion of the phrase, pulling off his pea-jacket, and laying aside his souwester ; " a capful of wind, with just enough drizzle to take the comfort out of a man, and lacker him down like a boot."

" The ship has gone about ? "

" Like a dancing-master with two toes. We have got her head to the southward and westward again ; another reef in the topsails "(which word Mr. Truck pronounced " tawsails," with great unction), " England well under our lee, and the Atlantic ocean right before us. Six hours on this course, and we make a fair wind of it."

"And the sloop?"

"Well, Mr. Blunt, I can give no direct account of her. She has dropped in along-shore, I suspect, where she is clawing off, like a boy climbing a hillock of ice on his hands and knees; or is flying about among the other *foam*, somewhere in the latitude of the Lizard. An easy pillow to you, Mr. Blunt, and no tacking till the first nap 's up."

"And the poor wretches in the Foam?"

"Why, the Lord have mercy on their souls!"

# CHAPTER IX.

"The moon was now
Rising full orbed, but broken by a cloud.
The wind was hushed, and the sea mirror-like."

*Italy.*

MOST of the passengers appeared on deck soon after Saunders was again heard rattling among his glasses. The day was sufficiently advanced to allow a distinct view of all that was passing, and the wind had shifted. The change had not occurred more than ten minutes, and as most of the inmates of the cabin poured up the cabin-stairs nearly in a body, Mr. Leach had just got through with the necessary operation of bracing the yards about, for the breeze, which was coming stiff, now blew from the northwest. No land was visible, and the mate was just giving his opinion that they were up with Scilly, as Captain Truck appeared in the group.

One glance aloft, and another at the heavens, sufficed to let the experienced master into all the secrets of his present situation. His next step was to jump into the rigging, and to take a look at the sea, in the direction of the Lizard. There, to his extreme disappointment, appeared a ship with everything set that would draw, and with a studding-sail flapping, before it could be drawn, which he knew in an instant to be the Foam. At this spectacle Mr. Truck compressed his lips, and made an inward imprecation, that it would ill comport with our notions of propriety to repeat.

"Turn the hands up, and shake out the reefs, sir," he said coolly to his mate, for it was a standing rule of the captain's to seem calmest when he was in the greatest rage. "Turn them up, sir, and show every rag that will draw, from the truck to the lower studding-sail boom, and be d——d to them!"

On this hint Mr. Leach bestirred himself, and the men were quickly on the yards, casting loose gaskets and reef points. Sail opened after sail, and as the steerage passengers, who could show a force of thirty or forty men, aided with their strength, the Montauk was soon running dead before the wind, under everything that would draw, and with studding-sails on both sides. The mates looked surprised, the seamen cast inquiring glances aft, but Mr. Truck lighted a cigar.

"Gentlemen," said the captain, after a few philosophical whiffs, "to go to America with yonder fellow on my weather beam is quite out of the question; he would be up with me, and in possession, before ten o'clock, and my only play is to bring the wind right over the taffrail, where, luckily, we have got it. I think we can bother him at this sport, for your sharp bottoms are not as good as your kettle-bottoms in ploughing a full furrow. As for bearing her canvas, the Montauk will stand it as long as any ship in King William's navy, before the gale. And on one thing you may rely; I'll carry you all into Lisbon, before that tobacco-hating rover shall carry you back to Portsmouth. This is a category to which I will stick."

This characteristic explanation served to let the passengers understand the real state of the case. No one remonstrated, for all preferred a race to being taken; and even the Englishmen on board began again to take sides with the vessel they were in, and this the more readily, as Captain Truck freely admitted that their cruiser was too much for him on every tack but the one he was about to try. Mr. Sharp hoped that they might now escape, and as for Sir George Templemore, he generously repeated his offer to pay, out of his own pocket, all the port-charges in any French, Spanish, or Portuguese harbor the master would enter, rather than see such an outrage done a foreign vessel in a time of profound peace.

The expedient of Captain Truck proved his judgment, and his knowledge of his profession. Within an hour it was apparent that if there was any essential difference in the sailing of the two ships, under the present circumstances, it was slightly in favor of the Montauk. The Foam now set her ensign for the first time, a signal that she wished to speak the ship in sight. At this Captain Truck chuckled, for he pronounced it a sign that she was conscious she could not get them within range of her guns.

"Show him the gridiron," cried the captain, briskly; "it will not do to be beaten in civility by a man who has beaten us already on so many other tacks ; but keep all fast as a church-door on a week-day."

This latter comparison was probably owing to the circumstance of the master's having come from a part of the country where all the religion is compressed into the twenty-four hours that commence on Saturday night at sunset, and end at sunset the next day : at least, this was his own explanation of the matter. The effect of success was always to make Mr. Truck loquacious, and he now began to tell many excellent anecdotes, of which he had stores, all of events that had happened to him in person, or of which he had been an eye-witness ; and on which his hearers, as Sancho said, might so certainly depend as true, that, if they chose, they might safely swear they had seen them themselves.

"Speaking of churches and doors, Sir George," he said, between the puffs of the cigar, "were you ever in Rhode Island ?"

"Never, as this is my first visit to America, captain."

"True ; well, you will be likely to go there, if you go to Boston, as it is the best way ; unless you would prefer to run over Nantucket shoals, and a hundred miles of ditto, as Mr. Dodge calls it."

"*Ditter*, captain, if you please—*ditter*; it is the continental word for round-about."

"The d——l it is ! it is worth knowing, however. And what may be the French for pea-jacket ?"

"You mistake me, sir—*ditter*, a circuit, or the longer way."

"That is the road we are now travelling, by George ! I say, Leach, do you happen to know that we are making a ditter to America ?"

"You were speaking of a church, Captain Truck," politely interposed Sir George, who had become rather intimate with his fellow-occupant of the state-room.

"I was travelling through that State, a few years since, on my way from Providence to New London, at a time when a new road had just been opened. It was on a Sunday, and the stage—a four-horse power, you must know—had never yet run through on the Lord's day. Well, we might be, as it were, off here at right angles to our course, and there was a short turn in the road, as one would say, out yonder. As we hove in sight of the turn, I saw a chap at the masthead of a tree; down he slid, and away he went right before it, towards a meeting-house two or three cables'-length down the road. We followed at a smart jog, and just before we got the church abeam, out poured the whole congregation, horse and foot, parson and idlers, sinners and hypocrites, to see the four-horse power go past. Now this is what I call keeping the church-door open on a Sunday."

We might have hesitated about recording this anecdote of the captain's, had we not received an account of the same occurrence from a quarter that left no doubt that his version of the affair was substantially correct. This and a few similar adventures, some of which he invented, and all of which he swore were literal, enabled the worthy master to keep the quarter-deck in good humor, while the ship was running at the rate of ten knots the hour in a line so far diverging from her true course. But the relief to landsmen is so great, in general, in meeting with a fair wind at sea, that few are disposed to quarrel with its consequences. A bright day, a steady ship, the pleasure of motion as they raced with the combing seas, and the interest of the chase, set every one at ease; and even Steadfast Dodge was less devoured with envy, a jealousy of his own deservings, and the desire of management, than usual. Not an introduction occurred, and yet the little world of the ship got to be better acquainted with each other in the course of that day, than would have happened in months of the usual collision on land.

The Montauk continued to gain on her pursuer until the

sun set, when Captain Truck began once more to cast about
him for the chances of the night.    He knew that the ship
was running into the mouth of the Bay of Biscay, or at
least was fast approaching it, and he bethought him of the
means of getting to the westward.    The night promised to
be anything but dark, for though a good many wild-looking
clouds were by this time scudding athwart the heavens, the
moon diffused a sort of twilight gleam in the air.    Waiting
patiently, however, until the middle watch was again called,
he reduced sail, and hauled the ship off to a southwest course,
hoping by this slight change insensibly to gain an offing before the Foam was aware of it ; a scheme that he thought
more likely to be successful, as by dint of sheer driving
throughout the day, he had actually caused the courses of
that vessel to dip before the night shut in.

Even the most vigilant become weary of watching, and
Captain Truck was unpleasantly disturbed next morning by
an alarm that the Foam was just out of gunshot, coming up
with them fast.    On gaining the deck, he found the fact in-
disputable.    Favored by the change in the course, the cruiser
had been gradually gaining on the Montauk ever since the
first watch was relieved, and had indeed lessened the distance
between the respective ships by two thirds.    No remedy remained but to try the old expedient of getting the wind over
the taffrail once more, and of showing all the canvas that
could be spread.    As like causes are known to produce
like effects, the expedient brought about the old results.
The packet had the best of it, and the sloop-of-war slowly
fell astern.    Mr. Truck now declared he would make a
" regular business of it," and accordingly he drove the ship
in that direction throughout the day, the following night, and
until near noon of the day which succeeded, varying his
course slightly to suit the wind, which he studiously kept so
near aft as to allow the studding-sails to draw on both sides.
At meridian, on the fourth day out, the captain got a good
observation, and ascertained that the ship was in the latitude
of Oporto, with an offing of less than a degree.    At this
time the topgallant sails of the Foam might be discovered
from the deck, resembling a boat clinging to the watery

horizon. As he had fully made up his mind to run into port in preference to being overhauled, the master had kept so near the land, with an intention of profiting by his position, in the event of any change favoring his pursuers; but he now believed that at sunset he should be safe in finally shaping his course for America.

"There must be double-fortified eyes aboard that fellow, to see what we are about at this distance, when the night is once shut in," he said to Mr. Leach, who seconded all his orders with obedient zeal, "and we will watch our moment to slip out fairly into the great prairie, and then we shall discover who best knows the trail! You 'll be for trotting off to the prairies, Sir George, as soon as we get in, and for trying your hand at the buffaloes, like all the rest of them. Ten years since, if an Englishman came to look at us, he was afraid of being scalped in Broadway, and now he is never satisfied unless he is a-straddle of the Rocky Mountains in the first fortnight. I take over lots of cockney-hunters every summer, who just get a shot at a grizzly bear or two, or at an antelope, and come back in time for the opening of Drury Lane."

"Should we not be more certain of accomplishing your plans, by seeking refuge in Lisbon for a day or two? I confess now I should like to see Lisbon; and as for the port-charges, I would rather pay them twice, than that this poor man should be torn from his wife. On this point I hope, Captain Truck, I have made myself sufficiently explicit."

Captain Truck shook the baronet heartily by the hand, as he always did when this offer was renewed, declaring that his feelings did him honor.

"Never fear for Davis," he said. "Old Grab shall not have him this tack, nor the Foam neither. I 'll throw him overboard before such a disgrace befall us or him. Well, this leech has driven us from the old road, and nothing now remains but to make the southern passage, unless the wind prevail at south."

The Montauk, in truth, had not much varied from a course that was once greatly in favor with the London ships, Lisbon and New York being nearly in the same parallel of latitude, and the currents, if properly improved, often favoring the run. It is true, the Montauk had kept closer in with the Continent by a long distance than was usual, even for the passage he had named; but the peculiar circumstances of the chase had left no alternative, as the master explained to his listeners.

"It was a coasting voyage, or a tow back to Portsmouth, Sir George," he said, "and of the two, I know you like the Montauk too well to wish to be quit of her so soon."

To this the baronet gave a willing assent, protesting that his feelings had got so much enlisted on the side of the vessel he was in, that he could cheerfully forfeit a thousand pounds rather than be overtaken. The master assured him that was just what he liked, and swore that he was the sort of passenger he most delighted in.

"When a man puts his foot on the deck of a ship, Sir George, he should look upon her as his home, his church, his wife and children, his uncles and aunts, and all the other lumber ashore. This is the sentiment to make seamen. Now, I entertain a greater regard for the shortest ropeyarn aboard this ship, than for the topsail-sheets or best bower of any other vessel. It is like a man's loving his own finger, or toe, before any other person's. I have heard it said that one should love his neighbor as well as himself; but for my part, I love my ship better than my neighbor's, or my neighbor himself; and I fancy, if the truth were known, my neighbor pays me back in the same coin! For my part, I like a thing because it is mine."

A little before dark the head of the Montauk was inclined towards Lisbon, as if her intention was to run in; but the moment the dark spot that pointed out the position of the Foam was lost in the haze of the horizon, Captain Truck gave the order to "*wear*," and sail was made to the westsouthwest.

Most of the passengers felt an intense curiosity to know the state of things on the following morning, and all the men among them were dressed and on deck just as the day began to break. The wind had been fresh and steady all night, and as the ship had been kept with her yards a little checked, and topmast studding-sails set, the officers reported her to be at least a hundred miles to the westward of the spot where she veered. The reader will imagine the disappointment the latter experienced, then, when they beheld the Foam a little on their weather-quarter, edging away for them as assiduously as she had been hauling up for them the night they sailed from Portsmouth, distant little more than a league!

"This is, indeed, extraordinary perseverance," said Paul Blunt to Eve, at whose side he was standing at the moment the fact was ascertained, "and I think our captain might do well to heave-to and ascertain its cause."

"I hope not," cried his companion with vivacity. "I confess to an *esprit de corps*, and a gallant determination to 'see it out,' as Mr. Leach styles his own resolution. One does not like to be followed about the ocean in this manner, unless it be for the interest it gives the voyage. After all, how much better is this than dull solitude, and what a zest it gives to the monotony of the ocean!"

"Do you then find the ocean a scene of monotony?"

"Such it has oftener appeared to me than anything else, and I give it a fair trial, never having *le mal de mer*. But I acquit it of this sin now; for the interest of a chase, in reasonably good weather, is quite equal to that of a horse-race, which is a thing I delight in. Even Mr. John Effingham can look radiant under its excitement."

"And when this is the case, he is singularly handsome; a nobler outline of face is seldom seen than that of Mr. John Effingham."

"He has a noble outline of soul, if he did but know it himself," returned Eve, warmly: "I love no one as much as him, with the exception of my father, and, as Mademoiselle Viefville would say, *pour cause.*"

The young man could have listened all day, but Eve smiled, bowed gracefully, though with a glistening eye, and hastily left the deck, conscious of having betrayed some of her most cherished feelings to one who had no claim to share them.

8

Captain Truck, while vexed to his heart's core, or, as he expressed it himself, "struck aback, like an old lady shot off a hand-sled in sliding down hill," was prompt in applying the old remedy to the evil. The Montauk was again put before the wind, sail was made, and the fortunes of the chase were once more cast on the "play of the ship."

The commander of the Foam certainly deprecated this change, for it was hardly made before he set his ensign, and fired a gun. But of these signals no other notice was taken than to show a flag in return, when the captain and his mates proceeded to get the bearings of the sloop-of-war. Ten minutes showed they were gaining; twenty did better; and in an hour she was well on the quarter.

Another day of strife succeeded, or rather of pure sailing, for not a rope was started on board the Montauk, the wind still standing fresh and steady. The sloop made many signals, all indicating a desire to speak the Montauk, but Captain Truck declared himself too experienced a navigator to be caught by bunting, and in too great a hurry to stop and chat by the way.

"Vattel has laid down no law for such a piece of complaisance, in a time of profound peace. I am not to be caught by that category."

The result may be anticipated from what has been already related. The two ships kept before the wind until the Foam was again far astern, and the observations of Captain Truck told him he was as far south as the Azores. In one of these islands he was determined to take refuge, provided he was not favored by accident, for going farther south was out of the question, unless absolutely driven to it. Calculating his distance, on the evening of the sixth day out, he found that he might reach an anchorage at Pico, before the sloop-of-war could close with him, even allowing the necessity of hauling up again by the wind.

But Providence had ordered differently. Towards midnight, the breeze almost failed and became baffling, and when the day dawned the officer of the watch reported that it was ahead. The pursuing ship, though still in sight, was luckily so far astern and to leeward as to prevent any danger from a visit by boats, and there was leisure to make the preparations that might become necessary on the springing up of a new breeze. Of the speedy occurrence of such a change there was now every symptom, the heavens lighting up at the northwest, a quarter from which the genius of the storms mostly delights in making a display of his power.

# CHAPTER X.

"I come with mightier things;
Who calls me silent? I have many tones;
The dark sky thrills with low, mysterious moans,
Borne on my sweeping winds."

MRS. HEMANS.

THE awaking of the winds on the ocean is frequently
attended with signs and portents as sublime as any
the fancy can conceive. On the present occasion, the
breeze that had prevailed so steadily for a week was
succeeded by light, baffling puffs, as if, conscious of the mighty
powers of the air that were assembling in their strength,
these inferior blasts were hurrying to and fro for a refuge.
The clouds, too, were whirling about in uncertain eddies,
many of the heaviest and darkest descending so low along
the horizon, that they had an appearance of settling on the
waters in quest of repose. But the waters themselves were
unnaturally agitated. The billows, no longer following each
other in long, regular waves, were careering upward, like
fiery coursers suddenly checked in their mad career. The
usual order of the eternally unquiet ocean was lost in a
species of chaotic tossings of the element, the seas heaving
themselves upward, without order, and frequently without
visible cause. This was the reaction of the currents, and
of the influence of breezes still older than the last. Not
the least fearful symptom of the hour was the terrific calmness of the air amid such a scene of menacing wildness.
Even the ship came into the picture to aid the impression
of intense expectation; for with her canvas reduced, she,
too, seemed to have lost that instinct which had so lately
guided her along the trackless waste, and was "wallowing,"

nearly helpless, among the confused waters. Still she was a beautiful and a grand object, perhaps more so at that moment than at any other ; for her vast and naked spars, her well-supported masts, and all the ingenious and complicated hamper of the machine, gave her a resemblance to some sinewy and gigantic gladiator, pacing the arena, in waiting for the conflict that was at hand.

"This is an extraordinary scene," said Eve, who clung to her father's arm, as she gazed around her equally in admiration and in awe ; "a dreadful exhibition of the sublimity of nature!"

"Although accustomed to the sea," returned Mr. Blunt, "I have witnessed these ominous changes but twice before, and I think this the grandest of them all."

"Were the others followed by tempests?" inquired the anxious parent.

"One brought a tremendous gale, while the other passed away like a misfortune of which we get a near view, but are permitted to escape the effects."

"I do not know that I wish such to be entirely our present fortune," rejoined Eve, "for there is so much sublimity in this view of the ocean unaroused, that I feel desirous of seeing it when aroused."

"We are not in the hurricane latitudes, or hurricane months," resumed the young man, "and it is not probable that there is anything more in reserve for us than a hearty gale of wind, which may, at least, help us to get rid of yonder troublesome follower."

"Even that I do not wish, provided he will let us continue the race on our proper route. A chase across the Atlantic would be something to enjoy at the moment, gentlemen, and something to talk of in after life."

"I wonder if such a thing be possible!" exclaimed Mr. Sharp ; "it would indeed be an incident to recount to another generation!"

"There is little probability of our witnessing such an exploit," Mr. Blunt remarked, "for gales of wind on the ocean have the same separating influence on consorts of the sea, that domestic gales have on consorts of the land. Nothing is more difficult than to keep ships and fleets in sight of each other in very heavy weather, unless, indeed, those of the best qualities are disposed to humor those of the worst."

"I know not which may be called the best, or which the worst, in this instance, for our tormentor appears to be as much better than ourselves in some particulars, as we are better than he in others. If the humoring is to come from our honest captain, it will be some such humoring as the spoiled child gets from a capricious parent in moments of anger."

Mr. Truck passed the group at that instant, and heard his name coupled with the word honest, in the mouth of Eve, though he lost the rest of the sentence.

"Thank you for the compliment, my dear young lady," he said; "and I wish I could persuade Captain Somebody, of his Britannic Majesty's ship Foam, to be of the same way of thinking. It is all because he will not fancy me honest in the article of tobacco, that he has got the Montauk down here, on the Spanish coast, where the man who built her would not know her; so unnatural and unseemly is it to catch a London liner so far out of her track. I shall have to use double care to get the good craft home again."

"And why this particular difficulty, captain?" Eve, who was amused with Mr. Truck's modes of speech, pleasantly inquired. "Is it not equally easy to go from one part of the ocean as from another?"

"Equally easy! Bless you, my dear young lady, you never made a more capital mistake in your life. Do you imagine it is as easy to go from London to New York, now, as to go from New York to London?"

"I am so ignorant as to have made this ridiculous mistake, if mistake it be; nor do I now see why it should be otherwise."

"Simply because it is up-hill, ma'am. As for our position here to the eastward of the Azores, the difficulty is soon explained. By dint of coaxing I had got the good old ship so as to know every inch of the road on the northern passage, and now I shall be obliged to wheedle her along on a new route, like a shy horse getting through a new stable-door. One might as well think of driving a pig from his sty, as to get a ship out of her track."

"We trust to you to do all this and much more at need. But to what will these grand omens lead? Shall we have a gale, or is so much magnificent menacing to be taken as an empty threat of Nature's?"

"That we shall know in the course of the day, Miss Effingham, though Nature is no bully, and seldom threatens in vain. There is nothing more curious to study, or which needs a nicer eye to detect, than your winds."

"Of the latter I am fully persuaded, captain, for they are called the 'viewless winds,' you will remember, and the greatest authority we possess, speaks of them as being quite beyond the knowledge of man: that we may hear the sound of the wind, but cannot tell whence it cometh or whither it goeth."

"I do not remember the writer you mean, my dear young lady," returned Mr. Truck, quite innocently; "but he was a sensible fellow, for I believe Vattel has never yet dared to grapple with the winds. There are people who fancy the weather is foretold in the almanac; but, according to my opinion, it is safer to trust a rheumatis' of two or three years' standing. A good, well-established, old-fashioned rheumatis'—I say nothing of your new-fangled diseases, like the cholera, and varioloid, and animal magnitudes— but a good old-fashioned rheumatis', such as people used to have when I was a boy, is as certain a barometer as that which is at this moment hanging up in the coach-house here, within two fathoms of the very spot where we are standing. I once had a rheumatis', that I set much store by, for it would let me know when to look out for easterly weather, quite as infallibly as any instrument I ever sailed with. I never told you the story of the old Connecticut horse-jockey, and the typhoon, I believe; and as we are doing nothing but waiting for the weather to make up its mind—"

"The weather to make up its mind!" exclaimed Eve, looking around her in awe at the sublime and terrific grandeur of the ocean, of the heavens, and of the pent and moody air; "is there an uncertainty in this?"

"Lord bless you! my dear young lady, the weather is often as uncertain, and as undecided, and as hard to please, too, as an old girl who gets sudden offers on the same day, from a widower with ten children, an attorney with one leg, and the parson of the parish. Uncertain, indeed! Why, I have known the weather in this grandiloquent condition for a whole day. Mr. Dodge, there, will tell you it is making up its mind which way it ought to blow, to be popular; so, as we have nothing better to do, Mr. Effingham, I will tell you the story about my neighbor, the horse-jockey. Hauling yards when there is no wind, is like playing on a Jew's-harp, at a concert of trombones."

Mr. Effingham made a complaisant sign of assent, and pressed the arm of the excited Eve for patience.

"You must know, gentlemen," the captain commenced, looking round to collect as many listeners as possible,—for he excessively disliked lecturing to small audiences, when he had anything to say that he thought particularly clever, —"you must know that we had formerly many craft that went between the river and the islands—"

"The river?" interrupted the amused Mr. Sharp.

"Certain; the Connecticut, I mean; we all call it the river down our way—between the river and the West Indies, with horses, cattle, and other knick-knacks of that description. Among others was old Joe Bunk, who had followed the trade in a high-decked brig for some twenty-three years, he and the brig having grown old in company, like man and wife. About forty years since, our river ladies began to be tired of their bohea, and as there was a good deal said in favor of souchong in those days, an excitement was got up on the subject, as Mr. Dodge calls it, and it was determined to make an experiment in the new quality, before they dipped fairly into the trade. Well, what do you suppose was done in the premises, as Vattel says, my dear young lady?"

Eve's eyes were still on the grand and portentous aspect of the heavens, but she civilly answered,—

"No doubt they sent to a shop and purchased a sample."

"Not they; they knew too much for that, since any

rogue of a grocer might cheat them. When the excitement had got a little headway on it, they formed a tea society, with the parson's wife for presidentess, and her oldest daughter for secretary. In this way they went to work, until the men got into the fever too, and a project was set afoot to send a craft to China for a sample of what they wanted."

"China!" exclaimed Eve, this time looking the captain fairly in the face.

"China, certain; it lies off hereaway, you know, round on the other side of the earth. Well, whom should they choose to go on the errand but old Joe Bunk. The old man had been so often to the islands and back, without knowing anything of navigation, they thought he was just their man, as there was no such thing as losing him."

"One would think he was the very man to get lost," observed Mr. Effingham, while the captain fitted a fresh cigar; for smoke he would, and did, in any company, that was out of the cabin, although he always professed a readiness to cease, if any person disliked the fragrance of tobacco.

"Not he, sir; he was just as well off in the Indian Ocean as he would be here, for he knew nothing about either. Well, Joe fitted up the brig; the Seven Dollies was her name; for you must know, we had seven ladies in the town, who were called Dolly, and they each of them used to send a colt, or a steer, or some other delicate article to the islands by Joe, whenever he went; so he fitted up the Seven Dollies, hoisted in his dollars, and made sail. The last that was seen or heard of the old man for eight months, was off Montauk, where he was fallen in with, two days out, steering southeasterly by compass."

"I should think," observed John Effingham, who began to arouse himself as the story proceeded, "that Mrs. Bunk must have been very uneasy all this time?"

"Not she; she stuck to the bohea in hopes the souchong would arrive before the restoration of the Jews. Arrive it did, sure enough, at the end of eight months, and a capital adventure it proved for all concerned. Old Joe got a great name in the river for the exploit, though how he got to

China no one could say, or how he got back again ; or, for
a long time, how he got the huge, heavy silver teapot, he
brought home with him."

"A silver teapot?"

"Exactly that article. At last the truth came to be
known ; for it is not an easy matter to hide anything of that
nature down our way ; it is aristocratic, as Mr. Dodge says,
to keep a secret. At first they tried Joe with all sorts of
questions, but he gave them 'guess' for 'guess.' Then
people began to talk, and finally it was fairly whispered that
the old man had stolen the teapot. This brought him
before the meeting. Law was out of the question, you will
understand, as there was no evidence ; but the meeting
don't stick much at particulars, provided people talk a good
deal."

"And the result?" asked John Effingham ; "I suppose
the parish took the teapot and left Joe the grounds."

"You are as far out of the way as we are here down on
the coast of Spain! The truth is just this. The Seven
Dollies was lying among the rest of them, at anchor, below
Canton, with the weather as fine as young girls love to see
it in May, when Joe began to get down his yards, to house
his masts, and to send out all his spare anchors. He even
went so far as to get two hawsers fastened to a junk that
had grounded a little ahead of him. This made a talk
among the captains of the vessels, and some came on board
to ask the reason. Joe told them he was getting ready for
the typhoon ; but when they inquired his reasons for believing there was to be a typhoon at all, Joe looked solemn,
shook his head, and said he had reasons enough, but they
were his own. Had he been explicit, he would have been
laughed at, but the sight of an old gray-headed man, who
had been at sea forty years, getting ready in this serious
manner, set the others at work too ; for ships follow each
other's movements, like sheep running through a breach in
the fence. Well, that night the typhoon came in earnest,
and it blew so hard, that Joe Bunk said he could see the
houses in the moon, all the air having blown out of the
atmosphere."

"But what has this to do with the teapot, Captain Truck?"

"It is the life and soul of it. The captains in port were so delighted with Joe's foreknowledge, that they clubbed, and presented him this pot as a testimony of their gratitude and esteem. He'd got to be popular among them, Mr. Dodge, and that was the way they proved it."

"But, pray, how did he know the storm was approaching?" asked Eve, whose curiosity had been awakened in spite of herself. "It could not have been that his 'foreknowledge' was supernatural."

"That no one can say, for Joe was Presbyterian-built, as we say, kettle-bottomed, and stowed well. The truth was not discovered until ten years afterwards, when the old fellow got to be a regular cripple, what between rheumatis', old age, and steaming. One day he had an attack of the first complaint, and in one of its most severe paroxysms, when nature is apt to wince, he roared three times, 'A typhoon! a typhoon! a typhoon!' and the murder was out. Sure enough, the next day we had a regular northeaster; but old Joe got no sign of popularity that time. And now, when you get to America, gentlemen and ladies, you will be able to say you have heard the story of Joe Bunk and his teapot."

Thereupon Captain Truck took two or three hearty whiffs of the cigar, turned his face upwards and permitted the smoke to issue forth in a continued stream until it was exhausted, but still keeping his head raised in the inconvenient position it had taken. The eye of the master, fastened in this manner on something aloft, was certain to draw other eyes in the same direction, and in a few seconds all around him were gazing in the same way, though none but himself could tell why.

"Turn up the watch below, Mr. Leach," Captain Truck at length called out, and Eve observed that he threw away the cigar, although a fresh one; a proof, as she fancied, that he was preparing for duty.

The people were soon at their places, and an effort was made to get the ship's head round to the southward.

Although the frightful stillness of the atmosphere rendered the manœuvre difficult, it succeeded in the end, by profiting by the passing and fitful currents, that resembled so many sighings of the air. The men were then sent on the yards, to furl all the canvas, with the exception of the three topsails and the fore-course, most of it having been merely hauled up to await the result. All those who had ever been at sea before, saw in these preparations proof that Captain Truck expected the change would be sudden and severe; still, as he betrayed no uneasiness, they hoped his measures were merely those of prudence. Mr. Effingham could not refrain from inquiring, however, if there existed any immediate motives for the preparations that were so actively, though not hurriedly, making.

"This is no affair for the rheumatis'," returned the facetious master, "for, look you here, my worthy sir, and you, my dear young lady,"—this was a sort of parental familiarity the honest Jack fancied he had a right to take with all his unmarried female passengers, in virtue of his office, and of his being a bachelor drawing hard upon sixty,—"look you here, my dear young lady, and you, too Ma'amselle, for you can understand the clouds, I take it, if they are not French clouds; do you not see the manner in which those black-looking rascals are putting their heads together? They are plotting something quite in their own way, I'll warrant you."

"The clouds are huddling, and rolling over each other, certainly," returned Eve, who had been struck with the wild beauty of their evolutions, "and a noble, though fearful picture they present; but I do not understand the particular meaning of it, if there be any hidden omen in their airy flights."

"No rheumatis' about you, young lady," said the captain, jocularly; "too young, and handsome, and too modern, too, I dare say, for that old-fashioned complaint. But on one category you may rely, and that is, that nothing in nature conspires without an object."

"But I do not think vapor whirling in a current of air is a conspiracy," answered Eve, laughing, "though it may be a category."

"Perhaps not,—who knows, however? for it is as easy to suppose that objects understand each other, as that horses and dogs understand each other. We know nothing about it, and, therefore, it behooves us to say nothing. If mankind conversed only of the things they understood, half the words might be struck out of the dictionaries. But, as I was remarking, those clouds, you can see, are getting together, and are making ready for a start, since here they will not be able to stay much longer."

"And what will compel them to disappear?"

"Do me the favor to turn your eyes here, to the nor'-west. You see an opening there that looks like a crouching lion; is it not so?"

"There is certainly a bright, clear streak of sky along the margin of the ocean, that has quite lately made its appearance; does it prove that the wind will blow from that quarter?"

"Quite as much, my dear young lady, as when you open your window it proves that you mean to put your head out of it."

"An act a well-bred young woman very seldom performs," observed Mademoiselle Viefville; "and never in a town."

"No? Well, in our town on the river, the women's heads are half the time out of the windows. But I do not pretend, Ma'amselle, to be expert in proprieties of this sort, though I can venture to say that I am somewhat of a judge of what the winds would be about when they open *their* shutters. This opening to the nor'west, then, is a sure sign of something coming out of the window, well-bred or not."

"But," added Eve, "the clouds above us, and those farther south, appear to be hurrying towards your bright opening, captain, instead of from it."

"Quite in nature, gentlemen; quite in nature, ladies. When a man has fully made up his mind to retreat, he blusters the most; and one step forward often promises two backward. You often see the stormy petrel sailing at a ship as if he meant to come aboard, but he takes good care to put his helm down before he is fairly in the rigging. So it is with clouds, and all other things in nature. Vattel says you may make a show of fight when your necessities require it, but that a neutral cannot fire a gun, unless against pirates. Now, these clouds are putting the best face on the matter, but in a few minutes you will see them wheeling as St. Paul did before them."

"St. Paul, Captain Truck!"

"Yes, my dear young lady; to the right-about."

Eve frowned, for she disliked some of these nautical images, though it was impossible not to smile in secret at the queer associations that so often led the well-meaning master's discursive discourse. His mind was a strange jumble of an early religious education,—religious as to externals and professions, at least,—with subsequent loose observation and much worldly experience, and he drew on his stock of information, according to his own account of the matter, "as Saunders, the steward, cut the butter from the firkins, or as it came first."

His prediction concerning the clouds proved to be true, for half an hour did not pass before they were seen "scampering out of the way of the nor'wester," to use the captain's figure, "like sheep giving play to the dogs." The horizon brightened with a rapidity almost supernatural, and, in a surprisingly short space of time, the whole of that frowning vault that had been shadowed by murky and menacing vapor, sporting its gambols in ominous wildness, was cleared of everything like a cloud, with the exception of a few white, rich, fleecy piles, that were grouped in the north, like a battery discharging its artillery on some devoted field.

The ship betrayed the arrival of the wind by a cracking of the spars, as they settled into their places, and then the huge hull began to push aside the waters, and to come under control. The first shock was far from severe, though, as the captain determined to bring his vessel up as near his course as the direction of the breeze would permit, he soon found he had as much canvas spread as she could bear. Twenty minutes brought him to a single reef, and half an hour to a second.

By this time attention was drawn to the Foam. The

old superiority of that cruiser was now apparent again, and calculations were made concerning the possibility of avoiding her, if they continued to stand on much longer on the present course. The captain had hoped the Montauk would have the advantage from her greater bulk, when the two vessels should be brought down to close-reefed topsails, as he foresaw would be the case; but he was soon compelled to abandon even that hope. Farther to the southward he was resolved he would not go, as it would be leading him too far astray, and, at last, he came to the determination to stand towards the islands, which were as near as might be in his track, and to anchor in a neutral roadstead, if too hard pressed.

" He cannot get up with us before midnight, Leach," he concluded the conference held with the mate by saying; " and by that time the gale will be at its height, if we are to have a gale, and then the gentleman will not be desirous of lowering his boats. In the meantime we shall be driving in towards the Azores, and it will be nothing out of the course of nature, should I find an occasion to play him a trick. As for offering up the Montauk a sacrifice on the altar of tobacco, as old Deacon Hourglass used to say in his prayers, it is a category to be averted by any catastrophe short of condemnation."

# CHAPTER XI.

"I, that shower dewy light
Through slumbering leaves, bring storms!—the tempest birth
Of memory, thought, remorse. Be holy, Earth!
I am the solemn Night!"

MRS. HEMANS.

IN this instance, it is not our task to record any of the phenomena of the ocean, but a regular, though fierce, gale of wind. One of the first signs of its severity was the disappearance of the passengers from the deck, one shutting himself in his room after another, until none remained visible but John Effingham and Paul Blunt. Both these gentlemen, as it appeared, had made so many passages, and had got to be so familiar with ships, that sea-sickness and alarms were equally impotent as respected their constitutions and temperaments.

The poor steerage passengers were no exception, but they stole for refuge into their dens, heartily repentant, for the time being, at having braved the dangers and discomforts of the sea. The gentle wife of Davis would now willingly have returned to meet the resentment of her uncle; and as for the bridegroom himself, as Mr. Leach, who passed through this scene of abominations to see that all was right, described him, "Mr. Grab would not wring him for a dishcloth, if he could see him in his present pickle."

Captain Truck chuckled a good deal at this account, for he had much the same sympathy for ordinary cases of sea-sickness, as a kitten feels in the agony of the first mouse it has caught, and which it is its sovereign pleasure to play with, instead of eating.

"It serves him right, Mr. Leach, for getting married; and

mind you don't fall into the same abuse of your opportunities," he said, with an air of self-satisfaction, while comparing three or four cigars in the palm of his hand, doubtful which of the fragrant plump rolls to put into his mouth. "Getting married, Mr. Blunt, commonly makes a man a fit subject for nausea, and nothing is easier than to set the stomach-pump in motion in one of your bridegrooms ; is not this true as the gospel, Mr. John Effingham? "

Mr. John Effingham made no reply ; but the young man who at the moment was admiring his fine form and the noble outline of his features, was singularly struck with the bitterness, not to say anguish, of the smile with which he bowed a cold assent. All this was lost on Captain Truck, who proceeded *con amore*.

"One of the first things that I ask concerning my passengers is, Is he married? when the answer is ' No,' I set him down as a good companion in a gale like this, or as one who can smoke, or crack a joke when a topsail is flying out of a bolt-rope—a companion for a category. Now, if either of you gentlemen had a wife, she would have you under hatches to-day, lest you should slip through a scupper-hole, or be washed overboard with the spray, or have your eyebrows blown away in such a gale, and then I should lose the honor of your company. Comfort is too precious to be thrown away in matrimony. A man may gain foreknowledge by a wife, but he loses free agency. As for you, Mr. John Effingham, you must have coiled away about half a century of life, and there is not much to fear on your account ; but Mr. Blunt is still young enough to be in danger of a mishap. I wish Neptune would come aboard of us, hereaway, and swear you to be true and constant to yourself, young gentleman."

Paul laughed, colored slightly, and then rallying he replied in the same voice,—

"At the risk of losing your good opinion, captain, and even in the face of this gale, I shall avow myself an advocate of matrimony."

"If you will answer me one question, my dear sir, I will tell you whether the case is, or is not, hopeless."

9

"In order to assent to this, you will of course see the necessity of letting me know what the question is."

"Have you made up your mind who the young woman shall be? If that point is settled, I can only recommend to you some of Joe Bunk's souchong, and advise you to submit, for there is no resisting one's fate. The reason your Turks yield so easily to predestination and fate, is the number of their wives. Many a book is written to show the cause of their submitting their necks so easily to the sword and bowstring. I've been in Turkey, gentlemen, and know something of their ways. The reason of their submitting so quietly to be beheaded is, that they are always ready to hang themselves. How is the fact, sir? Have you settled upon the young lady in your own mind, or not?"

Although there was nothing in all this but the permitted trifling of boon-companions on shipboard, Paul Blunt received it with an awkwardness one would hardly have expected in a young man of his knowledge of the world. He reddened, laughed, made an effort to throw the captain to a greater distance by reserve, and in the end fairly gave up the matter, by walking to another part of the deck. Luckily, the attention of the honest master was drawn to the ship, at that instant, and Paul flattered himself he was unperceived; but the shadow of a figure at his elbow startled him, and, turning quickly, he found Mr. John Effingham at his side.

"Her mother was an angel," said the latter, huskily. "I, too, love her; but it is as a father."

"Sir!—Mr. Effingham!—these are sudden and unexpected remarks, and such as I am not prepared for."

"Do you think one as jealous of that fair creature as I, could have overlooked your passion? She is loved by *both* of you, and she merits the warmest affection of a thousand. Persevere, for while I have no voice, and, I fear, little influence on her decision, some strange sympathy causes me to wish you success. My own man told me that you have met before, and with her father's knowledge, and this is all I ask, for my kinsman is discreet. He probably knows you, though I do not."

The face of Paul glowed like fire, and he almost gasped

for breath. Pitying his distress, Effingham smiled kindly, and was about to quit him, when he felt his hand convulsively grasped by those of the young man.

"Do not quit me, Mr. Effingham, I entreat you," he said rapidly; " it is so unusual for me to hear words of confidence, or even of kindness, that they are most precious to me!  I have permitted myself to be disturbed by the random remarks of that well-meaning, but unreflecting man; but in a moment I shall be more composed—more manly—less unworthy of your attention and pity."

"Pity is a word I should never have thought of applying to the person, character, attainments, or as I hoped, fortunes of Mr. Blunt; and I sincerely trust that you will acquit me of impertinence.  I have felt an interest in you, young man, that I have long ceased to feel in most of my species, and I trust this will be some apology for the liberty I have taken. Perhaps the suspicion that you were anxious to stand well in the good opinion of my little cousin was at the bottom of it all."

"Indeed you have not misconceived my anxiety, sir; for who is there that could be indifferent to the good opinion of one so simple and yet so cultivated; with a mind in which nature and knowledge seem to struggle for the possession. One, Mr. Effingham, so little like the cold sophistication and heartlessness of Europe on the one hand, and the unformed girlishness of America, on the other; one, in short, so every way what the fondest father or the most sensitive brother could wish."

John Effingham smiled, for to smile at any weakness was with him a habit; but his eye glistened.  After a moment of doubt, he turned to his young companion, and with a delicacy of expression and a dignity of manner that none could excel him in, when he chose, he put a question that for several days had been uppermost in his thoughts, though no fitting occasion had ever before offered, on which he thought he might venture.

"This frank confidence emboldens me—one who ought to be ashamed to boast of his greater experience, when every day shows him to how little profit it has been turned

—to presume to render our acquaintance less formal, by al-
luding to interests more personal than strangers have a right
to touch on. You speak of the two parts of the world just
mentioned, in a way to show me you are equally acquainted
with both."

" I have often crossed the ocean, and, for so young a man,
have seen a full share of their societies. Perhaps it increases
my interest in your lovely kinswoman, that, like myself, she
properly belongs to neither."

" Be cautious how you whisper that in her ear, my youthful friend ; for Eve Effingham fancies herself as much
American in character as in birth. Single-minded and
totally without management, devoted to her duties, religious
without cant, a warm friend of liberal institutions, without
the slightest approach to the impracticable, in heart and soul
a woman, you will find it hard to persuade her, that with all
her practice in the world, and all her extensive attainments,
she is more than a humble copy of her own great *beau idéal.*"

Paul smiled, and his eyes met those of John Effingham.
The expression of both satisfied the parties that they thought
alike in more things than in their common admiration of the
subject of their discourse.

" I feel I have not been as explicit as I ought to be with
you, Mr. Effingham," the young man resumed, after a
pause ; "but on a more fitting occasion, I shall presume on
your kindness to be less reserved. My lot has thrown me
on the world, almost without friends, quite without relatives,
so far as intercourse with them is concerned ; and I have
known little of the language or the acts of the affections."

John Effingham pressed his hand, and from that time he
cautiously abstained from any allusion to his personal concerns ; for a suspicion crossed his mind that the subject was
painful to the young man. He knew that thousands of
well-educated and frequently of affluent people, of both
sexes, were to be found in Europe, to whom, from the circumstance of having been born out of wedlock, through
divorces, or other family misfortunes, their private histories
were painful, and he at once inferred that some such event,
quite probably the first, lay at the bottom of Paul Blunt's

peculiar situation. Notwithstanding his warm attachment to Eve, he had too much confidence in her own as well as in her father's judgment, to suppose an acquaintance of any intimacy would be lightly permitted ; and as to the mere prejudices connected with such subjects, he was quite free from them. Perhaps his masculine independence of character caused him, on all such points, to lean to the side of the *ultra* in liberality.

In this short dialogue, with the exception of the slight though unequivocal allusion of John Effingham, both had avoided any further allusions to Mr. Sharp, or to his supposed attachment to Eve. Both were confident of its existence, and this perhaps was one reason why neither felt any necessity to advert to it ; for it was a delicate subject, and one, under the circumstances, that they would mutually wish to forget in their cooler moments. The conversation then took a more general character, and for several hours that day, while the rest of the passengers were kept below by the state of the weather, these two were together, laying what perhaps it was now too late to term the foundation of a generous and sincere friendship. Hitherto Paul had regarded John Effingham with distrust and awe, but he found him a man so different from what report and his own fancy had pictured, that the reaction in his feelings served to heighten them, and to aid in increasing his respect. On the other hand, the young man exhibited so much modest good sense, a fund of information so much beyond his years, such integrity and justice of sentiment, that when they separated for the night, the old bachelor was full of regret that nature had not made him the parent of such a son.

All this time the business of the ship had gone on. The wind increased steadily, until, as the sun went down, Captain Truck announced it, in the cabin, to be a "regular-built gale of wind." Sail after sail had been reduced or furled, until the Montauk was lying-to under her foresail, a close-reefed main-topsail, a fore-topmast staysail, and a mizzen-staysail. Doubts were even entertained whether the second of these sails would not have to be handed soon, and the foresail itself reefed.

The ship's head was to the south-southwest, her drift considerable, and her way of course barely sufficient to cause her to feel her helm. The Foam had gained on her several miles during the time sail could be carried; but she, also, had been obliged to heave-to, at the same increase of the sea and wind as that which had forced Mr. Truck to lash his wheel down. This state of things made a considerable change in the relative positions of the two vessels again; the next morning showing the sloop-of-war hull down, and well on the weather-beam of the packet. Her sharper mould and more weatherly qualities had done her this service, as became a ship intended for war and the chase.

At all this, however, Captain Truck laughed. He could not be boarded in such weather, and it was matter of indifference where his pursuer might be, so long as he had time to escape, when the gale ceased. On the whole, he was rather glad than otherwise of the present state of things, for it offered a chance to slip away to leeward as soon as the weather would permit, if, indeed, his tormentor did not altogether disappear in the northern board, or to windward.

The hopes and fears of the worthy master, however, were poured principally into the ears of his two mates; for few of the passengers were visible until the afternoon of the second day of the gale; then, indeed, a general relief to their physical suffering occurred, though it was accompanied by apprehensions that scarcely permitted the change to be enjoyed. About noon, on that day, the wind came with such power, and the seas poured down against the bows of the ship with a violence so tremendous, that it got to be questionable whether she could any longer remain with safety in her present condition. Several times in the course of the morning, the waves had forced her bows off, and before the ship could recover her position, the succeeding billow would break against her broadside, and throw a flood of water on her decks. This is a danger peculiar to lying-to in a gale; for if the vessel get into the trough of the sea, and is met in that situation by a wave of unusual magnitude, she runs the double risk of being thrown on her beam-ends, and of having her decks cleared of everything, by the cataract of water that washes athwart them. Landsmen entertain little notion of the power of the waters, when driven before a tempest, and are often surprised, in reading of naval catastrophes, at the description of the injuries done. But experience shows that boats, hurricanehouses, guns, anchors of enormous weight, bulwarks, and planks, are even swept off into the ocean, in this manner, or are ripped up from their fastenings.

The process of lying-to has a double advantage, so long as it can be maintained, since it offers the strongest portion of the vessel to the shock of the seas, and has the merit of keeping her as near as possible to the desired direction. But it is a middle course, being often adopted as an expedient of safety when a ship cannot scud ; and then, again, it is abandoned for scudding when the gale is so intensely severe that it becomes in itself dangerous. In nothing are the high qualities of ships so thoroughly tried as in their manner of behaving, as it is termed, in these moments of difficulty ; nor is the seamanship of the accomplished officer so triumphantly established in any other part of his professional knowledge, as when he has had an opportunity of showing that he knows how to dispose of the vast weight his vessel is to carry, so as to enable her mould to exhibit its perfection, and on occasion to turn both to the best account.

Nothing will seem easier to a landsman than for a vessel to run before the wind, let the force of the gale be what it may. But his ignorance overlooks most of the difficulties, nor shall we anticipate their dangers, but let them take their places in the regular thread of the narrative.

Long before noon, or the hour mentioned, Captain Truck foresaw that, in consequence of the seas that were constantly coming on board of her, he should be compelled to put his ship before the wind. He delayed the manœuvre to the last moment, however, for what he deemed to be sufficient reasons. The longer he kept the ship lying-to, the less he deviated from his proper course to New York, and the greater was the probability of his escaping, stealthily and without observation, from the Foam, since the latter, by maintaining her position better, allowed the Montauk to drift gradually to leeward, and, of course, to a greater distance.

But the crisis would no longer admit of delay. All hands were called ; the main-topsail was hauled up, not without much difficulty, and then Captain Truck reluctantly gave the order to haul down the mizzen-staysail, to put the helm hard up, and to help the ship round with the yards. This is at all times a critical change, as has just been mentioned, for the vessel is exposed to the ravages of any sea, larger than common, that may happen to strike her as she lies, nearly motionless, with her broadside exposed to its force. To accomplish it, therefore, Captain Truck went up a few ratlines in the fore-rigging (he was too nice a calculator to offer even a surface as small as his own body to the wind, in the after-shrouds), whence he looked out to windward for a lull, and a moment when the ocean had fewer billows than common of the larger and more dangerous kind. At the desired instant he signed with his hand, and the wheel was shifted from hard-down to hard-up.

This is always a breathless moment in a ship, for as none can foresee the result, it resembles the entrance of a hostile battery. A dozen men may be swept away in an instant, or the ship herself hove over on her side. John Effingham and Paul, who of all the passengers were alone on deck, understood the hazards, and they watched the slightest change with the interest of men who had so much at stake. At first, the movement of the ship was sluggish, and such as ill suited the eagerness of the crew. Then her pitching ceased, and she settled into the enormous trough bodily, or the whole fabric sank, as it were, never to rise again. So low did she fall, that the foresail gave a tremendous flap ; one that shook the hull and spars from stem to stern. As she rose on the next surge, happily its foaming crest slid beneath her, and the tall masts rolled heavily to windward. Recovering her equilibrium, the ship started through the brine and as the succeeding roller came on, she was urging ahead fast. Still, the sea struck her abeam, forcing her bodily to leeward, and heaving the lower yard-arms into the ocean. Tons of water fell on her decks, with the dull sound of the clod on the coffin. At this grand movement, old Jack Truck, who was standing in the rigging, dripping with the spray, that had washed over him, with a naked head, and his gray hair glistening, shouted like a Stentor, "Haul in your fore-braces, boys! away with the yard, like a fiddle-stick!" Every nerve was strained; the unwilling yards, pressed upon by an almost irresistible column of air, yielded slowly, and as the sail met the gale more perpendicularly, or at right angles to its surface, it dragged the vast hull through the sea with a power equal to that of a steam-engine. Ere another sea could follow, the Montauk was glancing through the ocean at a furious rate, and though offering her quarter to the billows, their force was now so much diminished by her own velocity, as to deprive them of their principal danger.

The motion of the ship immediately became easy, though her situation was still far from being without risk. No longer compelled to buffet the waves, but sliding along in their company, the motion ceased to disturb the systems of the passengers, and ten minutes had not elapsed before most of them were again on deck, seeking the relief of the open air. Among the others was Eve, leaning on the arm of her father.

It was a terrific scene, though one might now contemplate it without personal inconvenience. The gentlemen gathered around the beautiful and appalled spectatress of this grand sight, anxious to know the effect it might produce on one of her delicate frame and habits. She expressed herself as awed, but not alarmed; for the habits of dependence usually leave females less affected by fear, in such cases, than those who, by their sex, are supposed to be responsible.

"Mademoiselle Viefville has promised to follow me," she said, "and as I have a national claim to be a sailor, you are not to expect hysterics or even ecstasies from me; but reserve yourselves, gentlemen, for the *Parisienne*."

The *Parisienne*, sure enough, soon came out of the hurricane-house, with elevated hands, and eyes eloquent of admiration, wonder, and fear. Her first exclamations were those of terror, and then turning a wistful look on Eve, she burst into tears. "*Ah, ceci est décisif!*" she exclaimed. "When we part, we shall be separated for life."

"Then we will not part at all, my dear Mademoiselle; you have only to remain in America, to escape all future inconveniences of the ocean. But forget the danger, and admire the sublimity of this terrific panorama."

Well might Eve thus term the scene. The hazards now to be avoided were those of the ship's broaching-to, and of being pooped. Nothing may seem easier, as has been said, than to "sail before the wind," the words having passed into a proverb; but there are times when even a favoring gale becomes prolific of dangers, that we shall now briefly explain.

The velocity of the water, urged as it is before a tempest, is often as great as that of the ship, and at such moments the rudder is useless, its whole power being derived from its action as a moving body against the element in comparative repose. When ship and water move together, at an equal rate, in the same direction, of course this power of the helm is neutralized, and then the hull is driven much at the mercy of the winds and waves. Nor is this all; the rapidity of the billows often exceeds that of a ship, and then the action of the rudder becomes momentarily reversed, producing an effect exactly opposite to that which is desired. It is true, this last difficulty is never of more than a few moments' continuance, else indeed would the condition of the mariner be hopeless; but it is of constant occurrence, and so irregular as to defy calculations and defeat caution. In the present instance, the Montauk would seem to fly through the water, so swift was her progress; and then, as a furious surge overtook her in the chase, she settled heavily into the element, like a wounded animal, that, despairing of escape, sinks helplessly into the grass, resigned to fate. At such times the crests of the waves swept past her, like vapor in the atmosphere; and one unpractised would be apt to think the ship stationary, though in truth whirling along in company with a frightful momentum.

It is scarcely necessary to say, that the process of scudding

requires the nicest attention to the helm, in order that the
hull may be brought speedily back to the right direction,
when thrown aside by the power of the billows; for, besides
losing her way in the caldron of water—an imminent danger
of itself—if left exposed to the attack of the succeeding
wave, her decks at least would be swept, even should she
escape a still more serious calamity.

Pooping is a hazard of another nature, and is also peculiar
to the process of scudding. It merely means the ship's
being overtaken by the waters when running from them,
when the crest of a sea, broken by the resistance, is thrown
inboard, over the taffrail or quarter. The term is derived
from the name of that particular portion of the ship. In
order to avoid this risk, sail is carried on the vessel as long
as possible, it being deemed one of the greatest securities of
scudding, to force the hull through the water at the greatest attainable rate. In consequence of these complicated
risks, ships that sail the fastest and steer the easiest, scud
the best. There is, however, a species of velocity that
becomes of itself a source of new danger; thus, exceedingly
sharp vessels have been known to force themselves so far
into the watery mounds in their front, and to receive so
much of the element on their decks as never to rise again.
This is a fate to which those who attempt to sail the American clipper without understanding its properties are peculiarly liable. On account of this risk, however, there was
now no cause of apprehension, the full-bowed, kettle-bottomed Montauk being exempt from the danger; though
Captain Truck intimated his doubts whether the corvette
would like to brave the course he had himself adopted.

In this opinion, the fact would seem to sustain the master
of the packet; for when the night shut in, the spars of the
Foam were faintly discernible, drawn like spiders' webs on
the bright streak of the evening sky. In a few more minutes, even this tracery, which resembled that of a magic-
lantern, vanished from the eyes of those aloft; for it had
not been seen by any on deck for more than an hour.

The magnificent horrors of the scene increased with the
darkness. Eve and her companions stood supported by the

hurricane-house, watching it for hours, the supernatural-looking light, emitted by the foaming sea, rendering the spectacle one of attractive terror. Even the consciousness of the hazards heightened the pleasure; for there was a solemn and grand enjoyment mingled with it all, and the first watch had been set an hour, before the party had resolution enough to tear themselves from the sublime sight of a raging sea.

# CHAPTER XII.

" *Touch.* Wast ever in court, shepherd?
  *Cor.* No, truly.
  *Touch.* Then thou art damn'd.
  *Cor.* Nay, I hope—
  *Touch.* Truly, thou art damn'd, like an ill-roasted egg, all on one
side."

*As You Like It.*

NO one thought of seeking his berth when all the passengers were below. Some conversed in broken, half-intelligible dialogues, a few tried unavailingly to read, and more sat looking at each other in silent misgivings, as the gale howled through the cordage and spars, or among the angles and bulwarks of the ship. Eve was seated on a sofa in her own apartment, leaning on the breast of her father, gazing silently through the open doors into the forward cabin; for all idea of retiring within one's self, unless it might be to secret prayer, was banished from the mind. Even Mr. Dodge had forgotten the gnawings of envy, his philanthropical and exclusive democracy, and, what was perhaps more convincing still of his passing views of this sublunary world, his profound deference for rank, as betrayed in his strong desire to cultivate an intimacy with Sir George Templemore. As for the baronet himself, he sat by the cabin-table with his face buried in his hands, and once he had been heard to express a regret that he had ever embarked.

Saunders broke the moody stillness of this characteristic party, with preparations for a supper. He took but one end of the table for his cloth, and a single cover showed that Captain Truck was about to dine, a thing he had not

yet done that day. The attentive steward had an eye to
his commander's tastes; for it is not often one sees a better
garnished board than was spread on this occasion, so far at
least as quantity was concerned. Besides the usual solids
of ham, corned-beef, and roasted shoat, there were carcasses
of ducks, pickled oysters—a delicacy almost peculiar to
America—and all the minor condiments of olives, anchovies, dates, figs, almonds, raisins, cold potatoes, and puddings, displayed in a single course, and arranged on the
table solely with regard to the reach of Captain Truck's
arm. Although Saunders was not quite without taste, he
too well knew the propensities of his superior to neglect
any of these important essentials, and great care was had,
in particular, so to dispose of everything as to render the
whole so many *radii* diverging from a common centre,
which centre was the stationary arm-chair that the master
of the packet loved to fill in his hours of ease.

"You will make many voyages, Mr. Toast,"—the steward affectedly gave his subordinate, or as he was sometimes
facetiously called, the steward's mate, reason to understand,
when they had retired to the pantry to await the captain's
appearance,—"before you accumulate all the niceties of a
gentleman's dinner. Every *plat*" (Saunders had been in
the Havre line, where he had caught a few words of this
nature), "every *plat* should be within reach of the *convive's*
arm, and particularly if it happen to be Captain Truck,
who has a great awersion to delays at his diet. As for the
*entremets*, they may be scattered miscellaneously with the
salt and the mustard, so that they can come with facility in
their proper places."

"I don't know what an *entremet* is," returned the subordinate, "and I exceedingly desire, sir, to receive my orders
in such English as a gentleman can diwine."

"An *entremet*, Mr. Toast, is a mouthful thrown in pro-
miscuously between the reliefs of the solids. Now, suppose
a gentleman begins on pig; when he has eaten enough of
this, he likes a little brandy and water, or a glass of porter,
before he cuts into the beef; and while I 'm mixing the
first, or starting the cork, he refreshes himself with an *en-*

*tremel*, such as a wing of a duck, or perhaps a plate of pickled oysters. You must know that there is great odds in passengers; one set eating and jollifying, from the hour we sail till the hour we get in, while another takes the ocean as it might be sentimentally."

"Sentimentally, sir! I s'pose those be they as uses the basins uncommon?"

"That depends on the weather. I 've known a party not eat as much as would set one handsome table in a week, and then, when they convalesced, it was intimidating how they devoured. It makes a great difference, too, whether the passengers acquiesce well together or not, for agreeable feelings give a fine appetite. Lovers make cheap passengers always."

"That is extr'or'nary, for I thought such as they was always hard to please, with everything but one another."

"You never were more mistaken. I 've seen a lover who could n't tell a sweet potato from an onion, or a canvas-back from an old-wife. But of all mortals in the way of passengers, the bagman or go-between is my greatest animosity. These fellows will sit up all night, if the captain consents, and lie abed next day, and do nothing but drink in their berths. Now, this time we have a compliable set, and on the whole, it is quite a condescension and pleasure to wait on them."

"Well, I think, Mr. Saunders, they is n't alike as much as they might be nother."

"Not more so than wenison and pig. Perfectly correct, sir; for this cabin is a lobscouse as regards deportment and character. I set all the Effinghams down as tip-tops, or, A No. 1, as Mr. Leach calls his ship: and then Mr. Sharp and Mr. Blunt are quite the gentlemen. Nothing is easier, Mr. Toast, than to tell a gentleman; and as you have set up a new profession,—in which I hope, for the credit of the color, you will be prosperous,—it is well worth your while to know how this is done, especially as you need never expect much from a passenger, that is not a true gentleman, but trouble. There is Mr. John Effingham, in particular; his man says he never anticipates change, and if a coat confines his arm, he repudiates it on the spot."

"Well, it must be a satisfaction to serve such a companion. I think Mr. Dodge, sir, quite a feller."

"Your taste, Toast, is getting to be observable, and by cultivating it, you will soon be remarkable for a knowledge of mankind. Mr. Dodge, as you werry justly insinuate, is not werry refined, or particularly well suited to figure in genteel society."

"And yet he seems attached to it, Mr. Saunders, for he has purposed to establish five or six societies since we sailed."

"Werry true, sir; but then every society is not genteel. When we get back to New York, Toast, I must see and get you into a better set than the one you occupied when we sailed. You will not do yet for our circle, which is altogether conclusive; but you might be elevated. Mr. Dodge has been electioneering with me, to see if we cannot inwent a society among the steerage passengers for the abstinence of liquors, and another for the perpetration of the morals and religious principles of our forefathers. As for the first, Toast, I told him it was sufficiently indurable to be confined in a hole like the steerage, without being precluded from the consolation of a little drink; and as for the last, it appeared to me that such a preposition inwolved an attack on liberty of conscience."

"There you giv'd him, sir, quite as good as he sent," returned the steward's mate, chuckling, or perhaps sniggering would be a word better suited to his habits of cachinnation, "and I should have been glad to witness his confusion. It seems to me, Mr. Saunders, that Mr. Dodge loves to get up his societies in support of liberty and religion, that he may predominate over both by his own inwentions."

Saunders laid his long yellow finger on the broad, flat nose of his mate, with an air of approbation, as he replied—

"Toast, you have hit his character as pat as I touch your Roman. He is a man fit to make proselytes among the wulgar and Irish,"—the Hibernian peasant and the American negro are sworn enemies,—"but quite unfit for anything respectable or decent. Were it not for Sir George, I would scarcely descend to clean his state-room."

"What is your sentiments, Mr. Saunders, respecting Sir George?"

"Why, Sir George is a titled gentleman, and of course is not to be strictured too freely. He has complimented me already with a sovereign, and apprised me of his intention to be more particular when we get in."

"I feel astonished such a gentleman should neglect to insure a state-room to his own convenience."

"Sir George has elucidated all that in a conversation we had in his room, soon after our acquaintance commenced. He is going to Canada on public business, and sailed at an hour's interval. He was too late for a single room, and his own man is to follow with most of his effects by the next ship. O! Sir George may be safely put down as respectable and liberalized, though thrown into disparagement perhaps by forty circumstances."

Mr. Saunders, who had run his vocabulary hard in this conversation, meant to say "fortuitous"; and Toast thought that so many circumstances might well reduce a better man to a dilemma. After a moment of thought, or what in his orbicular shining features he fancied passed for thought, he said,—

"I seem to diwine, Mr. Saunders, that the Effinghams do not much intimate Sir George."

Saunders looked out of the pantry-door to reconnoitre, and finding the sober quiet already described reigning, he opened a drawer, and drew forth a London newspaper.

"To treat you with the confidence of a gentleman in a situation as respectable and responsible as the one you occupy, Mr. Toast," he said, "a little ewent has transpired in my presence yesterday, that I thought sufficiently particular to be designated by retaining this paper. Mr. Sharp and Sir George happened to be in the cabin together, alone, and the last, as it suggested to me, Toast, was desirous of removing some of the haughter of the first, for you may have observed that there has been no conversation between any of the Effinghams, or Mr. Blunt, or Mr. Sharp, and the baronet; and so, to break the ice of his haughter, as it might be, Sir George says, 'Really, Mr. Sharp, the papers have got to be so personally particular, that one cannot run into the country for a mouthful of fresh air that they don't record it. Now, I thought not a soul knew of my departure for America, and yet here you see they have mentioned it, with more particulars than are agreeable.' On concluding, Sir George gave Mr. Sharp this paper, and indicated this here paragraph. Mr. Sharp perused it, laid down the paper, and retorted coldly, 'It is indeed quite surprising, sir; but impudence is a general fault of the age.' And then he left the cabin *solus*. Sir George was so wexed, he went into his state-room and forgot the paper, which fell to the steward, you know, on a principle laid down in Wattel, Toast."

Here the two worthies indulged in a smothered merriment of their own, at the expense of their commander; for, though a dignified man in general, Mr. Saunders could laugh, on occasion, and, according to his own opinion of himself, he danced particularly well.

"Would you like to read the paragraph, Mr. Toast?"

"Quite unnecessary, sir; your account will be perfectly legible and satisfactory."

By this touch of politeness, Mr. Toast, who knew as much of the art of reading as a monkey commonly knows of mathematics, got rid of the awkwardness of acknowledging the careless manner in which he had trifled with his early opportunities. Luckily, Mr. Saunders, who had been educated as a servant in a gentleman's family, was better off, and as he was vain of all his advantages, he was particularly pleased to have an opportunity of exhibiting them. Turning to the paragraph, he read the following lines, in that sort of didactic tone and elaborate style with which gentlemen who commence the graces after thirty are a little apt to make bows :—

"We understand Sir George Templemore, Bart., the member for Boodleigh, is about to visit our American colonies, with a view to make himself intimately acquainted with the merits of the unpleasant questions by which they are just now agitated, and with the intention of entering into the debates in the House on that interesting subject, on his

return. We believe that Sir George will sail in the packet
of the first from Liverpool, and will return in time to be in
his seat after the Easter holidays. His people and effects
left town yesterday by the Liverpool coach. During the
baronet's absence, his county will be hunted by Sir Gervaise
de Brush, though the establishment at Templemore Hall
will be kept up."

"How came Sir George here, then?" Mr. Toast very
naturally inquired.

"Having been kept too late in London, he was obliged to
come this way or be left. It is sometimes as close work to
get the passengers on board, Mr. Toast, as to get the people.
I have often admired how gentlemen and ladies love procras-
tinating, when dishes that ought to be taken hot, are getting
to be quite insipid and uneatable."

"Saunders!" cried the hearty voice of Captain Truck,
who had taken possession of what he called his throne in the
cabin. All the steward's elegant diction and finish of demeanor vanished at the well-known sound, and, thrusting
his head out of the pantry-door, he gave the prompt ship-
answer to a call,—

"Ay, ay, sir!"

"Come, none of your dictionary in the pantry there, but
show your physiognomy in my presence. What the devil
do you think Vattel would say to such a supper as this?"

"I think, sir, he would call it a werry good supper for a
ship in a hard gale of wind. That's my honest opinion,
Captain Truck, and I never deceive any gentleman in a
matter of food. I think Mr. Wattel would approve of that
there supper, sir."

"Perhaps he might, for he has made blunders as well as
another man. Go, mix me a glass of just what I love, when
I've not had a drop all day. Gentlemen, will any of you
honor me, by sharing in a cut? This beef is not indigesti-
ble, and here is a real Marylander in the way of a ham; no
want of oakum to fill up the chinks with, either."

Most of the gentlemen were too full of the gale to wish
to eat; besides, they had not fasted, like Captain Truck,
since morning. But Mr. Monday, the bagman, as John

Effingham had termed him, and who had been often enough at sea to know something of its varieties, consented to take a glass of brandy and water, as a corrective of the Madeira he had been swallowing. The appetite of Captain Truck was little affected by the state of the weather, however; for though too attentive to his duties to quit the deck until he had ascertained how matters were going on, now that he had fairly made up his mind to eat, he set about it with a heartiness and simplicity that proved his total disregard of appearances when his hunger was sharp. For some time he was too much occupied to talk, making regular attacks upon the different *plats*, as Mr. Saunders called them, without much regard to the cookery or the material. The only pauses were to drink, and this was always done with a steadiness that never left a drop in the glass Still Mr. Truck was a temperate man; for he never consumed more than his physical wants appeared to require, or his physical energies knew how to dispose of. At length, however, he came to the steward's *entremets*, or he began to stuff what he himself had called " oakum," into the chinks of his dinner.

Mr. Sharp had watched the whole process from the ladies' cabin, as indeed had Eve; and thinking this a favorable occasion to ascertain the state of things on deck, the former came into the main cabin commissioned by the latter, to make the inquiry.

" The ladies are desirous of knowing where we are, and what is the state of the gale, Captain Truck," said the gentleman, when he had seated himself near the throne.

" My dear young lady," called out the captain, by way of cutting short the diplomacy of employing ambassadors between them, " I wish in my heart I could persuade you and Mademoiselle V. A. V." (for so he called the governess, in imitation of Eve's pronunciation of her name), " to try a few of these pickled oysters; they are as delicate as yourselves, and worthy to be set before a mermaid, if there were any such thing."

" I thank you for the compliment, Captain Truck; and while I ask leave to decline it, I beg leave to refer you to the plenipotentiary Mademoiselle Viefville" (Eve would not say herself) "has intrusted with her wishes."

"Thus you perceive, sir," interposed Mr. Sharp again, "you will have to treat with me, by all the principles laid down by Vattel."

"And treat you too, my good sir. Let me persuade you to try a slice of this anti-abolitionist," laying his knife on the ham, which he still continued to regard, himself, with a sort of melancholy interest. "No? well, I hold over-persuasion as the next thing to neglect. I am satisfied, sir, after all, as Saunders says, that Vattel himself, unless more unreasonable at his grub than in matters of state, would be a happier man after he had been at his table twenty minutes, than before he sat down."

Mr. Sharp, perceiving that it was idle to pursue his inquiry while the other was in one of his discursive humors, determined to let things take their course, and fell into the captain's own vein.

"If Vattel would approve of the repast, few men ought to repine at their fortune in being so well provided."

"I flatter myself, sir, that I understand a supper, especially in a gale of wind, as well as Mr. Vattel, or any other man could do."

"And yet Vattel was one of the most celebrated cooks of his day."

Captain Truck stared, looked his grave companion steadily in the eye, for he was too much addicted to mystifying, not to distrust others, and picked his teeth with redoubled diligence.

"Vattel a cook! This is the first I ever heard of it."

"There was a Vattel, in a former age, who stood at the head of his art as a cook; this I can assure you, on my honor: he may not have been your Vattel, however."

"Sir, there never were two Vattels. This is extraordinary news to me, and I scarcely know how to receive it."

"If you doubt my information, you may ask any of the other passengers. Either of the Mr. Effinghams, or Mr. Blunt, or Miss Effingham, or Mademoiselle Viefville, will confirm what I tell you, I think ; especially the latter, for he was her countryman.''

Hereupon Captain Truck began to stuff in the oakum again, for the calm countenance of Mr. Sharp produced an effect ; and as he was pondering on the consequences of his oracle's turning out to be a cook, he thought it not amiss to be eating, as it were, incidentally. After swallowing a dozen olives, six or eight anchovies, as many pickled oysters, and raisins and almonds, as the advertisements say, *à volonté*, he suddenly struck his fist on the table, and announced his intention of putting the question to both the ladies.

"My dear young lady," he called out, "will you do me the honor to say whether you ever heard of a cook of the name of Vattel ?"

Eve laughed, and her sweet tones were infectious amid the dull howling of the gale, which was constantly heard in the cabins like a bass accompaniment, or the distant roar of a cataract among the singing of birds.

"Certainly, captain," she answered ; "Mr. Vattel was not only a cook, but perhaps the most celebrated on record, for sentiment at least, if not for skill.''

"I make no doubt the man did his work well, let him be set about what he might ; and, Mademoiselle, he was a countryman of yours, they tell me ?''

"*Assurement*, Monsieur Vattel has left more distinguished *souvenirs* than any other cook in France.''

Captain Truck turned quickly to the elated and admiring Saunders, who felt his own glory enhanced by this important discovery, and said in that short-hand way he had of expressing himself to the chief of the pantry,—

"Do you hear that, sir? see and find out what they are, and dress me a dish of these *souvenirs* as soon as we get in. I dare say they are to be had at the Fulton Market ; and mind, while there, to look out for some tongues and sounds. I 've not made half a supper to-night, for the want of them. I dare say these *souvenirs* are capital eating, if Monsieur Vattel thought so highly of them. Pray, Mademoiselle, is the gentleman dead?''

" *Hélas, oui !* How could he live with a sword run through his body ? "

" Ha ! killed in a duel, I declare ; died fighting for his principles, if the truth were known ! I shall have a double respect for his opinion, for this is the touchstone of a man's honesty. Mr. Sharp, let us take a glass of Geissenheimer to his memory ; we might honor a less worthy man."

As the captain poured out the liquor, a fall of several tons of water on the deck shook the entire ship, and one of the passengers in the hurricane-house, opening a door to ascertain the cause, the sound of the hissing waters and of the roaring winds came fresher and more distinct into the cabin. Mr. Truck cast an eye at the tell-tale over his head to ascertain the course of the ship, and paused just an instant, and then tossed off his wine.

" This hint reminds me of my mission," Mr. Sharp rejoined. " The ladies desire to know your opinion of the state of the weather ? "

" I owe them an answer, if it were only in gratitude for the hint about Vattel. Who the devil would have supposed the man ever was a cook ! But these Frenchmen are not like the rest of mankind, and half the nation are cooks, or live by food, in some way or other."

" And very good cooks, too, Monsieur le Capitaine," said Mademoiselle Viefville. " Monsieur Vattel did die for the honor of his art. He fell on his own sword, because the fish did not arrive in season for the dinner of the king."

Captain Truck looked more astonished than ever. Then turning short round to the steward, he shook his head and exclaimed,—

" Do you hear that, sir ? How often would you have died, if a sword had been run through you every time the fish was forgotten, or was too late ? Once, to a dead certainty, about these very tongues and sounds."

" But the weather ? " interrupted Mr. Sharp.

" The weather, my dear sir ; the weather, my dear ladies, is very good weather, with the exception of winds and waves, of which, unfortunately, there are just now more of both than we want. The ship must scud ; and as we go like a race-horse, without stopping to take breath, we may see the Canary Islands before the voyage is over. Of danger there is none in this ship, as long as we can keep clear of the land ; and in order that this may be done, I will just step into my state-room and find out exactly where we are."

On receiving this information, the passengers retired for the night, Captain Truck setting about his task in good earnest. The result of his calculations showed that they would run westward of Madeira, which was all he cared about immediately, intending always to haul up to his course on the first good occasion.

## CHAPTER XIII.

"There are yet two things in my destiny—
A world to roam o'er, and a home with thee."

BYRON.

EVE EFFINGHAM slept little: although the motion of the ship had been much more severe and uncomfortable while contending with head-winds, on no other occasion were there so many signs of a fierce contention of the elements as in this gale. As she lay in her berth, her ear was within a foot of the roaring waters without, and her frame trembled as she heard them gurgling so distinctly, that it seemed as if they had already forced their way through the seams of the planks, and were filling the ship. Sleep she could not, for a long time, therefore, and during two hours she remained with closed eyes an entranced and yet startled listener of the fearful strife that was raging over the ocean. Night had no stillness, for the roar of the winds and waters was incessant, though deadened by the intervening decks and sides; but now and then an open door admitted, as it might be, the whole scene into the cabins. At such moments every sound was fresh, and frightfully grand,—even the shout of the officer coming to the ear like a warning cry from the deep.

At length Eve, wearied by her apprehensions even, fell into a troubled sleep, in which her frightened faculties, however, kept so much on the alert, that at no time was the roar of the tempest entirely lost to her sense of hearing. About midnight the glare of a candle crossed her eyes, and she was broad awake in an instant. On rising in her berth she found Nanny Sidley, who had so often and so long watched over her infant and childish slumbers, standing at her side, and gazing wistfully in her face.

"'Tis a dreadful night, Miss Eve," half whispered the appalled domestic. "I have not been able to sleep for thinking of you, and of what might happen on these wide waters!"

"And why of me particularly, my good Nanny?" returned Eve, smiling in the face of her old nurse as sweetly as the infant smiles in its moments of tenderness and recollection. "Why so much of me, my excellent Ann?—are there not others, too, worthy of your care? my beloved father—your own good self—Mademoiselle Viefville—cousin Jack—and"—the warm color deepened on the cheek of the beautiful girl, she scarcely knew why, herself—"and many others in the vessel, that one, kind as you, might think of, I should hope, when your thoughts become apprehensions, and your wishes prayers."

"There are many precious souls in the ship, ma'am, out of all question; and I'm sure no one wishes them all safe on land again more than myself; but it seems to me, no one among them all is so much loved as you."

Eve leaned forward playfully, and drawing her old nurse towards her, kissed her cheek, while her own eyes glistened, and then she laid her flushed cheek on that bosom which had so frequently been its pillow before. After remaining a minute in this affectionate attitude, she rose and inquired if her nurse had been on deck.

"I go every half hour, Miss Eve; for I feel it as much my duty to watch over you here, as when I had you all to myself in the cradle. I do not think your father sleeps a great deal to-night, and several of the gentlemen in the other cabins remain dressed; they ask me how you spend the time in this tempest, whenever I pass their state-room doors."

Eve's color deepened, and Ann Sidley thought she had never seen her child more beautiful, as the bright, luxuriant golden hair, which had strayed from the confinement of the cap, fell on the warm cheek, and rendered eyes that were always full of feeling, softer and more brilliant even than common.

"They conceal their uneasiness for themselves under an affected concern for me, my good Nanny," she said hurriedly; "and your own affection makes you an easy dupe to the artifice."

"It may be so, ma'am, for I know but little of the ways of the world. It is fearful, is it not, Miss Eve, to think that we are in a ship, so far from any land, whirling along over the bottom as fast as a horse could plunge?"

"The danger is not exactly of that nature, perhaps, Nanny."

"There is a bottom to the ocean, is there not? I have heard some maintain there is no bottom to the sea—and that would make the danger so much greater. I think, if I felt certain that the bottom was not very deep, and there was only a rock to be seen now and then, I should not find it so very dreadful."

Eve laughed like a child, and the contrast between the sweet simplicity of her looks, her manners, and her more cultivated intellect, and the matronly appearance of the less instructed Ann, made one of those pictures in which the superiority of mind over all other things becomes most apparent.

"Your notions of safety, my dear Nanny," she said, "are not precisely those of a seaman; for I believe there is nothing of which they stand more in dread than of rocks and the bottom."

"I fear I'm but a poor sailor, ma'am, for in my judgment we could have no greater consolation in such a tempest than to see them all around us. Do you think, Miss Eve, that the bottom of the ocean, if there is truly a bottom, is whitened with the bones of shipwrecked mariners, as people say?"

"I doubt not, my excellent Nanny, that the great deep might give up many awful secrets; but you ought to think less of these things, and more of that merciful Providence, which has protected us through so many dangers since we have been wanderers. You are in much less danger now than I have known you to be, and escape unharmed."

"I, Miss Eve! Do you suppose that I fear for myself?

What matters it if a poor old woman like me die a few years sooner or later, or where her frail old body is laid? I have never been of so much account when living as to make it of consequence where the little which will remain to decay when dead, moulders into dust. Do not, I implore you, Miss Effingham, suppose me so selfish as to feel any uneasiness to-night on my own account."

" It is then, as usual, all for me, my dear, my worthy old nurse, that you feel this anxiety? Put your heart at ease, for they who know best betray no alarm; and you may observe that the captain sleeps as tranquilly this night as on any other."

" But he is a rude man, and accustomed to danger. He has neither wife nor children, and I 'll engage has never given a thought to the horrors of having a form precious as this floating in the caverns of the ocean, amidst ravenous fish and sea-monsters."

Here her imagination overcame poor Nanny Sidley, and she folded her arms about the beautiful person of Eve, and sobbed violently. Her young mistress, accustomed to similar exhibitions of affection, soothed her with blandishments and assurances that soon restored her self-command, when the dialogue was resumed with a greater appearance of tranquillity on the part of the nurse. They conversed a few minutes on the subject of their reliance on God, Eve returning fourfold, or with the advantages of a cultivated intellect, many of those simple lessons of faith and humility that she had received from her companion when a child; the latter listening, as she always did, to these exhortations, which sounded in her ears like the echoes of all her own better thoughts, with a love and reverence no other could awaken. Eve passed her small, white hand over the wrinkled cheek of Nanny in kind fondling, as it had been passed a thousand times when a child, an act she well knew her nurse delighted in, and continued,—

" And now, my good old Nanny, you will set your heart at ease, I know; for though a little too apt to trouble yourself about one who does not deserve half your care, you are much too sensible and too humble to feel distrust out of reason. We will talk of something else a few minutes, and then you will lie down and rest your weary body.''

"Weary! I should never feel weary in watching, when I thought there was a cause for it."

Although Nanny made no allusion to herself, Eve understood in whose behalf this watchfulness was meant. She drew the face of the old woman towards her, and left a kiss on each cheek ere she continued :—

"These ships have other things to talk about, besides their dangers," she said. "Do you not find it odd, at least, that a vessel of war should be sent to follow us about the ocean in this extraordinary way?"

"Quite so, ma'am, and I did intend to speak to you about it, some time when I saw you had nothing better to think of. At first I fancied, but I believe it was a silly thought, that some of the great English lords and admirals that used to be so much about us at Paris, and Rome, and Vienna, had sent this ship to see you safe to America, Miss Eve ; for I never supposed they would make so much fuss concerning a poor runaway couple, like these steerage passengers."

Eve did not refrain from laughing again, at this conceit of Nanny's, for her temperament was gay as childhood, though well restrained by cultivation and manner, and once more she patted the cheek of her nurse kindly.

"Those great lords and admirals are not great enough for that, dear Nanny, even had they the inclination to do so silly a thing. But has no other reason suggested itself to you, among the many curious circumstances you may have had occasion to observe in the ship?"

Nanny looked at Eve, and turned her eyes aside, glanced furtively at the young lady again, and at last felt compelled to answer.

"I endeavor, ma'am, to think well of everybody, though strange thoughts will sometimes arise without our wishing it. I suppose I know to what you allude ; but I don't feel quite certain it becomes me to speak."

"With me at least, Nanny, you need have no reserves, and I confess a desire to learn if we have thought alike

about some of our fellow-passengers.  Speak freely, then;
for you can have no more apprehension in communicating
all your thoughts to me, than in communicating them to
your own child."

"Not as much, ma'am, not half as much; for you are
both child and mistress to me, and I look quite as much to
receiving advice as to giving it.   It is odd, Miss Eve, that
gentlemen should not pass under their proper names, and I
have had unpleasant feelings about it, though I did not
think it became me to be the first to speak, while your
father was with you, and Mamerzelle," for so Nanny always
styled the governess, "and Mr. John, all of whom love you
almost as much as I do, and all of whom are so much better judges of what is right.   But now you encourage me
to speak my mind, Miss Eve, I will say I should like that
no one came near you who does not carry his heart in his
open hand, that the youngest child might know his character and understand his motives."

Eve smiled as her nurse grew warm, but she blushed in
spite of an effort to seem indifferent.

"This would be truly a vain wish, dear Nanny, in the
mixed company of a ship," she said.  "It is too much to
expect that strangers, will throw aside all their reserves, on
first finding themselves in close communion.   The well-
bred and prudent will only stand more on their guard under
such circumstances."

"Strangers, ma'am!"

"I perceive that you recollect the face of one of our
shipmates.   Why do you shake your head?"   The tell-tale
blood of Eve again mantled over her lovely countenance.
"I suppose I ought to have said *two* of our shipmates,
though I had doubted whether you retained any recollection
of one of them."

"No gentleman ever speaks to you twice, Miss Eve, that
I do not remember him."

"Thank you, dearest Nanny, for this and a thousand
other proofs of your never-ceasing interest in my welfare;
but I had not believed you so vigilant as to take heed of
every face that happens to approach me."

"Ah, Miss Eve! neither of these gentlemen would like to be mentioned by you in this careless manner, I 'm sure. They both did a great deal more than 'happen to approach you'; for as to—"

"Hist! dear Nanny; we are in a crowded place, and you may be overheard. You will use no names, therefore, as I believe we understand each other without going into all these particulars. Now, my dear nurse, would I give something to know which of these young men has made the most favorable impression on your upright and conscientious mind!"

"Nay, Miss Eve, what is my judgment in comparison with your own, and that of Mr. John Effingham, and—"

"My cousin Jack! In the name of wonder, Nanny, what has he to do with the matter?"

"Nothing, ma'am: only I can see he has his favorites as well as another, and I 'll venture to say Mr. Dodge is not the greatest he has in this ship."

"I think you might add Sir George Templemore, too," returned Eve, laughing.

Ann Sidley looked hard at her young mistress, and smiled before she answered; and then she continued the discourse naturally, as if there had been no interruption.

"Quite likely, ma'am; and Mr. Monday, and all the rest of that set. But you see how soon he discovers a real gentleman; for he is quite easy and friendly with Mr. Sharp and Mr. Blunt, particularly the last."

Eve was silent, for she did not like the open introduction of these names, though she scarce knew why, herself.

"My cousin is a man of the world," she resumed, on perceiving that Nanny watched her countenance with solicitude as if fearful of having gone too far; "and there is nothing surprising in his discovering men of his own class. We know both these persons to be not exactly what they seem, though I think we know no harm of either, unless it be the silly change of names. It would have been better had they come on board, bearing their proper appellations; to us, at least, it would have been more respectful, though both affirm they were ignorant that my father had taken

passage in the Montauk,—a circumstance that may very
well be true, as you know we got the cabin that was first
engaged by another party.''

"I should be sorry, ma'am, if either failed in respect.''

"It was not quite adulatory to make a young woman the
involuntary keeper of the secrets of two unreflecting young
men ; that is all, my good Nanny. We cannot well betray
them, and we are consequently their confidants *par force*.
The most amusing part of the thing is, that they are masters of each other's secrets, in part at least, and feel a delightful awkwardness in a hundred instances. For my own
part, I pity neither, but think that each is fairly enough
punished. They will be fortunate if their servants do not
betray them before we reach New York.''

"No fear of that, ma'am, for they are discreet, cautious
men, and if disposed to blab, Mr. Dodge has given both
good opportunities already, as I believe he has put to them
as many questions as there are speeches in the catechism.''

"Mr. Dodge is a vulgar man.''

"So we all say, ma'am, in the servants' cabin, and everybody is so set against him there, that there is little chance
of his learning much. I hope, Miss Eve, Mamerzelle does
not distrust either of the gentlemen ?''

"Surely you cannot suspect Mademoiselle Viefville of
indiscretion, Nanny ; a better spirit, or a better tone than
hers, does not exist.''

"No, ma'am, 'tis not that : but I should like to have one
more secret with you, all to myself. I honor and respect
Mamerzelle, who has done a thousand times more for you
than a poor, ignorant woman like me could have done, with
all my zeal ; but I do believe, Miss Eve, I love your shoe-
tie better than she loves your pure and beautiful spirit.''

"Mademoiselle Viefville is an excellent woman, and I
believe is sincerely attached to me.''

"She would be a wretch else. I do not deny her attachment, but I only say it is nothing, it ought to be nothing,
it can be nothing, it shall be nothing, compared to that of
the one who first held you in her arms, and who has always
held you in her heart. Mamerzelle can sleep such a night

as this, which I 'm sure she could not do were she as much concerned for you as I am."

Eve knew that jealousy of Mademoiselle Viefville was Nanny's greatest weakness, and drawing the old woman to her, she entwined her arms around her neck, and complained of drowsiness. Accustomed to watching, and really unable to sleep, the nurse now passed a perfectly happy hour in holding her child, who literally dropped asleep on her bosom; after which Nanny slid into the berth beneath, in her clothes, and finally lost the sense of her apprehensions in perturbed slumbers.

A cry on deck awoke all in the cabins early on the succeeding morning. It was scarcely light, but a common excitement seized every passenger, and ten minutes had not elapsed when Eve and her governess appeared in the hurricane-house, the last of those who came from below. Few questions had been asked, but all hurried on deck with their apprehensions, awakened by the gale, increased to the sense of some positive and impending danger.

Nothing, however, was immediately apparent to justify all this sudden clamor. The gale continued, if anything, with increased power; the ocean was rolling over its cataracts of combing seas, with which the ship was still racing, driven under the strain of a reefed forecourse, the only canvas that was set. Even with this little sail the hull was glancing through the seas, or rather in their company, at a rate a little short of ten miles in the hour.

Captain Truck was in the mizzen-rigging, bareheaded, every lock of hair he had blowing out like a pennant. Occasionally he signed to the man at the wheel which way to put the helm; for instead of sleeping, as many had supposed, he had been conning the ship for hours in the same situation. As Eve appeared, he was directing the attention of several of the gentlemen to some object astern, but a very few moments put all on deck in possession of the facts.

About a cable's-length, on one of the quarters of the Montauk, was a ship careering before the gale like themselves, though carrying more canvas, and consequently driving faster through the water. The sudden appearance of

this vessel in the sombre light of the morning, when objects
were seen distinctly, but without the glare of day ; the dark
hull, relieved by a single narrow line of white paint, dotted
with ports ; the glossy hammock-cloths, and all those other
coverings of dark, glistening canvas which give to a cruiser
an air of finish and comfort, like that of a travelling carriage ; the symmetry of the spars, and the gracefulness of all
the lines, whether of the hull or hamper, told all who knew
anything of such subjects, that the stranger was a vessel of
war.    To this information Captain Truck added that it was
their old pursuer, the Foam.

"She is corvette-built," said the master of the Montauk,
"and is obliged to carry more canvas than we, in order to
keep out of the way of the seas ; for, if one of these big
fellows should overtake her, and throw its crest into her
waist, she would become like a man who has taken too much
Saturday night, and with whom a second dose might settle
the purser's books forever."

Such in fact was the history of the sudden appearance of
this ship.   She had lain-to as long as possible, and on being driven to scud, carried a close-reefed main-topsail, a
show of canvas that urged her through the water about two
knots to the hour faster than the rate of the packet.   Necessarily following the same course, she overtook the latter
just as the day began to dawn.   The cry had arisen on her
sudden discovery, and the moment had now arrived when
she was about to come up, quite abreast of her late chase.
The passage of the Foam, under such circumstances, was
a grand but thrilling thing.   Her captain, too, was seen in
the mizzen-rigging of his ship, rocked by the gigantic billows over which the fabric was careering.   He held a
speaking-trumpet in his hand, as if still bent on his duty, in
the midst of that awful warring of the elements.   Captain
Truck called for a trumpet in his turn, and, fearful of consequences, he waved it to the other to keep more aloof.
The injunction was either misunderstood, the man-of-war's-
man was too much bent on his object, or the ocean was too
uncontrollable for such a purpose, the corvette driving up
on a sea quite abeam of the packet, and in fearful prox-

imity. The Englishman applied the trumpet, and words
were heard amid the roaring of the winds. At that time
the white field of old Albion, with the St. George's cross,
rose over the bulwarks, and by the time it had reached the
gaff-end, the bunting was whipping in ribbons.

"Show 'em the gridiron!" growled Captain Truck
through his trumpet, "with its mouth turned inboard."

As everything was ready, this order was instantly
obeyed, and the stripes of America were soon seen fluttering nearly in separate pieces. The two ships now ran a
short distance in parallel lines, rolling from each other so
heavily that the bright copper of the corvette was seen
nearly to her keel. The Englishman, who seemed a portion of his ship, again tried his trumpet; the detached
words of "lie-by,"—"orders,"—"communicate," were
caught by one or two, but the howling of the gale rendered
all connection in the meaning impossible. The Englishman
ceased his efforts to make himself heard, for the two ships
were now rolling-to, and it appeared as if their spars would
interlock. There was an instant when Mr. Leach had his
hand on the main-brace to let it go; but the Foam started
away on a sea, like a horse that feels the spur, and dis-
obeying her helm, shot forward, as if about to cross the
Montauk's forefoot.

A breathless instant followed, for all on board the two
ships thought they must now inevitably come foul of each
other, and this the more so, because the Montauk took the
impulse of the sea just as it was lost to the Foam, and
seemed on the point of plunging directly into the stern of
the latter. Even the seamen clenched the ropes around
them convulsively, and the boldest held their breaths for a
time. The "P-o-r-t, hard a-port, and be d——d to you!"
of Captain Truck, and the "S-t-a-r-b-o-a-r-d, starboard
hard!" of the Englishman, were both distinctly audible to
all in the two ships; for this was a moment in which seamen can speak louder than the tempest. The affrighted
vessels seemed to recede together, and they shot asunder in
diverging lines, the Foam leading. All further attempts at
a communication were instantly useless; the corvette being

half a mile ahead in a quarter of an hour, rolling her yard-
arms nearly to the water.

Captain Truck said little to his passengers concerning
this adventure ; but when he had lighted a cigar, and was
discussing the matter with his chief mate, he told the latter
there was "just one minute when he would not have given a
ship's biscuit for both vessels, nor much more for their car-
goes. A man must have a small regard for human souls,
when he puts them, and their bodies too, in so much jeopardy for a little tobacco."

Throughout the day it blew furiously, for the ship was
running into the gale, a phenomenon that we shall explain,
as most of our readers may not comprehend it. All gales
of wind commence to leeward ; or, in other words, the wind
is first felt at some particular point, and later, as we recede from that point, proceeding in the direction from which
the wind blows. It is always severest near the point where
it commences, appearing to diminish in violence as it re-
cedes. This, therefore, is an additional motive for mariners to lie-to, instead of scudding, since the latter not only
carries them far from their true course, but it carries them
also nearer to the scene of the greatest fury of the elements.

## CHAPTER XIV.

"Good boatswain, have care."

*Tempest.*

AT sunset, the speck presented by the reefed topsail of the corvette had sunk beneath the horizon, in the southern board, and that ship was seen no longer. Several islands had been passed, looking tranquil and smiling amid the fury of the tempest ; but it was impossible to haul up for any one among them. The most that could be done was to keep the ship dead before it, to prevent her broaching-to, and to have a care that she kept clear of those rocks and of that bottom, for which Nanny Sidley had so much pined.

Familiarity with the scene began to lessen the apprehensions of the passengers, and as scudding is an easy process for those who are liable to sea-sickness, ere another night shut in, the principal concern was connected with the course the ship was compelled to steer. The wind had so far hauled to the westward as to render it certain that the coast of Africa would lie in their way, if obliged to scud many hours longer ; for Captain Truck's observations actually placed him to the southward and eastward of the Canary Islands. This was a long distance out of his course, but the rate of sailing rendered the fact sufficiently clear.

This, too, was the precise time when the Montauk felt the weight of the tempest, or rather, when she experienced the heaviest portion of that which it was her fate to feel. Lucky was it for the good ship that she had not been in this latitude a few hours earlier, when it had blown something very like a hurricane. The responsibility and danger of his situation now began seriously to disturb Captain

Truck, although he kept his apprehensions to himself, like a prudent officer. All his calculations were gone over again with the utmost care, the rate of sailing was cautiously estimated, and the result showed that ten or fifteen hours more would inevitably produce shipwreck of another sort, unless the wind moderated.

Fortunately, the gale began to break about midnight. The wind still blew tremendously, but it was less steadily, and there were intervals of half an hour at a time when the ship might have carried much more canvas, even on a bowline: of course her speed abated in proportion, and, after the day had dawned, a long and anxious survey from aloft showed no land to the eastward. When perfectly assured of this important fact, Captain Truck rubbed his hands with delight, ordered a coal for his cigar, and began to abuse Saunders about the quality of the coffee during the blow.

"Let there be something creditable this morning, sir," added the captain, after a sharp rebuke; "and remember, we are down here in the neighborhood of the country of your forefathers, where a man ought, in reason, to be on his good behavior. If I hear any more of your washy compounds, I'll put you ashore, and let you run naked a summer or two with the monkeys and orang-outangs."

"I endeavor, on all proper occasions, to render myself agreeable to you, Captain Truck, and to all those with whom I have the happiness to sail," returned the steward; "but the coffee, sir, cannot be very good, sir, in such weather, sir. I do diwine that the wind must blow away its flavor, for I am ready to confess it has not been as odorous as it usually is, when I have had the honor to prepare it. As for Africa, sir, I flatter myself, Captain Truck, that you esteem me too highly to believe I am suited to consort or resort with the ill-formed and inedicated men who inhabit that wild country. I misremember whether my ancestors came from this part of the world or not; but if they did, sir, my habits and profession entirely unqualify me for their company, I hope. I know I am only a poor steward, sir, but you'll please to recollect that your great Mr. Vattel was nothing but a cook."

" D——n the fellow, Leach ; I believe it is this conceit that has spoiled the coffee the last day or two ! Do you suppose it can be true that a great writer like this man could really be no better than a cook, or was that English-man roasting me, by way of showing how cooking was done ashore ? If it were not for the testimony of the ladies, I might believe it ; but they would not share in such an in-decent trick. What are you lying-by for, sir ? Go to your pantry, and remember that the gale is broken, and we shall all sit down to table this morning, as keen-set as a party of your brethren ashore here, who had a broiled baby for breakfast."

Saunders, who *ex-officio* might be said to be trained in similar lectures, went pouting to his work, taking care to expend a proper part of his spleen on Mr. Toast, who, quite as a matter of course, suffered in proportion as his superior was made to feel, in his own person, the weight of Captain Truck's authority. It is perhaps fortunate that nature points out this easy and self-evident mode of relief, else would the rude habits of a ship sometimes render the relations between him who orders and him whose duty it is to obey, too nearly approaching to the intolerable.

The captain's squalls, however, were of short duration, and on the present occasion he was soon in even a better humor than common, as every minute gave the cheering assurance that the tempest was fast coming to a close. He had finished his third cigar, and was actually issuing his orders to turn the reef out of the foresail, and to set the main-topsail close reefed, when most of the passengers appeared on deck, for the first time that morning.

" Here we are, gentlemen ! " cried Captain Truck, in the way of salutation, "nearer to Guinea than I could wish, with every prospect now of soon working our way across the Atlantic, and possibly of making a thirty or thirty-five days' passage of it yet. We have this sea to quiet ; and then I hope to show you what the Montauk has in her, be-sides her passengers and cargo. I think we have now got rid of the Foam, as well as of the gale. I did believe, at one time, her people might be walking and wading on the coast of Cornwall; but I now believe they are more likely to try the sands of the great Desert of Sahara."

"It is to be hoped they have escaped the latter calamity, as fortunately as they escaped the first," observed Mr. Effingham.

"It may be so; but the wind has got round to nor'west, and has not been sighing these last twelve hours. Cape Blanco is not a hundred leagues from us, and, at the rate he was travelling, that gentleman with the speaking-trumpet may now be philosophizing over the fragments of his ship, unless he had the good sense to haul off more to the westward than he was steering when last seen. His ship should have been christened the 'Scud,' instead of the 'Foam.'"

Every one expressed the hope that the ship, to which their own situation was fairly enough to be ascribed, might escape this calamity; and all faces regained their cheerfulness as they saw the canvas fall, in sign that their own danger was past. So rapidly, indeed, did the gale now abate, that the topsails were hardly hoisted before the order was given to shake out another reef, and within an hour all the heavier canvas that was proper to carry before the wind was set, solely with a view to keep the ship steady. The sea was still fearful, and Captain Truck found himself obliged to keep off from his course, in order to avoid the danger of having his decks swept.

The racing with the crest of the waves, however, was quite done, for the seas soon cease to comb and break, after the force of the wind is expended.

At no time is the motion of the vessel more unpleasant, or, indeed, more dangerous, than in the interval that occurs between the ceasing of a violent gale, and the springing up of a new wind. The ship is unmanageable, and falling into the troughs of the sea, the waves break in upon her decks, often doing serious injury, while the spars and rigging are put to the severest trial by the sudden and violent surges which they have to withstand. Of all this Captain Truck was fully aware, and when he was summoned to breakfast, he gave many cautions to Mr. Leach before quitting the deck.

" I do not like the new shrouds we got up in London,"
he said, "for the rope has stretched in this gale in a way to
throw too much strain on the old rigging ; so see all ready
for taking a fresh drag on them, as soon as the people have
breakfasted. Mind and keep her out of the trough, sir, and
watch every roller that you find comes tumbling upon us."

After repeating these injunctions in different ways, looking to the windward some time, and aloft five or six minutes,
Captain Truck finally went below, to pass judgment on Mr.
Saunders' coffee. Once on his throne, at the head of the
long table, the worthy master, after a proper attention to
his passengers, set about the duty of restoration, as the steward affectedly called eating, with a zeal that never failed him
on such occasions. He had just swallowed a cup of the
coffee, about which he had lectured Saunders, when a heavy
flap of the sails announced the sudden failure of the wind.

" That is bad news," said Captain Truck, listening to the
fluttering blows of the canvas against the masts. " I never
like to hear a ship shaking its wings while there is a heavy
sea on ; but this is better than the Desert of Sahara, and so,
my dear young lady, let me recommend to you a cup of
this coffee, which is flavored this morning by a dread of
orang-outangs, as Mr. Saunders will have the honor to inform you—"

A jerk of the whole ship was followed by a report like
that made by a musket. Captain Truck rose, and stood
leaning on one hand in a bent attitude, expectation and distrust intensely portrayed in every feature. Another helpless
roll of the ship succeeded, and three or four similar reports
were immediately heard, as if large ropes had parted in quick
succession. A rending of wood followed, and then came a
chaotic crash in which the impending heavens seemed to fall
on the devoted ship. Most of the passengers shut their eyes,
and when they were opened again, or a moment afterwards,
Mr. Truck had vanished.

It is scarcely necessary to describe the confusion that followed. Eve was frightened, but she behaved well, though
Mademoiselle Viefville trembled so much as to require the
assistance of Mr. Effingham.

"We have lost our masts," John Effingham coolly remarked; "an accident that will not be likely to be very dangerous, though by prolonging the passage a month or two, it may have the merit of making this good company more intimately acquainted with each other, a pleasure for which we cannot express too much gratitude."

Eve implored his forbearance by a glance, for she saw his eye was unconsciously directed towards Mr. Monday and Mr. Dodge, for both of whom she knew her kinsman entertained an incurable dislike. His words, however, explained the catastrophe, and most of the men hastened on deck to assure themselves of the fact.

John Effingham was right. The new rigging which had stretched so much during the gale, had permitted too much of the strain, in the tremendous rolls of the ship, to fall upon the other ropes. The shroud most exposed had parted first; three or four more followed in succession, and before there was time to secure anything, the remainder had gone together, and the mainmast had broken at a place where a defect was now seen in its heart. Falling over the side, the latter had brought down with it the mizzen-mast and all its hamper, and as much of the foremast as stood above the top. In short, of all the complicated tracery of ropes, the proud display of spars, and the broad folds of canvas that had so lately overshadowed the deck of the Montauk, the mutilated foremast, the foreyard and sail, and the fallen head-gear alone remained. All the rest either cumbered the deck, or was beating against the side of the ship, in the water.

The hard, red, weather-beaten face of Captain Truck was expressive of mortification and concern, for a single instant, when his eye glanced over the ruin we have just described. His mind then seemed made up to the calamity, and he ordered Toast to bring him a coal of fire, with which he quietly lighted a cigar.

"Here is a category, and be d——d to it, Mr. Leach," he said, after taking a single whiff. "You are doing quite right, sir; cut away the wreck and force the ship free of it, or we shall have some of those sticks poking themselves through the planks. I always thought the chandler in London, into whose hands the agent has fallen, was a —— rogue, and now I know it well enough to swear to it. Cut away, carpenter, and get us rid of all this thumping as soon as possible. A very capital vessel, Mr. Monday, or she would have rolled the pumps out of her, and capsized the galley."

No attempt being made to save anything, the wreck was floating astern in five minutes, and the ship was fortunately extricated from this new hazard. Mr. Truck, in spite of his acquired coolness, looked piteously at all that gallant hamper, in which he had so lately rejoiced, as yard-arm, cross-trees, tressel-trees, and tops rose on the summits of swells or settled in the troughs, like whales playing their gambols. But habit is a seaman's philosophy, and in no one feature is his character more respectable than in that manliness which disinclines him to mourn over a misfortune that is inevitable.

The Montauk now resembled a tree stripped of its branches, or a courser crippled in his sinews; her glory had, in a great degree, departed. The foremast alone remained, and of this even the head was gone, a circumstance of which Captain Truck complained more than any other, as, to use his own expressions, "it destroyed the symmetry of the spar, which had proved itself to be a good stick." What, however, was of more real importance, it rendered it difficult, if not impossible, to get up a spare topmast forward. As both the main and mizzen-mast had gone quite near the deck, this was almost the only tolerably easy expedient that remained; and, within an hour of the accident, Mr. Truck announced his intentions to stand as far south as he could to strike the trades, and then to make a fair wind of it across the Atlantic, unless, indeed, he might be able to fetch into the Cape de Verde Islands, where it would be possible, perhaps, to get something like a new outfit.

"All I now ask, my dear young lady," he said to Eve, who ventured on deck to look at the desolation, as soon as the wreck was cut adrift, "all I now ask, my dear young lady, is an end to westerly winds for two or three weeks, and I will promise to place you all in America yet, in time to eat your Christmas dinner. I do not think Sir George will shoot many white bears among the Rocky Mountains this year, but then there will be so many more left for another season. The ship is in a category, and he will be an impudent scoundrel who denies it; but worse categories than this have been reasoned out of countenance. All head-sail is not a convenient show of cloth to claw off a lee-shore with; but I still hope to escape the misfortune of laying eyes on the coast of Africa."

"Are we far from it?" asked Eve, who sufficiently understood the danger of being on an uninhabitable shore in their present situation; one in which it was vain to seek for a port. "I would rather be in the neighborhood of any other land, I think, than that of Africa."

"Especially Africa between the Canaries and Cape Blanco," returned Captain Truck, with an expressive shrug. "More hospitable regions exist, certainly; for, if accounts are to be credited, the honest people alongshore never get a Christian that they do not mount him on a camel, and trot him through the sands a thousand miles or so, under a hot sun, with a sort of haggis for food, that would go nigh to take away even a Scotchman's appetite."

"And you do not tell us how far we are from this frightful land, Monsieur le Capitaine?" inquired Mademoiselle Viefville.

"In ten minutes you shall know, ladies, for I am about to observe for the longitude. It is a little late, but it may yet be done."

"And we may rely on the fidelity of your information?"

"On the honor of a sailor and a man."

The ladies were silent, while Mr. Truck proceeded to get the sun and the time. As soon as he had run through his calculations, he came to them with a face in which the eye was roving, though it was still good-humored and smiling.

"And the result?" said Eve.

"Is not quite as flattering as I could wish. We are materially within a degree of the coast; but, as the wind is gone, or nearly so, we may hope to find a shift that will shove us farther from the land. And now I have dealt

frankly with you, let me beg you will keep the secret, for
my people will be dreaming of Turks, instead of working, if
they know the fact."

It required no great observation to discover that Captain
Truck was far from satisfied with the position of his ship.
Without any after-sail, and almost without the means of
making any, it was idle to think of hauling off from the
land, more especially against the heavy sea that was still
rolling in from the northwest; and his present object was
to make the Cape de Verdes, before reaching which he
would be certain to meet the trades, and where, of course,
there would be some chance of repairing damages. His
apprehensions would have been much less were the ship a
degree farther west, as the prevailing winds in this part of
the ocean are from the northward and eastward; but it was
no easy matter to force a ship that distance under a foresail,
the only regular sail that now remained in its place. It is
true, he had some of the usual expedients of seamen at his
command, and the people were immediately set about them;
but in consequence of the principal spars having gone so
near the decks, it became exceedingly difficult to rig jury-
masts.

Something must be attempted, however, and the spare
spars were got out, and all the necessary preparations were
commenced, in order that they might be put into their places
and rigged, as well as circumstances would allow. As soon
as the sea went down, and the steadiness of the ship would
permit, Mr. Leach succeeded in getting up an awkward lower
studding-sail, and a sort of staysail forward, and with these
additions to their canvas, the ship was brought to head south
with the wind light at the westward. The sea was greatly
diminished about noon; but a mile an hour, for those who
had so long a road before them, and who were so near a coast
that was known to be fearfully inhospitable, was a cheerless
progress, and the cry of "Sail, ho!" early in the afternoon,
diffused a general joy in the Montauk.

The stranger was made to the southward and eastward,
and was standing on a course that must bring her quite near
to their own track, as the Montauk then headed. The wind

was so light, however, that Captain Truck gave it as his opinion they could not speak until night had set in.

"Unless the coast has brought him up, yonder flaunting gentleman. who seems to have had better luck with his light canvas than ourselves, must be the Foam," he said. "Tobacco or no tobacco, bride or bridegroom, the fellow has us at last, and all the consolation that is left is, that we shall be much obliged to him, now, if he will carry us to Portsmouth, or into any other Christian haven. We have shown him what a kettle-bottom can do before the wind, and now let him give us a tow to windward like a generous antagonist. That is what I call Vattel, my dear young lady."

"If he do this, he will indeed prove himself a generous adversary," said Eve, "and we shall be certain to speak well of his humanity, whatever we may think of his obstinacy."

"Are you quite sure the ship in sight is the corvette?" asked Paul Blunt.

"Who else can it be? Two vessels are quite sufficient to be jammed down here on the coast of Africa, and we know that the Englishman must be somewhere to leeward of us; though, I will confess, I had believed him much farther, if not plump up among the Mohammedans, beginning to reduce to a featherweight, like Captain Riley, who came out with just his skin and bones, after a journey across the desert."

"I do not think those topgallant-sails have the symmetry of the canvas of a ship-of-war."

Captain Truck looked steadily at the young man an instant, as one regards a sound criticism, and then he turned his eye towards the object of which they were speaking.

"You are right, sir," he rejoined, after a moment of examination; "and I have had a lesson in my own trade from one young enough to be my son. The stranger is clearly no cruiser, and as there is no port in-shore of us anywhere near this latitude, he is probably some trader who has been driven down here, like ourselves."

"And I 'm very sure, captain," put in Sir George Templemore, "we ought to rejoice sincerely that, like ourselves, he has escaped shipwreck. For my part, I pity the poor wretches on board the Foam most sincerely, and could almost wish myself a Catholic, that one might yet offer up sacrifices in their behalf."

"You have shown yourself a Christian throughout all that affair, Sir George, and I shall not forget your handsome offers to befriend the ship, rather than let us fall into the jaws of the Philistines. We were in a category more than once, with that nimble-footed racer in our wake, and you were the man, Sir George, who manifested the most hearty desire to get us out."

"I ever feel an interest in the ship in which I embark," returned the gratified baronet, who was not displeased at hearing his liberality so openly commended; "and I would cheerfully have given a thousand pounds in preference to being taken. I rather think, now, that is the true spirit for a sportsman!"

"Or for an admiral, my good sir. To be frank with you, Sir George, when I first had the honor of your acquaintance, I did not think you had so much in you. There was a sort of English attention to small wares, a species of knee-buckleism about your *début*, as Mr. Dodge calls it, that made me distrust your being the whole-souled and one-idea'd man I find you really are."

"O! I *do* like my comforts," said Sir George, laughing.

"That you do, and I am only surprised you don't smoke. Now, Mr. Dodge, your room-mate, there, tells me you have six-and-thirty pair of breeches!"

"I have—yes, indeed, I have. One would wish to go abroad decently clad."

"Well! if it should be our luck to travel in the deserts, your wardrobe would rig out a whole harem."

"I wish, captain, you would do me the favor to step into our state-room, some morning; I have many curious things I should like to show you. A set of razors, in particular—and a dressing-case—and a pair of patent pistols—and that life-preserver that you admire so much, Mr. Dodge. Mr. Dodge has seen most of my curiosities, I believe, and will tell you some of them are really worth a moment's examination."

"Yes, captain, I must say," observed Mr. Dodge,—for

this conversation was held apart between the three, the mate keeping an eye the while on the duty of the ship, for habit had given Mr. Truck the faculty of driving his people while he entertained his passengers,—" yes, captain, I must say I have met no gentleman who is better supplied with necessaries, than *my* friend, Sir George. But English gentlemen are curious in such things, and I admit that I admire their ingenuity."

" Particularly in breeches, Mr. Dodge. Have you coats to match, Sir George?"

" Certainly, sir. One would be a little absurd in his shirt sleeves. I wish, captain, we could make Mr. Dodge a little less of a republican. I find him a most agreeable roommate, but rather annoying on the subject of kings and princes."

" You stick up for the people, Mr. Dodge, or to the old category?"

" On that subject, Sir George and I shall never agree, for he is obstinately monarchical ; but I tell him we shall treat him none the worse for that, when he gets among us. He has promised me a visit in our part of the country, and I have pledged myself to his being unqualifiedly well received ; and I think I know the whole meaning of a pledge."

" I understand Mr. Dodge," pursued the baronet, " that he is the editor of a public journal, in which he entertains his readers with an account of his adventures and observations during his travels. " ' The Active Inquirer,' is it not, Mr. Dodge?"

" That is the name, Sir George. ' The Active Inquirer ' is the present name, though when we supported Mr. Adams it was called ' The Active Enquirer,' with an E."

" A distinction without a difference ; I like that," interrupted Captain Truck. " This is the second time I have had the honor to sail with Mr. Dodge, and a more active inquirer never put foot in a ship, though I did not know the use he put his information to before. It is all in the way of trade, I find."

" Mr. Dodge claims to belong to a profession, captain, and is quite above trade. He tells me many things have occurred on board this ship, since we sailed, that will make very eligible paragraphs."

"The d——l he does! I should like particularly well, Mr. Dodge, to know what you will find to say concerning this category in which the Montauk is placed."

"O! captain, no fear of me, when you are concerned. You know I am a friend, and you have no cause to apprehend anything: though I 'll not answer for everybody else on board: for there are passengers in this ship to whom I have decided antipathies, and whose deportment meets with my unqualified disapprobation."

"And you intend to paragraph them?"

Mr. Dodge was now swelling with the conceit of a vulgar and inflated man, who not only fancies himself in possession of a power that others dread, but was so far blinded to his own qualities as to think his opinion of importance to those whom he felt, in the minutest fibre of his envious and malignant system, to be in every essential his superiors. He did not dare express all his rancor, while he was unequal to suppressing it entirely.

"These Effinghams, and this Mr. Sharp, and that Mr. Blunt," he muttered, "think themselves everybody's betters; but we shall see! America is not a country in which people can shut themselves up in rooms, and fancy they are lords and ladies."

"Bless my soul!" said Captain Truck, with his affected simplicity of manner; "how did you find this out, Mr. Dodge? What a thing it is, Sir George, to be an active inquirer!"

"O! I know when a man is blown up with notions of his own importance. As for Mr. John Effingham, he has been so long abroad that he has forgotten that he is a-going home to a country of equal rights!"

"Very true, Mr. Dodge; a country in which a man cannot shut himself up in his room, whenever the notion seizes him. This is the spirit, Sir George, to make a great nation, and you see that the daughter is likely to prove worthy of the old lady. But, my dear sir, are you quite sure that Mr. John Effingham has absolutely so high a sentiment in his

12

own favor ? It would be awkward business to make a blunder in such a serious matter, and murder a paragraph for
nothing. You should remember the mistake of the Irishman !"

"What was that ?"asked the baronet, who was completely
mystified by the indomitable gravity of Captain Truck,
whose character might be said to be actually formed by
the long habit of treating the weaknesses of his fellow-
creatures with cool contempt. "We hear many good things
at our club; but I do not remember the mistake of the
Irishman."

"He merely mistook the drumming in his own ear, for
some unaccountable noise that disturbed his companions."

Mr. Dodge felt uncomfortable; but there is no one of
whom a vulgar-minded man stands so much in awe as an
immovable quiz, who has no scruple in using his power.
He shook his head, therefore, in a menacing manner, and
affecting to have something to do he went below, leaving the
baronet and captain by themselves.

"Mr. Dodge is a stubborn friend of liberty," said the
former, when his room-mate was out of hearing.

"That he is, and you have his own word for it. He has no
notion of letting a man do as he has a mind to ! We are full
of such active inquirers in America, and I don't care how
many you shoot before you begin upon the white bears, Sir
George."

"But it would be more gracious in the Effinghams, you
must allow, captain, if they shut themselves up in their
cabin less, and admitted us to their society a little oftener.
I am quite of Mr. Dodge's way of thinking, that exclusion
is excessively odious."

"There is a poor fellow in the steerage, Sir George, to
whom I have given a piece of canvas to repair a damage to
his mainsail, who would say the same thing, did he know of
your six-and-thirtys. Take a cigar, my dear sir, and smoke
away sorrow."

"Thankee, captain : I never smoke. We never smoke at
our club, though some of us go, at times, to the divan to
try a chibouk."

"We can't all have cabins to ourselves, or no one would live forward. If the Effinghams like their own apartment, I do honestly believe it is for a reason as simple as that it is the best in the ship. I'll warrant you, if there were a better, that they would be ready enough to change. I suppose when we get in, Mr. Dodge will honor you with an article in 'The Active Inquirer'?"

"To own the truth, he has intimated some such thing."

"And why not? A very instructive paragraph might be made about the six-and-thirty pair of breeches, and the patent razors, and the dressing-case, to say nothing of the Rocky Mountains, and the white bears."

Sir George now began to feel uncomfortable, and making a few unmeaning remarks about the late accident, he disappeared.

Captain Truck, who never smiled except at the corner of his left eye, turned away, and began rattling off his people, and throwing a hint or two to Saunders, with as much indifference as if he were a firm believer in the unfailing orthodoxy of a newspaper, and entertained a profound respect for the editor of the "Active Inquirer," in particular.

The prognostic of the master concerning the strange ship proved true, for about nine at night she came within hail, and backed her main-topsail. This vessel proved to be an American in ballast, bound from Gibraltar to New York; a return storeship from the squadron kept in the Mediterranean. She had met the gale to the westward of Madeira, and after holding on as long as possible, had also been compelled to scud. According to the report of her officers, the Foam had run in much closer to the coast than herself, and it was their opinion she was lost. Their own escape was owing entirely to the wind's abating, for they had actually been within sight of the land, though having received no injury, they had been able to haul off in season.

Luckily, this ship was ballasted with fresh water, and Captain Truck passed the night in negotiating a transfer of his steerage passengers, under an apprehension that, in the crippled state of his own vessel, his supplies might be ex-

hausted before he could reach America. In the morning,
the offer of being put on board the storeship was made to
those who chose to accept it, and all in the steerage, with
most from the cabin, profited by the occasion to exchange a
dismasted vessel for one that was, at least, full rigged.
Provisions were transferred accordingly, and by noon next
day the stranger made sail on a wind, the sea being tolerably smooth, and the breeze still ahead. In three hours
she was out of sight to the northward and westward, the
Montauk holding her own dull course to the southward,
with the double view of striking the trades, or of reaching
one of the Cape de Verdes.

## CHAPTER XV.

*" Steph.* His forward voice now is to speak well of his friend; his backward voice is to utter foul speeches, and to detract."

*Tempest.*

THE situation of the Montauk appeared more desolate than ever, after the departure of so many of her passengers. So long as her decks were thronged, there was an air of life about her that served to lessen disquietude, but now that she was left by all in the steerage, and by so many in the cabins, those who remained began to entertain livelier apprehensions of the future. When the upper sails of the storeship sunk as a speck in the ocean, Mr. Effingham regretted that he, too, had not overcome his reluctance to a crowded and inconvenient cabin, and gone on board her, with his own party. Thirty years before he would have thought himself fortunate in finding so good a ship, and accommodations so comfortable ; but habit and indulgence change all our opinions, and he had now thought it next to impossible to place Eve and Mademoiselle Viefville in a situation that was so common to those who travelled by sea at the commencement of the century.

Most of the cabin passengers, as has just been stated, decided differently, none remaining but the Effinghams, and their party, Mr. Sharp, Mr. Blunt. Sir George Templemore, Mr. Dodge, and Mr. Monday. Mr. Effingham had been influenced by the superior comforts of the packet, and his hopes that a speedy arrival at the islands would enable the ship to refit, in time to reach America almost as soon as the dull-sailing vessel which had just left them. Mr. Sharp and

Mr. Blunt had both expressed a determination to share his fortunes, which was indirectly saying that they would share the fortunes of his daughter. John Effingham remained, as a matter of course, though he had made a proposition to the stranger to tow them into port, an arrangement that failed in consequence of the two captains disagreeing as to the course proper to be steered, as well as to a more serious obstacle in the way of compensation, the stranger throwing out some pretty plain hints about salvage ; and Mr. Monday staying from an inveterate attachment to the steward's stores, more of which, he rightly judged, would now fall to his share than formerly.

Sir George Templemore had gone on board the storeship, and had given some very clear demonstrations of an intention to transfer himself and the thirty-six pair of breeches to that vessel ; but on examining her comforts, and particularly the confined place in which he should be compelled to stow himself and his numerous curiosities, he was unequal to the sacrifice. On the other hand, he knew an entire state-room would now fall to his share, and this self-indulged and feeble-minded young man preferred his immediate comfort, and the gratification of his besetting weakness, to his safety.

As for Mr. Dodge, he had the American mania of hurry, and was one of the first to propose a general swarming, as soon as it was known the stranger could receive them. During the night, he had been actively employed in fomenting a party to "resolve" that prudence required the Montauk should be altogether abandoned, and even after this scheme failed, he had dwelt eloquently in corners (Mr. Dodge was too meek, and too purely democratic, ever to speak aloud, unless under the shadow of public opinion), on the propriety of Captain Truck's yielding his own judgment to that of the majority. He might as well have scolded against the late gale, in the expectation of outrailing the tempest, as to make such an attempt on the firm-set notions of the old seaman concerning his duty ; for no sooner was the thing intimated to him than he growled a denial in a tone that he was little accustomed to use to his passengers, and one that effectually silenced remonstrance.

When these two plans had failed, Mr. Dodge endeavored
strenuously to show Sir George that his interests and safety
were on the side of a removal; but with all his eloquence,
and with the hold that incessant adulation had actually
given him on the mind of the other, he was unable to overcome his love of ease, and chiefly the passion for the enjoyment of the hundred articles of comfort and curiosity in
which the baronet so much delighted. The breeches might
have been packed in a trunk, it is true, and so might the
razors, and the dressing-case, and the pistols, and most of
the other things; but Sir George loved to look at them
daily, and as many as possible were constantly paraded
before his eyes.

To the surprise of every one, Mr. Dodge, on finding it
impossible to prevail on Sir George Templemore to leave
the packet, suddenly announced his own intention to remain
also. Few stopped to inquire into his motives in the hurry
of such a moment. To his room-mate he affirmed that the
strong friendship he had formed for him, could alone induce
him to relinquish the hope of reaching home previously to
the autumn elections.

Nor did Mr. Dodge greatly color the truth in making
this statement. He was an American demagogue precisely
in obedience to those feelings and inclinations which would
have made him a courtier anywhere else. It is true, he
had travelled, or thought he had travelled, in a *diligence*
with a countess or two, but from these he had been obliged
to separate early on account of the force of things; while
here he had got a *bond-fide* English baronet all to himself,
in a confined state-room, and his imagination revelled in the
glory and gratification of such an acquaintance. What were
the proud and distant Effinghams to Sir George Templemore! He even ascribed their reserve with the baronet to
envy, a passion of whose existence he had very lively per-
ceptions, and he found a secret charm in being shut up in so
small an apartment with a man who could excite envy in an
Effingham. Rather than abandon his aristocratical prize,
therefore, whom he intended to exhibit to all his democratic
friends in his own neighborhood, Mr. Dodge determined to

abandon his beloved hurry, looking for his reward in the future pleasure of talking of Sir George Templemore and his curiosities, and of his sayings and his jokes, in the circle at home. Odd, moreover, as it may seem, Mr. Dodge had an itching desire to remain with the Effinghams; for while he was permitting jealousy and a consciousness of inferiority to beget hatred, he was willing at any moment to make peace, provided it could be done by a frank admission into their intimacy. As to the innocent family that was rendered of so much account to the happiness of Mr. Dodge, it seldom thought of that individual at all, little dreaming of its own importance in his estimation, and merely acted in obedience to its own cultivated tastes and high principles in disliking his company. It fancied itself, in this particular, the master of its own acts, and this so much the more, that with the reserve of good-breeding its members seldom indulged in censorious personal remarks, and never in gossip.

As a consequence of these contradictory feelings of Mr. Dodge, and of the fastidiousness of Sir George Templemore, the interest her two admirers took in Eve, the devotion of Mr. Monday to sherry and champagne, and the decision of Mr. Effingham, these persons therefore remained the sole occupants of the cabins of the Montauk. Of the *oi polloi* who had left them, we have hitherto said nothing, because this separation was to remove them entirely from the interest of our incidents.

If we were to say that Captain Truck did not feel melancholy as the store-ship sunk beneath the horizon, we should represent that stout-hearted mariner as more stoical than he actually was. In the course of a long and adventurous professional life, he had encountered calamities before, but he had never before been compelled to call in assistance to deliver his passengers at the stipulated port, since he had commanded a packet. He felt the necessity, in the present instance, as a sort of stain upon his character as a seaman, though in fact the accident which had occurred was chiefly to be attributed to a concealed defect in the mainmast. The honest master sighed often, smoked nearly double the usual number of cigars in the course of the afternoon, and

when the sun went down gloriously in the distant west, he
stood gazing at the sky in melancholy silence, as long as
any of the magnificent glory that accompanies the decline
of day lingered among the vapors of the horizon. He then
summoned Saunders to the quarter-deck, where the following dialogue took place between them : --

"This is a devil of a category to be in, Master Steward !"

"Well, he might be better, sir. I only wish the good
butter may endure until we get in."

"If it fail, I shall go nigh to see you clapped into the
State Prison, or at least into that Gothic cottage on Black-
well's Island."

"There is an end to all things, Captain Truck, if you
please, sir, even to butter. I presume, sir, Mr. Vattel, if he
know anything of cookery, will admit that."

"Harkee, Saunders, if you ever insinuate again that
Vattel belonged to the coppers, in my presence, I 'll take the
liberty to land you on the coast here, where you may amuse
yourself in stewing young monkeys for your own dinner.
I saw you aboard the other ship, sir, overhauling her arrangements; what sort of a time will the gentlemen be
likely to have in her ?"

"Atrocious, sir ! I give you my honor, as a real gentleman, sir. Why, would you believe it, Captain Truck, the
steward is a downright nigger, and he wears ear-rings, and
a red flannel shirt, without the least edication. As for the
cook, sir, he would n't pass an examination for Jemmy
Ducks aboard here, and there is but one camboose, and one
set of coppers."

"Well, the steerage passengers, in that case, will fare as
well as the cabin."

"Yes, sir, and the cabin as bad as the steerage ; and for
my part, I abomernate liberty and equality."

"You should converse with Mr. Dodge on that subject,
Master Saunders, and let the hardest fend off in the argument. May I inquire, sir, if you happen to remember the
day of the week ? "

" Beyond controversy, sir ; to-morrow will be Sunday,
Captain Truck, and I think it a thousand pities we have

not an opportunity to solicit the prayers and praises of the Church, sir, in our behalf, sir."

"If to-morrow will be Sunday, to-day must be Saturday, Mr. Saunders, unless this last gale has deranged the calendar."

"Quite naturally, sir, and werry justly remarked. Everybody admits there is no better navigator than Captain Truck, sir."

"This may be true, my honest fellow," returned the captain, moodily, after making three or four heavy puffs at the cigar; "but I am sadly out of my road down here in the country of your amiable family, just now. If this be Saturday, there will be a Saturday night before long, and look to it, that we have our 'sweethearts and wives.' Though I have neither myself, I feel the necessity of something cheerful, to raise my thoughts to the future."

"Depend on my discretion, sir, and I rejoice to hear you say it; for I think, sir, a ship is never so respectable and genteel as when she celebrates all the anniversaries. You will be quite a select and agreeable party to-night, sir."

With this remark Mr. Saunders withdrew, to confer with Toast on the subject, and Captain Truck proceeded to give his orders for the night to Mr. Leach. The proud ship did indeed present a sight to make a seaman melancholy; for to the only regular sail that stood, the foresail, by this time was added a lower studding-sail, imperfectly rigged, and which would not resist a fresh puff, while a very inartificial jurytopmast supported a topgallant-sail, that could only be carried in a free wind. Aft, preparations were making of a more permanent nature, it is true. The upper part of the mainmast had been cut away, as low as the steerage deck, where an arrangement had been made to step a spare topmast. The spar itself was lying on the deck rigged, and a pair of sheers were in readiness to be hoisted, in order to sway it up; but night approaching, the men had been broken off, to rig the yards, bend the sails, and to fit the other spars it was intended to use, postponing the last act, that of sending all up, until morning.

"We are likely to have a quiet night of it," said the captain, glancing his eyes round at the heavens; "and at eight o'clock to-morrow let all hands be called, when we will turn-to with a will, and make a brig of the old hussy. This topmast will do to bear the strain of the spare main-yard, unless there come another gale, and by reefing the new mainsail we shall be able to make something out of it. The topgallant-mast will fit of course above, and we may make out, by keeping a little free, to carry the sail : at need, we may possibly coax the contrivance into carrying a studding-sail also. We have sticks for no more, though we 'll endeavor to get up something aft, out of the spare spars obtained from the store-ship. You may knock off at four bells, Mr. Leach, and let the poor fellows have their Saturday night in peace. It is a misfortune enough to be dismasted, without having one's grog stopped.''

The mate of course obeyed, and the evening shut in beautifully and placid, with all the glory of a mild night, in a latitude as low as that they were in. They who have never seen the ocean under such circumstances, know little of its charms in its moments of rest. The term of sleeping is well applied to its impressive stillness, for the long, sluggish swells on which the ship rose and fell, hardly disturbed its surface. The moon did not rise until midnight, and Eve, accompanied by Mademoiselle Viefville and most of her male companions, walked the deck by the bright starlight, until fatigued with pacing their narrow bounds.

The song and the laugh rose frequently from the fore-castle, where the crew were occupied with their Saturday night; and occasionally a rude sentiment in the way of a toast was heard. But weariness soon got the better of merriment forward, and the hard-worked mariners who had the watch below soon went down to their berths, leaving those whose duty it was to remain to doze away the long hours in such places as they could find on deck.

" A white squall," said Captain Truck, looking up at the uncouth sails that hardly impelled the vessel a mile in the hour through the water, '' would soon furl all our canvas for us, and we are in the very place for such an interlude."

" And what would then become of us? " asked Mademoiselle Viefville quickly.

"You had better ask what would become of that apology for a topsail, Mam'selle, and yonder stunsail, which looks like an American in London without straps to his pantaloons. The canvas would play kite, and we should be left to renew our inventions. A ship could scarcely be in better plight than we are at this moment, to meet with one of these African flurries."

"In which case, captain," observed Mr. Monday, who stood by the skylight watching the preparations below, "we can go to our Saturday night without fear; for I see the steward has everything ready, and the punch looks very inviting, to say nothing of the champagne."

"Gentlemen, we will not forget our duty," returned the captain; "we are but a small family, and so much the greater need that we should prove a jolly one. Mr. Effingham, I hope we are to have the honor of your company at 'sweethearts and wives'?"

Mr. Effingham had no wife, and the invitation coming under such peculiar circumstances, produced a pang that Eve, who felt his arm tremble, well understood. She mildly intimated her intention to go below, however; the whole party followed, and lucky it was for the captain's entertainment that she quitted the deck, as few would otherwise have been present at it. By pressing the passengers to favor him with their company, he succeeded in the course of a few minutes in getting all the gentlemen seated at the cabin-table, with a glass of delicious punch before each man.

"Mr. Saunders may not be a conjurer or a mathematician, gentlemen," cried Captain Truck, as he ladled out the beverage, "but he understands the philosophy of sweet and sour, strong and weak; and I will venture to praise his liquor without tasting it. Well, gentlemen, there are better-rigged ships on the ocean than this of ours; but there are few with more comfortable cabins, or stouter hulls, or better company. Please God we can get a few sticks aloft again, now that we are quit of our troublesome shadow, I think I may flatter myself with a reasonable hope of landing you, that do me the honor to stand by me, in New

York, in less time than a common droger would make the passage, with all his legs and arms. Let our first toast be, if you please, ' A happy end to that which has had a disastrous beginning.' ''

Captain Truck's hard face twitched a little while he was making this address; and as he swallowed the punch, his eyes glistened in spite of himself. Mr. Dodge, Sir George, and Mr. Monday repeated the sentiment sonorously, word for word, while the other gentlemen bowed, and drank it in silence.

The commencement of a regular scene of merriment is usually dull and formal, and it was some time before Captain Truck could bring any of his companions up to the point where he wished to see them; for though a perfectly sober man, he loved a social glass, and particularly at those times and seasons which conformed to the practice of his calling. Although Eve and her governess had declined taking their seats at the table, they consented to place themselves where they might be seen, and where they might share occasionally in the conversation.

'' Here have I been drinking sweethearts and wives of a Saturday night, my dear young lady, these forty years and more,'' said Captain Truck, after the party had sipped their liquor for a minute or two, ''without ever falling into luck's latitude, or furnishing myself with either: but, though so negligent of my own interests and happiness, I make it an invariable rule to advise all my young friends to get spliced before they are thirty. Many is the man who has come aboard my ship a determined bachelor in his notions, who has left it at the end of the passage ready to marry the first pretty young woman he fell in with.''

As Eve had too much of the self-respect of a lady, and of the true dignity of her sex, to permit jokes concerning matrimony, or a treatise on love, to make a part of her conversation, and all the gentlemen of her party understood her character too well, to say nothing of their own habits, to second this attempt of the captain's, after a vapid remark or two from the others, this rally of the honest mariner produced no *suites*.

"Are we not unusually low, Captain Truck," inquired Paul Blunt, with a view to change the discourse, "not to have fallen in with the trades? I have commonly met with those winds on this coast as high as twenty-six or twenty-seven, and I believe you observed to-day, in twenty-four."

Captain Truck looked hard at the speaker, and when he had done, he nodded his head in approbation.

"You have travelled this road before, Mr. Blunt, I perceive. I have suspected you of being a brother chip, from the moment I saw you first put your foot on the side-cleets in getting out of the boat. You did not come aboard parrot-toed, like a country-girl waltzing; but set the ball of the foot firmly on the wood, and swung off the length of your arms, like a man who knows how to humor the muscles. Your present remark, too, shows you understand where a ship ought to be, in order to be in her right place. As for the trades, they are a little uncertain, like a lady's mind when she has more than one good offer; for I've known them to blow as high as thirty, and then again, to fail a vessel as low as twenty-three, or even lower. It is my private opinion, gentlemen, and I gladly take this opportunity to make it public, that we are on the edge of the trades, or in those light, baffling winds which prevail along their margin, as eddies play near the track of strong, steady currents in the ocean. If we can force the ship fairly out of this trimming region—that is the word, I believe, Mr. Dodge—we shall do well enough; for a northeast, or an east wind, would soon send us up with the islands, even under the rags we carry. We are very near the coast, certainly—much nearer than I could wish; but when we do get the good breeze, it will be all the better for us, as it will find us well to windward."

"But these trades, Captain Truck?" asked Eve; "if they always blow in the same direction, how is it possible that the late gale should drive a ship into the quarter of the ocean where they prevail?"

"Always, means sometimes, my dear young lady. Although light winds prevail near the edge of the trades, gales, and tremendous fellows too, sometimes blow there also, as we have just seen. I think we shall now have settled weather, and that our chance of a safe arrival, more particularly in some southern American port, is almost certain, though our chance for a speedy arrival be not quite as good. I hope, before twenty-four hours are passed, to see our decks white with sand."

"Is that a phenomenon seen here?" asked the father.

"Often, Mr. Effingham, when ships are close in with Africa, and are fairly in the steady winds. To say the truth, the country abreast of us, some twenty or thirty miles distant, is not the most inviting ; and though it may not be easy to say where the Garden of Eden is, it is not hazardous to say it is not there."

"If we are so very near the coast, why do we not see it?"

"Perhaps we might from aloft, if we had any aloft just now. We are to the southward of the mountains, however, and off a part of the country where the Great Desert makes from the coast. And now, gentlemen, I perceive Mr. Monday finds all this sand arid, and I ask permission to give you, one and all, ' Sweethearts and wives.' "

Most of the company drank the usual toast with spirit, though both the Effinghams scarce wetted their lips. Eve stole a timid glance at her father, and her own eyes were filled with tears as she withdrew them : for she knew that every allusion of this nature revived in him mournful recollections. As for her cousin Jack, he was so confirmed a bachelor that she thought nothing of his want of sympathy with such a sentiment.

"You must have a care for your heart in America, Sir George Templemore," cried Mr. Dodge, whose tongue loosened with the liquor he drank. "Our ladies are celebrated for their beauty, and are immensely popular, I can assure you."

Sir George looked pleased, and it is quite probable his thoughts ran on the one particular vestment of the six-and-thirty, in which he ought to make his first appearance in such a society.

"I allow the American ladies to be handsome," said Mr. Monday; "but I think no Englishman need be in any particular danger of his heart from such a cause, after having been accustomed to the beauty of his own island. Captain Truck, I have the honor to drink your health."

"Fairly said," cried the captain, bowing to the compliment; "and I ascribe my own hard fortune to the fact that I have been kept sailing between the two countries so much favored in this particular, that I have never been able to make up my mind which to prefer. I have wished a thousand times there was but one handsome woman in the world, when a man would have nothing to do but fall in love with her; and make up his mind to get married at once, or to hang himself."

"That is a cruel wish to us men," returned Sir George, "as we should be certain to quarrel for the beauty."

"In such a case," resumed Mr. Monday, "we common men would have to give way to the claims of the nobility and gentry, and satisfy ourselves with plainer companions; though an Englishman loves his independence, and might rebel. I have the honor to drink your health and happiness, Sir George."

"I protest against your principle, Mr. Monday," said Mr. Dodge, "which is an invasion of human rights. Perfect freedom of action is to be maintained in this matter as in all others. I acknowledge that the English ladies are extremely beautiful, but I shall always maintain the supremacy of the American fair."

"We will drink their healths, sir. I am far from denying their beauty, Mr. Dodge, but I think you must admit that they fade earlier than our British ladies. God bless them both, however, and I empty this glass to the two entire nations, with all my heart and soul."

"Perfectly polite, Mr. Monday; but as to the fading of the ladies, I am not certain that I can yield an unqualified approbation to your sentiment."

"Nay, sir, your climate, you will allow, is none of the best, and it wears out constitutions almost as fast as your States make them."

"I hope there is no real danger to be apprehended from the climate," said Sir George; "I particularly detest bad climates; and for that reason have always made it a rule never to go into Lincolnshire."

"In that case, Sir George, you had better have stayed at home. In the way of climate, a man seldom betters himself by leaving old England. Now this is the tenth time I've been in America, allowing that I ever reach there, and although I entertain a profound respect for the country, I find myself growing older every time I quit it. Mr. Effingham, I do myself the favor to drink your health and happiness."

"You live too well when amongst us, Mr. Monday," said the captain; "there are too many soft crabs, hard clams, and canvas-backs; too much old Madeira, and generous sherry, for a man of your well-known taste to resist them. Sit less time at table, and go oftener to church this trip, and let us hear your report of the consequences a twelvemonth hence."

"You quite mistake my habits, Captain Truck, I give you my honor. Although a judicious eater, I seldom take anything that is compounded, being a plain roast and boiled man; a true old-fashioned Englishman in this respect, satisfying my appetite with solid beef and mutton, and turkeys and pork, and puddings and potatoes, and turnips and carrots, and similar simple food; and then I *never* drink. Ladies, I ask the honor to be permitted to wish you a happy return to your native countries. I ascribe all the difficulty, sir, to the climate, which will not permit a man to digest properly."

"Well, Mr. Monday, I subscribe to most of your opinions, and I believe few men cross the ocean together that are more harmonious in sentiment, in general, than has proved to be the case between you and Sir George, and myself," observed Mr. Dodge, glancing obliquely and pointedly at the rest of the party, as if he thought they were in a decided minority; "but in this instance I feel constrained to record my vote in the negative. I believe America has as good a climate, and as good general digestion, as commonly falls to the lot of mortals ; more than this I do not claim for the country, and less than this I should be reluctant to maintain. I have travelled a little, gentlemen, not as much, perhaps, as the Messrs. Effingham ; but then a man can see no more than is to be seen ; and I do affirm, Captain Truck, that in my poor judgment, which I know is good for nothing—"

" Why do you use it, then ? " abruptly asked the straight-forward captain ; " why not rely on a better ? "

" We must use such as we have, or go without, sir ; and I suspect, in my very poor judgment, which is probably poorer than that of most others on board, that America is a very good sort of a country. At all events, after having seen something of other countries, and governments, and people, I am of opinion that America, as a country, is quite good enough for me."

" You never said truer words, Mr. Dodge, and I beg you will join Mr. Monday and myself in a fresh glass of punch, just to help on the digestion. You have seen more of human nature than your modesty allows you to proclaim ; and I dare say this company would be gratified if you would overcome all scruples, and let us know your private opinions of the different people you have visited. Tell us something of that *ditter* you made on the Rhine."

" Mr. Dodge intends to publish, it is to be hoped ! " observed Mr. Sharp ; " and it may not be fair to anticipate his matter."

" I beg, gentlemen, you will have no scruples on that score, for my work will be rather philosophical and general, than of the particular nature of private anecdotes. Saunders, hand me the manuscript journal you will find on the shelf of our state-room, next to Sir George's patent tooth-pick case. This is the book ; and now, gentlemen and ladies, I beg you to remember that these are merely the ideas as they arose, and not my more mature reflections."

" Take a little punch, sir," interrupted the captain again, whose hard nor' west face was set in the most demure attention. " There is nothing like punch to clear the voice, Mr. Dodge ; the acid removes the huskiness, the sugar softens the tones, the water mellows the tongue, and the Jamaica braces

the muscles. With a plenty of punch, a man soon gets to be
another I forget the name of that great orator of antiquity
—it was n't Vattel, however.''

"You mean Demosthenes, sir; and, gentlemen, I beg you
to remark that this orator was a republican : but there can
be no question that liberty is favorable to the encouragement of all the higher qualities. Would you prefer a few
notes on Paris, ladies, or shall I commence with some extracts about the Rhine?''

"Oh! de grace, Monsieur, be so very kind as not to overlook Paris!'' said Mademoiselle Viefville.

Mr. Dodge bowed graciously, and turning over the
leaves of his private journal, he alighted in the heart of the
great city named. After some preliminary hemming, he
commenced reading in a grave didactic tone, that sufficiently
showed the value he had attached to his own observations.

"'Déjjuned at ten, as usual, an hour that I find exceedingly unreasonable and improper, and one that would meet
with general disapprobation in America. I do not wonder
that a people gets to be immoral and depraved in their practices, who keep such improper hours. The mind acquires
habits of impurity, and all the sensibilities become blunted,
by taking the meals out of the natural seasons. I impute
much of the corruption of France to the periods of the day
in which the food is taken—''

"Voilà une drole d'idée!'' ejaculated Mademoiselle Viefville.

"'In which food is taken,' '' repeated Mr. Dodge, who
fancied the involuntary exclamation was in approbation of
the justice of his sentiments. "'Indeed, the custom of taking wine at this meal, together with the immorality of the
hour, must be chief reasons why the French ladies are so
much in the practice of drinking to excess.' ''

"Mais, Monsieur!''

"You perceive, Mademoiselle calls in question the accuracy of your facts," observed Mr. Blunt, who, in common
with all the listeners, Sir George and Mr. Monday excepted,
began to enjoy a scene which at first had promised nothing
but ennui and disgust.

" I have it on the best authority, I give you my honor, or I would not introduce so grave a charge in a work of this contemplated importance. I obtained my information from an English gentleman who has resided twelve years in Paris ; and he informs me that a very large portion of the women of fashion in that capital, let them belong to what country they will, are dissipated."

" *A la bonne heure, Monsieur !—mais*, to drink, it is very different."

" Not so much so, Mademoiselle, as you imagine," rejoined John Effingham. " Mr. Dodge is a purist in language as well as in morals, and he uses terms differently from us less instructed prattlers. By dissipated, he understands a drunkard."

" *Comment !* "

" Certainly ; Mr. John Effingham, I presume, will at least give us the credit in America of speaking our language better than any other known people. 'After dejjunying, took a *phyacre* and rode to the palace, to see the king and royal family leave for Nully.' "

" *Pour où ?* "

" *Pour Neuilly, Mademoiselle*," Eve quietly answered.

" ' For Nully. His majesty went on horseback, preceding his illustrious family and all the rest of the noble party, dressed in a red coat, laced with white on the seams, wearing blue breeches and a cocked hat.' "

" *Ciel !* "

" ' I made the king a suitable republican reverence as he passed, which he answered with a gracious smile, and a benignant glance of his royal eye. The Hon. Louis Philippe Orleans, the present sovereign of the French, is a gentleman of portly and commanding appearance, and in his state attire, which he wore on this occasion, looks " every inch a king." He rides with grace and dignity, and sets an example of decorum and gravity to his subjects, by the solemnity of his air, that it is to be hoped will produce a beneficial and benign influence during this reign, on the manners of the nation. His dignity was altogether worthy of the schoolmaster of Haddonfield.' "

" *Par exemple !* "

" Yes, Mam'selle, in the way of example, it is that I mean. ' Although a pure democrat, and every way opposed to exclusion, I was particularly struck with the royalty of his majesty's demeanor, and the great simplicity of his whole deportment. I stood in the crowd next to a very accomplished countess, who spoke English, and she did me the honor to invite me to pay her a visit at her hotel, in the vicinity of the Bourse.' "

" *Mon Dieu—mon Dieu—mon Dieu!* "

" 'After promising my fair companion to be punctual, I walked as far as Notter Dam—' "

" I wish Mr. Dodge would be a little more distinct in his names," said Mademoiselle Viefville, who had begun to take an interest in the subject, that even valueless opinions excite in us concerning things that touch the affections.

" Mr. Dodge is a little profane, Mademoiselle," observed the captain; "but his journal probably was not intended for the ladies, and you must overlook it. Well, sir, you went to that naughty place ·"

" To Notter Dam, Captain Truck, if you please, and I flatter myself that is pretty good French."

" I think, ladies and gentlemen, we have a right to insist on a translation; for plain roast and boiled men, like Mr. Monday and myself, are sometimes weeping when we ought to laugh, so long as the discourse is in anything but old-fashioned English. Help yourself, Mr. Monday, and remember, you *never* drink."

" *Notter Dam*, I believe, Mam'selle, means our Mother, the Church of our Mother. Notter, or Noster, our,—Dam, Mother: Notter Dam. ' Here I was painfully impressed with the irreligion of the structure, and the general absence of piety in the architecture. Idolatry abounded, and so did holy water. How often have I occasion to bless Providence for having made me one of the descendants of those pious ancestors who cast their fortunes in the wilderness in preference to giving up their hold on faith and charity! The building is much inferior in comfort and true taste to the commoner American churches, and met with my unqualified disapprobation.' "

" *Est-il possible que cela soit vrai, ma chère !* "

" *Je l'espère, bien, Mademoiselle.* "

" You may *despair bien*, cousin Eve," said John Effingham, whose fine curvilinear face curled even more than usual with contempt.

The ladies whispered a few explanations, and Mr. Dodge, who fancied it was only necessary to resolve to be perfect to achieve his end, went on with his comments, with all the self-satisfaction of a provincial critic.

" ' From Notter Dam I proceeded in a *cabrioly* to the great national burying-ground, Pere la Chaise, so termed from the circumstance that its distance from the capital renders chaises necessary for the *convoys*—' "

" How 's this, how 's this ! " interrupted Mr. Truck ; " is one obliged to sail under a convoy about the streets of Paris ? "

" *Monsieur Dodge veut dire, convoi.* Mr. Dodge means to say, *convoi*," kindly interposed Mademoiselle Viefville.

" Mr. Dodge is a profound republican, and is an advocate for rotation in language, as well as in office : I must accuse you of inconstancy, my dear friend, if I die for it. You certainly do not pronounce your words always in the same way, and when I had the honor of carrying you out this time six months, when you were practising the continentals as you call them, you gave very different sounds to many of the words I then had the pleasure and gratification of hearing you use."

" We all improve by travelling, sir, and I make no question that my knowledge of foreign language is considerably enlarged by practice in the countries in which they are spoken."

Here the reading of the journal was interrupted by a digression on language, in which Messrs. Dodge, Monday, Templemore, and Truck were the principal interlocutors, and during which the pitcher of punch was twice renewed. We shall not record much of this learned discussion, which was singularly commonplace, though a few of the remarks may be given as a specimen of the whole.

" I must be permitted to say," replied Mr. Monday to

one of Mr. Dodge's sweeping claims to superiority in favor of his own nation, "that I think it quite extraordinary an Englishman should be obliged to go out of his own country in order to hear his own language spoken in purity ; and as one who has seen your people, Mr. Dodge, I will venture to affirm that nowhere is English better spoken than in Lancashire. Sir George, I drink your health !"

"More patriotic than just, Mr. Monday ; everybody allows that the American of the Eastern States speaks the best English in the world, and I think either of these gentlemen will concede that."

"Under the penalty of being nobody," cried Captain Truck : "for my own part, I think, if a man wishes to hear the language in perfection, he ought to pass a week or ten days in the river. I must say, Mr Dodge, I object to many of your sounds, particularly that of inyon, which I myself heard you call onion, no later than yesterday."

"Mr. Monday is a little peculiar in fancying that the best English is to be met with in Lancashire," observed Sir George Templemore ; "for I do assure you that, in town, we have difficulty in understanding gentlemen from your part of the kingdom."

This was a hard cut from one in whom Mr. Monday expected to find an ally, and that gentleman was driven to washing down the discontent it excited, in punch.

"But all this time we have interrupted the *convoi*, or convoy, captain," said Mr. Sharp ; "and Mr. Dodge, to say nothing of the mourners, has every right to complain. I beg that gentleman will proceed with his entertaining extracts."

Mr Dodge hemmed, sipped a little more liquor, blew his nose, and continued : —

"'The celebrated cemetery is, indeed, worthy of its high reputation. The utmost republican simplicity prevails in the interments, ditches being dug, in which the bodies are laid, side by side, without distinction of rank, and with regard only to the order in which the convoys arrive.' I think this sentence, gentlemen, will have great success in America, where the idea of any exclusiveness is quite odious to the majority."

"Well, for my part," said the captain, "I should have no particular objection to being excluded from such a grave: one would be afraid of catching the cholera in so promiscuous a company."

Mr. Dodge turned over a few leaves, and gave other extracts.

"'The last six hours have been devoted to a profound investigation of the fine arts. My first visit was to the *gullyteen*; after which I passed an instructive hour or two in the galleries of the Musy—'"

"*Où, donc?*"

"*Le Musée, Mademoiselle.*"

"'Where I discovered several very extraordinary things, in the way of sculpture and painting. I was particularly struck with the manner in which a plate was portrayed in the celebrated "Marriage of Cana," which might very well have been taken for real Delft, and there was one finger on the hand of a lady that seemed actually fitted to receive and to retain the hymeneal ring.'"

"Did you inquire if she were engaged? Mr. Monday, we will drink her health."

"'St. Michael and the Dragon' is a *shefdowrry*—"

"*Un quoi?*"

"*Un chéf-d'œuvre, Mademoiselle.*"

"'The manner in which the angel holds the dragon with his feet, looking exactly like a worm trodden on by the foot of a child, is exquisitely plaintive and interesting. Indeed these touches of nature abound in the works of the old masters, and I saw several fruit-pieces that I could have eaten. One really gets an appetite by looking at many things here, and I no longer wonder at a Raphael, a Titian, a Correggio, a Guide-o—'"

"*Un qui?*"

"*Un Guido, Mademoiselle.*"

"'Or a Cooley.'"

"And pray who may he be?" asked Mr. Monday.

"A young genius in Dodgetown, who promises one day to render the name of an American illustrious. He has painted a new sign for the store, that in its way is quite equal to the 'Marriage of Cana.' 'I have stood, with tears, over the despair of a Niobe,' " continuing to read, " ' and witnessed the contortions of the snakes in the Laocoön with a convulsive eagerness to clutch them, that has made me fancy I could hear them hiss.' That sentence, I think, will be likely to be noticed even in the New-Old-New-Yorker, one of the very best reviews of our days, gentlemen."

"Take a little more punch, Mr. Dodge," put in the attentive captain ; " this grows affecting, and needs alleviation, as Saunders would say. Mr. Monday, you will get a bad name for being too sober, if you never empty your glass. Proceed, in the name of Heaven ! Mr. Dodge."

" ' In the evening I went to the Grand Opery—' "

" *Où, donc !* "

"Au grand Hoppery, Mademoiselle," replied John Effingham.

" ' To the *Grand Opery*,' " resumed Mr. Dodge, with emphasis, his eyes beginning to glisten by this time, for he had often applied to the punch for inspiration, " ' where I listened to music that is altogether inferior to that which we enjoy in America, especially at the general trainings, and on the Sabbath. The want of science was conspicuous ; and if *this* be music, then do I know nothing about it ! ' "

" A judicious remark ! " exclaimed the captain. " Mr. Dodge has great merit as a writer, for he loses no occasion to illustrate his opinions by the most unanswerable facts. He has acquired a taste for a Zip Coon and Long-tail Blue, and it is no wonder he feels a contempt for your inferior artists."

" ' As for the dancing,' " continued the editor of the " Active Inquirer," " ' it is my decided impression that nothing can be worse. The moment was more suited to a funeral than the ball-room, and I affirm, without fear of contradiction, that there is not an assembly in all America in which a *cotillion* would not be danced in one half the time the one was danced in the *bally* to-night.' "

" *Dans le quoi ?* "

" I believe I have not given the real Parisian pronunciation to this word, which the French call bal-*lay*," continued the reader, with great candor.

" Belay, or make all fast, as we say on shipboard. Mr.
Dodge, as master of this vessel, I beg to return you the
united, or as Saunders would say, the condensed thanks of
the passengers, for this information ; and next Saturday we
look for a renewal of the pleasure. The ladies are getting
to be sleepy, I perceive, and as Mr. Monday *never* drinks,
and the other gentlemen have finished their punch, we may
as well retire, to get ready for a hard day's work to-morrow."

Captain Truck made this proposal, because he saw that
one or two of the party were *plenum punch*, and that Eve
and her companion were becoming aware of the propriety
of retiring. It was also true that he foresaw the necessity
of rest, in order to be ready for the exertions of the morning.

After the party had broken up, which it did very contrary
to the wishes of Messrs. Dodge and Monday, Mademoiselle
Viefville passed an hour in the state-room of Miss Effingham, during which time she made several supererogatory
complaints of the manner in which the editor of the " Active
Inquirer " had viewed things in Paris, besides asking a good
many questions concerning his occupation and character.

" I am not quite certain, my dear Mademoiselle, that I
can give you a very learned description of the animal you
think worthy of all these questions, but, by the aid of Mr.
John Effingham's information, and a few words that have
fallen from Mr. Blunt, I believe it ought to be something
as follows : America once produced a very distinguished
philosopher, named Franklin—"

" *Comment, ma chère ! Tout le monde le connait !* "

"This Monsieur Franklin commenced life as a printer ;
but, living to a great age, and rising to high employments,
he became a philosopher in morals, as his studies had made
him one in physics. Now, America is full of printers, and
most of them fancy themselves Franklins, until time and
failures teach them discretion."

" *Mais*, the world has seen but *un seul Franklin !* "

" Nor is it likely to see another very soon. In America
the young men are taught, justly enough, that by merit they
may rise to the highest situations ; and, always according to

Mr. John Effingham, too many of them fancy that because they are at liberty to turn any high qualities they may happen to have to account, they are actually fit for anything. Even he allows this peculiarity of the country does much good, but he maintains that it also does much harm, by causing pretenders to start up in all directions. Of this class he describes Mr. Dodge to be. This person, instead of working at the mechanical part of a press, to which he was educated, has the ambition to control its intellectual, part and thus edits the ' Active Inquirer.' "

" It must be a very useful journal ! "

" It answers his purposes, most probably. He is full of provincial ignorance, and provincial prejudices, you perceive ; and, I dare say, he makes his paper the circulator of all these, in addition to the personal rancor, envy, and uncharitableness that usually distinguish a pretension that mistakes itself for ambition. My cousin Jack affirms that America is filled with such as he."

" And Monsieur Effingham ? "

" O! my dear father is all mildness and charity, you know, Mademoiselle, and he only looks at the bright side of the picture, for he maintains that a great deal of good results from the activity and elasticity of such a state of things. While he confesses to a great deal of downright ignorance, that is paraded as knowledge ; to much narrow intolerance, that is offensively prominent in the disguise of principle, and a love of liberty ; and to vulgarity and personalities, that wound all taste, and every sentiment of right, he insists on it that the main result is good."

" In such a case there is no need of an umpire. You mentioned the case of Mr. Blunt. *Comme ce jeune homme parle bien Français !* "

Eve hesitated, and she changed color slightly, before she answered.

" I am not certain that the opinion of Mr. Blunt ought to be mentioned in opposition to those of my father and cousin Jack, on such a subject," she said. " He is very young, and it is, now, quite questionable whether he is even an American at all."

" *Tant mieux, ma chère.* He has been much in the country, and it is not the native that makes the best judge, when the stranger has many opportunities of seeing."

" On this principle, Mademoiselle, you are, then, to give up your own judgment about France, on all those points in which I have the misfortune to differ from you," said Eve, laughing.

" *Pas tout à fait,*" returned the governess good-humoredly. " Age and experience must pass *pour quelque chose. Et Monsieur Blunt ?* "

" Monsieur Blunt leans nearer to the side of cousin Jack, I fear, than to that of my dear, dear father. He says men of Mr. Dodge's character, propensities, malignancy, intoler-ance, ignorance, vulgarity, and peculiar vices, abound in and about the American press. He even insists that they do an incalculable amount of harm, by influencing those who have no better sources of information ; by setting up low jealous-ies and envy in the place of principles and the right ; by substituting—I use his own words, Mademoiselle," said Eve, blushing with the consciousness of the fidelity of her memory —" by substituting uninstructed provincial notions for true taste and liberality ; by confounding the real principles of liberty with personal envies, and the jealousies of station ; and by losing sight entirely of their duties to the public, in the effort to advance their own interests. He says that the government is in truth a *press-ocracy,* and a press-ocracy, too, that has not the redeeming merit of either principles, tastes, talents, or knowledge."

" *Ce Monsieur Blunt* has been very explicit, and *suffisam-ment éloquent,*" returned Mademoiselle Viefville, gravely ; for the prudent governess did not fail to observe that Eve used language so very different from that which was habit-ual to her, as to make her suspect she quoted literally. For the first time the suspicion was painfully awakened, that it was her duty to be more vigilant in relation to the inter-course between her charge and the two agreeable young men whom accident had given them as fellow-passengers. After a short but musing pause, she again adverted to the subject of their previous conversation.

" *Ce Monsieur Dodge, est-il ridicule !* "

" On that point at least, my dear Mademoiselle, there can be no mistake. And yet cousin Jack insists that this stuff will be given to his readers, as views of Europe worthy of their attention."

"*Ce conte du roi !—mais, c'est trop fort !* "

" With the coat laced at the seams, and the cocked hat ! "

"*Et l'honorable Louis Philippe d'Orleans !* "

" Orleans, Mademoiselle ; d'Orleans would be anti-republican."

Then the two ladies sat looking at each other a few moments in silence, when both, although of a proper *retenue* of manner in general, burst into a hearty and long-continued fit of laughter. Indeed, so long did Eve, in the buoyancy of her young spirits, and her keen perception of the ludicrous, indulge herself, that her hair fell about her rosy cheeks, and her bright eyes fairly danced with delight.

## CHAPTER XVI.

" And there he went ashore without delay,
    Having no custom-house or quarantine,—
To ask him awkward questions on the way
    About the time and place where he had been."

                                        BYRON.

CAPTAIN TRUCK was in a sound sleep as soon as his head touched the pillow. With the exception of the ladies, the others soon followed his example; and as the people were excessively wearied, and the night was so tranquil, ere long only a single pair of eyes were open on deck; those of the man at the wheel. The wind died away, and even this worthy was not innocent of nodding at his post.

Under such circumstances, it will occasion no great surprise that the cabin was aroused next morning with the sudden and startling information that the land was close aboard the ship. Every one hurried on deck, where, sure enough, the dreaded coast of Africa was seen, with a palpable distinctness, within two miles of the vessel. It presented a long, broken line of sand-hills, unrelieved by a tree, or by so few as almost to merit this description, and with a hazy background of remote mountains to the northeast. The margin of the actual coast nearest to the ship was indented with bays; and even rocks appeared in places; but the general character of the scene was that of a fierce and burning sterility. On this picture of desolation all stood gazing in awe and admiration for some minutes, as the day gradually brightened, until a cry arose from forward, of "A ship!"

"Whereaway?" sternly demanded Captain Truck; for the sudden and unexpected appearance of this dangerous coast had awakened all that was forbidding and severe in the temperament of the old master ; " whereaway, sir ? "

" On the larboard quarter sir, and at anchor."

" She is ashore ! " exclaimed half a dozen voices at the same instant, just as the words came from the last speaker. The glass soon settled this important point. At the distance of about a league astern of them were, indeed, to be seen the spars of a ship, with the hull looming on the sands, in a way to leave no doubt of her being a wreck. It was the first impression of all, that this, at last, was the Foam ; but Captain Truck soon announced to the contrary.

" It is a Swede, or a Dane," he said, " by his rig and his model. A stout, solid, compact sea-boat, that is high and dry on the sands, looking as if he had been built there. He does not appear even to have bilged, and most of his sails, and all of his yards, are in their places. Not a living soul is to be seen about her ! Ha ! there are signs of tents made of sails on shore, and broken bales of goods ! Her people have been seized and carried into the desert, as usual, and this is a fearful hint that we must keep the Montauk off the bottom. Turn-to the people, Mr. Leach, and get up your sheers, that we may step our jury-masts at once ; the smallest breeze on the land would drive us ashore, without any after-sail."

While the mates and the crew set about completing the work they had prepared the previous day, Captain Truck and his passengers passed the time in ascertaining all they could concerning the wreck, and the reasons of their being themselves in a position so very different from what they had previously believed.

As respects the first, little more could be ascertained ; she lay absolutely high and dry on a hard, sandy beach, where she had probably been cast during the late gale, and sufficient signs were made out by the captain to prove to him that she had been partly plundered. More than this could not be discovered at that distance, and the work of the Montauk was too urgent to send a boat manned with her own people to examine. Mr. Blunt, Mr. Sharp, Mr. Monday, and the servants of the two former, however, volunteering to pull the cutter, it was finally decided to look more closely into the facts, Captain Truck himself taking charge of the expedition. While the latter is getting ready, a word of explanation will suffice to tell the reader the reason why the Montauk had fallen so much to leeward.

The ship being so near the coast, it became now very obvious she was driven by a current that set along the land, but which it was probable, had set towards it more in the offing. The imperceptible drift between the observation of the previous day and the discovery of the coast, had sufficed to carry the vessel a great distance ; and to this simple cause, coupled perhaps with some neglect in the steerage during the past night, was her present situation to be solely attributed. Just at this moment, the little air there was came from the land, and by keeping her head off shore, Captain Truck entertained no doubt of his being able to escape the calamity that had befallen the other ship in the fury of the gale. A wreck is always a matter of so much interest with mariners, therefore, that taking all these things into view, he had come to the determination we have mentioned, of examining into the history of the one in sight, so far as circumstances permitted.

The Montauk carried three boats ; the launch, a large, safe, and well-constructed craft, which stood in the usual chucks between the foremast and mainmast ; a jolly-boat, and a cutter. It was next to impossible to get the first into the water, deprived as the ship was of its mainmast ; but the others hanging at davits, one on each quarter, were easily lowered. The packets seldom carry any arms beyond a light gun to fire signals with, the pistols of the master, and perhaps a fowling-piece or two. Luckily the passengers were better provided : all the gentlemen had pistols, Mr. Monday and Mr. Dodge excepted, if indeed they properly belonged to this category, as Captain Truck would say, and most of them had also fowling-pieces. Although a careful examination of the coast with the glasses offered no signs of the presence of any danger from enemies, these arms were carefully collected, loaded, and deposited in the boats, in order to be prepared for the worst. Provisions and water were also provided, and the party were about to proceed.

Captain Truck and one or two of the adventurers were still on the deck, when Eve, with that strange love of excitement and adventure that often visits the most delicate spirits, expressed an idle regret that she could not make one in the expedition.

" There is something so strange and wild in landing on an African desert," she said ; " and I think a nearer view of the wreck would repay us, Mademoiselle, for the hazard."

The young men hesitated between their desire to have such a companion, and their doubts of the prudence of the step ; but Captain Truck declared there could be no risk, and Mr. Effingham consenting, the whole plan was altered so as to include the ladies ; for there was so much pleasure in varying the monotony of a calm, and escaping the confinement of a ship, that everybody entered into the new arrangement with zeal and spirit.

A single whip was rigged on the fore-yard, a chair was slung, and in ten minutes both ladies were floating on the ocean in the cutter. This boat pulled six oars, which were manned by the servants of the two Messrs. Effingham, Mr. Blunt, and Mr. Sharp, together with the two latter gentlemen in person. Mr. Effingham steered. Captain Truck had the jolly-boat, of which he pulled an oar himself, aided by Saunders, Mr. Monday, and Sir George Templemore, the mates and the regular crew being actively engaged in rigging their jury-mast. Mr. Dodge declined being of the party, feeding himself with the hope that the present would be a favorable occasion to peep into the state-rooms, to run his eye over forgotten letters and papers, and otherwise to increase the general stock of information of the editor of the " Active Inquirer."

" Look to your chains, and see all clear for a run of the anchors, Mr. Leach, should you set within a mile of the shore," called out the captain, as they pulled off from the vessel's side. " The ship is drifting along the land, but the wind you have will hardly do more than meet the send

14

of the sea, which is on shore : should anything go wrong, show an ensign at the head of the jury-stick forward."

The mate waved his hand, and the adventurers passed without the sound of the voice. It was a strange sensation to most of those in the boats, to find themselves in their present situation. Eve and Mademoiselle Viefville, in particular, could scarcely credit their senses, when they found the egg-shells that held them heaving and setting like bubbles on those long, sluggish swells, which had seemed of so little consequence while in the ship, but which now resembled the heavy respirations of a leviathan. The boats, indeed, though always gliding onward, impelled by the oars, appeared at moments to be sent helplessly back and forth, like playthings of the mighty deep, and it was some minutes before either obtained a sufficient sense of security to enjoy her situation. As they receded from the Montauk, too, their situation seemed still more critical ; and with her sex's love of excitement, Eve heartily repented of her undertaking before they had gone a mile. The gentlemen, however, were all in good spirits, and as the boats kept near each other, Captain Truck enlivening their way with his peculiar wit, and Mr. Effingham, who was influenced by a motive of humanity in consenting to come, being earnest and interesting, Eve soon began to entertain other ideas.

As they drew near the end of their little expedition, entirely new feelings got the mastery of the whole party. The solitary and gloomy grandeur of the coast, the sublime sterility,—for even naked sands may become sublime by their vastness,—the heavy moanings of the ocean on the beach, and the entire spectacle of the solitude, blended as it was with the associations of Africa, time, and the changes of history, united to produce sensations of a pleasing melancholy. The spectacle of the ship, bringing with it the images of European civilization, as it lay helpless and deserted on the sands, too, heightened all.

This vessel, beyond a question, had been driven up on a sea during the late gale, at a point where the water was of sufficient depth to float her, until within a few yards of the very spot where she now lay; Captain Truck giving the following probable history of the affair :—

"On all sandy coasts," he said, "the return waves that are cast on the beach form a bar, by washing back with them a portion of the particles. This bar is usually within thirty or forty fathoms of the shore, and there is frequently sufficient water within it to float a ship. As this bar, however, prevents the return of all the water, on what is called the under-tow, narrow channels make from point to point, through which this excess of the element escapes. These channels are known by the appearance of the water over them, the seas breaking less at those particular places than in the spots where the bottom lies nearer to the surface, and all experienced mariners are aware of the fact. No doubt, the unfortunate master of this ship, finding himself reduced to the necessity of running ashore to save the lives of his crew, has chosen such a place, and has consequently forced his vessel up to a spot where she has remained dry as soon as the sea fell. So worthy a fellow deserved a better fate; for this wreck is not three days old, and yet no signs are to be seen of any who were in that stout ship."

These remarks were made as the crew of the two boats lay on their oars, at a short distance without the line on the water, where the breaking of the sea pointed out the position of the bar. The channel, also, was plainly visible directly astern of the ship, the sea merely rising and falling in it without combing. A short distance to the southward, a few bold, black rocks thrust themselves forward, and formed a sort of bay, in which it was practicable to land without risk; for they had come on the coast in a region where the monotony of the sands, as it appeared when close in, was little relieved by the presence of anything else.

"If you will keep the cutter just without the breakers, Mr. Effingham," Captain Truck continued, after standing up awhile and examining the shore, "I will put into the channel, and land in yonder bay. If you feel disposed to follow, you may do so, by giving the tiller to Mr. Blunt, on receiving a signal to that effect from me. Be steady, gentlemen, at your oars, and look well to the arms on landing, for we are in a knavish part of the world. Should any of the monkeys or orang-outangs claim kindred with Mr. Saunders, we may find it no easy matter to persuade them to leave us the pleasure of his society."

The captain made a sign, and the jolly-boat entered the channel. Inclining south, it was seen rising and falling just within the breakers, and then it was hid by the rocks. In another minute, Mr. Truck, followed by all but Mr. Monday, who stood sentinel at the boat, was on the rocks, making his way towards the wreck. On reaching the latter, he ascended swiftly even to the main cross-trees. Here a long examination of the plain, beyond the bank that hid it from the view of all beneath, succeeded, and then the signal to come on was made to those who were still in the boat.

"Shall we venture?" cried Paul Blunt, soliciting an assent by the very manner in which he put the question.

"What say you, dear father?"

"I hope we may not yet be too late to succor some Christian in distress, my child. Take the tiller, Mr. Blunt, and in Heaven's good name, and for humanity's sake, let us proceed!

The boat advanced, Paul Blunt standing erect to steer, his ardor to proceed corrected by apprehensions on account of her precious freight. There was an instant when the ladies trembled, for it seemed as if the light boat was about to be cast upon the shore, like the froth of the sea that shot past them; but the steady hand of him who steered averted the danger, and in another minute they were floating at the side of the jolly-boat. The ladies got ashore without much difficulty, and stood on the summit of the rock.

"*Nous voici donc, en Afrique,*" exclaimed Mademoiselle Viefville, with that sensation of singularity that comes over all when they first find themselves in situations of extraordinary novelty.

"The wreck—the wreck," murmured Eve; "let us go to the wreck. There may be yet a hope of saving some wretched sufferer."

Towards the wreck they all proceeded, after leaving two of the servants to relieve Mr. Monday on his watch.

It was an impressive thing to stand at the side of a ship
on the sands of Africa, a scene in which the desolation of
an abandoned vessel was heightened by the desolation of a
desert. The position of the vessel, which stood nearly
erect, imbedded in the sands, rendered it less difficult than
might be supposed for the ladies to ascend to, and to walk
her decks, a rude staging having been made already to facil-
itate the passage. Here the scene became thrice exciting,
for it was the very type of a hastily deserted and cherished
dwelling.

Before Eve and Mademoiselle Viefville gained the deck,
the other party had ascertained that no living soul remained.
The trunks, chests, furniture, and other appliances of the
cabin, had been rummaged, and many boxes had been raised
from the hold, and plundered, a part of their contents still
lying scattered on the decks. The ship, however, had been
lightly freighted, and the bulk of her cargo, which was salt,
was apparently untouched. A Danish ensign was found
bent to the halyards, a proof that Captain Truck's original
conjecture concerning the character of the vessel was accurate. Her name, too, was ascertained to be the Carrier, as
translated into English, and she belonged to Copenhagen.
More than this it was not easy to ascertain. No papers
were found, and her cargo, or as much of it as remained,
was so mixed and miscellaneous, as Saunders called it, that
no plausible guess could be given as to the port where it
had been taken in, if indeed it had all been received on
board at the same place.

Several of the light sails had evidently been carried off,
but all the heavy canvas was left on the yards, which remained in their places. The vessel was large, exceedingly
strong, as was proved by the fact that she had not bilged in
breaching, and apparently well found. Nothing was wanting to launch her into the ocean but machinery and force,
and a crew to sail her, when she might have proceeded on
her voyage as if nothing unusual had occurred. But such
a restoration was hopeless, and this admirable machine, like
a man cut off in his youth and vigor, had been cast upon the
shores of this inhospitable region, to moulder where it lay,

unless broken up for the wood and iron by the wanderers
of the desert.

There was no object more likely to awaken melancholy
ideas in a mind resembling that of Captain Truck's, than a
spectacle of this nature. A fine ship, complete in nearly
all her parts, virtually uninjured, and yet beyond the chance
of further usefulness, in his eyes was a picture of the most
cruel loss. He cared less for the money it had cost than for
the qualities and properties that were thus destroyed.

He examined the bottom, which he pronounced capital
for stowing, and excellent as that of a sea-boat; he admired
the fastenings; applied his knife to try the quality of the
wood, and pronounced the Norway pine of the spars to be
almost equal to anything that could be found in our own
southern woods. The rigging, too, he regarded as one loves
to linger over the regretted qualities of a deceased friend.

The tracks of camels and horses were abundant on the
sands around the ship, and especially at the bottom of the
rude staging by which the party had ascended, and which had
evidently been hastily made in order to carry articles from
the vessel to the backs of the animals that were to bear
them into the desert. The footprints of men were also to
be seen, and there was a startling and mournful certainty
in distinguishing the marks of shoes, as well as those of
the naked foot.

Judging from all these signs, Captain Truck was of
opinion the wreck must have taken place but two or three
days before, and that the plunderers had not left the spot
many hours.

"They probably went off with what they could carry at
sunset last evening; and there can be no doubt that before
many days, they, or others in their place, will be back
again. God protect the poor fellows who have fallen into
this miserable bondage! What an occasion would there
now be to rescue one of them, should he happen to be hid
near this spot!"

The idea seized the whole party at once, and all eagerly
turned to examine the high bank, which rose nearly to the
summit of the masts, in the hope of discovering some con-

cealed fugitive. The gentlemen went below again, and Mr. Sharp and Mr. Blunt called out in German, and English, and French, to invite any one who might be secreted to come forth. No sound answered these friendly calls. Again Captain Truck went aloft to look into the interior, but he beheld nothing more than the broad and unpeopled desert.

A place where the camels had descended to the beach was at no great distance, and thither most of the party proceeded, mounting to the level of the plain beyond. In this little expedition Paul Blunt led the advance, and as he rose over the brow of the bank, he cocked both barrels of his fowling-piece, uncertain what might be encountered. They found, however, a silent waste, almost without vegetation, and nearly as trackless as the ocean that lay beyond them. At the distance of a hundred rods, an object was just discernible, lying on the plain, half-buried in sand, and thither the young men expressed a wish to go, first calling to those in the ship to send a man aloft to give the alarm, in the event of any party of the Mussulmans being seen. Mr. Effingham, too, on being told their intention, had the precaution to cause Eve and Mademoiselle Viefville to get into the cutter, which he manned, and caused to pull out over the bar, where she lay waiting the issue.

A camel's path, of which the tracks were nearly obliterated by the sands, led to the object; and after toiling along it, the adventurers soon reached the desired spot. It proved to be the body of a man who had died by violence. His dress and person denoted that of a passenger rather than that of a seaman, and he had evidently been dead but a very few hours, probably not twelve. The cut of a sabre had cleft his skull. Agreeing not to acquaint the ladies with this horrible discovery, the body was hastily covered with the sand, the pockets of the dead man having been first examined; for, contrary to usage, his person had not been stripped. A letter was found, written by a wife to her husband, and nothing more. It was in German, and its expressions and contents, though simple, were endearing and natural. It spoke of the traveller's return; for she who wrote it little thought of the miserable fate that awaited her beloved in this remote desert.

As nothing else was visible, the party returned hastily to the beach, where they found that Captain Truck had ended his investigation, and was impatient to return. In the interest of the scene, the Montauk had disappeared behind a headland, towards which she had been drifting when they left her. Her absence created a general sense of loneliness, and the whole party hastened into the jolly-boat, as if fearful of being left. When without the bar again, the cutter took in her proper crew, and the boats pulled away, leaving the Dane standing on the beach in his solitary desolation— a monument of his own disaster.

As they got farther from the land the Montauk came in sight again, and Captain Truck announced the agreeable intelligence that the jury mainmast was up, and that the ship had after-sail set, diminutive and defective as it might be. Instead of heading to the southward, however, as heretofore, Mr. Leach was apparently endeavoring to get back again to the northward of the headland that had shut in the ship, or was trying to retrace his steps. Mr. Truck rightly judged that this was proof his mate disliked the appearance of the coast astern of him, and that he was anxious to get an offing. The captain in consequence urged his men to row, and in little more than an hour the whole party were on the deck of the Montauk again, and the boats were hanging at the davits.

## CHAPTER XVII.

IF Captain Truck distrusted the situation of his own ship when he saw that the mate had changed her course, he liked it still less after he was on board, and had an opportunity to form a more correct judgment. The current had set the vessel not only to the southward, but in-shore, and the send of the ground-swell was gradually, but inevitably, heaving her in towards the land. At this point the coast was more broken than at the spot where the Dane had been wrecked, some signs of trees appearing, and rocks running off in irregular reefs into the sea. More to the south, these rocks were seen without the ship, while directly astern they were not half a mile distant. Still the wind was favorable, though light and baffling, and Mr. Leach had got up every stitch of canvas that circumstances would at all allow ; the lead, too, had been tried, and the bottom was found to be a hard sand mixed with rocks, and the depth of the water such as to admit of anchoring. It was a sign that Captain Truck did not absolutely despair after ascertaining all these facts, that he caused Mr. Saunders to be summoned ; for as yet, none of those who had been in the boats had break-fasted.

"Step this way, Mr. Steward," said the captain ; "and report the state of the coppers. You were rummaging, as usual, among the lockers of yonder unhappy Dane, and I desire to know what discoveries you have made ! You will please to recollect, that on all public expeditions of this nature, there must be no peculation or private journal kept. Did you see any stock-fish?"

"Sir, I should deem this ship disgraced by the admission into her pantry of such an article, sir. We have tongues and sounds in plenty, Captain Truck, and no gentleman that has such diet, need ambition a stock-fish!"

"I am not quite of your way of thinking; but the earth is not made of stock-fish! Did you happen to fall in with any butter?"

"Some, sir, that is scarcely fit to slush a mast with, and I do think, one of the most atrocious cheeses, sir, it was ever my bad fortune to meet with. I do not wonder the Africans left the wreck."

"You followed their example, of course, Mr. Saunders, and left the cheese."

"I followed my own judgment, sir, for I would not stay in the ship with such a cheese, Captain Truck, sir, even to have the honor of serving under so great a commander as yourself. I think it no wonder that vessel was wrecked. Even the sharks would abandon her. The very thoughts of her impurities, sir, make me feel unsettled in the stomach."

The captain nodded his head in approbation of this sentiment, called for a coal, and then ordered breakfast. The meal was silent, thoughtful, and even sad; every one was thinking of the poor Danes and their sad fate, while they who had been on the plain had the additional subject of the murdered man for their contemplation.

"Is it possible to do nothing to redeem these poor people, father, from captivity?" Eve at length demanded.

"I have been thinking of this, my child; but I see no other method than to acquaint their government of their situation."

"Might we not contribute something from our own means to that effect? Money, I fancy, is the chief thing necessary."

The gentlemen looked at each other in approbation, though a reluctance to be the first to speak kept most of them silent.

"If a hundred pounds, Miss Effingham, will be useful,"

Sir George Templemore said, after the pause had continued an awkward minute, laying a bank-note of that amount on the table, "and you will honor us by becoming the keeper of the redemption money, I have great pleasure in making the offer."

This was handsomely said, and as Captain Truck afterwards declared, handsomely done too, though it was a little abrupt, and caused Eve to hesitate and redden.

" I shall accept your gift, sir," she said; "and with your permission will transfer it to Mr. Effingham, who will better know what use to put it to, in order to effect our benevolent purpose. I think I can answer for as much more from himself."

" You may, with certainty, my dear—and twice as much, if necessary. John, this is a proper occasion for your interference."

" Put me down at what you please," said John Effingham, whose charities in a pecuniary sense were as unlimited, as in feeling they were apparently restrained. "One hundred or one thousand, to rescue that poor crew ! "

" I believe, sir, we must all follow so good an example," Mr. Sharp observed ; "and I sincerely hope that this scheme will not prove useless. I think it may be effected by means of some of the public agents at Mogadore."

Mr. Dodge raised many objections, for it really exceeded his means to give so largely, and his character was formed in a school too envious and jealous to confess an inferiority on a point even as worthless as that of money. Indeed, he had so long been accustomed to maintain that "one man was as good as another," in opposition to his senses, that, like most of those who belong to this impracticable school, he had tacitly admitted in his own mind, the general and vulgar ascendency of mere wealth ; and, quite as a matter of course, he was averse to confessing his own inferiority on a point that he had made to be all in all, while loudest in declaiming against any inferiority whatever. He walked out of the cabin, therefore, with strong heart-burnings and jealousies, because others had presumed to give that which it was not really in his power to bestow.

On the other hand, both Mademoiselle Viefville and Mr. Monday manifested the superiority of the opinions in which they had been trained. The first quietly handed a Napoleon to Mr. Effingham, who took it with as much attention and politeness as he received any of the larger contributions; while the latter produced a five-pound note, with a hearty good-will that redeemed the sin of many a glass of punch in the eyes of his companions.

Eve did not dare to look towards Paul Blunt, while this collection was making; but she felt regret that he did not join in it. He was silent and thoughtful, and even seemed pained, and she wondered if it were possible that one, who certainly lived in a style to prove that his income was large, could be so thoughtless as to have deprived himself of the means of doing that which he so evidently desired to do. But most of the company was too well-bred to permit the matter to become the subject of conversation, and they soon rose from table in a body. The mind of Eve, however, was greatly relieved when her father told her that the young man had put a hundred sovereigns in gold into his hands as soon as possible, and that he had seconded this offering with another, of embarking for Mogadore in person, should they get into the Cape de Verdes, or the Canaries, with a view of carrying out the charitable plan with the least delay.

"He is a noble-hearted young man," said the pleased father, as he communicated this fact to his daughter and cousin; "and I shall not object to the plan."

"If he offer to quit this ship one minute sooner than is necessary, he does, indeed, deserve a statue of gold," said John Effingham; "for it has all that can attract a young man like him, and all too that can awaken his jealousy."

"Cousin Jack!" exclaimed Eve reproachfully, quite thrown off her guard by the abruptness and plainness of this language.

The quiet smile of Mr. Effingham proved that he understood both, but he made no remark. Eve instantly recovered her spirits, and angry at herself for the girlish exclamation that had escaped her, she turned on her assailant. "I do not know that I ought to be seen in an aside with Mr. John Effingham," she said, "even when it is sanctioned with the presence of my own father."

"And may I ask why so much sudden reserve, my offended beauty?"

"Merely that the report is already active, concerning the delicate relation in which we stand towards each other."

John Effingham looked surprised, but he suppressed his curiosity from a long habit of affecting an indifference he did not always feel. The father was less dignified, for he quietly demanded an explanation.

"It would seem," returned Eve, assuming a solemnity suited to a matter of interest, "that our secret is discovered. While we were indulging our curiosity about this unfortunate ship, Mr. Dodge was gratifying the laudable industry of the Active Inquirer, by prying into our state-rooms."

"This meanness is impossible!" exclaimed Mr. Effingham.

"Nay," said John, "no meanness is impossible to a demagogue—a pretender to things of which he has even no just conception—a man who lives to envy and traduce; in a word, a *quasi*-gentleman. Let us hear what Eve has to say."

"My information is from Ann Sidley, who saw him in the act. Now the kind letter you wrote my father, cousin Jack, just before we left London, and which you wrote because you would not trust that honest tongue of yours to speak the feelings of that honest heart, is the subject of my daily study; not on account of its promises, you will believe me, but on account of the strong affection it displays to a girl who is not worthy of one half you feel and do for her."

"Pshaw!"

"Well, let it then be pshaw! I had read that letter this very morning, and carelessly left it on my table. This letter Mr. Dodge, in his undying desire to lay everything before the public, as becomes his high vocation, and as in duty bound, has read; and misconstruing some of the phrases, as will sometimes happen to a zealous circulator of news, he has drawn the conclusion that I am to be made a happy woman as soon as we reach America, by being con-verted from Miss Eve Effingham into Mrs. John Effing-ham."

"Impossible! No man can be such a fool, or quite so great a miscreant!"

"I should rather think, my child," added the milder father, "that injustice has been done Mr. Dodge. No per-son, in the least approximating to the station of a gentle-man, could even think of an act so base as this you mention."

"O! if this be all your objection to the tale," observed the cousin, "I am ready to swear to its truth. But Eve has caught a little of Captain Truck's spirit of mystifying, and is determined to make a character by a bold stroke in the beginning. She is clever, and in time may rise to be a quiz."

"Thank you for the compliment, cousin Jack, which, however, I am forced to disclaim, as I never was more serious in my life. That the letter was read, Nanny, who is truth itself, affirms she saw. That Mr. Dodge has since been industriously circulating the report of my great good fortune, she has heard from the mate, who had it from the highest source of information direct; and that such a man would be likely to come to such a conclusion, you have only to recall the terms of the letter yourself, to believe."

"There is nothing in my letter to justify any notion so silly."

"An Active Inquirer might make discoveries you little dream of, dear cousin Jack. You speak of its being time to cease roving, of settling yourself at last, of never parting, and, prodigal as you are, of making Eve the future mistress of your fortune. Now to all this, recreant, confess, or I shall never again put faith in man."

John Effingham made no answer, but the father warmly expressed his indignation, that any man of the smallest pre-tensions to be admitted among gentlemen, should be guilty of an act so base.

"We can hardly tolerate his presence, John, and it is almost a matter of conscience to send him to Coventry."

"If you entertain such notions of decorum, your wisest way, Edward, will be to return to the place whence you have come ; for, trust me, you will find scores of such gentlemen where you are going !"

"I shall not allow you to persuade me I know my own country so little. Conduct like this will stamp a man with disgrace in America as well as elsewhere."

"Conduct like this would, but it will no longer. The pell-mell that rages has brought honorable men into a sad minority, and even Mr. Dodge will tell you the majority must rule. Were he to publish my letter, a large portion of his readers would fancy he was merely asserting the liberty of the press. Heaven save us ! You have been dreaming abroad, Ned Effingham, while your country has retrograded, in all that is respectable and good, a century in a dozen years !"

As this was the usual language of John Effingham, neither of his listeners thought much of it, though Mr. Effingham more decidedly expressed an intention to cut off even the slight communication with the offender he had permitted himself to keep up since they had been on board.

"Think better of it, dear father," said Eve ; "for such a man is scarcely worthy of even your resentment. He is too much your inferior in principles, manners, character, station, and everything else, to render him of so much account ; and then, were we to clear up this masquerade into which the chances of a ship have thrown us, we might have our scruples concerning others, as well as concerning this wolf in sheep's clothing."

"Say rather an ass, shaved and painted to resemble a zebra," muttered John. "The fellow has no property as respectable as the basest virtue of a wolf."

"He has at least rapacity."

"And can howl in a pack. This much, then, I will concede to you ; but I agree with Eve, we must either punish him affirmatively, by pulling his ears, or treat him with contempt, which is always negative or silent. I wish he had entered the state-room of that fine young fellow, Paul Blunt, who is of an age and a spirit to give him a lesson that might make a paragraph for his 'Active Inquirer,' if not a scissors' extract of himself."

Eve knew that the offender had been there too, but she had too much prudence to betray him.

"This will only so much the more oblige him," she said, laughingly, "for Mr. Blunt, in speaking of the editor of the 'Active Inquirer,' said that he had the failing to believe that this earth, and all it contained, was created merely to furnish materials for newspaper paragraphs."

The gentlemen laughed with the amused Eve, and Mr. Effingham remarked, that "there did seem to be men so perfectly selfish, so much devoted to their own interests, and so little sensible of the rights and feelings of others, as to manifest a desire to render the press superior to all other power; not," he concluded, "in the way of argument, or as an agent of reason, but as a master, coarse, corrupt, tyrannical, and vile; the instrument of selfishness, instead of the right, and when not employed as the promoter of personal interests, to be employed as the tool of personal passions."

"Your father will become a convert to my opinions, Miss Effingham," said John, "and he will not be home a twelvemonth before he will make the discovery that the government is a press-ocracy, and its ministers, self-chosen and usurpers, composed of those who have the least at stake, even as to character.

Mr. Effingham shook his head in dissent, but the conversation changed in consequence of a stir in the ship. The air from the land had freshened, and even the heavy canvas on which the Montauk was now compelled principally to rely, had been asleep, as mariners term it, or had blown out from the mast, where it stood inflated and steady, a proof at sea, where the water is always in motion, that the breeze is getting to be fresh. Aided by this power, the ship had overcome the united action of the heavy ground-swell and of the current, and was stealing out from under the land, when the air murmured for an instant, as if about to blow still fresher, and then all the sails flapped. The wind had passed away like a bird, and a dark line to seaward denoted the approach of the breeze from the ocean. The stir in the vessel was occasioned by the preparations to meet this change.

The new wind brought little with it beyond the general danger of blowing on shore. The breeze was light, and not more than sufficient to force the vessel through the water, in her present condition, a mile and a half in the hour, and this too in a line nearly parallel with the coast. Captain Truck saw, therefore, at a glance, that he should be compelled to anchor. Previously, however, to doing this, he had a long talk with his mates, and a boat was lowered.

The lead was cast, and the bottom was found to be still good, though a hard sand, which is not the best holding-ground.

"A heavy sea would cause the ship to drag," Captain Truck remarked, "should it come on to blow, and the line of dark rocks astern of us would make chips of the Pennsylvania in an hour, were that great ship to lie on it."

He entered the boat, and pulled along the reefs to examine an inlet that Mr. Leach reported to have been seen, before he got the ship's head to the northward. Could an entrance be found at this point, the vessel might possibly be carried within the reef, and a favorite scheme of the captain's could be put in force, one to which he now attached the highest importance. A mile brought the boat up to the inlet, where Mr. Truck found the following appearances : the general formation of the coast in sight was that of a slight curvature, within which the ship had so far drifted as to be materially inside a line drawn from headland to headland. There was, consequently, little hope of urging a vessel, crippled like the Montauk, against wind, sea, and current, out again into the ocean. For about a league abreast of the ship the coast was rocky, though low, the rocks running off from the shore quite a mile in places, and everywhere fully half that distance. The formation was irregular, but it had the general character of a reef, the position of which was marked by breakers, as well as by the black heads of rocks that here and there showed themselves above the water. The inlet was narrow, crooked, and so far environed by rocks as to render it questionable whether there was a passage at all, though the smoothness of the water had raised hopes to that effect in Mr. Leach.

As soon as Captain Truck arrived at the mouth of this passage, he felt so much encouraged by the appearance of things, that he gave the concerted signal for the ship to veer round and to stand to the southward. This was losing ground in the way of offing, but tack the Montauk could not with so little wind, and the captain saw by the drift she had made since he left her, that promptitude was necessary. The ship might anchor off the inlet, as well as anywhere else, if reduced to anchoring outside at all, and then there was always the chance of entering.

As soon as the ship's head was again to the southward, and Captain Truck felt certain that she was lying along the reef at a reasonably safe distance, and in as good a direction as he could hope for, he commenced his examination. Like a discreet seaman, he pulled off from the rocks to a suitable distance, for should an obstacle occur outside, he well knew any depth of water farther in would be useless. The day was so fine, and in the absence of rivers, the ocean so limpid in that low latitude, that it was easy to see the bottom at a considerable depth. But to this sense, of course, the captain did not trust, for he kept the lead going constantly, although all eyes were also employed in searching for rocks.

The first cast of the lead was in five fathoms, and these soundings were held nearly up to the inlet, where the lead struck a rock in three fathoms and a half. At this point, then, a more careful examination was made; but three and a half was the shallowest cast. As the Montauk drew nearly a fathom less than this, the cautious old master proceeded closer in. Directly in the mouth of the inlet was a large flat rock, that rose nearly to the surface of the sea, and which, when the tide was low, was probably bare. This rock Captain Truck at first believed would defeat his hopes of success, which by this time were strong; but a closer examination showed him that on one side of it was a narrow passage, just wide enough to admit a ship.

From this spot the channel became crooked, but it was sufficiently marked by the ripple on the reef; and after a

careful investigation, he found it was possible to carry three
fathoms quite within the reef, where a large space existed
that was gradually filling up with sand, but which was
nearly all covered with water when the tide was in, as was
now the case, and which had channels, as usual, between
the banks. Following one of these channels a quarter of a
mile, he found a basin of four fathoms of water, large enough
to take a ship in, and, fortunately, it was in close proximity
to a portion of the reef that was always bare, when a heavy
sea was not beating over it. Here he dropped a buoy, for
he had come provided with several fragments of spars for
this purpose; and, on his return, the channel was similarly
marked off, at all the critical points. On the flat rock, in
the inlet, one of the men was left, standing up to his waist
in the water, it being certain that the tide was falling.

The boat now returned to the ship, which it met at the
distance of half a mile from the inlet. The current setting
southwardly, her progress had been more rapid than when
heading north, and her drift had been less towards the land.
Still there was so little wind, so steady a ground-swell, and
it was possible to carry so little after-sail, that great doubts
were entertained of being able to weather the rocks sufficiently to turn into the inlet. Twenty times in the next
half-hour was the order to let go the anchor on the point
of being given, as the wind baffled, and as often was it
countermanded, to take advantage of its reviving. These
were feverish moments, for the ship was now so near the
reef as to render her situation very insecure in the event
of the wind's rising, or of a sea's getting up, the sand of the
bottom being too hard to make good holding-ground. Still,
as there was a possibility, in the present state of the
weather, of kedging the ship off a mile into the offing, if
necessary, Captain Truck stood on with a boldness he might
not otherwise have felt. The anchor hung suspended by a
single turn of the stopper, ready to drop at a signal, and
Mr. Truck stood between the knight-heads, watching the
slow progress of the vessel, and accurately noticing every
foot of leeward set she made, as compared with the rocks.

All this time the poor fellow stood in the water, awaiting

the arrival of his friends, who, in their turn, were anxiously watching his features, as they gradually grew more distinct.

"I see his eyes," cried the captain, cheerily; "take a drag at the bowlines, and let her head up as much as she will, Mr. Leach, and never mind those sham topsails. Take them in at once, sir; they do us, now, more harm than good."

The clewline blocks rattled, and the topgallant-sails, which were made to do the duty of topsails, but which would hardly spread to the lower yards, so as to set on a wind, came rapidly in. Five minutes of intense doubt followed, when the captain gave the animating order to—

"Man the main clew-garnets, boys, and stand by to make a run of it!"

This was understood to be a sign that the ship was far enough to windward, and the command to "In mainsail," which soon succeeded, was received with a shout.

"Hard up with the helm, and stand by to lay the foreyard square!" cried Captain Truck, rubbing his hands. "Look that both bowers are clear for a run; and you, Toast, bring me the brightest coal in the galley."

The movements of the Montauk were necessarily slow; but she obeyed her helm, and fell off until her bows pointed in towards the sailor in the water. This fine fellow, the moment he saw the ship approaching, waded to the verge of the rock, where it went off perpendicularly to the bottom, and waved to them to come on without fear.

"Come within ten feet of me," he shouted. "There is nothing to spare on the other side."

As the captain was prepared for this, the ship was steered accordingly, and as she hove slowly past on the rising and falling water, a rope was thrown to the man, who was hauled on board.

"Port!" cried the captain, as soon as the rock was passed; "port your helm, sir, and stand for the first buoy."

In this manner the Montauk drove slowly but steadily on, until she had reached the basin, where one anchor was let go almost as soon as she entered. The chain was paid out until the vessel was forced over to some distance, and then the other bower was dropped. The foresail was hauled up and handed, and chain was given the ship, which was pronounced to be securely moored.

"Now," cried the captain, all his anxiety ceasing with the responsibility, "I expect to be made a member of the New York Philosophical Society, at least, which is learned company for a man who has never been at college, for discovering a port on the coast of Africa, which harbor, ladies and gentlemen, without too much vanity, I hope to be permitted to call Port Truck. If Mr. Dodge, however, should think this too anti-republican, we will compromise the matter by calling it Port Truck and Dodge; or the town that no doubt will sooner or later arise on its banks, may be called Dodgeborough, and I will keep the harbor to myself."

"Should Mr. Dodge consent to this arrangement, he will render himself liable to the charge of aristocracy," said Mr. Sharp; for as all felt relieved by finding themselves in a place of security, so all felt disposed to join in the pleasantry. "I dare say his modesty would prevent his consenting to the plan."

"Why, gentlemen," returned the subject of these remarks, "I do not know that we are to refuse honors that are fairly imposed on us by the popular voice; and the practice of naming towns and counties after distinguished citizens, is by no means uncommon with us. A few of my own neighbors have been disposed to honor me in this way already, and my paper is issued from a hamlet that certainly does bear my own unworthy name. So you perceive there will be no novelty in the appellation."

"I would have made oath to it," cried the captain, "from your well-established humility. Is the place as large as London?"

"It can boast of little more than my own office, a tavern, a store, and a blacksmith's shop, captain, as yet; but Rome was not built in a day."

"Your neighbors, sir, must be people of extraordinary discernment; but the name?"

"That is not absolutely decided. At first it was called

Dodgetown, but this did not last long, being thought vulgar and commonplace. Six or eight weeks afterwards, we—''

"We, Mr. Dodge!''

"I mean the people, sir,—I am so much accustomed to connect myself with the people, that whatever they do, I think I have a hand in.''

"And very properly, sir,'' observed John Effingham, "as probably without you, there would have been no people at all.''

"What may be the population of Dodgetown, sir?'' asked the persevering captain, on this hint.

"At the census of January, it was seventeen; but by the census of March, there were eighteen. I have made a calculation that shows, if we go on at this rate, or by arithmetical progression, it will be a hundred in about ten years, which will be a very respectable population for a country place. I beg pardon, sir, the people six or eight weeks afterwards, altered the name to Dodgeborough; but a new family coming in that summer, a party was got up to change it to Dodge-ville, a name that was immensely popular, as ville means city in Latin; but it must be owned the people like change, or rotation in names, as well as in office, and they called the place Butterfield Hollow, for a whole month, after the new inhabitant, whose name is Butterfield. He moved away in the fall; and so, after trying Belindy [*Anglice* Belinda], Nineveh, Grand Cairo, and Pumpkin Valley, they made me the offer to restore the ancient name, provided some *addendum* more noble and proper could be found than town, or ville, or borough; it is not yet determined what it shall be, but I believe we shall finally settle down in Dodgeople, or Dodgeopolis.''

"For the season; and a very good name it will prove for a short cruise, I make no question. The Butterfield Hollow was a little like rotation in office, in truth, sir.''

"I did n't like it, captain, so I gave Squire Butterfield to understand, privately; for as he had a majority with him, I did n't approve of speaking too strongly on the subject. As soon as I got him out of the tavern, however, the current set the other way.''

" You fairly uncorked him ! "

" That I did, and no one ever heard of him, or of his hollow, after his retreat. There are a few discontented and arrogant innovators, who affect to call the place by its old name of Morton ; but these are the mere vassals of a man who once owned the patent, and who has now been dead these forty years. We are not the people to keep his old musty name, or to honor dry bones."

" Served him right, sir, and like men of spirit ! If he wants a place called after himself, let him live, like other people. A dead man has no occasion for a name, and there should be a law passed, that when a man slips his cables, he should bequeath his name to some honest fellow who has a worse one. It might be well to compel all great men in particular, to leave their renown to those who cannot get any for themselves."

" I will venture to suggest an improvement on the name, if Mr. Dodge will permit me," said Mr. Sharp, who had been an amused listener to the short dialogue. " Dodge-ople is a little short, and may be offensive by its *brusquerie*. By inserting two letters, it will become Dodge-people, or, there is the alternative of Dodge-adrianople, which will be a truly sonorous and republican title. Adrian was an emperor, and even Mr. Dodge might not disdain the conjunction."

By this time, the editor of the " Active Inquirer " began to be extremely elevated—for this was assailing him on his weakest side—and he laughed and rubbed his hands as if he thought the joke particularly pleasant. This person had also a peculiarity of judgment that was singularly in opposition to all his open professions, a peculiarity, however, that belongs rather to his class than to the individual member of it. Ultra as a democrat and an American, Mr. Dodge had a sneaking predilection in favor of foreign opinions. Although practice had made him intimately acquainted with all the frauds, deceptions, and vileness of the ordinary arts of paragraph-making, he never failed to believe religiously in the veracity, judgment, good faith, honesty, and talents of anything that was imported in the form of types. He had been weekly, for years, accusing his nearest brother of the craft, of lying, and he could not be altogether ignorant of his own propensity in the same way; but, notwithstanding all his experience in the secrets of the trade, whatever reached him from a European journal, he implicitly swallowed whole. One, who knew little of the man, might have supposed he feigned credulity to answer his own purposes; but this would be doing injustice to his faith, which was perfect, being based on that provincial admiration, and provincial ignorance, that caused the countryman, who went to London for the first time, to express his astonishment at finding the king a man. As was due to his colonial origin, his secret awe and reverence for an Englishman was exactly in proportion to his protestations of love for the people, and his deference for rank was graduated on a scale suited to the heart-burning and jealousies he entertained for all whom he felt to be his superiors. Indeed, one was the cause of the other; for they who really are indifferent to their own social position, are usually equally indifferent to that of others, so long as they are not made to feel the difference by direct assumptions of superiority.

When Mr. Sharp, whom even Mr. Dodge had discovered to be a gentleman,—and an English gentleman of course, —entered into the trifling of the moment, therefore, so far from detecting the mystification, the latter was disposed to believe himself a subject of interest with this person, against whose exclusiveness and haughty reserve, notwithstanding, he had been making side-hits ever since the ship had sailed. But the avidity with which the Americans of Mr. Dodge's temperament are apt to swallow the crumbs of flattery that fall from the Englishman's table, is matter of history, and the editor himself was never so happy as when he could lay hold of a paragraph to republish, in which a few words of comfort were doled out by the condescending mother to the never-dying faith of the daughter. So far, therefore, from taking umbrage at what had been said, he continued the subject long after the captain had gone to his duty, and with so much perseverance that Paul Blunt, as soon as Mr. Sharp escaped, took an occasion to compliment that gentleman on his growing intimacy with the refined and single-minded champion of the people. The other admitted his indiscretion; and if the affair had no other consequences, it afforded these two fine young men a moment's merriment, at a time when anxiety had been fast getting the ascendency over their more cheerful feelings. When they endeavored to make Miss Effingham share in the amusement, however, that young lady heard them with gravity; for the meanness of the act discovered by Nanny Sidley had indisposed her to treat the subject of their comments with the familiarity of even ridicule. Perceiving this, though unable to account for it, the gentlemen changed the discourse, and soon became sufficiently grave by contemplating their own condition.

The situation of the Montauk was now certainly one to excite uneasiness in those who were little acquainted with the sea, as well as in those who were. It was very much like that for which Miss Effingham's nurse had pined, having many rocks and sands in sight, with the land at no great distance. In order that the reader may understand it more clearly, we shall describe it with greater minuteness.

To the westward of the ship lay the ocean, broad, smooth, glittering, but heaving and setting, with its eternal breathings, which always resemble the respiration of some huge monster. Between the vessel and this waste of water, and within three hundred feet of the first, stretched an irregular line of ripple, dotted here and there with the heads of low, naked rocks, marking the presence and direction of the reef.

This was all that would interpose between the basin and the raging billows, should another storm occur; but Captain Truck thought this would suffice so far to break the waves as to render the anchorage sufficiently secure. Astern of the ship, however, a rounded ridge of sand began to appear as the tide fell, within forty fathoms of the vessel, and as the bottom was hard, and difficult to get an anchor into it, there was the risk of dragging on this bank. We say that the bottom was hard, for the reader should know that it is not the weight of the anchor that secures the ship, but the hold its pointed fluke and broad palm get of the ground. The coast itself was distant less than a mile, and the entire basin within the reef was fast presenting spits of sand, as the water fell on the ebb. Still there were many channels, and it would have been possible, for one who knew their windings, to have sailed a ship several leagues among them, without passing the inlet; these channels forming a sort of intricate network, in every direction from the vessel.

When Captain Truck had coolly studied all the peculiarities of his position, he set about the duty of securing his ship, in good earnest. The two light boats were brought under the bows, and the stream anchor was lowered, and fastened to a spar that lay across both. This anchor was carried to the bank astern, and, by dint of sheer strength, it was laid over its summit with a fluke buried to the shank in the hard sand. By means of a hawser, and a purchase applied to its end, the men on the banks next roused the chain out, and shackled it to the ring. The bight was hove-in, and the ship secured astern, so as to prevent a shift of wind, off the land, from forcing her on the reef. As no sea could come from this quarter, the single anchor and chain were deemed sufficient for this purpose. As soon as the boats were at liberty, and before the chain had been got ashore, two kedges were carried to the reef, and laid among the rocks, in such a way that their flukes and stocks equally got hold of the projections. To these kedges lighter chains were secured; and when all the bights were hove-in, to as equal a strain as possible, Captain Truck pronounced his ship in readiness to ride out any gale that would be likely to blow. So far as the winds and waves might affect her, the Montauk was, in truth, reasonably safe; for on the side where danger was most to be apprehended, she had two bowers down, and four parts of smaller chain were attached to the two kedges. Nor had Captain Truck fallen into the common error of supposing he had so much additional strength in his fastenings, by simply running the chains through the rings, but he had caused each to be separately fastened, both in-board and to the kedges, by which means each length of the chain formed a distinct and independent fastening of itself.

So absolute is the sovereignty of a ship, that no one had presumed to question the master as to his motives for all this extraordinary precaution, though it was the common impression that he intended to remain where they were until the wind became favorable, or at least, until all danger of being thrown upon the coast, from the currents and the ground-swell, should have ceased. Paul Blunt observed, that he fancied it was the intention to take advantage of the smooth water within the reef, to get up a better and a more efficient set of jury-masts. But Captain Truck soon removed all doubts by letting the truth be known. While on board the Danish wreck, he had critically examined her spars, sails, and rigging, and, though adapted for a ship two hundred tons smaller than the Montauk, he was of opinion they might be fitted to the latter vessel, and made to answer all the necessary purposes for crossing the ocean, provided the Mussulmans and the weather would permit the transfer.

"We have smooth water and light airs," he said, when concluding his explanation, "and the current sets southwardly along this coast; by means of all our force, hard working, a kind Providence, and our own enterprise, I hope yet to see the Montauk enter the port of New York, with royals set, and ready to carry sail on a wind. The seaman who cannot rig his ship with sticks and ropes and blocks enough, might as well stay ashore, Mr. Dodge, and publish an hebdomadal. And so, my dear young lady, by looking along the land, the day after to-morrow, in the northern board here, you may expect to see a raft booming down upon you that will cheer your heart, and once more raise the hope of a Christmas dinner in New York, in all lovers of good fare."

# CHAPTER XVIII.

"Here, in the sands,
Thee I'll rake up."

*Lear.*

HIS mind made up, his intentions announced, and his ship in readiness, Captain Truck gave his orders to proceed with promptitude and clearness. The ladies remaining behind, he observed that the two Messrs. Effingham, as a matter of course, would stay with them as protectors, though little could harm them where they were.

"I propose to leave the ship in the care of Mr. Blunt," he said, "for I perceive something about that gentleman which denotes a nautical instinct. If Mr. Sharp choose to remain also, your society will be the more agreeable, and in exchange, gentlemen, I ask the favor of the strong arms of all your servants. Mr. Monday is my man in fair or foul, and so, I flatter myself, will be Sir George Templemore; and as for Mr. Dodge, if he stay behind, why the 'Active Inquirer' will miss a notable paragraph, for there shall be no historian to the expedition, but one of my own appointing. Mr. Saunders shall have the honor of cooking for you in the meanwhile, and I propose taking every one else to the Dane."

As no serious objections could be made to this arrangement, within an hour of the time when the ship was fastened, the cutter and jolly-boat departed, it being the intention of Captain Truck to reach the wreck that evening, in season to have his sheers ready to raise by daylight in the morning; for he hoped to be back again in the course of the succeeding day. No time was to be lost, he knew, the return of the Arabs being hourly expected, and the tranquillity of the open sea being at all times a matter of the greatest uncertainty. With the declared view of making quick work, and with the secret apprehension of a struggle with the owners of the country, the captain took with him every officer and man in his ship that could possibly be spared, and as many of the passengers as he thought might be useful. As numbers might be important in the way of intimidation, he cared almost as much for appearances as for anything else, or certainly he would not have deemed the presence of Mr. Dodge of any great moment; for to own the truth, he expected the editor of the "Active Inquirer" would prove the quality implied by the first word of the title of his journal, as much in any other way as in fighting.

Neither provisions nor water, beyond what might be necessary in pulling to the wreck, nor ropes, nor blocks, nor anything but arms and ammunition, were taken in the boats; for the examination of the morning had shown the captain that, notwithstanding so much had been plundered, a sufficiency still remained in the stranded vessel. Indeed, the fact that so much had been left was one of his reasons for hastening off himself, as he deemed it certain that they who had taken away what was gone, would soon return for the remainder. The fowling-pieces and pistols, with all the powder and ball in the ship, were taken; a light gun that was on board, for the purpose of awaking sleepy pilots, being left loaded, with the intention of serving for a signal of alarm, should any material change occur in the situation of the ship.

The party included thirty men, and as most had fire-arms of one sort or another, they pulled out of the inlet with spirit and great confidence in their eventual success. The boats were crowded, it is true, but there was room to row, and the launch had been left in its place on deck, because it was known that two boats were to be found in the wreck, one of which was large : in short, as Captain Truck had meditated this expedient from the moment he ascertained the situation of the Dane, he now set about carrying it into effect with method and discrimination. We shall first accompany him on his way, leaving the small party in the Montauk for our future attention in another chapter.

The distance between the two vessels was about four leagues, and a headland intervening, those in the boats in less than an hour lost sight of their own ship, as she lay shorn of her pride, anchored within the reef. At almost the same moment, the wreck came in view, and Captain Truck applied his glass with great interest, in order to ascertain the state of things in that direction. All was tranquil—no signs of any one having visited the spot since morning being visible. The intelligence was given to the people, who pulled at their oars the more willingly under the stimulus of probable success, driving the boats ahead with increasing velocity.

The sun was still some distance above the horizon, when the cutter and jolly-boat rowed through the narrow channel astern of the wreck, and brought up as before by the side of the rocks. Leaping ashore, Captain Truck led the way to the vessel, and, in five minutes, he was seen in the forward cross-trees, examining the plain with his glass. All was as solitary and deserted as when before seen, and the order was immediately given to commence operations without delay.

A gang of the best seamen got out the spare topmast and lower yard of the Dane, and set about fitting a pair of sheers, a job that would be likely to occupy them several hours. Mr. Leach led a party up forward, and the second mate went up with another farther aft, each proceeding to send down its respective topgallant-mast, topsail-yard and topmast; while Captain Truck, from the deck, superintended the same work on the mizzen-mast. As the men worked with spirit, and a strong party remained below to give the drags, and to come up the lanyards, spar came down after spar with rapidity, and just as the sun dipped into the ocean to the westward, everything but the lower masts was lying on the sands, alongside of the ship; nothing having been permitted to touch the decks in descending. Previously, however, to sending down the lower-yards, the launch had been lifted from its bed and landed also by the side of the vessel.

All hands were now mustered on the sands, and the boat was launched, an operation of some delicacy, as heavy rollers were occasionally coming in. As soon as it floated, this powerful auxiliary was swept up to the rocks, and then the men began to load it with the standing rigging and the sails, the latter having been unbent, as fast as each spar came down. Two kedges were found, and a hawser was bent to one, when the launch was carried outside of the bar and anchored. Lines being brought in, the yards were hauled out to the same place, and strongly lashed together for the night. A great deal of running rigging, many blocks, and divers other small articles, were put into the boats of the Montauk ; and the jolly-boat of the wreck, which was still hanging at her stern, was also lowered and got into the water. With these acquisitions the party had now four boats, one of which was heavy, and capable of carrying considerable freight.

By this time it was so late and so dark, that Captain Truck determined to suspend his labors until morning. In the course of a few hours of active toil, he had secured all the yards, the sails, the standing and running rigging, the boats, and many of the minor articles of the Dane ; and nothing of essential importance remained but the three lower masts. These, it is true, were all in all to him, for without them he would be but little better off than he was before, since his own ship had spare canvas and spare yards enough to make a respectable show above the foundation. This foundation, however, was the great requisite ; and his principal motive in taking the other things was to have a better fit than could be obtained by using spars and sails that were not intended to go together.

At eight o'clock, the people got their suppers, and prepared to turn in for the night. Some conversation passed between Captain Truck and his mates, concerning the manner of disposing of the men while they slept, which resulted in the former's keeping a well-armed party of ten with him in the ship, while the remainder were put in the boats, all of which were fastened to the launch, as she lay anchored off the bar. Here they made beds of the sails, and setting a watch, the greater portion of both gangs were soon as quietly asleep as if lying in their own berths on board the Montauk. Not so with Captain Truck and his mates. They walked the deck of the Dane fully an hour after the men were silent, and for some time after Mr. Monday had finished the bottle of wine he had taken the precaution to bring with him from the packet, and had bestowed his person among some old sails in the cabin. The night was a bright starlight, but the moon was not to be expected until near morning. The wind came off the sands of the interior in hot puffs, but so lightly as to sound, that it breathed past them like the sighings of the desert.

"It is lucky, Mr. Leach," said the captain, continuing the discourse he had been holding with his mate in a low voice, under the sense of the insecurity of their situation, "it is lucky, Mr. Leach, that we got out the stream anchor astern, else we should have had the ship rubbing her copper against the corners of the rocks. This air seems light, but under all her canvas the Montauk would soon flap her way out from this coast, if all were ready."

"Ay, ay, sir, if all were ready!" repeated Mr. Leach, as if he knew how much honest labor was to be expended before that happy moment could arrive.

"If all were ready. I think we may be able to whip these three sticks out of this fellow by breakfast-time in the morning, and then a couple of hours will answer for the raft ; after which, a pull of six or eight more will take us back to our own craft."

"If all goes well, it may be done, sir."

"Well or ill, it must be done. We are not in a situation to play at jack-straws !"

"I hope it may be done, sir."

"Mr. Leach !"

"Captain Truck !"

"We are in a d——le category, sir, if the truth must be spoken."

"That is a word I am not much acquainted with, but we have an awkward berth of it here, if that be what you mean !"

A long pause, during which these two seamen, one of whom was old, the other young, paced the deck diligently.

"Mr. Leach!"

"Captain Truck!"

"Do you ever pray?"

"I have done such a thing in my time, sir; but since I have sailed with you, I have been taught to work first and pray afterwards; and when the difficulty has been gotten over by the work, the prayers have commonly seemed surplusage."

"You should take to your thanksgivings. I think your grandfather was a parson, Leach?"

"Yes, he was, sir; and I have been told your father followed the same trade."

"You have been told the truth, Mr. Leach. My father was as meek, and pious, and humble a Christian as ever thumped a pulpit. A poor man, and, if truth must be spoken, a poor preacher too; but a zealous one, and thoroughly devout. I ran away from him at twelve, and never passed a week at a time under his roof afterwards. He could not do much for me, for he had little education and no money, and, I believe, carried on the business pretty much by faith. He was a good man, Leach, notwithstanding there might be a little of a take-in for such a person to set up as a teacher; and, as for my mother, if ever there was a pure spirit on earth, it was in her body!"

"Ay, that is the way commonly with the mothers, sir."

"She taught me to pray," added the captain, speaking a little thick, "but since I've been in this London line, to own the truth, I find but little time for anything but hard work, until, for want of practice, praying has got to be among the hardest things I can turn my hand to."

"That is the way with all of us; it is my opinion, Captain Truck, these London and Liverpool liners will have a good many lost souls to answer for."

"Ay, ay, if we could put it on them, it would do well enough; but my honest old father always maintained that every man must stand in the gap left by his own sins; though he did assert, also, that we were all foreordained to

16

shape our courses starboard or port, even before we were launched."

"That doctrine makes an easy tide's-way of life; for I see no great use in a man's carrying sail and jamming himself up in the wind, to claw off immoralities, when he knows he is to fetch up upon them after all his pains."

"I have worked all sorts of traverses to get hold of this matter, and never could make anything of it. It is harder than logarithms. If my father had been the only one to teach it, I should have thought less about it, for he was no scholar, and might have been paying it out just in the way of business; but then my mother believed it, body and soul, and she was too good a woman to stick long to a course that had not truth to back it."

"Why not believe it heartily, sir, and let the wheel fly? One gets to the end of the v'y'ge on this tack as well as on another."

"There is no great difficulty in working up to, or even through the passage of death, Leach, but the great point is to know the port we are to moor in finally. My mother taught me to pray, and when I was ten I had underrun all the Commandments, knew the Lord's Creed, and the Apostles' Prayer, and had made a handsome slant into the Catechism; but, dear me, dear me, it has all oozed out of me, like the warmth from a Greenlander."

"Folks were better educated in your time, Captain Truck, than they are nowadays, by all I can learn."

"No doubt of that in the world. In my time, younkers were taught respect for their betters, and for age, and their Catechism, and piety, and the Apostles' Prayer, and all those sort of things. But America has fallen astern sadly in manners within the last fifty years. I do not flatter myself with being as good as I was when under my excellent dear mother's command, but there are worse men in the world, and out of Newgate, too, than John Truck. Now, in the way of vices, Leach, I never swear."

"Not you, sir; and Mr. Monday never drinks."

As the protestation of sobriety on the part of their passenger had got to be a joke with the officers and men of the ship, Captain Truck had no difficulty in understanding his mate, and though nettled at a retort that was like usurping his own right to the exclusive quizzing of the vessel, he was in a mood much too sentimental and reflecting to be angry. After a moment's pause, he resumed the dialogue, as if nothing had been said to disturb its harmony.

"No, I *never* swear; or, if I do, it is in a small, gentlemanly way, and with none of your foul-mouthed oaths, such as are used by the horse-jockeys that formerly sailed out of the river."

"Were they hard swearers?"

"Is a nor'wester a hard wind? Those fellows, after they have been choked off and jammed by the religion ashore for a month or two, would break out like a hurricane when they had made an offing, and were once fairly out of hearing of the parsons and deacons. It is said that old Joe Bunk began an oath on the bar that he did not get to the end of until his brig was off Montauk. I have my doubts, Leach, if anything be gained by screwing down religion and morals, like a cotton-bale, as is practised in and about the river."

"A good many begin to be of the same way of thinking; for when our people *do* break out, it is like the small-pox."

"I am an advocate for education; nor do I think I was taught in my own case more than was reasonable. I think even a prayer is of more use to a shipmaster than Latin, and I often have, even now, recourse to one, though it may not be exactly in Scripture language. I seldom want a wind without praying for it, mentally, as it might be; and as for the rheumatis', I am always praying to be rid of it, when I'm not cursing it starboard and larboard. Has it never struck you that the world is less moral since steamboats were introduced than formerly?"

"The boats date from before my birth, sir."

"Very true—you are but a boy. Mankind appear to be hurried, and no one likes to stop to pray, or to foot up his sins, as used to be the case. Life is like a passage at sea. We feel our way cautiously until off soundings on our own coast, and then we have an easy time of it in the deep water ; but when we get near the shoals again, we take out the lead, and mind a little how we steer. It is the going off and coming on the coast, that gives us all the trouble."

" You had some object in view, Captain Truck, when you asked me if I ever prayed ? "

" Certain. If I were to set to work to pray myself, just now, it would be for smooth water to-morrow, that we may have a good time in towing the raft to the ship—hist ! Leach, did you hear nothing ? "

" There was a sound different from what is common in the air, from the land ! It is probably some savage beast, for Africa is full of them."

" I think we might manage a lion from this fortress. Unless the fellow found the stage, he could hardly board us ; and a plank or two thrown from that, would make a drawbridge of it at once. Look yonder ! there is something moving on the bank, or my eyes are two jewel-blocks."

Mr. Leach looked in the required direction, and he, too, fancied he saw something in motion on the margin of the bank. At the point where the wreck lay, the beach was far from wide, and her flying jib-boom, which was still out, pro-jected so near the low acclivity, where the coast rose to the level of the desert, as to come within ten feet of the bushes by which the latter was fringed. Although the spar had dropped a little in consequence of having lost the support of the stays, its end was still sufficiently high to rise above the leaves, and to permit one seated on it to overlook the plain, as well as the starlight would allow. Believing the duty to be important, Captain Truck, first giving his orders to Mr. Leach, as to the mode of alarming the men, should it become necessary, went cautiously out on the bowsprit, and thence by the foot-ropes, to the farther extremity of the booms. As this was done with the steadiness of a seaman, and with the utmost care to prevent discovery, he was soon stretched on the spar, balancing his body by his legs beneath, and casting eager glances about, though prevented by the obscurity from seeing either far or very distinctly.

After lying in this position a minute, Captain Truck discovered an object on the plains, at the distance of a hundred yards from the bushes, that was evidently in motion. He was now all watchfulness, for, had he not seen the proofs that the Arabs or Moors had already been at the wreck, he knew that parties of them were constantly hovering along the coast, especially after every heavy gale that blew from the westward, in the hope of booty. As all his own people were asleep, the mates excepted, and the boats could just be discovered by himself, who knew their position, he was in hopes that, should any of the barbarians be near, the presence of his own party could hardly be known. It is true, the alteration in the appearance of the wreck, by the removal of the spars, must strike any one who had seen it before, but this change might have been made by another party of marauders, or those who had now come, if any there were, might see the vessel for the first time.

While such thoughts were rapidly glancing through his mind, the reader will readily imagine that the worthy master was not altogether at his ease. Still he was cool, and, as he was resolved to fight his way off, even against an army, he clung to the spar with a species of physical resolution that would have done credit to a tiger. The object on the plain moved once more, and the clouds opening beyond, he plainly made out the head and neck of a dromedary. There was but one, however; nor could the most scrupulous examination show him a human being. After remaining a quarter of an hour on the boom, during all which time the only sounds that were heard were the sighings of the night-air, and the sullen and steady wash of the surf, Captain Truck came on deck again, where he found his mate waiting his report with intense anxiety. The former was fully aware of the importance of his discovery, but, being a cool man, he had not magnified the danger to himself.

"The Moors are down on the coast," he said, in an undertone; "but I do not think there can be more than two or three of them at the most; probably spies or scouts, and, could we seize them, we may gain a few hours on their comrades, which will be all we want; after which they shall be welcome to the salt and the other damage of the poor Dane. Leach, are you the man to stand by me in this affair?"

"Have I ever failed you, Captain Truck, that you put the question?"

"That you have never, my fine fellow; give me a squeeze of your honest hand, and let there be a pledge of life or death in it."

The mate met the iron grasp of his commander, and each knew that he received an assurance on which he might rely.

"Shall I awake the men, sir?" asked Mr. Leach.

"Not one of them. Every hour of sleep the people get will be a lower-mast saved. These sticks that still remain are our foundation, and even one of them is of more account to us, just now, than a fleet of ships might be at another time. Take your arms and follow me; but first we will give a hint to the second mate of what we are about."

This officer was asleep on the deck, for he had been so much wearied with his great exertions that afternoon as to catch a little rest as the sweetest of all gifts. It had been the intention of Captain Truck to dismiss him to the boats; but observing him to be overcome with drowsiness, he had permitted him to catch a nap where he lay. The lookout, too, was also slumbering under the same indulgence; but both were now awakened, and made acquainted with the state of things on shore.

"Keep your eyes open, but keep a dead silence," concluded Captain Truck; "for it is my wish to deceive these scouts, and to keep them ignorant of our presence. When I cry out 'Alarm!' you will muster all hands, and clear away for a brush, but not before. God bless you, my lads! mind and keep your eyes open. Leach, I am ready."

The captain and his companion cautiously descended to the sands, and passing astern of the ship, they first took their way to the jolly-boat, which lay at the rocks in readiness to carry off the two officers to the launch. Here they found the two men in charge so soundly asleep, that nothing would have been easier than to bind them without giving the alarm. After a little hesitation, it was determined to let them dream away their sorrows, and to proceed to the spot where the bank was ascended.

At this place it became necessary to use the greatest precaution, for it was literally entering the enemy's country. The steepness of the short ascent requiring them to mount nearly on their hands and feet, this part of their progress was made without much hazard, and the two adventurers stood on the plain, sheltered by some bushes.

"Yonder is the camel," whispered the captain; "you see his crooked neck, with the head tossing at moments. The fellow is not fifty yards from the body of the poor German! Now let us follow along this line of bushes, and keep a sharp lookout for the rider."

They proceeded in the manner mentioned, until they came to a point where the bushes ceased, and there was an opening that overlooked the beach quite near the wreck.

"Do you see the boats, Leach, hereaway, in a line with the starboard davit of the Dane? They look like dark spots on the water, and an ignorant Arab might be excused for taking them for rocks."

"Except that they rise and fall with the rollers; he must be doubly a Turk who could make such a blunder!"

"Your wanderers of the desert are not so particular. The wreck has certainly undergone some changes since yesterday, and I should not wonder if even a Mussulman found them out, but—"

The gripe of Mr. Leach, whose fingers almost entered the flesh of his arm, and a hand pointed towards the bushes on the other side of the opening, silenced the captain's whisper. A human form was seen standing on the fringe of the bank, directly opposite the jib-boom. It was swaddled in a sort of cloak, and the long musket that was borne in a hollow of an arm, was just discernible, diverging from the line of the figure. The Arab, for such it could only be, was evidently gazing on the wreck, and presently he ventured out more boldly, and stood on the spot that was clear of bushes. The deathlike stillness on the beach deceived him, and he advanced with less caution towards the spot where the two officers were in ambush, still keep-ing his own eye on the ship. A few steps brought him within reach of Captain Truck, who drew back his arm until the elbow reached his own hip, when he darted it forward, and dealt the incautious barbarian a severe blow between the eyes. The Arab fell like a slaughtered ox, and before his senses were fairly recovered, he was bound hands and feet, and rolled over the bank down upon the beach, with little ceremony, his fire-arms remaining with his captors.

"That lad is in a category," whispered the captain; "it now remains to be seen if there is another."

A long search was not rewarded with success, and it was determined to lead the camel down the path, with a view to prevent his being seen by any wanderer in the morning.

"If we get the lower masts out betimes," continued the captain, "these land pirates will have no beacons in sight to steer by, and, in a country in which one grain of sand is so much like another, they might hunt a week before they made a happy landfall."

The approach of the two towards the camel was made with less caution than usual, the success of their enterprise throwing them off their guard, and exciting their spirits. They believed, in short, that their captive was either a solitary wanderer, or that he had been sent ahead as a scout, by some party that would be likely to follow in the morning.

"We must be up and at work before the sun, Mr. Leach," said the captain, speaking clearly, but in a low tone, as they approached the camel. The head of the animal was tossed; then it seemed to snuff the air, and it gave a shriek. In the twinkling of an eye an Arab sprang from the sand, on which he had been sleeping, and was on the creature's back. He was seen to look around him, and before the startled mar-iners had time to decide on their course, the beast, which was a dromedary trained to speed, was out of sight in the darkness. Captain Truck had thrown forward his fowling-piece, but he did not fire.

"We have no right to shoot the fellow," he said, "and

our hope is now in the distance he will have to ride to join
his comrades. If we have got a chief, as I suspect, we will
make a hostage of him, and turn him to as much account as
he can possibly turn one of his own camels. Depend on it,
we shall see no more of them for several hours, and we will
seize the opportunity to get a little sleep. A man must have
his watch below, or he gets to be as dull and as obstinate as
a top-maul."

The captain having made up his mind to this plan, was
not slow in putting it in execution. Returning to the beach,
they liberated the legs of their prisoner, whom they found
lying like a log on the sands, and made him mount the
staging to the deck of the ship. Leading the way into the
cabin, Mr. Truck examined the fellow by a light, turning
him round and commenting on his points very much as he
might have done had the captive been any other animal of
the desert.

The Arab was a swarthy, sinewy man of forty, with all his
fibres indurated and worked down to the whip-cord meagre-
ness and rigidity of a racer, his frame presenting a perfect
picture of the sort of being one would fancy suited to the
exhausting motion of a dromedary, and to the fare of a
desert. He carried a formidable knife, in addition to the
long musket of which he had been deprived, and his principal
garment was the coarse mantle of camel's hair, that served
equally for cap, coat, and robe. His wild, dark eyes gleamed,
as Captain Truck passed the lamp before his face, and it was
sufficiently apparent that he fancied a very serious misfortune
had befallen him. As any verbal communication was out of
the question, some abortive attempts were essayed by the two
mariners to make themselves understood by signs, which,
like some men's reasoning, produced results exactly contrary
to what had been expected.

"Perhaps the poor fellow fancies we mean to eat him,
Leach," observed the captain, after trying his skill in pantomime for some time without success ; " and he has some
grounds for the idea, as he was felled like an ox that is bound
to the kitchen. Try and let the miserable wretch understand,
at least, that we are not cannibals."

Hereupon the mate commenced an expressive pantomime, which described, with sufficient clearness, the process of skinning, cutting up, cooking, and eating the carcass of the Arab, with the humane intention of throwing a negative over the whole proceeding, by a strong sign of dissent at the close; but there are no proper substitutes for the little monosyllables of "yes" and "no," and the meaning of the interpreter got to be so confounded that the captain himself was mystified.

"D——n it, Leach," he interrupted, "the man fancies that he is not good eating, you make so many wry and out-of-the-way contortions. A sign is a jury-mast for the tongue; and every seaman ought to know how to practise them, in case he should be wrecked on a savage and unknown coast. Old Joe Bunk had a dictionary of them, and in calm weather he used to go among his horses and horned cattle, and talk with them by the hour. He made a diagram of the language, and had it taught to all us younkers who were exposed to the accidents of the sea. Now I will try my hand on this Arab, for I could never go to sleep while the honest black imagined we intended to breakfast on him."

The captain now recommenced his own explanations in the language of nature. He too described the process of cooking and eating the prisoner—for this he admitted was indispensable by way of preface—and then, to show his horror of such an act, he gave a very good representation of a process he had often witnessed among his sea-sick passengers, by way of showing his loathing of cannibalism in general, and of eating this Arab in particular. By this time the man was thoroughly alarmed, and by way of commentary on the captain's eloquence, he began to utter wailings in his own language, and groans that were not to be mistaken. To own the truth, Mr. Truck was a good deal mortified with this failure, which, like all other unsuccessful persons, he was ready to ascribe to anybody but himself.

"I begin to think, Mr. Leach," he said, "that this fellow is too stupid for a spy or a scout, and that, after all, he is not more than a driveller who has strayed from his tribe, from a want of sense to keep the road in a desert. A man of the smallest information must have understood me, and yet you perceive by his lamentations and outcries that he knows no more what I said than if he were in another parallel of latitude. The chap has quite mistaken my character ; for if I really did intend to make a beast of myself, and devour my species, no one of the smallest knowledge of human nature would think I'd begin on a nigger ! What is your opinion of the man's mistake, Mr. Leach?"

" It is very plain, sir, that he supposes you mean to broil him, and then to eat so much of his steaks, that you will be compelled to heave up like a marine two hours out ; and, if I must say the truth, I think most people would have inferred the same thing from your signs, which are as plainly cannibal as anything of the sort I ever witnessed."

"And what the devil did he make of yours, Master Cookery Book?" cried the captain with some heat. " Did he fancy you meant to mortify the flesh with a fortnight's fast? No, no, sir; you are a very respectable first officer, but are no more acquainted with Joe Bunk's principles of signs, than this editor here knows of truth and propriety. It is your blundering manner of soliloquizing that has set the lad on a wrong traverse. He has just grafted your own idea on my communication, and has got himself into a category that a book itself would not reason him out of, until his fright is passed. Logic is thrown away on all ' skeary animals,' said old Joe Bunk. Harkee, Leach, I've a mind to set the rascal adrift, condemning the gun and the knife for the benefit of the captors. I think I should sleep better for the certainty that he was trudging along the sand, satisfied that he was not to be barbecued in the morning."

"There is no use in detaining him, sir, for his messmate, who went off on the dromedary, will sail a hundred feet to his one ; and if an alarm is really to be given to their party, it will not come from this chap. He will be unarmed, and by taking away his pouch, we shall get some ammunition for this gun of his, which will throw a shot as far as Queen Anne's pocket-piece. For my part, sir, I think there is no great use in keeping him, for I do not think he would understand us if he stayed a month, and went to school the whole time."

"You are quite right, and as long as he is among us, we shall be liable to unpleasant misconceptions; so cut his lashings and set him adrift, and be d——d to him."

The mate, who by this time was drowsy, did as desired, and in a moment the Arab was at liberty. At first the poor creature did not know what to make of his freedom; but a smart application, *à posteriori*, from the foot of Captain Truck, whose humanity was of the rough quality of the seas, soon set him in motion up the cabin-ladder. When the two mariners reached the deck, their prisoner was already leaping down the staging, and in another minute his active form was obscurely seen clambering up the bank, on gaining which he plunged into the desert, and was seen no more.

None but men indurated in their feelings by long exposure would be likely to sleep under the circumstances in which these two seamen were placed; but they were both too cool, and too much accustomed to arouse themselves on sudden alarms, to lose the precious moments in womanish apprehensions, when they knew that all their physical energies would be needed on the morrow, whether the Arabs arrived or not. They accordingly regulated the lookouts, gave strong admonitions of caution to be passed from one to another, and then the captain stretched himself in the berth of the poor Dane, who was now a captive in the desert, while Mr. Leach got into the jolly-boat, and was pulled off to the launch. Both were sound asleep in less than five minutes after their heads touched their temporary pillows.

## CHAPTER XIX.

"Aye, he does well enough, if he be disposed,
And so do I too ; he does it with a better grace, but
I do it more natural."

*Twelfth Night.*

THE sleep of the weary is sweet. Of all the party that lay thus buried in sleep, on the verge of the Great Desert, exposed at any moment to an assault from its ruthless and predatory occupants, but one bethought him of the danger; though *he* was, in truth, so little exposed as to have rendered it of less moment to himself than to most of the others, had he not been the possessor of a fancy that served oftener to lead him astray than for any purposes that were useful or pleasing. This person was in one of the boats, and as they lay at a reasonable distance from the land, and the barbarians would not probably have known how to use any craft had they even possessed one, he was consequently safe from everything but a discharge from their long muskets. But this remote risk sufficed to keep him awake, it being very different things to foster malice, circulate gossip, write scurrilous paragraphs, and cant about the people, and to face a volley of fire-arms. For the one employment, nature, tradition, education, and habit, had expressly fitted Mr. Dodge ; while for the other, he had not the smallest vocation. Although Mr. Leach, in setting his lookouts on board the boats, had entirely overlooked the editor of the "Active Inquirer," never before had that vigilant person's inquiries been more active than they were throughout the whole of that long night ; and twenty times would he have aroused the party on false alarms, but for the cool indifference of the phlegmatic seamen, to whom the duty more properly belonged. These brave fellows knew too well the precious qualities of sleep to allow that of their shipmates to be causelessly disturbed by the nervous apprehensions of one who carried with him an everlasting stimulant to fear in the consciousness of demerit. The night passed away undisturbed, therefore, nor was the order of the regular watch broken until the lookouts in the wreck, agreeably to their orders, awoke Captain Truck and his mates.

It was now precisely at the moment when the first, and as it might be the fugitive, rays of the sun glide into the atmosphere, and, to use a quaint expression, "dilute its darkness." One no longer saw by starlight, or by moonlight, though a little of both were still left; but objects, though indistinct and dusky, had their true outlines, while every moment rendered their surfaces more obvious.

When Captain Truck appeared on deck, his first glance was at the ocean; for, were its tranquillity seriously disturbed, it would be a death-blow to all his hopes. Fortunately, in this particular, there was no change.

"The winds seem to have put themselves out of breath in the last gale, Mr. Leach," he said, "and we are likely to get the spars round as quietly as if they were so many sawlogs floating in a mill-pond. Even the ground-swell has lessened, and the breakers on the bar look like the ripple of a wash-tub. Turn the people up, sir, and let us have a drag at these sticks before breakfast, or we may have to broil an Arab yet."

Mr. Leach hailed the boats, and ordered them to send their gang of laborers on shore. He then gave the accustomed raps on the deck, and called "all hands" in the ship. In a minute the men began to appear, yawning and stretching their arms—for no one had thrown aside his clothes—most of them launching their sea-jokes right and left, with as much indifference as if they lay quietly in the port to which they were bound. After some eight or ten minutes to shake themselves, and to get "aired," as Mr. Leach expressed it, the whole party was again mustered on the deck of the Dane, with the exception of a hand or two in the launch, and Mr. Dodge. The latter had assumed the office of sentinel over the jolly-boat, which, as usual, lay at the rocks, to carry such articles off as might be wanted.

"Send a hand up into the foretop, Mr. Leach," said the captain, gaping like a greyhound; "a fellow with sharp eyes; none of your chaps who read with their noses down in the cloudy weather of an almanac; and let him take a look at the desert, in search of Arabs."

Although the lower rigging was down and safe in the launch, a girt-line, or, as Captain Truck in the true Doric of his profession announced it, a "*gunt*-line," was rove at each mast, and a man was accordingly hauled up forward as soon as possible. As it was still too dusky to distinguish far with accuracy, the captain hailed him, and bade him stay where he was until ordered down, and to keep a sharp lookout.

"We had a visit from one chap in the night," he added, "and as he was a hungry-looking rascal, he is a greater fool than I think him, or he will be back before long, after some of the beef and stock-fish of the wreck. Keep a bright lookout."

The men, though accustomed to their commander's manner, looked at each other more seriously, glanced around at their arms, and then the information produced precisely the effect that had been intended, that of inducing them to apply to their work with threefold vigor.

"Let the boys chew up that, instead of their tobacco," observed the captain to Mr. Leach, as he hunted for a good coal in the galley to light his cigar with. "I'll warrant you the sheers go up none the slower for the information, desperate philosophers as some of these gentry are."

This prognostic was true enough, for instead of gaping and stretching themselves about the deck, as had been the case with most of them a minute before, the men now commenced their duty in good earnest, calling to each other to come to the falls and the capstan-bars, and to stand by the heels of the sheers.

"Heave away!" cried the mate, smiling to see how quick the captain's hint had been taken; "heave round with a will, men, and let us set these legs on end, that they may walk."

As the order was obeyed to the letter, the day had not fairly opened when the sheers were in their places and secured. Every man was all activity, and as their work was directed by those whose knowledge was never at fault, a landsman would have been surprised at the readiness with which the crew next raised a spar as heavy as the mainmast, and had it suspended, top and all, in the air, high enough to be borne over the side. The lowering was a trifling affair, and the massive stick was soon lying at its length on the sands. Captain Truck well knew the great importance of this particular spar, for he might make out with the part of the foremast that remained in the packet, whereas, without this mast, he could not possibly rig anything of much available use aft. He called out to the men, therefore, as he sprang from the staging, to follow him and to launch the spar into the water before they breakfasted.

"Let us make sure of this fellow, men," he added, "for it is our mainstay. With this stick fairly in our raft, we may yet make a passage; no one must think of his teeth till it is out of all risk. The stick we must have, if we make war on the Emperor of Morocco for its possession."

The people knew the necessity for exertion, and they worked accordingly. The top was knocked off, and carried down to the water; the spar was then cut round, and rolled after it, not without trouble, however, as the trestle-trees were left on; but the descent of the sands favored the labor. When on the margin of the sea, by the aid of handspikes, the head was got afloat, or so nearly so, as to require but little force to move it, when a line from the boats was fastened to the outer end, and the top was secured alongside.

"Now, clap your handspikes under it, boys, and heave away!" cried the captain. "Heave together and keep the stick straight—heave, and his head is afloat! Haul, haul away in the boat!—heave all at once, and as if you were giants! you gained three feet that tug, my hearties: try him again, gentlemen, as you are—and move together, like girls in a *cotillion*—Away with it! What the devil are you staring at, in the foretop there? Have you nothing better to do than to amuse yourself in seeing us heave our insides out?"

The intense interest attached to the securing of this spar had extended to the lookout in the top, and instead of keeping his eye on the desert, as ordered, he was looking down at the party on the beach, and betraying his sympathy in their efforts by bending his body, and appearing to heave in common with his messmates. Admonished of his neglect by this sharp rebuke, he turned round quickly towards the desert, and gave the fearful alarm of "The Arabs!"

Every man ceased his work, and the whole were on the point of rushing in a body towards their arms, when the greater steadiness of Captain Truck prevented it.

"Whereaway?" he demanded sternly.

"On the most distant hillock of sand, may be a mile and a half inland."

"How do they head?"

"Dead down upon us, sir."

"How do they travel?"

"They have camels, and horses: all are mounted, sir."

"What is their number?"

The man paused, as if to count, and then he called out—

"They are strong-handed, sir; quite a hundred, I think. They have brought up, sir, and seem to be sounding about them for an anchorage."

Captain Truck hesitated, and he looked wistfully at the mast.

"Boys!" said he, shaking his hand over the bit of massive wood, with energy, "this spar is of more importance to us than our mother's milk in infancy. It is our victuals and drink, life and hopes. Let us swear we will have it in spite of a thousand Arabs. Stoop to your handspikes, and heave at the word—heave as if you had a world to move—heave, men, heave!"

The people obeyed, and the mast advanced more than half the necessary distance into the water. But the man now called out that the Arabs were advancing swiftly towards the ship.

17

"One more effort, men," said Captain Truck, reddening
in the face with anxiety, and throwing down his hat to set
the example in person,—"heave!"

The men hove, and the spar floated.

"Now to your arms, boys, and you, sir, in the top, keep
yourself hid behind the head of the mast. We must be
ready to show these gentry we are not afraid of them." A
sign of the hand told the men in the launch to haul away,
and the all-important spar floated slowly across the bar, to
join the raft.

The men now hurried up to the ship, a post that Captain
Truck declared he could maintain against a whole tribe,
while Mr. Dodge began incontinently to scull the jolly-boat,
in the best manner he could, off to the launch. All remonstrance was useless, as he had got as far as the bar before
he was perceived. Both Sir George Templemore and Mr.
Monday loudly denounced him for deserting the party on the
shore in this scandalous manner, but quite without effect.
Mr. Dodge's skill, unfortunately for his success, did not quite
equal his zeal; and finding, when he got on the bar, that he
was unable to keep the boat's head to the sea, or indeed to
manage it at all, he fairly jumped into the water and swam
lustily towards the launch. As he was expert at this exercise, he arrived safely, cursing in his heart all travelling,
the desert, the Arabs, and mankind in general, wishing himself quietly back in Dodgeopolis again, among his beloved
people. The boat drove upon the sands, of course, and was
eventually taken care of by two of the Montauk's crew.

As soon as Captain Truck found himself on the deck of the
Dane, the arms were distributed among the people. It was
clearly his policy not to commence the war, for he had nothing, in an affirmative sense, to gain by it, though, without
making any professions, his mind was fully made up not to
be taken alive, as long as there was a possibility of averting
such a disaster. The man aloft gave constant notice of the
movements of the Arabs, and he soon announced that they
had halted at a pistol shot from the bank, where they were
securing their camels, and that his first estimate of their
force was true.

In the meantime, Captain Truck was far from satisfied with his position. The bank was higher than the deck of the ship, and so near it as to render the bulwarks of little use, had those of the Dane been of any available thickness, which they were not. Then, the position of the ship, lying a little on one side, with her bows towards the land, exposed her to being swept by a raking fire; a cunning enemy having it in his power, by making a cover of the bank, to pick off his men, with little or no exposure to himself. The odds were too great to sally upon the plain, and although the rocks offered a tolerable cover towards the land, they had none towards the ship. Divide his force he dared not do,—and by abandoning the ship, he would allow the Arabs to seize her, thus commanding the other position, besides the remainder of the stores, which he was desirous of securing.

Men think fast in trying circumstances; and although the captain was in a situation so perfectly novel, his practical knowledge and great coolness rendered him an invaluable commander to those under his orders.

"I do not know, gentlemen," he said, addressing his passengers and mates, "that Vattel has laid down any rule to govern this case. These Arabs, no doubt, are the lawful owners of the country, in one sense; but it is a desert —and a desert, like a sea, is common property for the time being, to all who find themselves in it. There are no wreckmasters in Africa, and probably no law concerning wrecks, but the law of the strongest. We have been driven in here, moreover, by stress of weather—and this is a category on which Vattel has been very explicit. We have a *right* to the hospitality of these Arabs, and if it be not freely accorded, d——n me, gentlemen, but I feel disposed to take just as much of it as I find I shall have occasion for! Mr. Monday, I should like to hear your sentiments on this subject."

"Why, sir," returned Mr. Monday, "I have the greatest confidence in your knowledge, Captain Truck, and am equally ready for peace or war, although my calling is for the first. I should try negotiation to begin with, sir, if it be practicable, and you will allow me to express an opinion ; after which I would offer war.''

" I am quite of the same mind, sir ; but in what way are we to negotiate with a people we cannot make understand a word we say ? It is true, if they were versed in the science of signs, one might do something with them ; but I have reason to know that they are as stupid as boobies on all such subjects. We shall get ourselves into a category at the first *protocol*, as the writers say.''

Now, Mr. Monday thought there was a language that any man might understand, and he was strongly disposed to profit by it. In rummaging the wreck, he had discovered a case of liquor, besides a cask of Hollands, and he thought an offering of these might have the effect to put the Arabs in good-humor at least.

" I have known men, who, treated with dry, in matters of trade, were as obstinate as mules, become reasonable and pliable, sir, over a bottle,'' he said, after explaining where the liquor was to be found ; "and I think, if we offer the Arabs this, after they have been in possession a short time, we shall find them better disposed towards us. If it should not prove so, I confess, for one, I should feel less reluctance in shooting them than before.''

" I have somewhere heard that the Mussulmans never drink,'' observed Sir George ; " in which case we shall find our offering despised. Then there is the difficulty of a first possession ; for, if these people are the same as those that were here before, they may not thank us for giving them so small a part of that, of which they may lay claim to all. I 'm very sure, were any one to offer me my patent pistols, as a motive for letting him carry away my patent razors, or the East India dressing-case, or anything else I own, I should not feel particularly obliged to him.''

" Capitally put, Sir George, and I should be quite of your way of thinking, if I did not believe these Arabs might really be mollified by a little drink. If I had a proper ambassador to send with the offering, I would resort to the plan at once.''

Mr. Monday, after a moment's hesitation, spiritedly of-

fered to be one of two, to go to the Arabs with the proposal, for he had sufficient penetration to perceive that there
was little danger of his being seized, while an armed party
of so much strength remained to be overcome—and he had
sufficient nerve to encounter the risk. All he asked was a
companion, and Captain Truck was so much struck with
the spirit of the volunteer, that he made up his mind to
accompany him himself. To this plan, however, both the
mates and all the crew stoutly but respectfully objected.
They felt his importance too much to consent to this exposure, and neither of the mates, even, would be allowed to go
on an expedition of so much hazard, without a sufficient
motive. They might fight, if they pleased, but they should
not run into the mouth of the lion unarmed and unresisting.

"It is of no moment," said Mr. Monday; "I could have
liked a gentleman for my companion; but no one of the
brave fellows will have any objection to passing an hour in
company with an Arab sheik over a bottle. What say you,
my lads, will any one of you volunteer?"

"Ay, ay, sir!" cried a dozen in a breath.

"This will never do," interrupted the captain: "I have
need of the men, for my heart is still set on these two sticks
that remain, and we have a head-sea and a stiff breeze to
struggle with in getting back to the ship. By George, I
have it! What do you say to Mr. Dodge for a companion,
Mr. Monday? He is used to committees, and likes the
service; and then he has need of some stimulant, after the
ducking he has received. Mr. Leach, take a couple of
hands, and go off in the jolly-boat and bring Mr. Dodge on
shore. My compliments to him, and tell him he has been
unanimously chosen to a most honorable and lucrative—
ay, and a popular employment."

As this was an order, the mate did not scruple about
obeying it. He was soon afloat, and on his way towards
the launch. Captain Truck now hailed the top, and inquired
what the Arabs were about. The answer was satisfactory,
as they were still busy with their camels and in pitching
their tents. This did not look much like an immediate war,
and bidding the man aloft to give timely notice of their ap-

proach, Mr. Truck fancied he might still have time to shift his sheers, and to whip out the mizzen-mast, and he accordingly set about it without further delay.

As every one worked, as it might be for life, in fifteen minutes this light spar was suspended in the falls. In ten more its heel was clear of the bulwarks, and it was lowered on the sands almost by the run. To knock off the top and roll it down to the water took but a few minutes longer, and then the people were called to their breakfast ; the sentinel aloft reporting that the Arabs were employed in the same manner, and in milking their camels. This was a fortunate relief, and everybody ate in peace, and in the full assurance that those whom they so much distrusted were equally engaged in the same pacific manner.

Neither the Arabs nor the seamen, however, lost any unnecessary time at the meal. The former were soon reported to be coming and going in parties of fifteen or twenty, arriving and departing in an eastern direction. Occasionally a single runner went or came alone, on a fleet dromedary, as if communications were held with other bodies which lay deeper in the desert. All this intelligence rendered Captain Truck very uneasy, and he thought it time seriously to take some decided measures to bring this matter to an issue. Still, as time gained was all in his favor, if improved, he first ordered the men to begin to shift the sheer forward, in hopes of being yet able to carry off the foremast ; a spar that would be exceedingly useful, as it would save the necessity of fishing a new head to the one which still stood in the packet. He then went aside with his two ambassadors, with a view to give his instructions.

Mr. Dodge had no sooner found himself safe in the launch than he felt his courage revive, and with his courage, his ingenuity, self-love, and assurance. While in the water, a meeker man there was not on earth ; he had even some doubts as to the truth of all his favorite notions of liberty and equality, for men think fast in danger, and there was an instant when he might have been easily persuaded to acknowledge himself a demagogue and a hypocrite in his ordinary practices ; one whose chief motive was self, and whose besetting passions were envy, distrust, and malice ; or, in other words, very much the creature he was. Shame came next, and he eagerly sought an excuse for the want of manliness he had betrayed ; but, passing over the language he had held in the launch, and the means Mr. Leach found to persuade him to land again, we shall give his apology in his own words, as he now somewhat hurriedly delivered it to Captain Truck, in his own person.

"I must have misunderstood your arrangement, captain," he said ; "for somehow, though how I do not exactly know —but somehow the alarm of the Arabs was no sooner given than I felt as if I ought to be in the launch to be at my post ; but I suppose it was because I knew that the sails and spars that brought us here are mostly there, and that this was the spot to be most resolutely defended. I *do* think, if they had waded off to us, I should have fought like a tiger ! "

"No doubt you would, my dear sir, and like a wild-cat too ! We all make mistakes in judgment, in war, and in politics, and no fact is better known than that the best soldiers in the end are they who give a little ground at the first attack. But Mr. Leach has explained to you the plan of Mr. Monday, and I rely on your spirit and zeal, which there is now an excellent opportunity to prove, as before it was only demonstrated."

"If it were only an opportunity of meeting the Arabs sword in hand, captain."

"Pooh ! pooh ! my dear friend, take two swords if you choose. One who is full of fight can never get the battle on his own terms. Fill the Arabs with the schnapps of the poor Dane, and if they should make the smallest symptom of moving down towards us, I rely on you to give the alarm, in order that we may be ready for them. Trust to us for the overture of the piece, as I trust to you for the overtures of peace."

"In what way can we possibly do this, Mr. Monday? How can we give the alarm in season ? "

"Why," interposed the unmoved captain, "you may just shoot the sheik, and that will be killing two birds with one stone ; you will take your pistols, of course, and blaze away upon them, starboard and larboard ; rely on it, we shall hear you."

"Of that I make no doubt, but I rather distrust the prudence of the step. That is, I declare, Mr. Monday, it looks awfully like tempting Providence ! I begin to have conscientious scruples. I hope you are quite certain, captain, there is nothing in all this against the laws of Africa? Good moral and religious influences are not to be overlooked. My mind is quite exercised in the premises ! "

"You are much too conscientious for a diplomatic man," said Mr. Truck, between the puffs at a fresh cigar. "You need not shoot any of the women, and what more does a man want. Come, no more words, but to the duty heartily. Every one expects it of you, since no one can do it half so well ; and if you ever get back to Dodgeopolis, there will be matter for a paragraph every day of the year for the next six months. If anything serious happen to you, trust to me to do your memory justice."

"Captain, captain, this trifling with the future is blasphemous ! Men seldom talk of death with impunity, and it really hurts my feelings to touch on such awful subjects so lightly. I will go, for I do not well see how the matter is to be helped ; but let us go amicably, and with such presents as will secure a good reception and a safe return."

"Mr. Monday takes the liquor-case of the Dane, and you are welcome to anything that is left, but the foremast. That I shall fight for, even if lions come out of the desert to help the Arabs."

Mr. Dodge had many more objections, some of which he urged openly, and more of which he felt in his inmost spirit. But for the unfortunate dive into the water, he certainly would have pleaded his immunities as a passenger, and plumply refused to be put forward on such an occasion ; but he felt that he was a disgraced man, and that some decided act of spirit was necessary to redeem his character. The neutrality observed by the Arabs, moreover, greatly encouraged him ; for he leaned to an opinion Captain Truck had expressed, that so long as a strong-armed party remained in the wreck, the sheik, if a man of any moderation and policy, would not proceed to violence.

"You may tell him, gentlemen," continued Mr. Truck, "that as soon as I have whipped the foremast out of the Dane, I will evacuate, and leave him the wreck, and all it contains. The stick can do him no good, and I want it in my heart's core. Put this matter before him plainly, and there is no doubt we shall part the best friends in the world. Remember one thing, however: we shall set about lifting the spar the moment you quit us, and should there be any signs of an attack, give us notice in season, that we may take to our arms."

By this reasoning Mr. Dodge suffered himself to be persuaded to go on the mission, though his ingenuity and fears supplied an additional motive that he took very good care not to betray. Should there be a battle, he knew he would be expected to fight, if he remained with his own party, and if with the other, he might plausibly secrete himself until the affair was over; for, with a man of his temperament, eventual slavery had less horrors than immediate death.

When Mr. Monday and his co-commissioner ascended the bank, bearing the case of liquors and a few light offerings that the latter had found in the wreck, it was just as the crew, assured that the Arabs still remained tranquil, had seriously set about pursuing their great object. On the margin of the plain, Captain Truck took his leave of the ambassadors, though he remained some time to reconnoitre the appearance of things in the wild-looking camp, which was placed within two hundred yards of the spot on which he stood. The number of the Arabs had not certainly been exaggerated, and what gave him the most uneasiness was the fact that parties appeared to be constantly communicating with more, who probably lay behind a ridge of sand that bounded the view less than a mile distant inland, as they all went and came in that direction. After waiting to see his two *envoyés* in the very camp, he stationed a lookout on the bank, and returned to the wreck, to hurry on the all-important work.

Mr. Monday was the efficient man of the two commissioners, so soon as they were fairly embarked in their enterprise. He was strong of nerves, and without imagination to fancy dangers where they were not very obvious, and had a great faith in the pacific virtues of the liquor-case. An Arab advanced to meet them, when near the tents; and although conversation was quite out of the question, by pure force of gesticulations, aided by the single word "sheik," they succeeded in obtaining an introduction to that personage.

The inhabitants of the desert have been so often described that we shall assume they are known to our readers, and proceed with our narrative the same as if we had to do with Christmas. Much of what has been written of the hospitality of the Arabs, if true of any portion of them, is hardly true of those tribes which frequent the Atlantic coast, where the practice of wrecking would seem to have produced the same effect on their habits and morals that it is known to produce elsewhere. But a ship protected by a few weatherworn and stranded mariners, and a ship defended by a strong and an armed party, like that headed by Captain Truck, presented very different objects to the cupidity of these barbarians. They knew the great advantage they possessed by being on their own ground, and were content to await events, in preference to risking a doubtful contest. Several of the party had been at Mogadore, and other parts, and had acquired tolerably accurate ideas of the power of vessels; and as they were confident the men now at work at the wreck had not the means of carrying away the cargo, their own principal object, curiosity and caution, connected with certain plans that were already laid among their leaders, kept them quiet, for the moment at least.

These people were not so ignorant as to require to be told that some other vessel was at no great distance, and their scouts had been out in all directions to ascertain the fact, previously to taking their ultimate measures; for the sheik himself had some pretty just notions of the force of a vessel of war, and the danger of contending with one. The result of his policy, therefore, will better appear in the course of the narrative.

The reception of the two envoys of Captain Truck was masked by that smiling and courteous politeness which seems to diminish as one travels west, and to increase as he goes eastward ; though it was certainly less elaborate than would have been found in the palace of an Indian rajah. The sheik was not properly a sheik, nor was the party composed of genuine Arabs, though we thus have styled them from usage. The first, however, was a man in authority, and he and his followers possessed enough of the origin and characteristics of the tribes east of the Red Sea, to be sufficiently described by the appellation we have adopted.

Mr. Monday and Mr. Dodge were invited by signs to be seated, and refreshments were offered. As the last were not particularly inviting, Mr. Monday was not slow in producing his own offering, and in recommending its quality, by setting example of the way in which it ought to be treated. Although Mussulmans, the host did not scruple about tasting the cup, and ten minutes of pantomime, potations, and grimaces, brought about a species of intimacy between the parties.

The man who had been so unceremoniously captured the previous night by Captain Truck, was now introduced, and much curiosity was manifested to know whether his account of the disposition in the strangers to eat their fellow-creatures was true. The inhabitants of the desert, in the course of ages, had gleaned certain accounts of mariners eating their shipmates, from their different captives, and vague traditions to that effect existed among them, which the tale of this man had revived. Had the sheik kept a journal, like Mr. Dodge, the result of these inquiries would probably have been some entries concerning the customs and characters of the Americans, that were quite as original as those of the editor of the "Active Inquirer" concerning the different nations he had visited.

Mr. Monday paid great attention to the pantomime of the Arab, in which that worthy endeavored to explain the disposition of Captain Truck to make a barbecue of him ; when it was ended, he gravely informed his companion that the sheik had invited them to stay for dinner,—a proposition that he was disposed to accept; but the sensitiveness of Mr. Dodge viewed the matter otherwise, for, with a conformity of opinion that really said something in favor of the science of signs, he arrived at the same conclusion as the poor Arab himself—with the material difference, that he fancied that the Arabs were disposed to make a meal of himself. Mr. Monday, who was a hearty beef and brandy personage, scouted the idea, and thought the matter settled, by pointing to two or three young camels, and asking the editor if he thought any man, Turk or Christian, would think of eating one so lank, meagre, and uninviting, as himself, when they had so much capital food of another sort at their elbow. "Take your share of the liquor while it is passing, man, and set your heart at ease as to the dinner, which I make no doubt will be substantial and decent. Had I known of the favor intended us, I should have brought out the sheik a service of knives and forks from Birmingham; for he really seems a well-disposed and gentleman-like man. A very capital fellow, I dare say, we shall find him, after he has had a few camel's steaks, and a proper allowance of schnapps. Mr. Sheik, I drink your health with all my heart."

The accidents of life could scarcely have brought together, in circumstances so peculiar, men whose characters were more completely the converse of each other than Mr. Monday and Mr. Dodge. They were perfect epitomes of two large classes in their respective nations, and so diametrically opposed to each other, that one could hardly recognize in them scions from a common stock. The first was dull, obstinate, straight-forward, hearty in his manners, and not without sincerity, though wily in a bargain, with all his seeming frankness; the last, distrustful, cunning rather than quick of comprehension, insincere, fawning when he thought his interests concerned, and jealous and detracting at all other times, with a coldness of exterior that had at least the merit of appearing to avoid deception. Both were violently prejudiced, though in Mr. Monday it was the prejudice of old dogmas in religion, politics, and morals; and in the other, it was the vice of provincialism, and an education that was not entirely free from the fanaticism of the seventeenth century. One consequence of this discrepancy of character was a perfectly opposite manner of viewing matters in this interview. While Mr. Monday was disposed to take things amicably, Mr. Dodge was all suspicion; and had they then returned to the wreck, the last would have called to arms, while the first would have advised Captain Truck to go out and visit the sheik, in the manner one would visit a respectable and agreeable neighbor.

## CHAPTER XX.

"'Tis of more worth than kingdoms! far more precious
Than all the crimson treasures of life's fountain!
O, let it not elude thy grasp!"

COTTON.

THINGS were in this state, the sheik and his guests communicating by signs, in such a way as completely to mystify each other; Mr. Monday drinking, Mr. Dodge conjecturing, and parties quitting the camp and arriving every ten minutes, when an Arab pointed eagerly with his finger in the direction of the wreck. The head of the foremast was slowly rising, and the lookout in the top was clinging to the spar, which began to cant, in order to keep himself from falling. The sheik affected to smile; but he was evidently disturbed, and two or three messengers were sent out into the camp. In the meanwhile, the spar began to lower, and was soon entirely concealed beneath the bank.

It was now apparent that the Arabs thought the moment had arrived when it was their policy to interfere. The sheik, therefore, left his guests to be entertained by two or three others who had joined in the potations, and making the best assurances he could by means of signs, of his continued amity, he left the tent. Laying aside all his arms, attended by two or three old men like himself, he went boldly to the plank, and descended quietly to the sands, where he found Captain Truck busied in endeavoring to get the spar into the water. The top was already afloat, and the stick itself was cut round in the right position for rolling, when the foul, but grave-looking barbarians appeared among the workmen. As the latter had been apprised of their ap-

proach, and of the fact of their being unarmed, no one left
his employment to receive them, with the exception of Captain Truck himself.

"Bear a hand with the spar, Mr. Leach," he said, "while
I entertain these gentlemen. It is a good sign that they
come to us without arms, and it shall never be said that we
are behind them in civility. Half an hour will settle our
affairs, when these gentry are welcome to what will be left
of the Dane. Your servant, gentlemen; I'm glad to see
you, and beg the honor to shake hands with all of you, from
the oldest to the youngest."

Although the Arabs understood nothing that was said,
they permitted Captain Truck to give each of them a hearty
shake of the hand, smiling and muttering their own compliments with as much apparent good-will as was manifested
by the old seaman himself.

"God help the Danes, if they have fallen into servitude
among these blackguards!" said the captain, aloud, while
he was shaking the sheik a second time most cordially by
the hand, "for a fouler set of thieves I never laid eyes on,
Leach. Mr. Monday has tried the virtue of the schnapps
on them, notwithstanding, for the odor of gin is mingled
with that of grease, about the old scoundrel. Roll away at
the spar, boys! half a dozen more such heaves, and you will
have him in his native element, as the newspapers call it.
I'm glad to see you, gentlemen; we are badly off as to
chairs, on this beach, but to such as we have you are heartily
welcome. Mr. Leach, the Arab sheik—Arab sheik, Mr.
Leach. On the bank there!"

"Sir!"

"Any movement among the Arabs?"

"About thirty have just ridden back into the desert,
mounted on camels, sir; nothing more."

"No signs of our passengers?"

"Ay, ay, sir. Here comes Mr. Dodge under full sail, heading for the bank, as straight as he can lay his course!"

"Ha!—is he pursued?"

The men ceased their work, and glanced aside at their
arms.

"Not at all, sir. Mr. Monday is calling after him, and the Arabs seem to be laughing. Mr. Monday is just splicing the main-brace with one of the rascals."

"Let the Atlantic Ocean, then, look out for itself, for Mr. Dodge will be certain to run over it. Heave away, my hearties, and the stick will be afloat yet before that gentleman is fairly docked."

The men worked with good-will, but their zeal was far less efficient than that of the editor of the "Active Inquirer," who now broke through the bushes, and plunged down the bank with a velocity which, if continued, would have carried him to Dodgeopolis itself within the month. The Arabs started at this sudden apparition, but perceiving that those around them laughed, they were disposed to take the interruption in good part. The lookout now announced the approach of Mr. Monday, followed by fifty Arabs; the latter, however, being without arms, and the former without his hat. The moment was critical, but the steadiness of Captain Truck did not desert him. Issuing a rapid order to the second mate, with a small party previously selected for that duty, to stand by the arms, he urged the rest of the people to renewed exertions. Just as this was done, Mr. Monday appeared on the bank, with a bottle in one hand and a glass in the other, calling aloud to Mr. Dodge to return and drink with the Arabs.

"Do not disgrace Christianity in this unmannerly way," he said; "but show these gentlemen of the desert that we know what propriety is. Captain Truck, I beg of you to urge Mr. Dodge to return. I was about to sing the Arabs 'God save the King,' and in a few more minutes we should have had 'Rule Britannia,' when we should have been the best friends and companions in the world. Captain Truck, I've the honor to drink your health."

But Captain Truck viewed the matter differently. Both his ambassadors were now safely back, for Mr. Monday came down upon the beach, followed, it is true, by all the Arabs, and the mast was afloat. He thought it better, therefore, that Mr. Dodge should remain, and that the two parties should be as quietly, but as speedily as possible, separated. He ordered the hauling line to be fastened to the mast, and as the stick was slowly going out through the surf, he issued the order for the men to collect their implements, take their arms, and to assemble in a body at the rocks, where the jolly-boat still lay.

" Be quick, men, but be steady ; for there are a hundred of these rascals on the beach already, and all the last-comers are armed. We might pick up a few more useful things from the wreck, but the wind is coming in from the westward, and our principal concern now will be to save what we have got. Lead Mr. Monday along with you, Leach, for he is so full of diplomacy and schnapps just now that he forgets his safety. As for Mr. Dodge, I see he is stowed away in the boat already, as snug as the ground-tier in a ship loaded with molasses. Count the men off, sir, and see that no one is missing."

By this time, the state of things on the beach had undergone material changes. The wreck was full of Arabs, some of whom were armed and some not ; while mauls, crows, handspikes, purchases, coils of rigging, and marline-spikes, were scattered about on the sands, just where they had been dropped by the seamen. A party of fifty Arabs had collected around the rocks, where, by this time, all the mariners were assembled, intermingling with the latter, and apparently endeavoring to maintain the friendly relations which had been established by Mr. Monday. As a portion of these men were also armed, Captain Truck disliked their proceedings ; but the inferiority of his numbers, and the disadvantage under which he was placed, compelled him to resort to management rather than force, in order to extricate himself.

The Arabs now crowded around and intermingled with the seamen, thronged the ship, and lined the bank, to the number of more than two hundred. It became evident that their true force had been underrated, and that additions were constantly making to it, from those who lay behind the ridges of sand. All those who appeared last had arms of one kind or another, and several brought fire-arms, which they gave to the sheik, and to those who had first descended

18

to the beach. Still, every face seemed amicable, and the men were scarcely permitted to execute their orders, from the frequent interruptions to exchange tokens of friendship.

But Captain Truck fully believed that hostilities were intended, and although he had suffered himself in some measure to be surprised, he set about repairing his error with great judgment and admirable steadiness. His first step was to extricate his own people from those who pressed upon them, a thing that was effected by causing a few to take a position, that might be defended, higher among the rocks, as they afforded a good deal of cover, and which communicated directly with the place where they had landed; and then ordering the remainder of the men to fall back singly. To prevent an alarm, each man was called off by name, and in this manner the whole party had got within the prescribed limits, before the Arabs, who were vociferating and talking all together, seemed to be aware of the movement. When some of the latter attempted to follow, they were gently repulsed by the sentinels. All this time Captain Truck maintained the utmost cordiality towards the sheik, keeping near him, and amongst the Arabs himself. The work of plunder, in the meantime, had begun in earnest in the wreck, and this he thought a favorable symptom, as men thus employed would be less likely to make a hostile attack. Still he knew that prisoners were of great account among these barbarians, and that an attempt to tow the raft off from the land, in open boats, where his people would be exposed to every shot from the wreck, would subject them to the greatest danger of defeat, were the former disposed to prevent it.

Having reflected a few minutes on his situation, Captain Truck issued his final orders. The jolly-boat might carry a dozen men at need, though they would be crowded and much exposed to fire; and he therefore, caused eight to get into her, and to pull out to the launch. Mr. Leach went with this party, for the double purpose of directing its movements, and of being separated from his commander, in order that one of those who were of so much importance to the packet, might at least stand a chance of being saved,

This separation also was effected without alarming the Arabs, though Captain Truck observed that the sheik watched the proceeding narrowly.

As soon as Mr. Leach had reached the launch, he caused a light kedge to be put into the jolly-boat, and coils of the lightest rigging he had were laid on the top of it, or were made on the bows of the launch. As soon as this was done, the boat was pulled a long distance off from the land, paying out the ropes first from the launch, and then from the boat itself, until no more of the latter remained. The kedge was then dropped, and the men in the launch began to haul in upon the ropes that were attached to it. As the jolly-boat returned immediately, and her crew joined in the work, the line of boats, the kedge by which they had previously ridden having been first raised, began slowly to recede from the shore. Captain Truck had rightly conjectured the effect of this movement. It was so unusual and so gradual, that the launch and the raft were warped up to the kedge before the Arabs fully comprehended its nature. The boats were now more than a quarter of a mile from the wreck, for Mr. Leach had run out quite two hundred fathoms of small rope, and, of course, so distant as greatly to diminish the danger from the muskets of the Arabs, though still within reach of their range. Near an hour was passed in effecting this point, which, as the sea and wind were both rising, could not probably have been effected in any other manner half as soon, if at all.

The state of the weather, and the increasing turbulence of the barbarians, now rendered it extremely desirable to all on the rocks to be in their boats again. A very moderate blow would compel them to abandon their hard-earned advantages, and it began to be pretty evident, from the manners of those around them that amity could not much longer be maintained. Even the old sheik retired, and, instead of going to the wreck, he joined the party on the beach where he was seen in earnest conversation with several other old men, all of whom gesticulated vehemently, as they pointed towards the boats and to the party on the rocks.

Mr. Leach now pulled in towards the bar, with both the jolly-boats and the cutter, having only two oars each, half his men being left in the launch. This was done that the people might not be crowded at the critical moment, and that, at need, there might be room to fight as well as to row; all these precautions having been taken in consequence of Captain Truck's previous orders. When the boats reached the rocks, the people did not hurry into them; but a quarter of an hour was passed in preparations, as if they were indifferent about proceeding, and even then the jolly-boat alone took in a portion, and pulled leisurely without the bar. Here she lay on her oars, in order to cover the passage of the other boats, if necessary, with her fire. The cutter imitated this manœuvre, and the boat of the wreck went last. Captain Truck quitted the rock after all the others, though his embarkation was made rapidly by a prompt and sudden movement.

Not a shot was fired, however, and, contrary to his own most ardent hopes, the captain found himself at the launch, with all his people unhurt, and with all the spars he had so much desired to obtain. The forbearance of the Arabs was a mystery to him, for he had fully expected hostilities would commence, every moment, for the last two hours. Nor was he yet absolutely out of danger, though there was time to pause and look about him, and to take his succeeding measures more deliberately. The first report was a scarcity of both food and water. For both these essentials the men had depended on the wreck, and, in the eagerness to secure the foremast, and subsequently to take care of themselves, these important requisites had been overlooked, quite probably, too, as much from a knowledge that the Montauk was so near, as from hurry. Still both were extremely desirable, if not indispensable, to men who had the prospect of many hours' hard work before them; and Captain Truck's first impulse was to despatch a boat to the ship for supplies. This intention was reluctantly abandoned, however, on account of the threatening appearance of the weather.

There was no danger of a gale, but a smart sea-breeze

was beginning to set in, and the surface of the ocean was, as usual, getting to be agitated. Changing all his plans, therefore, the captain turned his immediate attention to the safety of the all-important spars.

"We can eat to-morrow, men," he said; "but if we lose these sticks, our chance for getting any more will indeed be small. Take a gang on the raft, Mr. Leach, and double all the lashings, while I see that we get an offing. If the wind rises any more, we shall need it, and even then be worse off than we could wish."

The mate passed upon the raft, and set about securing all the spars by additional fastenings; for the working, occasioned by the sea, already rendered them loose, and liable to separate. While this was in train, the two jolly-boats took in lines and kedges, of which, luckily, they had one that was brought from the packet, besides two found in the wreck, and pulled off into the ocean. As soon as one kedge was dropped, that by which the launch rode was tripped, and the boats were hauled up to it, the other jolly-boat proceeding on to renew the process. In this manner, in the course of two more hours, the whole, raft and all, were warped broad off from the land, and to windward, quite two miles, when the water became so deep that Captain Truck reluctantly gave the order to cease.

"I would gladly work our way into the offing in this mode, three or four leagues," he said, "by which means we might make a fair wind of it. As it is, we must get all clear, and do as well as we can. Rig the masts in the launch, Mr. Leach, and we will see what can be done with this dull craft we have in tow."

While this order was in course of execution, the glass was used to ascertain the manner in which the Arabs were occupied. To the surprise of all in the boats, every soul of them had disappeared. The closest scrutiny could not detect one near the wreck, on the beach, nor even at the spot where the tents had so lately stood.

"They are all off, by George!" cried Captain Truck, when fully satisfied of the fact. "Camels, tents, and Arabs! The rascals have loaded their beasts already, and most probably have gone to hide their plunder, that they may be back and make sure of a second haul, before any of their precious brother vultures, up in the sands, get a scent of the carrion. D——n the rogues! I thought at one time they had me in a category! Well, joy be with them! Mr. Monday, I return you my hearty thanks for the manly, frank, and diplomatic manner in which you have discharged the duties of your mission. Without you, we might not have succeeded in getting the foremast. Mr. Dodge, you have the high consolation of knowing that, throughout this trying occasion, you have conducted yourself in a way no other man of the party could have done."

Mr. Monday was sleeping off the fumes of the schnapps, but Mr. Dodge bowed to the compliment, and foresaw many capital things for the journal, and for the columns of the "Active Inquirer." He even began to meditate a book.

Now commenced much the most laborious and critical part of the service that Captain Truck had undertaken, if we except the collision with the Arabs—that of towing all the heavy spars of a large ship, in one raft, in the open sea, near a coast, and with a wind blowing on shore. It is true he was strong-handed, being able to put ten oars in the launch, and four in all the other boats; but, after making sail, and pulling steadily for an hour, it was discovered that all their exertions would not enable them to reach the ship, if the wind stood, before the succeeding day. The drift to leeward, or towards the beach, was seriously great, every heave of the sea setting them bodily down before it; and by the time they were half a mile to the southward, they were obliged to anchor, in order to keep clear of the breakers, which by this time extended fully a mile from shore.

Decision was fortunately Captain Truck's leading quality. He foresaw the length and severity of the struggle that was before them; and the men had not been pulling ten minutes, before he ordered Mr. Leach, who was in the cutter, to cast off his line and to come alongside the launch.

"Pull back to the wreck, sir," he said, "and bring off all you can lay hands on, in the way of bread, water, and other comforts. We shall make a night of it, I see. We will keep a lookout for you, and if any Arabs heave in sight on the plain, a musket will be fired ; if so many as to render a hint to abscond necessary, two muskets will be fired, and the mainsail of the launch will be furled for two minutes ; more time than that we cannot spare you."

Mr. Leach obeyed this order, and with great success. Luckily the cook had left the coppers full of food, enough to last twenty-four hours, and this had escaped the Arabs, who were ignorant where to look for it. In addition, there was plenty of bread and water ; and "a hull of Jamaica" had been discovered, by the instinct of one of the hands, which served admirably to keep the people in good humor. This timely supply had arrived just as the launch anchored, and Mr. Truck welcomed it with all his heart ; for without it, he foresaw he should soon be obliged to abandon his precious prize.

When the people were refreshed, the long and laborious process of warping off the land was resumed, and in the course of two hours more, the raft was got fully a league into the offing, a shoal permitting the kedges to be used farther out this time than before. Then sail was again made, and the oars were once more plied. But the sea still proved their enemy, though they had struck the current which began to set them south. Had there been no wind and sea, the progress of the boats would now have been comparatively easy and quick ; but these two adverse powers drove them in towards the beach so fast, that they had scarcely made two miles from the wreck when they were compelled a second time to anchor.

No alternative remained but to keep warping off in this manner, and then to profit by the offing they had made as well as they could, the result bringing them at sunset nearly up with the headland that shut out the view of their own vessel, from which Captain Truck now calculated that he was distant a little less than two leagues. The wind had freshened, and though it was not by any means so strong as to render the sea dangerous, it increased the toil of the men to such a degree, that he reluctantly determined to seek out a proper anchorage, and to give his wearied people some rest.

It was not in the power of the seamen to carry their raft into any haven, for to the northward of the headland, or on the side on which they were, there was no reef, nor any bay to afford them shelter. The coast was one continued waving line of sand-banks, and in most places, when there was a wind, the water broke at the distance of a mile from the beach; the precise spot where the Dane had stranded his vessel, having most probably been chosen for that purpose, with a view to save the lives of the people. Under these circumstances nothing remained but to warp off again to a safe distance, and to secure the boats as well as they could for the night. This was effected by eight o'clock, and Captain Truck gave the order to let go two additional kedges, being determined not to strike adrift in the darkness, if it was in his power to prevent it. When this was done, the people had their suppers, a watch was set, and the remainder went to sleep.

As the three passengers had been exempted from the toil, they volunteered to look out for the safety of the boats until midnight, in order that the men might obtain as much rest as possible; and half an hour after the crew were lost in the deep slumber of seamen, Captain Truck and these gentlemen were seated in the launch, holding a dialogue on the events of the day.

"You found the Arabs conversable and ready at the cup, Mr. Monday?" observed the captain, lighting a cigar, which with him was a never-failing sign for a gossip: "men that, if they had been sent to school young, taught to dance, and were otherwise civilized, might make reasonably good shipmates, in this roving world of ours?"

"Upon my word, sir, I look upon the sheik as uncommon gentlemanlike, and altogether as a good fellow. He took his glass without any grimaces, smiled whenever he said anything, though I could not understand a word he said, and answered all my remarks quite as civilly as if he spoke English. I must say, I think Mr. Dodge manifested a want of consideration in quitting his company with so little ceremony. The gentleman was hurt, I'll answer for it, and he would say as much if he could only make out to explain

himself on the subject. Sir George, I regret we had not
the honor of your company on the occasion, for I have
been told these Arabs have a proper respect for the nobility
and gentry. Mr. Dodge and myself were but poor substitutes for a gentleman like yourself."

The trained humility of Mr. Monday was little to the
liking of Mr. Dodge, who by the sheer force of the workings of envy had so long been endeavoring to persuade
others that he was the equal of any and every other man—
a delusion, however, which he could not succeed in persuading himself to fall into—and he was not slow in exhibiting the feeling it awakened.

"Sir George Templemore has too just a sense of the
rights of nations to make this distinction, Mr. Monday,"
he said. " If I left the Arab sheik a little abruptly, it was
because I disliked his ways; for I take it Africa is a free
country, and that no man is obliged to remain longer in a
tent than it suits his own convenience. Captain Truck knows
that I was merely running down the beach to inform him
that the sheik intended to follow, and he no doubt appreciates my motive."

"If not, Mr. Dodge," put in the captain, "like other
patriots, you must trust to posterity to do you justice. The
joints and sinews are so differently constructed in different
men, that one never knows exactly how to calculate on
speed; but this much I will make affidavit to, if you wish
it, on reaching home, and that is, that a better messenger
could not be found than Mr. Steadfast Dodge, for a man in
a hurry. Sir George Templemore, we have had but a few
of your opinions since you came out on this expedition, and
I should be gratified to hear your sentiments concerning
the Arabs, and anything else that may suggest itself at the
moment."

"O, captain I I think the wretches odiously dirty, and
judging from appearances, I should say sadly deficient in
comforts."

" In the way of breeches in particular; for I am inclined
to think, Sir George, you are master of more than are to
be found in their whole nation. Well, gentlemen, one must

certainly travel who wishes to see the world ; but for this sheer down here upon the coast of Africa, neither of us might have ever known how an Arab lives, and what a nimble wrecker he makes. For my own part, if the choice lay between filling the office of Jemmy Ducks, on board the Montauk, and that of sheik in this tribe, I should, as we say in America, Mr. Dodge, leave it to the people, and do all in my power to obtain the first situation. Sir George, I'm afraid all these *county tongues*, as Mr. Dodge calls them, in the way of wind and weather, will quite knock the buffalo hunt on the prairies in the head, for this fall at least."

"I beg, Captain Truck, you will not discredit my French in this way. I do not call a disappointment '*county tongues*,' but '*contra toms*'; the phrase probably coming from some person of the name of *Tom*, who was *contra*, or opposed to every one else."

"Perfectly explained, and as clear as bilge-water. Sir George, has Mr. Dodge mentioned to you the manner in which these Arabs enjoy life? The gentlemen, by way of saving dishwater, eat half a dozen at a time out of the same plate. Quite republican, and altogether without pride, Mr. Dodge, in their notions."

"Why, sir, many of their habits struck me as being simple and praiseworthy, during the short time I remained in their country ; and I dare say, one who had leisure to study them might find materials for admiration. I can readily imagine situations in which a man has no right to appropriate a whole dish to himself."

"No doubt, and he who wishes a thing so unreasonable must be a great hog. What a thing is sleep! Here are these fine fellows as much lost to their dangers and toils as if at home, and tucked in by their careful and pious mothers. Little did the good souls who nursed them, and sung pious songs over their cradles, fancy the hardships they were bringing them up to! But we never know our fates, or miserable dogs most of us would be. Is it not so, Sir George?"

The baronet started at this appeal, which crossed the

quaint mind of the captain as a cloud darkens a sunny view, and he muttered a hasty expression of hope that there was now no particular reason to expect any more serious obstacles to their reaching the ship.

"It is not an easy thing to tow a heavy raft in light boats like these, exactly in the direction you wish it to go," returned the captain, gaping. "He who trusts to the winds and waves, trusts uncertain friends, and those who may fail him at the very moment when there is most need of their services. Fair as things now seem, I would give a thousand dollars of a small stock, in which no single dollar has been lightly earned, to see these spars safely on board the Montauk, and snugly fitted to their proper places. Sticks, gentlemen, are to a ship what limbs are to a man. Without them she rolls and tumbles about as winds, currents, and seas will; while with them she walks, and dances, and jumps Jim Crow; ay, almost talks. The standing rigging are the bones and gristle; the running gear the veins in which her life circulates; and the blocks the joints."

"And which is the heart?" asked Sir George.

"Her heart is the master. With an efficient commander no stout ship is ever lost, so long as she has a foot of water beneath her false keel, or a ropeyarn left to turn to account."

"And yet the Dane had all these."

"All but the water. The best craft that was ever launched, is of less use than a single camel, if laid high and dry on the sands of Africa. These poor wretches truly! And yet their fate might have been ours, though I thought little of the risk while we were in the midst of the Arabs. It is still a mystery to me why they let us escape, especially as they so soon deserted the wreck. They were strong-handed, too; counting all who came and went, I think not less than several hundreds."

The captain now became silent and thoughtful, and, as the wind continued to rise, he began to feel uneasiness about his ship. Once or twice he expressed a half-formed determination to pull to her in one of the light boats, in order to look after her safety in person, and then he abandoned it, as he witnessed the rising of the sea, and the manner in which the massive raft caused the cordage by which it was held to strain. At length he too fell asleep, and we shall leave him and his party for awhile, and return to the Montauk, to give an account of what occurred on board that ship.

# CHAPTER XXI.

"Nothing beside remains ! Round the decay
Of that colossal wreck, boundless and bare,
The lone and level sands stretch far away."

SHELLEY.

AS Captain Truck was so fully aware of the importance of rapid movements to the success of his
enterprise, it will be remembered that he left in
the ship no seaman, no servant, except Saunders
the steward, and, in short, no men but the two Messrs.
Effingham and Mr. Sharp, Mr. Blunt, and the other person
just mentioned. If to these be added, Eve Effingham,
Mademoiselle Viefville, Ann Sidley, and a French *femme
de chambre*, the whole party will be enumerated. At first,
it had been the intention of the master to leave one of his
mates behind him, but, encouraged by the secure berth he had
found for his vessel, the great strength of his moorings, the
little hold the winds and waves could get of spars so robbed
of their proportions, and of a hull so protected by the reef,
and feeling a certain confidence in the knowledge of Mr.
Blunt, who, several times during the passage, had betrayed
a great familiarity with ships, he came to the decision named,
and had formally placed the last-named gentleman in full
charge, *ad interim*, of the Montauk.

There was a solemn and exciting interest in the situation
of those who remained in the vessel, after the party of bustling seamen had left them. The night came in bland and
tranquil, and although there was no moon, they walked the
deck for hours with strange sensations of enjoyment, mingled
with those of loneliness and desertion. Mr. Effingham and
his cousin retired to their rooms long before the others, who

continued their exercise with a freedom and an absence of restraint that they had not before felt since subjected to the confinement of the ship.

"Our situation is at least novel," Eve observed, "for a party of Parisians, Viennois, Romans, or by whatever name we may be properly styled."

"Say Swiss, then," returned Mr. Blunt; "for I believe that even the cosmopolite has a claim to choose his favorite residence."

Eve understood the allusion, which carried her back to the weeks they had passed in company, among the grand scenery of the Alps; but she would not betray the consciousness, for, whatever may be the ingenuousness of a female, she seldom loses her sensitiveness on the subject of her more cherished feelings.

"And do you prefer Switzerland to all the other countries of your acquaintance?" asked Mr. Sharp. "England I leave out of the question, for, though we, who belong to the island, see so many charms in it, it must be conceded that strangers seldom join us very heartily in its praises. I think most travellers would give the palm to Italy."

"I am quite of the same opinion," returned the other "and were I to be confined to a choice of a residence for life, Italy should be my home. Still, I think that we like change in our residence, as well as in the seasons. Italy is summer, and one, I fear, would weary of even an eternal June."

"Is not Italy rather autumn, a country in which the harvest is gathered, and where one begins already to see the fall of the leaf?"

"To me," said Eve, "it would be an eternal summer; as things are eternal with young ladies. My ignorance would be always receiving instruction, and my tastes improvement. But, if Italy be summer, or autumn, what is poor America?"

"Spring, of course," civilly answered Mr. Sharp.

"And, do you, Mr. Blunt, who seem to know all parts of the world equally well, agree in giving *our* country, *my* country at least, this encouraging title?"

"It is merited in many respects, though there are others in which the term winter would, perhaps, be better applied.

America is a country not easily understood; for, in some particulars, like Minerva, it has been born full-grown; while, in others, it is certainly still an infant."

"In what particulars do you especially class it with the latter?" inquired Mr. Sharp.

"In strength, to commence," answered the other, slightly smiling; "in opinions, too, and in tastes, and perhaps in knowledge. As to the latter essential, however, and practical things as well as in the commoner comforts, America may well claim to be in midsummer, when compared with other nations. I do not think you Americans, Miss Effingham, at the head of civilization, certainly, as so many of your own people fancy; nor yet at the bottom, as so many of those of Mademoiselle Viefville and Mr. Sharp so piously believe."

"And what are the notions of the countrymen of Mr. Blunt, on the subject?"

"As far from the truth, perhaps, as any other. I perceive there exist some doubts as to the place of my nativity," he added, after a pause that denoted a hesitation, which all hoped was to end in his setting the matter at rest, by a simple statement of the fact; "and I believe I shall profit by the circumstance, to praise and condemn at pleasure, since no one can impeach my candor, or impute either to partialities or prejudices."

"That must depend on the justice of your judgments. In one thing, however, you will have me on your side, and that is in giving the *past* to delicious, dreamy Italy! Though Mademoiselle Viefville will set this down as *lèse majesté* against *cher Paris*; and I fear Mr. Sharp will think even London injured."

"Do you really hold London so cheap?" inquired the latter gentleman, with more interest than he himself was quite aware of betraying.

"Indeed, no. This would be to discredit my own tastes and knowledge. In a hundred things, I think London quite the finest town of Christendom. It is not Rome, certainly, and were it in ruins fifteen centuries, I question if people would flock to the banks of the Thames to dream

away existence among its crumbling walls ; but in conveniences, beauty of verdure, a mixture of park-like scenery and
architecture, and in magnificence of a certain sort, one would
hardly know where to go to find the equal of London."

"You say nothing of its society, Miss Effingham ?"

"It would be presuming, in a girl of my limited experience to speak of this. I hear so much of the good sense
of the nation, that I dare not say aught against its society,
and it would be affectation for me to pretend to commend it ;
but as for your females, judging by my own poor means,
they strike me as being singularly well cultivated and accomplished ; and yet—"

"Go on, I entreat you. Recollect, we have solemnly decided in a general congress of states to be cosmopolites, until
safe within Sandy Hook, and that *la franchise* is the *mot
d'ordre.*"

"Well, then, I should not certainly describe you English
as a talking people," continued Eve, laughing. "In the
way of society, you are quite as agreeable as a people who
never laugh and seldom speak can possibly make themselves."

"*Et les jeunes Américaines ?*" said Mademoiselle Viefville, laconically.

"My dear Mademoiselle, your question is terrific ! Mr.
Blunt has informed me that *they* actually giggle !"

"*Quelle horreur !*"

"It is bad enough, certainly ; but I ascribe the report to
calumny. No ; if I must speak, let me have Paris for its
society, and Naples for its nature. As respects New York,
Mr. Blunt, I suspend my judgment."

"Whatever may be the particular merit which shall most
attract your admiration in favor of the great emporium, as
the grandiloquent writers term the capital of your own
State, I think I can venture to predict it will be neither of
those just mentioned. Of society, indeed, New York has
positively none : like London, it has plenty of company,
which is disciplined something like a regiment of militia
composed of drafts from different brigades, and which sometimes mistakes the drum-major for the colonel."

"I had fancied you a New Yorker, until now," observed Mr. Sharp.

"And why not now? Is a man to be blind to facts as evident as the noonday sun, because he was born here or there? If I have told you an unpleasant truth, Miss Effingham, you must accuse *la franchise* of the offence. I believe *you* are not a Manhattanese?"

"I am a mountaineer; having been born at my father's country residence."

"This gives me courage, then, for no one here will have his filial piety shocked."

"Not even yourself?"

"As for myself," returned Paul Blunt, "it is settled I am a cosmopolite in fact, while you are only a cosmopolite by convention. Indeed, I question if I might take the same liberties with either Paris or London, that I am about to take with palmy Manhattan. I should have little confidence in the forbearance of my auditors; Mademoiselle Viefville would hardly forgive me, were I to attempt a criticism on the first, for instance."

"*C'est impossible!* you could not, Mousieur Blunt; *vous parlez trop bien Français* not to love *Paris*."

"I do love *Paris*, Mademoiselle; and what is more, I love *Londres*, or even *la Nouvelle Yorck*. As a cosmopolite, I claim this privilege, at least, though I can see defects in all. If you will recollect, Miss Effingham, that New York is a social bivouac, a place in which families encamp instead of troops, you will see the impossibility of its possessing a graceful, well ordered, and cultivated society. Then the town is commercial; and no place of mere commerce can well have a reputation for its society. Such an anomaly, I believe, never existed. Whatever may be the usefulness of trade, I fancy few will contend that it is very graceful."

"Florence of old?" said Eve.

"Florence and her commerce were peculiar, and the relations of things change with circumstances. When Florence was great, trade was a monopoly, in a few hands, and so conducted as to remove the principals from immediate contact with its affairs. The Medici traded in spices

19

and silks, as men traded in politics, through agents. They probably never saw their ships, or had any further connection with their commerce, than to direct its spirit. They were more like the legislator who enacts laws to regulate trade, than the dealer who fingers a sample, smells at a wine, or nibbles a grain. The Medici were merchants, a class of men altogether different from the mere factors, who buy of one to sell to another, at a stated advance in price, and all of whose enterprise consists in extending the list of safe customers, and of doing what is called a "regular business." Monopolies do harm on the whole, but they certainly elevated the favored few. The Medici and the Strozzi were both princes and merchants, while those around them were principally dependants. Competition, in our day, has let in thousands to share in the benefits; and the pursuit, while it is enlarged as a whole, has suffered in its parts by division."

"You surely do not complain that a thousand are comfortable and respectable to-day, for one that was *il magnifico* three hundred years since?"

"Certainly not. I rejoice in the change; but we must not confound names with things. If we have a thousand mere factors for one merchant, society, in the general signification of the word, is clearly a gainer; but if we had one Medici for a thousand factors, society, in its particular signification, might also be a gainer. All I mean is, that, in lowering the pursuit, we have necessarily lowered its qualifications; in other words, every man in trade in New York, is no more a Lorenzo, than every printer's devil is a Franklin."

"Mr. Blunt cannot be an American!" cried Mr. Sharp; "for these opinions would be heresy."

"*Jamais, jamais!*" joined the governess.

"You constantly forget the treaty of cosmopolitism. But a capital error is abroad concerning America on this very subject of commerce. In the way of merchandise alone, there is not a Christian maritime nation of any extent, that has a smaller portion of its population engaged in trade of this sort, than the United States of America. The

nation, as a nation, is agricultural, though the state of transition, in which a country in the course of rapid settlement
must always exist, causes more buying and selling of real
property than is usual. Apart from this peculiarity, the
Americans, as a whole people, have not the common European proportions of ordinary dealers.''

" This is not the prevalent opinion," said Mr. Sharp.

" It is not, and the reason is, that all American towns, or
nearly all that are at all known in other countries, are
purely commercial towns. The trading portion of a community is always the concentrated portion, too; and of
course, in the absence of a court of a political, or of a social
capital, it has the greatest power to make itself heard and
felt, until there is a direct appeal to the other classes. The
elections commonly show quite as little sympathy between
the majority and the commercial class as is consistent with
the public welfare. In point of fact, America has but a very
small class of real merchants, men who are the cause and
not a consequence of commerce, though she has exceeding
activity in the way of ordinary traffic. The portion of her
people who are engaged as factors—for this is the true calling of the man who is a regular agent between the common
producer and the common consumer—are of *a* high class as
factors, but not of *the* high class of merchants. The man
who orders a piece of silk to be manufactured at Lyons, at
three francs a yard, to sell it in the regular course of the
season to the retailer at three francs and a half, is no more
a true merchant than the attorney, who goes through the
prescribed forms of the court in his pleadings, is a barrister."

" I do not think these sentiments will be very popular at
home, as Mr. Dodge says," Eve laughingly remarked; " but
when shall we reach that home? While we are talking of
these things, here are we, in an almost deserted ship, within
a mile of the great Desert of Sahara! How beautiful are
the stars, Mademoiselle! we have never before seen a vault
so studded with brilliants."

" That must be owing to the latitude," Mr. Sharp observed.

" Certainly. Can any one say in what latitude we are

precisely?" As Eve asked this question, she unconsciously turned towards Mr. Blunt; for the whole party had silently come to the conclusion that he knew more of ships and navigation than all of them united.

"I believe we are not far from twenty-four, which is bringing us near the tropics, and places us quite sixteen degrees to the southward of our port. These two affairs of the chase and of the gale have driven us fully twelve hundred miles from the course we ought to have taken."

"Fortunately, Mademoiselle, there are none to feel apprehensions on our account, or none whose interest will be so keen as to create a very lively distress. I hope, gentlemen, you are equally at ease on this score?"

This was the first time Eve had ever trusted herself to put an interrogatory that might draw from Paul Blunt any communication that would directly touch upon his connections. She repented of the speech as soon as made, but causelessly, as it drew from the young man no answer. Mr. Sharp observed that his friends in England could scarcely know of their situation, until his own letters would arrive to relieve their minds. As for Mademoiselle Viefville, the hard fortune which reduced her to the office of a governess, had almost left her without natural ties.

"I believe we are to have watch and ward to-night," resumed Eve, after the general pause had continued some little time. "Is it not possible for the elements to put us in the same predicament as that in which we found the poor Dane?"

"Possible, certainly, but scarcely probable," returned Mr. Blunt. "The ship is well moored, and this narrow ledge of rocks, between us and the ocean, serves admirably for a breakwater. One would not like to be stranded, helpless as we are at this moment, on a coast like this!"

"Why so particularly helpless? You allude to the absence of our crew?"

"To that, and to the fact that, I believe, we could not muster as much as a pocket-pistol to defend ourselves with, everything in the shape of fire-arms having been sent with the party in the boats."

"Might we not lie on the beach, here, for days, even weeks," inquired Mr. Sharp, "without being discovered by the Arabs?"

"I fear not. Mariners have told me that the barbarians hover along the shores, especially after gales, in the hope of meeting with wrecks, and it is surprising how soon they gain intelligence of any disaster. It is seldom there is even an opportunity to escape in a boat."

"I hope here, at least, we are safe?" cried Eve, in a little terror, and shuddering, as much in playfulness as in real alarm.

"I see no grounds of concern where we are, so long as we can keep the ship off the shore. The Arabs have no boats, and if they had, they would not dare to attack a vessel that floated, in one, unless aware of her being as truly helpless as we happen at this moment to be."

"This is a chilling consolation, but I shall trust in your good care, gentlemen. Mademoiselle, it is drawing near midnight, I believe."

Eve and her companion then courteously wished the two young men good night, and retired to their state-rooms; Mr. Sharp remained an hour longer with Mr. Blunt, who had undertaken to watch the first few hours, conversing with a light heart and gayly; for, though there was a secret consciousness of rivalry between these two young men on the subject of Eve's favor, it was a generous and manly competition, in which each did the other ample justice. They talked of their travels, their views of customs and nations, their adventures in different countries, and of the pleasure each had felt in visiting spots renowned by association or the arts; but not a word was hazarded by either concerning the young creature who had just left them, and whom each still saw in his mind's eye, long after her light and graceful form had disappeared. At length Mr. Sharp went below, his companion insisting on being left alone, under the penalty of remaining up himself during the second watch. From this time, for several hours, there was no other noise in the ship than the tread of the solitary watchman. At the appointed period of the night, a change took place, and he who had watched, slept; while he who had slept, watched. Just as day dawned, however, Paul Blunt, who was in a deep sleep, felt a shake at his shoulder.

"Pardon me," cautiously whispered Mr. Sharp, "I fear we are about to have a most unpleasant interruption to our solitude."

"Heavenly powers! Not the Arabs?"

"I fear no less : but it is still too dark to be certain of the fact. If you will rise, we can consult on the situation in which we are placed. I beg you to be quick."

Paul Blunt had hastily risen on an arm, and he now passed a hand over his brow, as if to make certain that he was awake. He had not undressed himself, and in another moment he stood on his feet in the middle of the state-room.

"This is too serious to allow of mistake. We will not alarm her, then ; we will not give any alarm, sir, until certain of the calamity."

"In that I entirely agree with you," returned Mr. Sharp, who was perfectly calm, though evidently distressed. "I may be mistaken, and wish your opinion. All on board but us two are in a profound sleep."

The other drew on his coat, and in a minute both were on deck. The day had not yet dawned, and the light was scarce sufficient to distinguish objects even near as those on the reef, particularly when they were stationary. The rocks themselves, however, were visible in places, for the tide was out, and most of the upper portion of the ledge was bare. The two gentlemen moved cautiously to the bows of the vessel, and, concealed by the bulwarks, Mr. Sharp pointed out to his companion the objects that had given him the alarm.

"Do you see the pointed rock a little to the right of the spot where the kedge is placed?" he said, pointing in the direction that he meant. "It is now naked, and I am quite certain there was an object on it, when I went below, that has since moved away."

"It may have been a sea-bird ; for we are so near the day, some of them are probably in motion. Was it large?"

"Of the size of a man's head, apparently ; but this is by

no means all. Here, farther to the north, I distinguished three objects in motion, wading in the water, near the point where the rocks are never bare.''

"They may have been herons; the bird is often found in these low latitudes, I believe. I can discover nothing.''

"I would to God, I may have been mistaken, though I do not think I could be so much deceived.''

Paul Blunt caught his arm, and held it like one who listened intently.

"Heard you that?'' he whispered hurriedly.

"It sounded like the clanking of iron.''

Looking around, the other found a handspike, and passing swiftly up the heel of the bowsprit, he stood between the knightheads. Here he bent forward and looked intently towards the lines of chains which lay over the bulwarks, as bow-fasts. Of these chains the parts led quite near each other, in parallel lines, and as the ship's moorings were taut, they were hanging in merely a slight curve. From the rocks, or the place where the kedges were laid to a point within thirty feet of the ship, these chains were dotted with living beings crawling cautiously upward. It was even easy, at a second look, to perceive that they were men stealthily advancing on their hands and feet.

Raising the handspike, Mr. Blunt struck the chains several violent blows. The effect was to cause the whole of the Arabs—for it could be no others—suddenly to cease advancing, and to seat themselves astride the chains.

"This is fearful,'' said Mr. Sharp: "but we must die rather than permit them to reach the ship.''

"We must. Stand you here, and if they advance, strike the chains. There is not an instant to lose.''

Paul Blunt spoke hurriedly, and, giving the other the handspike, he ran down to the bits, and commenced loosening the chains from their fastenings. The Arabs heard the clanking of the iron rings, as he threw coil after coil on the deck, and they did not advance. Presently two parts yielded together beneath them, and then two more. These were the signals for a common retreat, and Mr. Sharp now plainly counted fifteen human forms as they scrambled back towards the reef, some hanging by their arms, some half in the water, and others lying along the chains, as best they might. Mr. Blunt having loosened the chains, so as to let their bights fall into the sea, the ship slowly drifted astern, and rode by her cables. When this was done, the two young men stood together in silence on the forecastle, as if each felt that all which had just occurred was some illusion.

"This is indeed terrible," exclaimed Paul Blunt. "We have not even a pistol left! No means of defence—nothing but this narrow belt of water between us and these barbarians! No doubt, too, they have fire-arms; and, as soon as it is light, they will render it unsafe to remain on deck."

Mr. Sharp took the hand of his companion and pressed it fervently. "God bless you!" he said in a stifled voice. "God bless you for even this brief delay. But for this happy thought of yours, Miss Effingham—the others—we should *all* have been by this time at the mercy of these remorseless wretches. This is not a moment for false pride or pitiful deceptions. I think either of us would willingly die to rescue that beautiful and innocent creature from a fate like this which threatens her in common with ourselves!"

"Cheerfully would I lay down my life to be assured that she was, at this instant, safe in a civilized and Christian country."

These generous young men squeezed each other's hands, and at that moment no feeling of rivalry, or of competition even entered the heart of either. Both were influenced by a pure and ardent desire to serve the woman they loved; and it would be true to say, that scarce a thought of any but Eve was uppermost in their minds. Indeed, so engrossing was their common care in her behalf, so much more terrible than that of any other person did her fate appear on being captured, that they forgot, for a moment, there were others in the ship, and others, too, who might be serviceable in arresting the very calamity they dreaded.

"They may not be a strong party," said Paul Blunt, after a little thought; "in which case, failing of a surprise, they may not be able to muster a force sufficient to hazard an open attack until the return of the boats. We have, God be

praised ! escaped being seized in our sleep, and made un-
conscious victims of so cruel a fate. Fifteen or twenty will
scarcely dare attempt a ship of this size, without a perfect
knowledge of our feebleness, and particularly of our want of
arms. There is a light gun on board, and it is loaded ; with
this too we may hold them at bay, by not betraying our
weakness. Let us awake the others, for this is not a moment for sleep. We are safe at least for an hour or two ;
since, without boats, they cannot possibly find the means to
board us in less than that time.''

The two young men went below, unconsciously treading
lightly, like those who moved about in the presence of an
impending danger. Paul Blunt was in advance, and, to his
great surprise, he met Eve at the door of the ladies' cabin,
apparently waiting their approach. She was dressed, for
apprehension, and the novelty of their situation, had caused
her to sleep in most of her clothes, and a few moments had
sufficed for a hasty adjustment of the toilet. Miss Effingham was pale, but a concentration of all her energies seemed
to prevent the exhibition of any womanly terror.

"Something is wrong !" she said, trembling in spite of
herself, and laying her hand unwittingly on the arm of Paul
Blunt ; "I heard the heavy fall of iron on the deck."

"Compose yourself, dearest Miss Effingham, compose
yourself, I entreat you. I mean, that we have come to
awaken the gentlemen.''

"Tell me the worst, Powis, I implore you. I am equal,
—I think I am equal, to hearing it.''

"I fear your imagination has exaggerated the danger.''

"The coast ? ''

"Of that there is no cause for apprehension. The sea is
calm, and our fasts are perfectly good.''

"The boats ? ''

"Will doubtless be back in good time.''

"Surely—surely," said Eve, recoiling a step, as if she saw
a monster, "not the Arabs ? ''

"They cannot enter the ship, though a few of them are
hovering about us. But for the vigilance of Mr. Sharp, indeed, we might have all been captured in our sleep. As it

is, we have warning, and there is now little doubt of our being able to intimidate the few barbarians who have shown themselves, until Captain Truck shall return."

"Then from my soul, I thank you, Sir George Templemore, and for this good office will you receive the thanks of a father, and the prayers of all whom you have so signally served."

"Nay, Miss Effingham, although I find this interest in me so grateful that I have hardly the heart to lessen your gratitude, truth compels me to give it a juster direction. But for the promptitude of Mr. Blunt—or as I now find I ought to address him, Mr. Powis—we should truly have all been lost."

"We will not dispute about your merits, gentlemen. You have both deserved our most heartfelt thanks, and if you will awaken my father and Mr. John Effingham, I will arouse Mademoiselle Viefville and my own woman. Surely, surely, this is no time to sleep!"

The summons was given at the state-room doors, and the two young men returned to the deck, for they felt it was not safe to leave it long at such a moment. All was quite tranquil above, however, nor could the utmost scrutiny now detect the presence of any person on the reef.

"The rocks are cut off from the shore, farther to the southward by deeper water," said Paul Blunt—for we shall continue to call both gentlemen, except on particular occasions, by their *noms de guerre*—"and when the tide is up the place cannot be forded. Of this the Arabs are probably aware; and having failed in their first attempt, they will probably retire to the beach as the water is rising, for they might not like to be left on the ribbon of rock that will remain, in the face of the force that would be likely to be found in such a vessel."

"May they not be acquainted with the absence of most of our people, and be bent upon seizing the vessel before they can return?"

"That indeed is the gloomy side of the conjecture, and it may possibly be too true; but as the day is beginning to break, we shall soon learn the worst, and anything is better than vague distrust."

For some time the two gentlemen paced the quarter-deck together in silence. Mr. Sharp was first to speak.

"The emotions natural to such an alarm," he said, "have caused Miss Effingham to betray an incognito of mine, that I fear you find sufficiently absurd. It is quite accidental, I do assure you; as much so, perhaps, as it was motiveless."

"Except as you might distrust American democracy," returned Paul, smiling, "and feel disposed to propitiate it by a temporary sacrifice of rank and title."

"I declare you do me injustice. My man, whose name *is* Sharp, had taken the state-room, and, finding myself addressed by his appellation, I had the weakness to adopt it, under the impression it might be convenient in a packet. Had I anticipated, in the least, meeting with the Effinghams, I should not have been guilty of the folly, for Mr. and Miss Effingham are old acquaintances."

"While you are thus apologizing for a venial offence, you forget it is to a man guilty of the same error. I knew your person, from having seen you on the Continent; and finding you disposed to go by the homely name of Sharp, in a moment of thoughtlessness, I took its counterpart, Blunt. A travelling name is sometimes convenient, though sooner or later I fancy all deceptions bring with them their own punishments."

"It is certain that falsehood requires to be supported by falsehood. Having commenced in untruth, would it not be expedient to persevere until we reach America? I, at least, cannot now assert a right to my proper name, without deposing a usurper!"

"It will be expedient for you, certainly, if it be only to escape the homage of that doubled-distilled democrat, Mr. Dodge. As for myself, few care enough about me to render it a matter of moment how I am styled; though, on the whole, I should prefer to let things stand as they are, for reasons I cannot well explain."

No more was said on the subject, though both understood that the old appellations were to be temporarily continued. Just as this brief dialogue ended, the rest of the party ap-

peared on deck.  All preserved a forced calmness, though
the paleness of the ladies betrayed the intense anxiety they
felt.  Eve struggled with her fears on account of her father,
who had trembled so violently, when the truth was first told
him, as to be quite unmanned, but who now comported himself with dignity, though oppressed with apprehension almost
to anguish.  John Effingham was stern, and in the bitterness of his first sensations he had muttered a few impreca-
tions on his own folly, in suffering himself to be thus caught
without arms.  Once the terrible idea of the necessity of
sacrificing Eve, in the last resort, as an expedient preferable
to captivity, had flashed across his mind ; but the real tenderness he felt for her, and his better nature, soon banished
the unnatural thought.  Still, when he joined the party on
deck, it was with a general but vague impression, that the
moment was at hand when circumstances had required that
they were all to die together.  No one was more seemingly
collected than Mademoiselle Viefville.  Her life had been
one of sacrifices, and she had now made up her mind that it
was to pass away in a scene of violence ; and, with a species
of heroism that is national, her feelings had been aroused to
a sort of Roman firmness, and she was prepared to meet her
fate with a composure equal to that of the men.

These were the first feelings and impressions of those who
had been awakened from the security of the night, to hear
the tale of their danger ; but they lessened as the party collected in the open air, and began to examine into their situation by means of the steadily increasing light.  As the day
advanced, Paul Blunt, in particular, carefully examined the
rocks near the ship, even ascending to the foretop, from
which elevation he overlooked the whole line of the reef ;
and something like hope revived in every bosom, when he
proclaimed the joyful intelligence that nothing having life
was visible in that direction.

"God be praised!" he said with fervor, as his foot
touched the deck again on descending ; "we have at least
a respite from the attacks of these barbarians.  The tide
has risen so high that they dare not stay on the rocks, lest
they might be cut off ; for they probably think us stronger

than we are, and armed. The light gun on the forecastle is loaded, gentlemen, though not shotted ; for there are no shot in the vessel, Saunders tells me ; and I would suggest the propriety of firing it, both to alarm the Arabs, and as a signal to our friends. The distance from the wreck is not so great but it might be heard, and I think they would at least send a boat to our relief. Sound flies fast, and a short time may bring us succor. The water will not be low enough for our enemies to venture on the reef again, under six or eight hours, and all may yet be well."

This proposal was discussed, and it proving, on inquiry, that all the powder in the ship, after loading the gun for this very purpose of firing a signal, had been taken in the boats, and that no second discharge could be made, it was decided to lose no more time, but to let their danger be known to their friends at once, if it were possible to send the sound so far. When this decision was come to, Mr. Blunt, aided by Mr. Sharp, made the necessary preparations without delay. The latter, though doing all he could to assist, envied the readiness, practical skill, and intelligence, with which his companion, a man of cultivated and polished mind in higher things, performed every requisite act that was necessary to effect their purpose. Instead of hastily discharging the piece, an iron four-pound gun, Mr. Blunt first doubled the wad, which he drove home with all his force, and then he greased the muzzle, as he said, to increase the report.

" I shall not attempt to explain the philosophy of this," he added with a mournful smile, " but all lovers of salutes and salvos will maintain that it is useful ; and be it so or not, too much depends on our making ourselves heard, to neglect anything that has even a chance of aiding that one great object. If you will now assist me, Sir George, we will run the gun over to starboard, in order that it may be fired on the side next the wreck."

"Judging from the readiness you have shown on several occasions, as well as your familiarity with the terms, I should think you had served," returned the real baronet, as he helped his companion to place the gun at a port on the northern side of the vessel.

"You have not mistaken my trade. I was certainly bred, almost born, a seaman; and though as a traveller I have now been many years severed from my early habits, little of what I knew has been lost. Were there five others here who had so much familiarity as myself with vessels, I think we would carry the ship outside the reef, crippled as she is, and set the Arabs at defiance. Would to God our worthy captain had never brought her inside!"

"He did all for the best, no doubt."

"Beyond a question; and no more than a commendable prudence required. Still he has left us in a most critical position. This priming is a little damp, and I distrust it. The coal, if you please."

"Why do you not fire?"

"At the last moment, I almost repent of my own expedient. Is it quite certain no pistols remain among any of our effects?"

"I fear not. Saunders reports that all, even to those of the smallest size, were put in requisition for the boats."

"The charge in this gun might serve for many pistols, or for several fowling-pieces. I might even sweep the reef, on an emergency, by using old iron for shot! It appears like parting with a last friend, to part with this single precious charge of gunpowder."

"Nay, you certainly know best; though I rather think the Messrs. Effingham are of your first opinion."

"It is puerile to waver on such a subject, and I will hesitate no longer. There are moments when the air seems to float in the direction of our friends; on the first return of one of those currents, I will fire."

A minute brought the opportunity, and Paul Blunt, or Paul Powis, as his real name would now appear to be, applied the coal. The report was sharp and lively; but as the smoke floated away, he again expressed his doubts of the wisdom of what had just been done. Had he then known that the struggling sounds had diffused themselves in their radii, without reaching the wreck, his regrets would have been increased fourfold. This was a fact, however, that could not be then ascertained, and those in the packet were compelled to wait two or three hours before they even got the certainty of their failure.

As the light increased, a view was obtained of the shore, which seemed as silent and deserted as the reef. For half an hour the whole party experienced the revulsion of feeling that accompanies all great changes of emotion, and the conversation had even got to be again cheerful, and to turn into its former channels, when suddenly a cry from Saunders renewed the alarm. The steward was preparing the breakfast in the galley, from which he gave occasional glances towards the land, and his quick eye had been the first to detect a new and still more serious danger that now menaced them.

A long train of camels was visible, travelling across the desert, and holding its way towards the part of the reef which touched the shore. At this point, too, were now to be seen some twenty Arabs, waiting the arrival of their friends; among whom, it was fair to conclude, were those who had attempted to carry the ship by surprise. As the events which next followed were closely connected with the policy and forbearance of the party of barbarians near the wreck, this will be a suitable occasion to explain the motives of the latter, in not assailing Captain Truck, and the real state of things among these children of the desert.

The Dane had been driven ashore, as conjectured, in the last gale, and the crew had immediately been captured by a small wandering party of the Arabs, with whom the coast was then lined; as is usually the case immediately after tempestuous weather. Unable to carry off much of the cargo, this party had secured the prisoners, and hurried inland to an oasis, to give the important intelligence to their friends; leaving scouts on the shore, however, that they might be early apprised of any similar disaster, or of any change in the situation of their present prize. These scouts had discovered the Montauk, drifting along the coast, dismasted and crippled, and they had watched her to her anchorage within the reef. The departure of her boats had been witnessed, and though unable to foresee the whole

object of this expedition, the direction taken pointed out
the wreck as the point of destination. All this, of course,
had been communicated to the chief men of the different
parties on the coast, of which there were several, who had
agreed to unite their forces to secure the second ship, and
then to divide the spoils.

When the Arabs reached the coast near the wreck that
morning, the elders among them were not slow in compre-
hending the motives of the expedition; and having gained
a pretty accurate idea of the number of men employed
about the Dane, they had come to the just conclusion that
few were left in the vessel at anchor. They had carried
off the spy-glass of their prize, too, and several among them
knew its use, from having seen similar things in other
stranded ships. By means of this glass, they discovered
the number and quality of those on board the Montauk,
as soon as there was sufficient light, and directed their
own operations accordingly. The parties that had appeared
and disappeared behind the sandy ridges of the desert, about
the time at which we have now arrived in the narrative,
and those who have been already mentioned in a previous
chapter, were those who came from the interior, and those
who went in the direction of the reef; the first of the latter
of which Saunders had just discovered. Owing to the
rounded formation of the coast, and to the intervention of
a headland, the distance of water between the two ships
was quite double that by land between the two encamp-
ments, and those who now arrived abreast of the packet,
deliberately pitched their tents, as if they depended more
on a display of their numbers for success than on conceal-
ment, and as if they felt no apprehension of the return of
the crew.

When the gentlemen had taken a survey of this strong
party, which numbered more than a hundred, they held a
consultation of the course it would be necessary to pursue. To Paul Blunt, as an avowed seaman, and as one who
had already shown the promptitude and efficiency of his resources, all eyes were turned in expectation of an opinion.

"So long as the tide keeps in," this gentleman observed,

"I see no cause for apprehensions. We are beyond the reach of musketry; or at all events, any fire of the Arabs at this distance must be uncertain and harmless, and we have always the hope of the arrival of the boats. Should this fail us, and the tide fall this afternoon as low as it fell in the morning, our situation will indeed become critical. The water around the ship may possibly serve as a temporary protection, but the distance to the reef is so small that it might be passed by swimming."

"Surely we could make good the vessel against men raising themselves out of the water, and clambering up a vessel's side?" said Mr. Sharp.

"It is probable we might, if unmolested from the shore. But, imagine twenty or thirty resolute swimmers to put off together for different parts of the vessel, protected by the long muskets these Arabs carry, and you will easily conceive the hopelessness of any defence. The first man among us, who should show his person to meet the boarders, would be shot down like a dog."

"It was a cruel oversight to expose us to this horrible fate!" exclaimed the appalled father.

"This is easier seen now than when the mistake was committed," observed John Effingham. "As a seaman, and with his important object in view, Captain Truck acted for the best, and we should acquit him of all blame, let the result be what it may. Regrets are useless, and it remains for us to devise some means to arrest the danger by which we are menaced, before it be too late. Mr. Blunt, you must be our leader and counsellor; is it not possible for us to carry the ship outside of the reef, and to anchor her beyond the danger of our being boarded?"

"I have thought of this expedient, and if we had a boat it might possibly be done, in this mild weather; without a boat, it is impossible."

"But we have a boat," glancing his eye towards the launch that stood in the chocks or chucks.

"One that would be too unwieldy for our purposes, could it be got into the water; a thing in itself that would be almost impracticable for us to achieve."

20

A long silence succeeded, during which the gentlemen were occupied in the bootless effort of endeavoring to devise expedients to escape the Arabs ; bootless, because on such occasions, the successful measure is commonly the result of a sort of sudden inspiration, rather than of continued and laborious thought.

## CHAPTER XXII.

" With religious awe
Grief heard the voice of Virtue. No complaint
The solemn silence broke. Tears ceased to flow."

GLOVER.

HOPE is the most treacherous of all human fancies. So long as there is a plausible ground to expect relief from any particular quarter, men will relax their exertions in the face of the most imminent danger, and they cling to their expectations long after reason has begun to place the chances of success on the adverse side of the scale. Thus it was with the party in the Montauk. Two or three precious hours were lost in the idle belief that the gun would be heard by Captain Truck, and that they might momentarily look for the appearance of, at least, one of the boats.

Paul Blunt was the first to relinquish this delusion. He knew that, if it reached their friends at all, the report must have been heard in a few seconds, and he knew, also, that it peculiarly belonged to the profession of a seaman to come to quick decisions. An hour of smart rowing would bring the cutter from the wreck to the headland, where it would be visible, by means of a glass, from the foretop. Two hours had now passed away and no signs of any boat were to be discovered, and the young man felt reluctantly compelled to yield all the strong hopes of timely aid that he had anticipated from this quarter. John Effingham, who had much more energy of character than his kinsman though not more personal fortitude and firmness, was watching the movements of their young leader, and he read the severe disappointment in his face, as he descended the last time from the top, where he had often been since the consultation, to look out for the expected succor.

"I see it in your countenance," said that gentleman; "we have nothing to look for from the boats. Our signal has not been heard."

"There is no hope, and we are now thrown altogether on our own exertions, aided by the kind providence of God."

"This calamity is so sudden and so dire, that I can scarcely credit it! Are we then truly in danger of becoming prisoners to barbarians? Is Eve Effingham, the beautiful, innocent, good, angelic daughter of my cousin, to be their victim!—perhaps the inmate of a seraglio!"

"There is the pang! Had I a thousand bodies, a thousand lives, I could give all of the first to unmitigated suffering—lay down all the last to avert so shocking a calamity. Do you think the ladies are sensible of their real situation?"

"They are uneasy rather than terrified. In common with us all, they have strong hopes from the boats, though the continued arrival of the barbarians, who are constantly coming into their camp, has helped to render them a little more conscious of the true nature of the danger."

Here Mr. Sharp, who stood on the hurricane-house, called out for the glass, in order to ascertain what a party of the Arabs, who were collected near the in-shore end of the reef, were about. Paul Blunt went up to him, and made the examination. His countenance fell as he gazed, and an expression like that of hopelessness was again apparent on his fine features, when he lowered the glass.

"Here is some new cause of uneasiness!"

"The wretches have got a number of spars, and are lashing them together to form a raft. They are bent on our capture, and I see no means of preventing it."

"Were we alone, men only, we might have the bitter consolation of selling our lives dearly; but it is terrible to have those with us whom we can neither save nor yet devote to a common destruction with our enemies!"

"It is indeed terrible, and the helplessness of our situation adds to its misery."

"Can we not offer terms? Might not a promise of ransom, with hostages, do something? I would cheerfully remain in the hands of the barbarians, in order to effect the release of the rest of the party."

Mr. Blunt grasped his hand, and for a moment he envied the other the generous thought. But smiling bitterly, he shook his head, as if conscious of the futility of even this desperate self-devotion.

"Gladly would I be your companion; but the project is, in every sense, impracticable. Ransom they might consent to receive with us all in their power, but not on the condition of our being permitted to depart. Indeed, no means of quitting them would be left; for once in possession of the ship, as in a few hours they must be, Captain Truck, though having the boats, will be obliged to surrender for want of food, or to run the frightful hazard of attempting to reach the islands, on an allowance scarcely sufficient to sustain life under the most favorable circumstances. These flint-hearted monsters are surrounded by the desolation of their desert, and they are aware of all their appalling advantages."

"The real state of things ought to be communicated to our friends, in order that they may be prepared for the worst."

To this Mr. Blunt agreed, and they went together to inform John Effingham of the new discovery. This stern-minded man was, in a manner, prepared for the worst, and he now agreed on the melancholy propriety of letting his kinsman know the actual nature of the new danger that threatened them.

"I will undertake this unpleasant office," he said, "though I could, in my inmost soul, pray that the necessity for it might pass away. Should the worst arrive, I have still hopes of effecting something by means of a ransom; but what will have been the fate of the youthful, and delicate, and lovely, ere we can make ourselves even comprehended by the barbarians? A journey in the desert, as these journeys have been described to me, would be almost certain death to all but the strongest of our party, and even gold may fail of its usual power, when weighed against the evil nature of savages.''

"Is there no hope, then, really left us?" demanded Mr. Sharp, when the last speaker had left them to descend to the cabins. "Is it not possible to get the boat into the water, and to make our escape in that?"

"That is an expedient of which I have thought, but it is next to impracticable. As anything is better than capture, however, I will make one more close examination of the proceedings of the demons, and look nearer into our own means."

Paul Blunt now got a lead and dropped it over the side of the ship, in the almost forlorn hope that possibly she might lie over some hole on the bottom. The soundings proved to be, as indeed he expected, but a little more than three fathoms.

"I had no reason to expect otherwise," he said, as he drew in the line, though he spoke like a disappointed man. "Had there been sufficient water the ship might have been scuttled, and the launch would have floated off the deck; but as it is, we should lose the vessel without a sufficient object. It would appear heroic were you and I to contrive to get on the reef, and to proceed to the shore with a view to make terms with the Arabs; but there could be no real use in it, as the treachery of their character is too well established to look for any benefit from such a step."

"Might they not be kept in play, until our friends returned? Providence may befriend us in some unexpected manner in our uttermost peril."

"We will examine them once more with the glass. By a movement among the Arabs, there has probably been a new accession to their numbers."

The two gentlemen now ascended to the top of the hurricane-house again, in feverish haste, and once more they applied the instrument. A minute of close study induced Mr. Blunt to drop the glass, with an expression that denoted increased concern.

"Can anything possibly make our prospects worse?" eagerly inquired his companion.

" Do you not remember a flag that was on board the Dane —that by which we identified his nation ?"

" Certainly : it was attached to the halyards, and lay on the quarter-deck."

" The flag is now flying in the camp of these barbarians ! You may see it, here, among the tents last pitched by the party that arrived while we were conversing forward."

" And from this you infer—"

" That our people are captives ! That flag was in the ship when we left it ; had the Arabs returned before our party got there, the captain would have been back long ere this ; and in order to obtain this ensign they must have obtained possession of the wreck, after the arrival of the boats ; an event that could scarcely occur without a struggle : I fear the flag is a proof on which side the victory has fallen."

" This then would seem to consummate our misfortunes !"

" It does indeed ; for the faint hope that existed, of being relieved by the boats, must now be entirely abandoned."

" In the name of God, look again, and see in what con-dition the wretches have got their raft !"

A long examination followed, for on this point did the fate of all in the ship now truly seem to depend.

" They work with spirit," said Mr. Blunt, when his ex-amination had continued a long time ; " but it seems less like a raft than before—they are lashing spars together length-wise—here is a dawning of hope, or what would be hope, rather, if the boats had escaped their fangs !"

" God bless you for the words !—what is there encour-aging ? "

" It is not much," returned Paul Blunt, with a mournful smile ; " but trifles become of account in moments of ex-treme jeopardy. They are making a floating stage, doubt-less with the intention to pass from the reef to the ship, and by veering on the chains we may possibly drop astern sufficiently to disappoint them in the length of their bridge. If I saw a hope of the final return of the boats, this expedi-ent would not be without its use, particularly if delayed to the last moment, as it might cause the Arabs to lose another tide ; and a reprieve of eight or ten hours is an age to men in our situation.''

Mr. Sharp caught eagerly at this suggestion, and the young men walked the deck together for half an hour, discussing its chances, and suggesting various means of turning it to the best account. Still, both felt convinced that the trifling delay which might thus be obtained would, in the end, be perfectly useless, should Captain Truck and his party have really fallen into the hands of the common enemy. They were thus engaged, sometimes in deep despondency, and sometimes buoyant with revived expectations, when Saunders, on the part of Mr. Effingham, summoned them below.

On reaching the cabin, whither both immediately hastened, the two gentlemen found the family party in the distress that the circumstances would naturally create. Mr. Effingham was seated, his daughter's head resting on a knee, for she had thrown herself on the carpet, by his side. Mademoiselle Viefville paced the cabin, occasionally stopping to utter a few words of consolation to her young charge, and then again reverting in her mind to the true dangers of their situation, with a force that completely undid all she had said, by betraying the extent of her own apprehensions. Ann Sidley knelt near her young mistress, sometimes praying fervently, though in silence, and at other moments folding her beloved in her arms, as if to protect her from the ruffian grasp of the barbarians. The *femme de chambre* was sobbing in a state-room, while John Effingham leaned with his arms folded against a bulkhead, a picture of stern submission rather than of despair. The whole party was now assembled, with the exception of the steward, whose lamentations throughout the morning had not been noiseless, but who was left on deck to watch the movements of the Arabs.

The moment was not one of idle forms, and Eve Effingham, who would have recoiled, under other circumstances, at being seen by her fellow-travellers in her present situation, scarce raised her head, in acknowledgment of their melancholy salute, as they entered. She had been weeping, and her hair had fallen in profusion around her shoulders. The tears fell no longer, but a warm, flushed look, one which denoted that a struggle of the mind had gotten the better of womanly emotions, had succeeded to deadly paleness, and rendered her loveliness of feature and expression bright and angelic. Both of the young men thought she had never seemed so beautiful, and both felt a secret pang, as the conviction forced itself on them, at the same instant, that this surpassing beauty was now likely to prove her most dangerous enemy.

"Gentlemen," said Mr. Effingham, with apparent calmness, and a dignity that no uneasiness could disturb, "my kinsman has acquainted us with the hopeless nature of our condition, and I have begged the favor of this visit on your own account. *We* cannot separate; the ties of blood and affection unite us, and our fate must be common; but, on *you* there is no such obligation. Young, bold, and active, some plan may suggest itself, by which you may possibly escape the barbarians, and at least save yourselves. I know that generous temperaments like yours will not be disposed to listen, at first, to such a suggestion; but reflection will tell you that it is for the interest of us all. You may let our fate be known earlier than it otherwise would be, to those who will take immediate measures to procure our ransoms."

"This is impossible!" Mr. Sharp said firmly. "We can never quit you; could never enjoy a moment's peace under the consciousness of having been guilty of an act so selfish!"

"Mr. Blunt is silent," continued Mr. Effingham, after a short pause, in which he looked from one of the young men to the other. "He thinks better of my proposition, and will listen to his own best interests."

Eve raised her head quickly, but without being conscious of the anxiety she betrayed, and gazed with melancholy intentness at the subject of this remark.

"I do credit to the generous feelings of Mr. Sharp," Paul Blunt now hurriedly answered, "and should be sorry to admit that my own first impulses were less disinterested;

but I confess I have already thought of this, and have
reflected on all the chances of success or failure. It might
be practicable for one who can swim easily to reach the
reef; thence to cross the inlet, and possibly to gain the
shore under the cover of the opposite range of rocks, which
are higher than those near us ; after which, by following the
coast, one might communicate with the boats by signal, or
even go quite to the wreck, if necessary. All of this I
have deliberated on, and once I had determined to propose
it ; but—"

"But what?" demanded Eve quickly. "Why not execute this plan, and save yourself? Is it a reason, because
our case is hopeless, that you should perish? Go, then, at
once, for the moments are precious ; an hour hence, it may
be too late."

"Were it merely to save myself, Miss Effingham, do you
really think me capable of this baseness?"

"I do not call it baseness. Why should we draw you
down with us in our misery? You have already served
us, Powis, in a situation of terrible trial, and it is not just
that you should always devote yourself in behalf of those
who seem fated never to do you good. My father will tell
you he thinks it your duty now to save yourself, if possible."

"I think it the duty of every man," mildly resumed Mr.
Effingham, "when no imperious obligation requires otherwise, to save the life and liberty which God has bestowed.
These gentlemen have doubtless ties and claims on them
that are independent of us, and why should they inflict a
pang on those who love them, in order to share in our disaster?"

"This is placing useless speculations before a miserable
certainty," observed John Effingham. "As there can be
no hope of reaching the boats, it is vain to discuss the propriety of the step."

"Is this true, Powis? Is there truly no chance of your
escaping? You will not deceive us—deceive yourself—on a
vain point of empty pride!"

"I can say with truth, almost with joy, for I thank God
I am spared the conflict of judging between my duty and

my feelings, that there can no longer be any chance of finding the wreck in the possession of our friends," returned Paul fervently. "There were moments when I thought the attempt should be made; and it would perhaps have properly fallen to my lot to be the adventurer; but we have now proof that the Arabs are masters; and if Captain Truck has escaped at all, it is under circumstances that scarcely admit the possibility of his being near the land. The whole coast must be watched and in possession of the barbarians, and one passing along it could hardly escape being seen."

"Might you not escape into the interior, notwithstanding?" asked Eve, impetuously.

"With what motive? To separate myself from those who have been my fellows in misfortune, only to die of want, or to fall into the hands of another set of masters? It is every way our interest to keep together, and to let those already on the coast become our captors, as the booty of two ships may dispose them to be less exacting with their prisoners."

"Slaves!" muttered John Effingham.

His cousin bowed his head over the delicate form of Eve, which he folded with his arms, as if to shield it from the blasts and evils of the desert.

"As we may be separated immediately on being taken" resumed Paul Blunt, "it will be well to adopt some common mode of acting, and a uniform account of ourselves, in order that we may impress the barbarians with the policy of carrying us, as soon as possible, into the vicinity of Mogadore, with a view to obtaining a speedy ransom."

"Can anything be better than the holy truth?" exclaimed Eve. "No, no, no! Let us not deform this chastening act of God, by coloring any thought or word with deception."

"Deception in our case will hardly be needed; but by understanding those facts which will most probably influence the Arabs, we may dwell the most on them. We cannot do better than by impressing on the minds of our captors the circumstance that this is no common ship, a fact their

own eyes will corroborate, and that we are not mere
mariners, but passengers, who will be likely to reward their
forbearance and moderation."

"I think, sir," interrupted Ann Sidley, looking up with
tearful eyes from the spot where she still knelt, "that if
these people knew how much Miss Eve is sought and
beloved, they might be led to respect her as she deserves
and this at least would 'temper the wind to the shorn
lamb'!"

"Poor Nanny!" murmured Eve, stretching forth a hand
towards her old nurse, though her face was still buried in
her own hair, "thou wilt soon learn that there is another
leveller besides the grave!"

"Ma'am!"

"Thou wilt find that Eve, in the hands of barbarians, is
not thy Eve. It will now become my turn to become a
handmaiden, and to perform for others offices a thousand
times more humiliating than any thou hast ever performed
for me."

Such a consummation of their misery had never struck
the imagination of the simple-minded Ann, and she gazed
at her child with tender concern, as if she distrusted her
senses.

"This is too improbable, dear Miss Eve," she said, "and
you will distress your father by talking so wildly. The
Arabs are human beings though they are barbarians, and
they will never dream of anything so wicked as this."

Mademoiselle Viefville made a rapid and fervent ejacula-
tion in her own language, that was keenly expressive of
her own sense of misery, and Ann Sidley, who always felt
uneasiness when anything was said affecting Eve that she
could not understand, looked from one to the other, as if
she demanded an explanation.

"I'm sure Mamerzelle cannot think any such thing likely
to take place," she continued, more positively; "and, sir,
you at least will not permit Miss Eve to torment herself
with any notions as unreasonable, as monstrous as this!"

"We are in the hands of God, my worthy Ann, and you
may live to see all your fixed ideas of propriety violated,"

returned Mr. Effingham. "Let us pray that we may not be separated, for there will at least be a tender consolation in being permitted to share our misery in company. Should we be torn asunder, then indeed will the infliction be one of insupportable agony."

"And who will think of such a cruelty, sir? *Me* they cannot separate from Miss Eve, for I am her servant, her own long-tried, faithful attendant, who first held her in arms, and nursed her when a helpless infant; and you too, sir, you are her father, her own beloved, revered parent; and Mr. John, is he not her kinsman, of her blood and name? And even Marmerzelle also has claims to remain with Miss Eve, for she has taught her many things, I dare say, that it is good to know. O! no, no, no! no one has a right to tear us asunder, and no one will have the heart to do it."

"Nanny, Nanny," murmured Eve, "you do not, cannot know the cruel Arabs!"

"They cannot be crueller and more unforgiving than our own savages, ma'am, and they keep the mother with the child; and when they spare life, they take the prisoners into their huts, and treat them as they treat their own. God has caused so many of the wicked to perish for their sins, in these eastern lands, that I do not think a man can be left that is wretch enough to harm one like Miss Eve. Take courage then, sir, and put your trust in his holy providence. I know the trial is hard to a tender father's heart, but should their customs require them to keep the men and women asunder, and to separate you from your daughter, for a short time, remember that I shall be with her, as I was in her childhood, when, by the mercy of God, we carried her through so many mortal diseases in safety, and have got her, in the pride of her youth, without a blemish or a defect, the perfect creature she is."

"If the world had no other tenants but such as you, devoted and simple-hearted woman, there would indeed be little cause for apprehension; for you are equally unable to imagine wrong yourself, or to conceive it in others. It would remove a mountain from my heart, could I indeed believe that even you will be permitted to remain near this dependent and fragile girl during the months of suffering and anguish that are likely to occur."

"Father," said Eve, hurriedly drying her eyes, and rising to her feet with a motion so easy, and an effort so slight, that it appeared like the power of mere volition—the superiority of the spirit over her light frame—"father, do not let a thought of me distress you at this awful moment. You have known me only in happiness and prosperity, an indulged and indolent girl; but I feel a force which is capable of sustaining me, even in this blank desert. The Arabs can have no other motive than to preserve us all, as captives likely to repay their care with a rich ransom. I know that a journey, according to their habits, will be painful and arduous, but it may be borne. Trust, then, more to my spirit than to my feeble body, and you will find that I am not as worthless as I fear you fancy."

Mr. Effingham passed his arm around the slender waist of his child and folded her almost frantically to his bosom. But Eve was aroused, and, gently extricating herself, with bright but tearless eyes, she looked around at her companions, as if she would reverse the order of their sympathies, and draw them to their own wants and hazards.

"I know you think me the most exposed by this dreadful disaster," she said; "that I may not be able to bear up against the probable suffering, and that I shall sink first, because I am the feeblest and frailest in frame; but God permits the reed to bend, when the oak is destroyed. I am stronger, able to bear more than you imagine, and we shall all live to meet again, in happier scenes, should it be our present hard fortune to be separated."

As Eve spoke, she cast affectionate looks on those dear to her by habit, and blood, and services; nor did she permit an unnecessary reserve at such a moment to prevent glances of friendly interest towards the two young men, whose very souls seemed wrapped in her movements. Words of encouragement from such a source, however, only served to set the frightful truth more vividly before the minds of her auditors, and not one of them heard what she said who did not feel an awful presentiment that a few weeks of the suffering of which she made so light, did she even escape a crueller fate, would consign that form, now so winning and lovely, to the sands. Mr. Effingham now arose, and for the first time the flood of sensations that had been so long gathering in his bosom, seemed ready to burst through the restraints of manhood. Struggling to command himself, he turned to his two young male companions, and spoke with an impressiveness and dignity that carried with them a double force, from the fact of his ordinary manners being so tempered and calm.

"Gentlemen," he said, "we may serve each other, by coming to an understanding in time; or at least you may confer on me a favor that a life of gratitude would not repay. You are young and vigorous, bold and intelligent, qualities that will command the respect of even savages. The chances that one of you will survive to reach a Christian land are much greater than those of a man of my years, borne down as I shall be with the never-dying anxieties of a parent!"

"Father! father!"

"Hush! darling: let me entreat these gentlemen to bear us in mind, should they reach a place of safety; for, after all, youth may do that in your behalf, which time will deny to John and myself. Money will be of no account, you know, to rescue my child from a fate far worse than death, and it may be some consolation to you, young men, to recollect, at the close of your own careers, which I trust will yet be long and happy, that a parent in his last moments found a consolation in the justifiable hopes he had placed on your generous exertions."

"Father, I cannot bear this! For you to be the victim of these barbarians is too much; and I would prefer trusting all to a raft on the terrible ocean, to incurring the smallest chance of such a calamity. Mademoiselle, you will join me in the entreaty to the gentlemen to prepare a few planks to receive us, where we can perish together, and at least have the consolation of knowing that our eyes will be closed by friends. The longest survivor will be surrounded and supported by the spirits of those who have gone before, into a world devoid of care."

"I have thought this from the first," returned Mademoiselle Viefville in French, with an energy of manner that betokened a high and resolved character: "I would not expose gentlewomen to the insults and outrages of barbarians; but did not wish to make a proposition that the feelings of others might reject."

"It is a thousand times preferable to capture, if indeed it be practicable," said John Effingham, looking inquiringly towards Paul. The latter, however, shook his head in the negative, for, the wind blowing on shore, he knew it would be merely meeting captivity without the appearance of a self-reliance and dignity, that might serve to impress their captors favorably.

"It is impossible," said Eve, reading the meaning of the glances, and dropping on her knees before Mr. Effingham; "well, then, may our trust be in God! We have yet a few minutes of liberty, and let them not be wasted idly, in vain regrets. Father, kiss me, and give me once more that holy and cherished blessing, with which you used to consign me to sleep, in those days when we scarce dreamed of, never realized, misfortune."

"Bless you, bless you, my babe; my beloved, my cherished Eve!" said the father, solemnly, but with a quivering lip. "May that dread Being, whose ways, though mysterious, are perfect wisdom and mercy, sustain you in this trial, and bring you at last, spotless in spirit and person, to his own mansions of peace. God took from me early thy sainted mother, and I had impiously trusted in the hope that thou wert left to be my solace in age. Bless you, my Eve; I shall pray God, without ceasing, that thou mayest pass away as pure and as worthy of his love as her to whom thou owest thy being."

John Effingham groaned; the effort he made to repress his feelings causing the out-breaking of his soul to be deep, though smothered.

"Father, let us pray together. Ann, my good Ann, thou who first taught me to lisp a thanksgiving and a request, kneel here by my side—and you, too, Mademoiselle; though of a different creed, we have a common God! Cousin John,

you pray often, I know, though so little apt to show your
emotions ; there is a place for you, too, with those of your
blood. I know not whether these gentlemen are too proud
to pray."

Both the young men knelt with the others, and there was
a long pause in which the whole party put up their supplications, each according to his or her habits of thought.

"Father!" resumed Eve, looking up as she still knelt
between the knees of Mr. Effingham, and smiling fondly in
the face of him she so piously loved, "there is one precious
hope of which even the barbarians cannot rob us: we
may be separated here, but our final meeting rests only with
God!"

Mademoiselle Viefville passed an arm round the waist of
her sweet pupil, and pressed her against her heart.

"There is but one abode for the blessed, my dear Mademoiselle, and one expiation for us all." Then rising from
her knees, Eve said, with the grace and dignity of a gentlewoman, "Cousin Jack, kiss me; we know not when another
occasion may offer to manifest to each other our mutual
regard. You have been a dear and an indulgent kinsman to
me, and should I live these twenty years a slave, I shall not
cease to think of you with kindness and regret."

John Effingham folded the beautiful and ardent girl in his
arms, with the freedom and fondness of a parent.

"Gentlemen," continued Eve, with a deepening color, but
eyes that were kind and grateful, "I thank you, too, for
lending your supplications to ours. I know that young men
in the pride of their security, seldom fancy such a dependence
on God necessary ; but the strongest are overturned, and
pride is a poor substitute for the hope of the meek. I believe you have thought better of me than I merit, and I
should never cease to reproach myself with a want of consideration, did I believe that anything more than accident
has brought you into this ill-fated vessel. Will you permit
me to add one more obligation to the many I feel to you
both?" advancing nearer to them, and speaking lower;
"you are young, and likely to endure bodily exposure
better than my father—that we shall be separated I feel per-

suaded—and it might be in your power to solace a heart-broken parent.    I see, I know, I may depend on your good offices.''

"Eve—my blessed daughter—my only, my beloved child !'' exclaimed Mr. Effingham, who overheard her lowest syllable, so death-like was the stillness of the cabin, "come to me, dearest, no power on earth shall ever tear us asunder ! ''

Eve turned quickly, and beheld the arms of her parent extended.    She threw herself into them, when the pent and irresistible emotions broke loose in both, for they wept together, as she lay on his bosom, with a violence that in a man it was awfully painful to witness.

Mr. Sharp had advanced to take the offered hand of Eve, when she suddenly left him for the purpose just mentioned, and he now felt the grasp of Paul's fingers on his arm, as if they were about to penetrate the bone.    Fearful of betraying the extent of their feelings, the two young men rushed on deck together, where they paced backward and forward for many minutes, quite unable to exchange a word or even a syllable.

## CHAPTER XXIII.

"O Domine Deus! speravi in te,
  O care mi Jesu, nunc libera me!
    In durâ catenâ,
    In miserâ pœnâ,
      Desidero te :
    Languendo, gemendo,
    Et genuflectendo,
  Adoro, imploro, ut liberes me."

*Mary Queen of Scots.*

THE sublime consolations of religion were little felt by either of the two generous-minded and ardent young men who were pacing the deck of the Montauk. The gentle and the plastic admit the most readily of the divine influence; and of all on board the devoted vessel at that moment, they who were the most resigned to their fate were those who by their physical force were the least able to endure it.

"This heavenly resignation," said Mr. Sharp, half whispering, "is even more heart-rending than the out-breakings of despair."

"It is frightful!" returned his companion. "Anything is better than passive submission in such circumstances. I see but little, indeed, no hope of escape; but idleness is torture. If I endeavor to raise this boat, will you aid me?"

"Command me like your slave. Would to Heaven there were the faintest prospects of success!"

"There is but little; and should we even succeed, there are no means of getting far from the ship in the launch, as all the oars have been carried off by the captain, and I can hear of neither masts nor sails. Had we the latter, with this wind which is beginning to blow, we might indeed prolong the uncertainty, by getting on some of those more distant spits of sand."

"Then, in the name of the blessed Maria!" exclaimed one behind them, in French, "delay not an instant, and all on board will join in the labor!"

The gentlemen turned in surprise, and beheld Mademoiselle Viefville standing so near them as to have overheard their conversation. Accustomed to depend on herself, coming of a people among whom woman is more energetic and useful, perhaps, than in any other Christian nation, and resolute of spirit naturally, this cultivated and generous female had come on deck purposely to see if indeed there remained no means by which they might yet escape the Arabs. Had her knowledge of a vessel at all equalled her resolution, it is probable that many fruitless expedients would already have been adopted; but finding herself in a situation so completely novel as that of a ship, until now she had found no occasion to suggest anything to which her companions would be likely to lend themselves. But, seizing the hint of Paul, she pressed it on him with ardor, and, after a few minutes of urging, by her zeal and persuasion she prevailed on the two gentlemen to commence the necessary preparations without further delay. John Effingham and Saunders were immediately summoned by Mademoiselle Viefville herself, who, once engaged in the undertaking, pursued it fervently, while she went in person into the cabins to make the necessary preparations connected with their subsistence and comforts, should they actually succeed in quitting the vessel.

No experienced mariner could set about the work with more discretion, or with a better knowledge of what was necessary to be done, than Mr. Blunt now showed. Saunders was directed to clear the launch, which had a roof on it, and still contained a respectable provision of poultry, sheep, and pigs. The roof he was told not to disturb, since it might answer as a substitute for a deck; but everything was passed rapidly from the inside of the boat, which the steward commenced scrubbing and cleaning with an assiduity that he seldom manifested in his cabins. Fortunately, the tackles with which Mr. Leach had raised the sheers and stepped the jury-mast the previous morning were still lying on the deck, and Paul was spared the labor of reeving new ones. He went to work, therefore, to get up two on the substitute for a mainstay ; a job that he had completed, through the aid of the two gentlemen on deck, by the time Saunders pronounced the boat to be in a fit condition to receive its cargo. The gripes were now loosened, and the fall of one of the tackles was led to the capstan.

By this time Mademoiselle Viefville, by her energy and decision, had so far aroused Eve and her woman, that Mr. Effingham had left his daughter, and appeared on deck among those who were assisting Paul. So intense was the interest, however, which all took in the result, that the ladies, and even Ann Sidley, with the *femme de chambre*, suspended their own efforts, and stood clustering around the capstan as the gentlemen began to heave, almost breathless between their doubts and hopes : for it was a matter of serious question whether there was sufficient force to lift so heavy a body at all. Turn after turn was made, the fall gradually tightening, until those at the bars felt the full strain of their utmost force.

"Heave together, gentlemen," said Paul Blunt, who directed everything, besides doing so much with his own hands. "We have its weight now, and all we gain is so much towards lifting the boat."

A steady effort was continued for two or three minutes, with but little sensible advantage, when all stopped for breath.

"I fear it will surpass our strength," observed Mr. Sharp. "The boat seems not to have moved, and the ropes are stretched in a way to menace parting."

"We want but the force of a boy added to our own," said Paul, looking doubtingly towards the females ; "in such cases, a pound counts for a ton."

"*Allons !*" cried Mademoiselle Viefville, motioning to the *femme de chambre* to follow ; "we will not be defeated for the want of such a trifle."

These two resolute women applied their strength to the bars, and the power, which had been so equally balanced, preponderated in favor of the machine. The capstan, which a moment before was scarcely seen to turn, and that only by short and violent efforts, now moved steadily but slowly round, and the end of the launch rose. Eve was only prevented from joining the laborers by Nanny, who held her folded in her arms, fearful that some accident might occur to injure her.

Paul Blunt now cheerfully announced the certainty that they had a force sufficient to raise the boat, though the operation would still be long and laborious. We say, cheerfully; for while this almost unhoped-for success promised little relief in the end, there is always something buoyant and encouraging in success of any sort.

"We are masters of the boat," he said, "provided the Arabs do not molest us; and we may drift away, by means of some contrivance of a sail, to such a distance as will keep us out of their power, until all chance of seeing our friends again is finally lost."

"This, then, is a blessed relief!" exclaimed Mr. Effingham; "and God may yet avert from us the bitterest portion of this calamity!"

The pent emotions again flowed, and Eve once more wept in her father's arms, a species of holy joy mingling with her tears. In the meantime, Paul having secured the fall by which they had just been heaving, brought the other to the capstan, when the operation was renewed with the same success. In this manner in the course of half an hour the launch hung suspended from the stay, at a sufficient height to apply the yard-tackles. As the latter, however, were not aloft, Paul having deemed it wise to ascertain their ability to lift the boat at all, before he threw away so much toil, the females renewed their preparations in the cabins, while the gentlemen assisted the young sailor in getting up the purchases. During this pause in the heaving, Saunders was sent below to search for sails and masts, both of which Paul thought must be somewhere in the ship, as he found the launch was fitted to receive them.

It was apparent, in the meantime, that the Arabs watched their proceedings narrowly ; for the moment Paul appeared on the yard a great movement took place among them, and several muskets were discharged in the direction of the ship, though the distance rendered the fire harmless. The gentlemen observed with concern, however, that the balls passed the vessel, a fearful proof of the extraordinary power of the arms used by these barbarians. Luckily the reef, which by this time was nearly bare ahead of the ship, was still covered in a few places nearer to the shore to a depth that forbade a passage, except by swimming. John Effing-ham, however, who was examining the proceedings of the Arabs with a glass, announced that a party appeared dis-posed to get on the naked rocks nearest the ship, as they had left the shore, dragging some light spars after them, with which they seemed to be about to bridge the different spots of deep water, most of which were sufficiently narrow to admit of being passed in this manner.

Although the operation commenced by the Arabs would necessarily consume a good deal of time, this intelligence quickened the movements of all in the ship. Saunders, in particular, who had returned to report his want of success, worked with redoubled zeal ; for, as is usual with those who are the least fortified by reason, he felt the greatest horror of falling into the hands of barbarians. It was a slow and laborious thing, notwithstanding, to get upon the yards the heavy blocks and falls ; and had not Paul Blunt been quite as conspicuous for personal strength as he was ready and expert in a knowledge of his profession, he would not have succeeded in the unaided effort ; unaided aloft, though the others, of course, relieved him much by working at the whips on deck. At length this important arrangement was effected, the young man descended, and the capstan was again manned.

This time the females were not required, it being in the power of the gentlemen to heave the launch out to the side of the ship, Paul managing the different falls so adroitly, that the heavy boat was brought so near, and yet so much above the rail, as to promise to clear it. John Effingham now stood at one of the stay-tackle falls, and Paul at the other, when the latter made a signal to ease away. The launch settled slowly towards the side of the vessel until it reached the rail, against which it lodged. Catching a turn with his fall, Mr Blunt sprang forward, and bending beneath the boat, he saw that its keel had hit a belaying-pin. One blow from a capstan-bar cleared away this obstruction, and the boat swung off. The stay-tackle falls were let go entirely, and all on board saw, with an exultation that words can scarcely describe, the important craft suspended directly over the sea. No music ever sounded more sweetly to the listeners than the first plash of the massive boat as it fell heavily upon the surface of the water. Its size, its roof, and its great strength gave it an appearance of security, that for a moment deceived them all; for, in contemplating the advantage they had so unexpectedly gained, they forgot the many obstacles that existed to their availing themselves of it.

It was not many minutes before Paul was on the roof of the launch, had loosened the tackles, and had breasted the boat to, at the side of the ship, in readiness to receive the stores that the females had collected. In order that the reader may better understand the nature of the ark that was about to receive those who remained in the Montauk, however, it may be well to describe it.

The boat itself was large, strong, and capable of resisting a heavy sea when well managed, and, of course, unwieldy in proportion. To pull it, at a moderate rate, eight or ten large oars were necessary; whereas, all the search of the gentlemen could not find one. They succeeded, however, in discovering a rudder and tiller, appliances not always used in launches, and Paul Blunt shipped them instantly. Around the gunwales of the boat, stanchions, which sustained a slight-rounded roof, were fitted, a provision that it is usual to make in the packets, in order to protect the stock they carry against the weather. This stock having been turned loose on the deck, and the interior cleaned, the latter now presented a snug and respectable cabin; one coarse and cramped, compared with those of the ship, cer-

tainly, but, on the other hand, one that might be well
deemed a palace by shipwrecked mariners.  As it would be
possible to retain this roof until compelled by bad weather
to throw it away, Paul, who had never before seen a boat
afloat with such a canopy, regarded it with delight ; for it
promised a protection to that delicate form he so much
cherished in his inmost heart, that he had not even dared
to hope for.  Between the roof and the gunwale of the
boat, shutters buttoned in, so as to fill the entire space ; and
when these were in their places, the whole of the interior
formed an inclosed apartment, of a height sufficient to allow
even a man to stand erect without his hat.  It is true, this
arrangement rendered the boat clumsy, and, to a certain
extent, top-heavy and unmanageable ; but so long as it
could be retained, it also rendered it infinitely more comfortable than it could possibly be without it.  The roof,
moreover, might be cut away in five minutes, at any time,
should circumstances require it.

Paul had just completed a hasty survey of his treasure,
for such he now began to consider the launch, when casting
his eye upward, with the intention to mount the ship's side,
he saw Eve looking down at him, as if to read their fate in
the expression of his own countenance.

"The Arabs," she hurriedly remarked, "are moving along
the reef, as my father says, faster than he could wish, and
all our hopes are centred in you and the boat.  The first,
I know, will not fail us, so long as means allow ; but can
we do anything with the launch ?"

"For the first time, dearest Miss Effingham, I see a little
chance of rescuing ourselves from the grasp of these barbarians.  There is no time to lose, but everything must be
passed into the boat with as little delay as possible."

"Bless you, bless you, Powis, for this gleam of hope !
Your words are cordials, and our lives can scarcely serve to
prove the gratitude we owe you."

This was said naturally, and as one expresses a strong
feeling, without reflection or much weighing of words ; but
even at that fearful moment it thrilled on every pulse of the
young man.  The ardent look that he gave the beautiful

girl caused her to redden to the temples, and she hastily withdrew.

The gentlemen now began to pass into the boat the different things that had been provided, principally by the foresight of Mademoiselle Viefville, where they were received by Paul, who thrust them beneath the roof without stopping to lose the precious moments in stowage. They included mattresses, the trunks that contained their ordinary sea-attire, or those that were not stowed in the baggage-room, blankets, counterpanes, potted meats, bread, wine, various condiments and prepared food, from the stores of Saunders, and generally such things as had presented themselves in the hurry of the moment. Nearly half of the articles were rejected by Paul as unnecessary, though he received many in consideration of the delicacy of his feebler companions, which would otherwise have been cast aside. When he found, however, that food enough had been passed into the boat to supply the wants of the whole party for several weeks, he solicited a truce, declaring it indiscreet to render themselves uselessly uncomfortable in this manner, to say nothing of the effect on the boat. The great requisite, water, was still wanting, and he now desired that the two domestics might get into the boat to arrange the different articles, while he endeavored to find something that might serve as a substitute for sails, and obtain the all-important supply.

His attention was first given to the water, without which all the other preparations would be rendered totally useless. Before setting about this, however, he stole a moment to look into the state of things among the Arabs. It was indeed time, for the tide had now fallen so low as to leave the rocks nearly bare, and several hundreds of the barbarians were advancing along the reef, towing their bridge, the slow progress of which alone prevented them from coming up at once to the point opposite the ship. Paul saw there was not a moment to lose, and, calling Saunders, he hurried below.

Three or four small casks were soon found, when the steward brought them to the tank to be filled. Luckily the

water had not to be pumped off, but it ran in a stream into
the vessel that was placed to receive it. As soon as one
cask was ready, it was carried on deck by the gentlemen,
and was struck into the boat with as little delay as possible.
The shouts of the Arabs now became audible, even to those
who were below, and it required great steadiness of nerve
to continue the all-important preparation. At length the
last of the casks was filled, when Paul rushed on deck, for,
by this time, the cries of the barbarians proclaimed their
presence near the ship. When he reached the rail, he found
the reef covered with them, some hailing the vessel, others
menacing, hundreds still busied with their floating bridge,
while a few endeavored to frighten those on board by discharging their muskets over their heads. Happily, aim was
impossible, so long as care was taken not to expose the body
above the bulwarks.

"We have not a moment to lose," cried Mr. Effingham,
on whose bosom Eve lay, nearly incapable of motion. "The
food and water are in the boat, and, in the name of a merciful God, let us escape from this scene of frightful bar-
barity."

"The danger is not yet so inevitable," returned Paul
steadily. "Frightful and pressing as it truly seems, we
have a few minutes to think in. Let me entreat that Miss
Effingham and Mademoiselle Viefville will receive a drop
of this cordial."

He poured into a glass a restorative from a bottle that
had been left on the capstan as superfluous, in the confusion
of providing stores, and held it to the pallid lips of Eve.
As she swallowed a mouthful, nearly as helpless as the infant
that receives nourishment from the hand of its nurse, the
blood returned, and raising herself from her father's arms, she
smiled, though with an effort, and thanked him for his care.

"It was a dread moment," she said, passing her hand over
her brow; "but it is past, and I am better. Mademoiselle
Viefville will be obliged to you, also, for a little of this."

The firm-minded and spirited Frenchwoman, though pale
as death, and evidently suffering under extreme apprehension,
put aside the glass courteously, declining its contents.

"We are sixty fathoms from the rocks," said Paul, calmly, "and they must cross this ditch yet, to reach us. None of them seem disposed to attempt it by swimming, and their bridge, though ingeniously put together, may not prove long enough."

"Would it be safe for the ladies to get into the boat where she lies, exposed as they would be to the muskets of the Arabs?" inquired Mr. Sharp."

"All that shall be remedied," returned Paul. "I cannot quit the deck : would you," slightly bowing to Mr. Sharp, "go below again, with Saunders, and look for some light sail? Without one, we cannot move away from the ship, even when in the boat. I see a suitable spar and necessary rigging on deck ; but the canvas must be looked for in the sail-room. It is a nervous thing, I confess, to be below at such a moment ; but you have too much faith in us to dread being deserted."

Mr. Sharp grasped the hand as a pledge of perfect reliance on the other's faith, but he could not speak. Calling Saunders, the steward received his instructions, when the two went hastily below.

"I could wish the ladies were in the boat with their women," said Paul, for Ann Sidley and the *femme de chambre* were still in the launch, busied in disposing of its mixed cargo of stores, though concealed from the Arabs by the roof and shutters ; "but it would be hazardous to attempt it while exposed to the fire from the reef. We shall have to change the position of the ship in the end, and it may as well be done at once."

Beckoning to John Effingham to follow, he went forward to examine into the movements of the Arabs once more before he took any decided step. The two gentlemen placed themselves behind the high defences of the forecastle, where they had a fair opportunity of reconnoitring their assailants, the greater height of the ship's deck completely concealing all that had passed on it from the sight of those on the rocks.

The barbarians, who seemed to be, and who in truth were, fully apprised of the defenceless and feeble condition of the party on board, were at work without the smallest apprehension of receiving any injury from that quarter. Their great object was to get possession of the ship before the returning water should again drive them from the rocks. In order to effect this, they had placed all who were willing and sufficiently subordinate on the bridge, though a hundred were idle, shouting, clapping their hands, menacing, and occasionally discharging a musket, of which there were probably fifty in their possession.

"They work with judgment at their pontoon," said Paul, after he had examined the proceedings of those on the reef, for a few minutes. "You may perceive that they have dragged the outer edge of the bridge up to windward, and have just shoved it from the rocks, with the intention to permit it to drift round until it shall bring up against the bows of the ship, when they will pour on board like so many tigers. It is a disjointed and loose contrivance, that the least sea would derange; but in this perfectly smooth water it will answer their purpose. It moves slowly, but will surely drift round upon us in the course of fifteen or twenty minutes more; and of this they appear to be quite certain themselves, for they seem as well satisfied with their work as if already assured of its complete success."

"It is, then, important to us to be prompt, since our time will be so brief."

"We will be prompt, but in another mode. If you will assist me a little, I think this effort, at least, may be easily defeated, after which it will be time enough to think of escape."

Paul, aided by John Effingham, now loosened the chains altogether from the bitts, and suffered the ship to drop astern. As this was done silently and stealthily, it occupied several minutes; but the wind being by this time fresh, the huge mass yielded to its power with certainty; and when the bridge floated round in a direct line from the reef, or dead to leeward, there was a space of water between its end and the ship of more than a hundred feet. The Arabs had rushed on it in readiness to board, but they set up a yell of disappointment as soon as the truth was discovered. A tumult followed ; several fell from the wet and slippery spars ; but, after a short time wasted in confusion and clamor, the directions of their chiefs were obeyed, and they set to work with energy to break up their bridge, in order to convert its materials into a raft.

By this time Mr. Sharp and Saunders had returned, bringing with them several light sails, such as spare royals and topgallant studding-sails. Paul next ordered a spare mizzen-topgallant-mast, with a topgallant studding-sail boom, and a quantity of light rope to be laid in the gang-way, after which he set about the final step. As time now pressed in earnest, the Arabs working rapidly and with increasing shouts, he called upon all the gentlemen for assist-ance, giving such directions as should enable them to work with intelligence.

" Bear a hand, Saunders," he said, having taken the stew-ard forward with him, as one more accustomed to ships than the others ; " bear a hand, my fine fellow, and light up this chain. Ten minutes just now are of more value than a year at another time."

" 'T is awful, Mr. Blunt, sir,—werry awful, I do con-firm," returned the steward, blubbering and wiping his eyes between the drags at the chains. " Such a fate to befall such cabins, sir ! And the crockery of the werry best quality out of London or New York ! Had I diwined such an issue for the Montauk, sir, I never would have counselled Captain Truck to lay in half the stores we did, and most essentially not the new lots of vines. O ! sir, it is truly awful to have such a calamity wisit so much elegant preparation ! "

" Forget it all, my fine fellow, and light up the chain. Ha ! she touches abaft ! Ten or fifteen fathoms more will answer."

" I 've paid great dewotion to the silver, Mr. Blunt, sir, for it 's all in the launch, even to the broken mustard-spoon ; and I do hope, if Captain Truck's soul is permitted to superintend the pantry any longer, it will be quite beatified and encouraged with my prudence and oversight. I left all the rest of the table furniture, sir ; though I suppose these *muscle*-men will not have much use for any but the oyster-knives, as I am informed they eat with their fingers. I declare it is quite oppressive and unhuman to have such wagabonds rummaging one's lockers!"

"Rouse away, my man, and light up! The ship has caught the breeze on her larboard bow, and begins to take the chain more freely. Remember that precious beings depend on us for safety."

"Ay, ay, sir; light up, it is. I feel quite a concern for the ladies, sir, and more especially for the stores we abandon to the underwriters. A better-found ship never came out of St. Catherine's Docks or the East River, particularly in the pantry department; and I wonder what these wretches will do with her. They will be quite abashed with her conveniences, sir, and unable to enjoy them. Poor Toast, too! he will have a monstrous unpleasant time with the *muscle*-men, for he never eats fish, and has quite a genteel and ameliorated way with him. I should n't wonder if he forgot all I have taken so much pains to teach him, sir, unless he 's dead; in which case it will be of no use to him in another world."

"That will do," interrupted Paul, ceasing his labor; "the ship is aground from forward aft. We will now hurry the spars and sails into the boat, and let the ladies get into her."

In order that the reader may better understand the present situation of the ship, it may be necessary to explain what Mr. Powis and the steward had been doing all this time. By paying out the chains, the ship had fallen farther astern, until she took the ground abaft on the edge of the sand-bank so often mentioned; and once fast at that end, her bows had fallen off, pressed by the wind, as long as the depth of the water would allow. She now lay aground forward and aft, with her starboard side to the reef, and the launch, between the vessel and the naked sands, was completely covered from the observations and assaults of the barbarians by the former.

Eve, Mademoiselle Viefville, and Mr. Effingham now got into the launch, while the others still remained in the ship to complete the preparations.

"They get on fast with their raft," said Paul, while he
both worked himself and directed the labor of the others,
"though we shall be safe here until they actually quit the
rocks. Their spars will be certain to float down upon the
ship, but the movement will necessarily be slow, as the
water is too deep to admit of setting, even if they had
poles, of which I see none. Throw these spare sails on
the roof of the launch, Saunders. They may be wanted
before we reach a port, should God protect us long enough
to effect so much. Pass two compasses also into the boat,
with all the carpenter's tools that have been collected."

While giving these orders, Paul was busied in sawing off
the larger end of the pole-mizzen-topgallant-mast, to convert it into a spar for the launch. This was done by the
time he ceased speaking; a step was made, and, jumping
down on the roof of the boat, he cut out a hole to receive
it, at a spot he had previously marked for that purpose.
By the time he had done, the spar was ready to be entered,
and in another minute they had the satisfaction of seeing a
very sufficient mast in its place. A royal was also stretched
to its yard, and halyards, tack, and sheet being bent, everything was ready to run up a sail at a moment's warning.
As this supplied the means of motion, the gentlemen began
to breathe more freely, and to bethink them of those minor
comforts and essentials that in the hurry of such a scene
would be likely to be overlooked. After a few more busy
minutes all was pronounced to be ready, and John Effingham began seriously to urge the party to quit the ship;
but Paul still hesitated. He strained his eyes in the direction of the wreck, in the vain hope of yet receiving succor
from that quarter; but, of course, uselessly, as it was about
the time when Captain Truck was warping off with his
raft, in order to obtain an offing. Just at this moment a
party of twenty Arabs got upon the spars, which they had
brought together into a single body, and began to drift
down slowly upon the ship.

Paul cast a look about him to see if anything else that
was useful could be found, and his eyes fell upon the gun.
It struck him that it might be made serviceable as a scare-

crow in forcing their way through the inlet, and he determined to lodge it on the roof of the launch, for the present, at least, and to throw it overboard as soon as they got
into rough water, if indeed they should be so fortunate as
to get outside of the reef at all. The stay and yard
tackles offered the necessary facilities, and he instantly
slung the piece. A few rounds of the capstan lifted it from
the deck, a few more bore it clear of the side, and then it
was easily lowered on the roof, Saunders being sent into
the boat to set up a stanchion beneath, in order that its
weight might do no injury.

The gentlemen at last got into the launch, with the exception of Paul, who still lingered in the ship watching the
progress of the Arabs, and making his calculations for the
future.

It required great steadiness of nerve, perfect self-reliance,
and an entire confidence in his resources and knowledge,
for one to remain a passive spectator of the slow drift of
the raft, while it gradually settled down on the ship. As
it approached, Paul was seen by those on it, and, with the
usual duplicity of barbarians, they made signs of amity and
encouragement. These signs did not deceive the young
man, however, who only remained to be a close observer
of their conduct, thinking some useful hint might thus be
obtained, though his calmness so far imposed on the Arabs
that they even made signs to him to throw them a rope.
Believing it now time to depart, he answered the signal
favorably, and disappeared from their sight.

Even in descending to the boat, this trained and cool
young seaman betrayed no haste. His movements were
quick, and everything was done with readiness and knowledge certainly, but no confusion or trepidation occasioned
the loss of a moment. He hoisted the sail, brought down
the tack, and then descended beneath the roof, having first
hauled in the painter, and given the boat a long and vigorous shove, to force it from the side of the vessel. By this
last expedient he at once placed thirty feet of water between the boat and the Montauk, a space that the Arabs
had no means of overcoming. As soon as he was beneath

the roof the sheet was hauled in, and Paul seized the tiller, which had been made, by means of a narrow cut in the boards, to play in one of the shutters. Mr. Sharp took a position in the bows, where he could see the sands and channels through the crevices, directing the other how to steer; and just as a shout announced the arrival of the raft at the other side of the ship, the flap of their sail gave those in the boat the welcome intelligence that they had got so far from her cover as to feel the force of the wind.

## CHAPTER XXIV.

"Speed, gallant bark ! richer cargo is thine,
  Than Brazilian gem, or Peruvian mine ;
  And the treasures thou bearest thy destiny wait,
  For they, if thou perish, must share in thy fate."

PARK.

THE departure of the boat was excellently timed. Had it left the side of the ship while the Arabs on the raft were unoccupied, and at a little distance, it would have been exposed to their fire ; for at least a dozen of those who boarded had muskets ; whereas the boat now glided away to leeward, while they were busy in getting up her side, or were so near the ship as not to be able to see the launch at all. When Paul Powis, who was looking astern through a crevice, saw the first Arab on the deck of the Montauk, the launch was already near a cable's-length from her, running with a fresh and free wind into one of the numerous little channels that intersected the naked banks of sand. The unusual construction of the boat, with its inclosed roof, and the circumstance that no one was visible on board her, had the effect to keep the barbarians passive, until distance put her beyond the reach of danger. A few muskets were discharged, but they were fired at random, and in the bravado of a semi-savage state of feeling.

Paul kept the launch running off free, until he was near a mile from the ship, when, finding he was approaching the reef to the northward and eastward, and that a favorable sand-bank lay a short distance ahead, he put down the helm, let the sheet fly, and the boat's forefoot shot upon the sands. By a little management, the launch was got broadside to the bank, the water being sufficiently deep, and, when it was secured, the females were enabled to land through the opening of a shutter.

The change from the apparent hopelessness of their situation was so great, as to render the whole party comparatively happy. Paul and John Effingham united in affirming it would be quite possible to reach one of the islands to leeward in so good a boat, and that they ought to deem themselves fortunate, under the circumstances, in being the masters of a little bark so well found in every essential. Eve and Mademoiselle Viefville, who had fervently returned their thanks to the Great Ruler of events, while in the boat, walked about the hard sand with even a sense of enjoyment, and smiles began again to brighten the beautiful features of the first. Mr. Effingham declared, with a grateful heart, that in no park, or garden, had he ever before met with a promenade that seemed so delightful as this spot of naked and moistened sand, on the sterile coast of the Great Desert. Its charm was its security, for its distance from every point that could be approached by the Arabs, rendered it, in their eyes, a paradise.

Paul Powis, however, though he maintained a cheerful air, and the knowledge that he had been so instrumental in saving the party lightened his heart of a load, and disposed him even to gayety, was not without some lingering remains of uneasiness. He remembered the boats of the Dane, and, as he thought it more than probable Captain Truck had fallen into the hands of the barbarians, he feared that the latter might yet find the means to lay hands on themselves. While he was at work fitting the rigging and preparing a jigger, with a view to render the launch more manageable, he cast frequent uneasy glances to the northward, with a feverish apprehension that one of the so-long-wished-for boats might at length appear. Their friends he no longer expected, but his fears were all directed towards the premature arrival of enemies from that quarter. None appeared, however, and Saunders actually lighted a fire on the bank, and prepared the grateful refreshment of tea for the whole party; none of which had tasted food since morning, though it was now drawing near night.

"Our caterers," said Paul, smiling, as he cast his eyes over the repast which Ann Sidley had spread on the roof of the boat, where they were all seated on stools, boxes, and trunks, "our caterers have been of the gentler sex, as any one may see, for we have delicacies that are fitter for a banquet than a desert."

"I thought Miss Eve would relish them, sir," Nanny meekly excused herself by saying: "she is not much accustomed to a coarse diet; and Mamerzelle, too, likes niceties, as I believe is the case with all of French extraction."

Eve's eyes glistened, though she felt it necessary to say something by the way of apology.

"Poor Ann has been so long accustomed to humor the caprices of a petted girl," she said, "that I fear those who will have occasion for all their strength may be the sufferers. I should regret it forever, Mr. Powis, if *you*, who are every way of so much importance to us, should not find the food you required."

"I have very inadvertently and unwittingly drawn down upon myself the suspicion of being one of Mr. Monday's *gourmets*, a plain roast and boiled person," the young man answered laughingly, "when it was merely my desire to express the pleasure I had in perceiving that those whose comfort and ease are of more account than anything else, have been so well cared for. I could almost starve with satisfaction, Miss Effingham, if I saw you free from suffering under the extraordinary circumstances in which we are placed."

Eve looked grateful, and the emotion excited by this speech restored all that beauty which had so lately been chilled by fear.

"Did I not hear a dialogue between you and Mr. Saunders touching the merits of sundry stores that had been left in the ship?" asked John Effingham, turning to Paul by way of relieving his cousin's distress.

"Indeed you might; he relieved the time we were rousing at the chains with a beautiful Jeremiad on the calamities of the lockers. I fancy, steward, that you consider the misfortunes of the pantry as the heaviest disaster that has befallen the Montauk!"

Saunders seldom smiled. In this particular he resembled Captain Truck; the one subduing all light emotions from an inveterate habit of serious comicality, and the responsibility of command; and the other having lost most of his disposition to merriment, as the cart-horse loses his propensity to kick, from being overworked. The steward, moreover, had taken up the conceit that it was indicative of a "nigger" to be merry; and, between dignity, a proper regard to his color,—which was about half-way between that of a Gold Coast inportation, and a rice-plantation overseer, down with the fever in his third season,—and dogged submission to unmitigated calls on his time, the prevailing character of the poor fellow's physiognomy was that of a dolorous sentimentality. He believed himself to be materially refined by having had so much intimate communication with gentlemen and ladies suffering under sea-sickness, and he knew that no man in the ship could use language like that he had always at his fingers' ends. While so strongly addicted to melancholy, therefore, he was fond of hearing himself talk; and, palpably encouraged as he had now been by John Effingham and Paul, and a little emboldened by the familiarity of a shipwreck, he did not hesitate about mingling in the discourse, though holding the Effinghams habitually in awe.

"I esteem it a great privilege, ladies and gentlemen," he observed, as soon as Paul ceased, "to have the honor of being *wracked* [for so the steward, in conformity with the Doric of the forecastle, pronounced the word] in such company. I should deem it a disgrace to be cast away in some society I could name, although I will predicate, as we say in America, nothing on their absence. As to what inwolves the stores, it surgested itself to me that the ladies would like delicate diet, and I intermated as much to Mrs. Sidley and t'other French waiting-woman. Do you imagine, gentlemen, that the souls of the dead are permitted to look back at such ewents of this life as touches their own private concerns and feelings?"

"That would depend, I should think, steward, on the nature of the employment of the souls themselves," returned John Effingham. "There must be certain souls to which

any occupation would be more agreeable than that of looking behind them.  But, may I ask why you inquire?''

"Because, Mr. John Effingham, sir, I do not believe
Captain Truck can ever be happy in heaven, as long as the
ship is in the hands of the Arabs!  If she had been hon-
orably and fairly wracked, and the captain suffercated by
drowning, he could go to sleep like another Christian ; but,
I do think, sir, if there be any special perdition for seamen,
it must be to see their vessel rummaged by Arabs.  I 'll
warrant, now, those blackguards have had their fingers in
everything already ; sugar, chocolate, raisins, coffee, cakes,
and all !  I wonder who they think would like to use
articles they have handled !  And there is poor Toast, gentlemen, an aspiring and improving young man ; one who
had the materials of a good steward in him, though I can
hardly say they were completely deweloped.  I did look
forward to the day when I could consign him to Mr. Leach
as my own predecessor, when Captain Truck and I should
retire, as I have no doubt we should have done on the
same day, but for this distressing accident.  I dewoutly
pray that Toast is deceased, for I would rather any misfortune shall befall him in the other world than that he should
be compelled to associate with Arab niggers in this.  Dead
or alive, ladies, I am an advocate for a man's keeping himself respectable, and in proper company.''

So elastic had the spirits of the whole become by their
unlooked-for escape, that Saunders was indulged to the top
of his humor, and while he served the meal, passing between his fire on the sands and the roof of the launch, he
enjoyed a heartier gossip than any he had had since they
left the dock ; not even excepting those sniggering scenes
with Mr. Toast in the pantry, in which he used to unbend
himself a little, forgetting his dignity as steward in the
native propensities of the black.

Paul Powis entered but a moment into the trifling, for on
him rested the safety of all.  He alone could navigate, or
even manage the boat in rough water ; and while the others
confided so implicitly in his steadiness and skill, he felt
the usual burden of responsibility.  When the supper was

ended, and the party were walking up and down the little islet of sand, he took his station on the roof, therefore, and examined the proceedings of the Arabs with the glass ; Mr. Sharp, with a species of chivalrous self-denial that was not lost on his companion, foregoing the happiness of walking at the side of Eve, to remain near him.

" The wretches have laid waste the cabins already ! " observed Mr. Sharp, when Paul had been looking at the ship some little time. " That which it took months to produce they will destroy in an hour."

" I do not see that," returned Paul ; " there are but about fifty in the ship, and their efforts seem to be directed to hauling her over against the rocks. They have no means of landing their plunder where she lies ; and I suspect there is a sort of convention that all are to start fair. One or two, who appear to be chiefs, go in and out of the cabins ; but the rest are actively engaged in endeavoring to move the ship."

" And with what success ? "

" None, apparently. It exceeds their knowledge of mechanics to force so heavy a mass from its position. The wind has driven the ship firmly on the bank, and nothing short of the windlass, or capstan, can remove her. These ignorant creatures have got two or three small ropes between the vessel and the reef, and are pulling fruitlessly at both ends ! But our chief concern will be to find an outlet into the ocean, when we will make the best of our way towards the Cape de Verdes."

Paul now commenced a long and close examination of the reef, to ascertain by what openings he might get the launch on the outside. To the northward of the great inlet there was a continued line of rocks, on which he was sorry to perceive armed Arabs beginning to show themselves ; a sign that the barbarians still entertained the hope of capturing the party. Southward of the inlet there were many places in which a boat might pass at half-tide, and he trusted to getting through one of them as soon as it became dark. As the escape in the boat could not have been foreseen, the Arabs had not yet brought down upon them the boats of the wreck; but should morning dawn and find them still within the reef, he saw no hope of final escape against boats that would possess the advantage of oars, ignorant as the barbarians might be of their proper use.

Everything was now ready. The interior of the launch was divided into two apartments by counterpanes, trunks, and boxes; the females spreading their mattresses in the forward room, and the males in the other. Some of those profound interpreters of the law, who illustrate legislation by the devices of trade, had shipped in the Montauk several hundred rude leaden busts of Napoleon, with a view to save the distinction in duties between the metal manufactured and the metal unmanufactured. Four or five of these busts had been struck into the launch as ballast. They were now snugly stowed, together with the water, and all the heavier articles, in the bottom of the boat. The jigger had been made and bent, and a suitable mast was stepped by means of the roof. In short, every provision for comfort or safety that Paul could think of had been attended to; and everything was in readiness to re-embark as soon as the proper hour should arrive.

The gentler portion of the party were seated on the edge of the roof, watching the setting sun, and engaged in a discourse with feelings more attempered to their actual condition than had been the case immediately after their escape. The evening had a little of that wild and watery aspect which, about the same hour, had given Captain Truck so much concern; but the sun dipped gorgeously into the liquid world of the West, and the whole scene, including the endless desert, the black reef, the stranded ship, and the movements of the bustling Arabs, was one of gloomy grandeur.

"Could we foretell the events of a month," said John Effingham, "with what different feelings from the present would life be checkered! When we left London, twenty days since, our eyes and minds were filled with the movements, cares, refinements, and interest of a great and polished capital; and here we sit, houseless wanderers, gazing at an eventide on the coast of Africa! In this way, young men, and young ladies too, will you find, as life glides away, that the future will disappoint the expectations of the present moment!"

"All futures are not gloomy, cousin Jack," said Eve; "nor is all hope doomed to meet with disappointment. A merciful God cares for us when we are reduced to despair on our own account, and throws a ray of unexpected light on our darkest hours. Certainly we, of all his creatures, ought not to deny this!"

"I do not deny it. We have been rescued in a manner so simple as to seem unavoidable, and yet so unexpected as to be almost miraculous. Had not Mr. Blunt, or Mr. Powis, as you call him—although I am not in the secret of the masquerade—but, had not this gentleman been a seaman, it would have surpassed all our means to get this boat into the water, or even to use her properly were she even launched. I look upon his profession as being the first great providential interference, or provision, in our behalf; and his superior skill and readiness in that profession as a circumstance of no less importance to us."

Eve was silent; but the glow in the western sky was scarcely more radiant and bright than the look she cast on the subject of the remark.

"It is no great merit to be a seaman, for the trade is like another, a mere matter of practice and education," observed Paul, after a moment of awkward hesitation. "If, as you say, I have been instrumental in serving you, I shall never regret the accidents—cruel accidents of my early life I had almost called them—that cast my fortunes so early on the ocean."

A falling pin would have been heard, and all hoped the young man would proceed; but he chose to be silent. Saunders happened to overhear the remark, for he was aiding Ann Sidley in the boat, and he took up the subject where it was left by the other, in a little aside with his companion.

"It is a misfortune that Mr. Dodge is not here to question the gentleman," said the steward to his assistant, "and then we might hear more of his adventures, which, I make

no doubt, have been werry pathetic and romantical. Mr.
Dodge is a genuine inquisitor, Mistress Ann; not such an
inquisitor as burns people and flays them in Spain, where I
have been, but such an inquisitor as torments people, and of
whom we have lots in America."

" Let the poor man rest in peace," said Nanny, sighing.
" He's gone to his great account, steward; and I fear we
shall none of us make as good a figure as we might at the
final settling. Besides, Miss Eve, I never knew a mortal
that was n't more or less a sinner."

" So they all say : and I must allow that my experience
leans to the wicked side of the question. Captain Truck,
now, was a worthy man ; but he had his faults, as well as
Toast. In the first place, he would swear when things took
him aback : and then, he had no prevarication about speaking his mind of a fellow-creature, if the coffee happened to be
thick, or the poultry did n't take fat kindly. I 've known him
box the compass with oaths if the ship was got in irons."

" It 's very sinful ; and it is to be feared that the poor
man was made to think of all this in his latter moments."

" If the Arabs undertook to cannibalize him, I think he
must have given it to them right and left," continued Saunders, wiping an eye, for between him and the captain there
had existed some such affection as the prisoner comes to feel
for the handcuffs with which he amuses his *ennui* ; "some
of his oaths would choke a dog."

" Well, let him rest -let him rest. Providence is kind,
and the poor man may have repented in season."

" And Toast, too ! I 'm sure, Mrs. Ann, I forgive Toast
all the little mistakes he made, from the bottom of my heart,
and particularly that affair of the beefsteak that he let fall
into the coffee the morning that Captain Truck took me so
flat aback about it ; and I pray most dewoutly that the
captain, now he has dropped this mortal coil, and that there
is nothing left of him but soul, may not find it out, lest it
should breed ill-blood between them in heaven."

" Steward, you scarcely know what you say," interrupted
Ann, shocked at his ignorance, "and I will speak of it no
more."

Mr. Saunders was compelled to acquiesce, and he amused himself by listening to what was said by those on the roof. As Paul did not choose to explain further, however, the conversation was resumed as if he had said nothing. They talked of their escape, their hopes, and of the supposed fate of the rest of the party ; the discourse leaving a feeling of sadness on all, that harmonized with the melancholy but not unpicturesque scene in which they were placed. At length the night set in ; and as it threatened to be dark and damp, the ladies early made their arrangements to retire. The gentlemen remained on the sands much later ; and it was ten o'clock before Paul Powis and Mr. Sharp, who had assumed the watch, were left alone.

This was about an hour later than the period already described as the moment when Captain Truck disposed himself to sleep in the launch of the Dane. The weather had sensibly altered in the brief interval, and there were signs that, to the understanding of our young seaman, denoted a change. The darkness was intense. So deep and pitchy black, indeed, had the night become, that even the land was no longer to be distinguished, and the only clues the two gentlemen had to its position, were the mouldering watch-fires of the Arab camp, and the direction of the wind.

"We will now make an attempt," said Paul, stopping in his short walk on the sand, and examining the murky vault overhead. "Midnight is near, and by two o'clock the tide will be entirely up. It is a dark night to thread these narrow channels in, and to go out upon the ocean, too, in so frail a bark ! But the alternative is worse."

"Would it not be better to allow the water to rise still higher ? I see by these sands that it has not yet done coming in."

"There is not much tide in these low latitudes, and the little rise that is left may help us off a bank, should we strike one. If you will get upon the roof, I will bring in the grapnels and force the boat off."

Mr. Sharp complied, and in a few minutes the launch was floating slowly away from the hospitable bank of sand.

Paul hauled out the jigger, a small spritsail, that kept itself
close-hauled from being fastened to a stationary boom, and
a little mast stepped quite aft, the effect of which was to
press the boat against the wind. This brought the launch's
head up, and it was just possible to see, by close attention,
that they had a slight motion through the water.

"I quit that bank of sand as one quits a tried friend,"
said Paul, all the conversation now being in little more
than whispers : "when near it, I know where we are ; but
presently we shall be absolutely lost in this intense darkness."

"We have the fires of the Arabs for light-houses still."

"They may give us some faint notions of our position ; but
light like that is a very treacherous guide in so dark a night.
We have little else to do but to keep an eye on the water, and
to endeavor to get to windward."

Paul set the lug-sail, into which he had converted the royal,
and seated himself directly in the eyes of the boat, with a leg
hanging down on each side of the cutwater. He had rigged
lines to the tiller, and with one in each hand, he steered
as if managing a boat with yoke-lines. Mr. Sharp was seated
at hand, holding the sheet of the mainsail ; a boat-hook and
a light spar lying on the roof near by, in readiness to be used
should they ground.

While on the bank, Paul had observed that by keeping
the boat near the wind, he might stretch through one of
the widest of the channels for near two miles, unless disturbed by currents, and that when at its southern end, he
should be far enough to windward to fetch the inlet, but for
the banks of sand that might lie in his way. The distance
had prevented his discerning any passage through the reef
at the farther end of this channel ; but this boat drawing
only two feet of water, he was not without hopes of being
able to find one. A chasm, that was deep enough to prevent the passage of the Arabs when the tide was in, would,
he thought, certainly suffice for their purpose. The progress of the boat was steady, and reasonably fast ; but it
was like moving in a mass of obscurity. The gentlemen
watched the water ahead intently, with a view to avoid the

banks, but with little success; for, as they advanced, it was merely one pile of gloom succeeding another. Fortunately the previous observation of Paul availed them, and for more than half an hour their progress was uninterrupted.

"They sleep in security beneath us," said Paul, "while we are steering almost at random. This is a strange and hazardous situation in which we are placed. The obscurity renders all the risks double."

"By the watch-fires, we must have nearly crossed the bay, and I should think we are now quite near the southern reef."

"I think the same; but I like not this baffling of the wind. It comes fresher at moments, but it is in puffs, and I fear there will be a shift. It is now my best pilot."

"That and the fires."

"The fires are treacherous always. It looks darker than ever ahead!"

The wind ceased blowing altogether, and the sail fell in heavily. Almost at the same moment the launch lost its way, and Paul had time to thrust the boat-hook forward just in season to prevent its striking a rock.

"This is a part of the reef, then, that is never covered," said he. "If you will get on the rocks and hold the boat, I will endeavor to examine the place for a passage. Were we one hundred feet to the southward and westward, we should be in the open ocean, and comparatively safe."

Mr. Sharp complied, and Paul descended carefully on the reef, feeling his way in the intense darkness by means of the boat-hook. He was absent ten minutes, moving with great caution, as there was the danger of his falling into the sea at every step. His friend began to be uneasy, and the whole of the jeopardy of their situation presented itself vividly to his mind in that brief space of time, should accident befall their only guide. He was looking anxiously in the direction in which Paul had disappeared, when he felt a gripe of his arm.

"Breathe even with care!" whispered Paul hurriedly. "These rocks are covered with Arabs, who have chosen to remain on the dry parts of the reef, in readiness for their

plunder in the morning. Thank Heaven! I have found
you again; for I was beginning to despair. To have called
to you would have been certain capture, as eight or ten of
the barbarians are sleeping within fifty feet of us. Get
on the roof with the least possible noise, and leave the rest
to me."

As soon as Mr. Sharp was in the boat, Paul gave it a
violent shove from the rocks, and sprang on the roof at the
same moment. This forced the launch astern, and procured
a momentary safety. But the wind had shifted. It now
came baffling, and in puffs, from the desert, a circumstance
that brought them again to leeward.

"This is the commencement of the trades," said Paul;
"they have been interrupted by the late gale, but are returning. Were we outside the reef, our prayers could not
be more kindly answered than by giving us this very wind;
but here, where we are, it comes unseasonably. Ha! this,
at least, helps her!"

A puff from the land filled the sails, and the ripple of the
water at the stern was just audible. The helm was attended
to, and the boat drew slowly from the reef and ahead.

"We have all reason for gratitude! That danger, at
least, is avoided. Ha! the boat is aground!"

Sure enough, the launch was on the sands. They were
still so near the rocks as to require the utmost caution in
their proceedings. Using the spar with great care, the gentlemen discovered that the boat hung astern, and there remained no choice but patience.

"It is fortunate the Arabs have no dogs with them on
the rocks: you hear them howling incessantly in their
camps."

"It is, truly. Think you we can ever find the inlet in
this deep obscurity?"

"It is our only course. By following the rocks we should
be certain to discover it; but you perceive they are already
out of sight, though they cannot be thirty fathoms from us.
The helm is free, and the boat must be clear of the bottom
again. This last puff has helped us."

Another silence succeeded, during which the launch

moved slowly onward, though whither, neither of the gentlemen could tell.   But a single fire remained in sight, and
that glimmered like a dying blaze.      At times the wind
came hot and arid, savoring of the desert, and then intervals
of death-like calm would follow.   Paul watched the boat
narrowly for half an hour, turning every breath of air to the
best account, though he was absolutely ignorant of his position.   The reef had not been seen again, and three several
times they grounded, the tide as often floating them off.
The course, too, had been repeatedly varied.   The result
was that painful and profound sensation of helplessness that
overcomes us all when the chain of association is broken,
and reason becomes an agent less useful than instinct.

"The last fire is out," whispered Paul.   "I fear that the
day will dawn and find us still within the reef."

"I see an object near us.   Can it be a high bank?"

The wind had entirely ceased, and the boat was almost
without motion.   Paul saw a darkness more intense even
than common ahead of him, and he leaned forward, naturally
raising a hand before him in precaution.   Something he
touched, he knew not what; but feeling a hard smooth surface, that he at first mistook for a rock, he raised his eyes
slowly, and discerned, by the little light that lingered in the
vault of heaven, a dim tracery that he recognized.   His
hand was on the quarter of the ship!

"'T is the Montauk!" he whispered breathlessly, "and
her decks must be covered with Arabs.   Hist! do you hear
nothing?"

They listened; and smothered voices, those of the watch,
mingled with low laughter, were quite audible.   This was a
crisis to disturb the coolness of one less trained and steady
than Paul; but he preserved his self-possession.

"There is good as well as evil in this," he whispered.
"I now know our precise position; and, God be praised!
the inlet is near, could we but reach it.   By a strong shove
we can always force the launch from the vessel's side, and
prevent their boarding us; and I think, with extreme caution, we may even haul the boat past the ship undetected."

This delicate task was undertaken.   It was necessary to

avoid even a tread heavier than common, a fall of the boat-hook, or a collision with the vessel, as the slightest noise became distinctly audible in the profound stillness of deep night. Once enlightened as to his real position, however, Paul saw with his mind's eye obstructions that another might not have avoided. He knew exactly where to lay his hand, when to bear off, and when to approach nearer to the side of the ship, as he warily drew the boat along the massive hull. The yard of the launch luckily leaned towards the reef, and offered no impediment. In this manner, then the two gentlemen hauled their boat as far as the bows of the ship, and Paul was on the point of giving a last push, with a view to shove it to as great a distance as possible ahead of the packet, when its movement was suddenly and violently arrested.

**23**

## CHAPTER XXV.

"And when the hours of rest
Come, like a calm upon the mid-sea brine,
    Hushing its billowy breast—
The quiet of that moment, too, is thine;
    It breathes of Him who keeps
The vast and helpless city while it sleeps."

BRYANT.

IT was chilling to meet with this unexpected and sudden check at so critical a moment. The first impression was, that some one of the hundreds of Arabs, who were known to be near, had laid a hand on the launch; but this fear vanished on examination. No one was visible, and the side of the boat was untouched. The boat-hook could find no impediment in the water, and it was not possible that they could again be aground. Raising the boat-hook over his head, Paul soon detected the obstacle. The line used by the barbarians in their efforts to move the ship, was stretched from the forecastle to the reef, and it lay against the boat's mast. It was severed with caution; but the short end slipped from the hand of Mr. Sharp, who cut the rope, and fell into the water. The noise was heard, and the watch on the deck of the ship made a rush towards her side.

No time was to be lost; but Paul, who still held the outer end of the line, pulled on it vigorously, hauling the boat swiftly from the ship, and, at the same time, a little in advance. As soon as this was done, he dropped the line and seized the tiller-ropes, in order to keep the launch's head in a direction between the two dangers—the ship and the reef. This was not done without some little noise; the footfall on the roof, and the plash of the water when it received the line, were audible ; and even the element washing under the bows of the boat was heard.  The Arabs of the ship called to those on the reef, and the latter answered. They took the alarm, and awoke their comrades, for, knowing as they did that the party of Captain Truck was still at liberty, they apprehended an attack.

The clamor and uproar that succeeded were terrific.  Muskets were discharged at random, and the noises from the camp echoed the cries and tumult from the vessel and the rocks.  Those who had been sleeping in the boat were rudely awaked, and Saunders joined in the cries through sheer fright.  But the two gentlemen on deck soon caused their companions to understand their situation, and to observe a profound silence.

"They do not appear to see us," whispered Paul to Eve, as he bent over, so as to put his head at an open window ; "and a return of the breeze may still save us.  There is a great alarm among them, and no doubt they know we are not distant ; but so long as they cannot tell precisely where, we are comparatively safe.  Their cries do us good service as landmarks, and you may be certain I shall not approach the spots where they are heard.  Pray Heaven for a wind, dearest Miss Effingham, pray Heaven for a wind !"

Eve silently, but fervently, did pray, while the young man gave all his attention again to the boat.  As soon as they were clear of the lee of the ship, the baffling puffs returned, and there were several minutes of a steady little breeze, during which the boat sensibly moved away from the noises of the ship.  On the reef, however, the clamor still continued, and the gentlemen were soon satisfied that the Arabs had stationed themselves along the whole line of rocks, wherever the latter were bare at high water, as was now nearly the case, to the northward as well as to the southward of the opening.

"The tide is still entering by the inlet," said Paul, "and we have its current to contend with.  It is not strong, but a trifle is important at a moment like this."

"Would it not be possible to reach the bank inside of

us, and to shove the boat ahead by means of these light spars?" asked Mr. Sharp.

The suggestion was a good one; but Paul was afraid the noise in the water might reach the Arabs, and expose the party to their fire, as the utmost distance between the reef and the inner bank at that particular spot did not exceed a hundred fathoms. At length another puff of air from the land pressed upon the sails, and the water once more rippled beneath the bows of the boat. Paul's heart beat hard, and, as he managed the tiller-lines, he strained his eyes uselessly in order to penetrate the massive-looking darkness.

"Surely," he said to Mr. Sharp, who stood constantly at his elbow, "these cries are directly ahead of us! We are steering for the Arabs!"

"We have got wrong in the dark, then. Lose not a moment to keep the boat away, for here to leeward there are noises."

As all this was self-evident, though confused in his reckoning, Paul put up the helm, and the boat fell off nearly dead before the wind. Her motion being now comparatively rapid, a few minutes produced an obvious change in the direction of the different groups of clamorous Arabs, though they also brought a material lessening in the force of the air.

"I have it!" said Paul, grasping his companion almost convulsively by the arm. "We are at the inlet, and heading, I trust, directly through it! You hear the cries on our right; they come from the end of the northern reef, while these on our left are from the end of the southern. The sounds from the ship, the direction of the land breeze, our distance—all confirm it, and Providence again befriends us!"

"It will be a fearful error should we be mistaken!"

"We cannot be deceived, since nothing else will explain the circumstances. There!—the boat feels the ground-swell—a blessed and certain sign that we are at the inlet! Would that this tide were done, or that we had more wind!"

Fifteen feverish minutes succeeded. At moments the

puffs of night air would force the boat ahead, and then again it was evident, by the cries, that she fell astern under the influence of an adverse current. Neither was it easy to keep her on the true course, for the slightest variation from the direct line in a tide's-way causes a vessel to sheer. To remedy the latter danger, Paul was obliged to watch his helm closely, having no other guide than the noisy and continued vociferations of the Arabs.

"These liftings of the boat are full of hope," resumed Paul; "I think, too, that they increase."

"I perceive but little difference, though I would gladly see all you wish."

"I am certain the swell increases, and that the boat rises and falls more frequently. You will allow there is a swell?"

"Quite obviously: I perceived it before we kept the boat away. This variable air is cruelly tantalizing."

"Sir George Templemore—Mr. Powis," said a soft voice at a window beneath them.

"Miss Effingham!" said Paul, so eager that he suffered the tiller-line to escape him.

"These are frightful cries! Shall we never be rid of them?"

"If it depended on me—on either of us—they should distress you no more. The boat is slowly entering the inlet, but has to struggle with a head tide. The wind baffles, and is light, or in ten minutes we should be out of danger."

"Out of this danger, but only to encounter another!"

"Nay, I do not think much of the risk of the ocean in so stout a boat. At the most, we may be compelled to cut away the roof, which makes our little bark somewhat clumsy in appearance, though it adds infinitely to its comfort. I think we shall soon get the trades, before which our launch, with its house even, will be able to make good weather."

"We are certainly nearer those cries than before!"

Paul felt his cheek glow, and his hand hurriedly sought the tiller-line, for the boat had sensibly sheered towards the northern reef. A puff of air helped to repair his oversight, and all in the launch soon perceived that the cries were gradually but distinctly drawing more aft.

"The current lessens," said Paul, "and it is full time, for it must be near high water. We shall soon feel it in our favor, when all will be safe."

"This is indeed blessed tidings; and no gratitude can ever repay the debt we owe you, Mr. Powis."

The puffs of air now required all the attention of Paul, for they again became variable, and at last the wind drew directly ahead in a continued current for half an hour. As soon as this change was felt, the sails were trimmed to it, and the boat began to stir the water under her bows.

"The shift was so sudden, that we cannot be mistaken in its direction," Paul remarked; "besides, those cries still serve as pilots. Never was uproar more agreeable."

"I feel the bottom with this spar!" said Mr. Sharp suddenly.

"Merciful Providence, protect and shield the weak and lovely—"

"Nay, I feel it no longer: we are already in deep water."

"It was the rock on which the seaman stood when we entered!" Paul exclaimed, breathing more freely. "I like those voices settling more under our lee, too. We will keep this tack" (the boat's head was to the northward) "until we hit the reef, unless warned off again by the cries."

The boat now moved at the rate of five miles in the hour, or faster than a man walks, even when in quick motion. Its rising and falling denoted the long, heavy swell of the ocean, and the wash of water began to be more and more audible, as she settled into the sluggish swells.

"That sounds like the surf on the reef," continued Paul; "everything denotes the outside of the rocks."

"God send it prove so!"

"That is clearly a sea breaking on a rock! It is awkwardly near, and to leeward, and yet it is sweet to the ear as music."

The boat stood steadily on, making narrow escapes from jutting rocks, as was evinced by the sounds, and once or twice by the sight even; but the cries shifted gradually, and were soon quite astern. Paul knew that the reef trended east soon after passing the inlet, and he felt the hope that they were fast leaving its western extremity, or the part that ran the farthest into the ocean ; after effecting which, there would be more water to leeward, his own course being nearly north, as he supposed.

The cries drew still farther aft, and more distant, and the sullen wash of the surf was no longer so near as to seem fresh and tangible.

"Hand me the lead and line, that lie at the foot of the mast, if you please," said Paul. "Our water seems sensibly to deepen, and the seas have become more regular."

He hove a cast, and found six fathoms of water ; a proof, he thought, that they were quite clear of the reef.

"Now, dear Mr. Effingham, Miss Effingham, Mademoiselle," he cried cheerfully, "now I believe we may indeed deem ourselves beyond the reach of the Arabs, unless a gale force us again on their inhospitable shores."

"Is it permitted to speak?" asked Mr. Effingham, who had maintained a steady but almost breathless silence.

"Freely : we are quite beyond the reach of the voice ; and this wind, though blowing from a quarter I do not like, is carrying us away from the wretches rapidly."

It was not safe in the darkness, and under the occasional heaves of the boat, for the others to come on the roof ; but they opened the shutters, and looked out upon the gloomy water with a sense of security they could not have deemed possible for people in their situation. The worst was over for the moment, and there is a relief in present escape that temporarily conceals future dangers. They could converse without the fear of alarming their enemies, and Paul spoke encouragingly of their prospects. It was his intention to stand to the northward until he reached the wreck, when, failing to get any tidings of their friends, they might make the best of their way to the nearest island to leeward.

With this cheering news the party below again disposed themselves to sleep, while the two young men maintained their posts on the roof.

"We must resemble an ark," said Paul, laughing, as he

seated himself on a box near the stem of the boat, "and I should think would frighten the Arabs from an attack, had they even the opportunity to make one. This house we carry will prove a troublesome companion, should we encounter a heavy and a head sea."

"You say it may easily be gotten rid of."

"Nothing would be easier, the whole apparatus being made to ship and unship. *Before* the wind we might carry it a long time, and it would even help us along; but *on* a wind it makes us a little top-heavy, besides giving us a leeward set. In the event of rain, or of bad weather of any sort, it would be a treasure to us all, more especially to the females, and I think we had better keep it as long as possible."

The half hour of breeze already mentioned sufficed to carry the boat some distance to the northward, when it failed, and the puffs from the land returned. Paul supposed they were quite two miles from the inlet, and, trying the lead, he found ten fathoms of water, a proof that they had also gradually receded from the shore. Still nothing but a dense darkness surrounded them, though there could no longer be the smallest doubt of their being in the open ocean.

For near an hour the light, baffling air came in puffs, as before, during which time the launch's head was kept, as near as the two gentlemen could judge, to the northward, making but little progress; and then the breeze drew gradually round into one quarter, and commenced blowing with a steadiness that they had not experienced before that night. Paul suspected this change, though he had no certain means of knowing it; for as soon as the wind baffled, his course had got to be conjectural again. As the breeze freshened, the speed of the boat necessarily augmented, though she was kept always on a wind; and after half an hour's progress, the gentlemen became once more uneasy as to the direction.

"It would be a cruel and awkward fate to hit the reef again," said Paul; "and yet I cannot be sure that we are not running directly for it."

"We have compasses ; let us strike a light and look into the matter."

"It were better had we done this more early, for a light might now prove dangerous, should we really have altered the course in this intense darkness. There is no remedy, however, and the risk must be taken. I will first try the lead again."

A cast was made, and the result was two and a half fathoms of water.

"Put the helm down !" cried Paul, springing to the sheet ; " lose not a moment, but down with the helm !"

The boat did not work freely under her imperfect sail and with the roof she carried, and a moment of painful anxiety succeeded. Paul managed, however, to get a part of the sail aback, and he felt more secure.

"The boat has stern-way : shift the helm, Mr. Sharp."

This was done, the yard was dipped, and the two young men felt a relief almost equal to that they had experienced on clearing the inlet, when they found the launch again drawing ahead, obedient to her rudder.

"We are near something, reef or shore." said Paul, standing with the lead-line in his hand, in readiness to heave. "I think it can hardly be the first, as we hear no Arabs."

Waiting a few minutes, he hove the lead, and, to his infinite joy, got three fathoms fairly.

"That is good news. We are hauling off the danger, whatever it may be," he said, as he felt the mark : " and now for the compass."

Saunders was called, a light was struck, and the compasses were both examined. These faithful but mysterious guides, which have so long served man while they have baffled all his ingenuity to discover the sources of their power, were, as usual, true to their governing principle. The boat was heading north-northwest ; the wind was at northeast, and before they tacked they had doubtless been standing directly for the beach, from which they could not have been distant a half quarter of a mile, if so much. A few more minutes would have carried them into the breakers, capsized the boat, and most probably drowned all below the roof, if not those on it.

Paul shuddered as these facts forced themselves on his attention, and he determined to stand on his present course for two hours, when daylight would render his return towards the land without danger.

"This is the trade," he said, "and it will probably stand. We have a current to contend with, as well as a head-wind; but I think we can weather the cape by morning, when we can get a survey of the wreck by means of the glass. If we discover nothing, I shall bear up at once for the Cape de Verdes."

The two gentlemen now took the helm in turns, he who slept fastening himself to the mast, as a precaution against being rolled into the sea by the motion of the boat. In fifteen fathoms water they tacked again, and stood to the east-southeast, having made certain, by a fresh examination of the compass, that the wind stood in the same quarter as before. The moon rose soon after, and, although the morning was clouded and lowering, there was then sufficient light to remove all danger from the darkness. At length this long and anxious night terminated in the usual streak of day, which gleamed across the desert.

Paul was at the helm, steering more by instinct than anything else, and occasionally nodding at his post; for two successive nights of watching, and a day of severe toil had overcome his sense of danger, and his care for others. Strange fancies beset men at such moments; and his busy imagination was running over some of the scenes of his early youth, when either his sense or his wandering faculties made him hear the usual brief, spirited hail of—

"Boat ahoy!"

Paul opened his eyes, felt that the tiller was in his hand, and was about to close the first again, when the words were more sternly repeated,—

"Boat ahoy! what craft's that? Answer, or expect a shot!"

This was plain English, and Paul was wide awake in an instant. Rubbing his eyes, he saw a line of boats anchored directly on his weather bow, with a raft of spars riding astern.

"Hurrah!" shouted the young man. "This is Heaven's own tidings! Are these the Montauks?"

"Ay, ay. Who the devil are you?"

The truth is, Captain Truck did not recognize his own launch in the royal, roof, and jigger. He had never before seen a boat afloat in such a guise; and in the obscurity of the hour, and fresh awakened from a profound sleep, like Paul, his faculties were a little confused. But the latter soon comprehended the whole matter. He clapped his helm down, let fly the sheet, and in a minute the launch of the packet was riding alongside of the launch of the Dane. Heads were out of the shutters, and every boat gave up its sleepers, for the cry was general throughout the little flotilla.

The party just arrived alone felt joy. They found those whom they had believed dead, or captives, alive and free; whereas the others now learned the extent of the misfortune that had befallen them. For a few minutes this contrast in feeling produced an awkward meeting; but the truth soon brought all down to the same sober level. Captain Truck received the congratulations of his friends like one in a stupor; Toast looked amazed as his friend Saunders shook his hand; and the gentlemen who had been to the wreck met the cheerful greetings of those who had just escaped the Arabs like men who fancied the others mad.

We pass over the explanations that followed, as every one will readily understand them. Captain Truck listened to Paul like one in a trance, and it was some time after the young man had done before he spoke. With a wish to cheer him, he was told of the ample provision of stores that had been brought off in the launch, of the trade-winds that had now apparently set in, and of the great probability of their all reaching the islands in safety. Still the old man made no reply; he got on the roof of his own launch, and paced backwards and forwards rapidly, heeding nothing. Even Eve spoke to him unnoticed, and the consolations offered by her father were not attended to. At length he stopped suddenly, and called for his mate.

"Mr. Leach!"

"Sir."

"Here is a category for you!"

"Ay, ay, sir; it's bad enough in its way; still, we are better off than the Danes."

"You tell me, sir," turning to Paul, "that these foul blackguards were actually on the deck of the ship?"

"Certainly, Captain Truck. They took complete possession; for we had no means of keeping them off."

"And the ship is ashore?"

"Beyond a question."

"Bilged?"

"I think not. There is no swell within the reef, and she lies on sand."

"We might have spared ourselves the trouble, Leach, of culling these cursed spars, as if they had been so many toothpicks."

"That we might, sir; for they will not now serve as oven-wood, for want of the oven."

"A damnable category, Mr. Effingham! I'm glad you are safe, sir; and you, too, my dear young lady—God bless you!—God bless you! It were better the whole line should be in their power than one like you!"

The old seaman's eyes filled as he shook Eve by the hand, and for a moment he forgot the ship.

"Mr. Leach!"

"Sir."

"Let the people have their breakfasts, and bear a hand about it. We are likely to have a busy morning, sir. Lift the kedge, too, and let us drift down towards these gentry, and take a look at them. We have both wind and current with us now, and shall make quick work of it."

The kedge was raised, the sails were all set, and, with the two launches lashed together, the whole line of boats and spars began to set to the southward at a rate that would bring them up with the inlet in about two hours.

"This is the course for the Cape de Verdes, gentlemen," said the captain bitterly. "We shall have to pass before our own door to go and ask hospitality of strangers. But let the people get their breakfasts, Mr. Leach; just let the boys have one comfortable meal before they take to their oars."

Eat himself, however, Mr. Truck would not. He chewed the end of a cigar, and continued walking up and down the roof.

In half an hour the people had ended their meal, the day had fairly opened, and the boats and raft had made good progress.

"Splice the main-brace, Mr. Leach," said the captain, "for we are a little jammed. And you, gentlemen, do me the favor to step this way for a consultation. This much is due to your situation."

Captain Truck assembled his male passengers in the stern of the Dane's launch, where he commenced the following address :—

"Gentlemen," he said, "everything in this world has its nature and its principles. This truth I hold you all to be too well informed and well educated to deny. The nature of a traveller is to travel, and see curiosities; the nature of old men is to think on the past, of a young man to hope for the future. The nature of a seaman is to stick by his ship, and of a ship to be treated like a vessel, and not to be ransacked like a town taken by storm, or a nunnery that is rifled. You are but passengers, and doubtless have your own wishes and occupations, as I have mine. Your wishes are, beyond question, to be safe in New York among your friends; and mine are to get the Montauk there too, in as little time and with as little injury as possible. You have a good navigator among you; and I now propose that you take the Montauk's launch, with such stores as are necessary, and fill away at once for the islands, where I pray God, you may all arrive in safety, and that when you reach America you may find all your relations in good health, and in no manner uneasy at this little delay. Your effects shall be safely delivered to your respective orders, should it please God to put it in the power of the line to honor your drafts."

"You intend to attempt recapturing the ship!" exclaimed Paul.

"I do, sir," returned Mr. Truck, who, having thus far opened his mind, for the first time that morning gave a vigorous hem! and set about lighting a cigar. "We may do it, gentlemen, or we may not do it. If we do it, you will hear further from me; if we fail, why, tell them at home that we carried sail as long as a stitch would draw."

The gentlemen looked at each other, the young waiting in respect for the counsel of the old, the old hesitating in deference to the pride and feelings of the young.

"We must join you in this enterprise, captain," said Mr. Sharp quietly, but with the manner of a man of spirit and nerve.

"Certainly, certainly," cried Mr. Monday; "we ought to make a common affair of it; as I dare say Sir George Templemore will agree with me in maintaining: the nobility and gentry are not often backward when their persons are to be risked."

The spurious baronet acquiesced in the proposal as readily as it had been made by him whom he had temporarily deposed; for, though a weak and a vain young man, he was far from being a dastard.

"This is a serious business," observed Paul, "and it ought to be ordered with method and intelligence. If we have a ship to care for, we have those also who are infinitely more precious."

"Very true, Mr. Blunt, very true," interrupted Mr. Dodge, a little eagerly. "It is my maxim to let well alone; and I am certain shipwrecked people can hardly be better off and more comfortable than we are at this very moment. I dare say these gallant sailors, if the question was fairly put to them, would give it by a handsome majority in favor of things as they are. I am a conservative, captain, and I think an appeal ought to be made to the ballot-boxes before we decide on a measure of so much magnitude."

The occasion was too grave for the ordinary pleasantry, and this singular proposition was heard in silence, to Mr. Dodge's great disgust.

"I think it is the duty of Captain Truck to endeavor to

retake his vessel," continued Paul ; "but the affair will be serious, and success is far from certain. The Montauk's launch ought to be left at a safe distance with all the females, and in prudent keeping ; for any disaster to the boarding party would probably throw the rest of the boats into the hands of the barbarians, and endanger the safety of those left in the launch. Mr. Effingham and Mr. John Effingham will of course remain with the ladies."

The father assented with the simplicity of one who did not distrust his own motives, but the eagle-shaped features of his kinsman curled with a cool and sarcastic smile.

"Will you remain in the launch?" the latter asked pointedly, turning towards Paul.

"Certainly it would be greatly out of character were I to think of it. My trade is war, and I trust that Captain Truck means to honor me with the command of one of the boats."

"I thought as much, by Jove!" exclaimed the captain, seizing a hand, which he shook with the utmost cordiality ; "I should as soon expect to see the sheet-anchor wink, or the best bower give a mournful smile, as to see you duck ! Still, gentlemen, I am well aware of the difference in our situations. I ask no man to forget his duties to those on shore on my account, and I fancy that my regular people, aided by Mr. Blunt, who can really serve me by his knowledge, will be as likely to do all that can be done as all of us united. It is not numbers that carry ships, as much as spirit, promptitude, and resolution."

"But the question has not yet been put to the people," said Mr. Dodge, who was a little mystified by the word last used, which he had yet to learn was strictly technical as applied to a vessel's crew.

"It shall, sir," returned Captain Truck, "and I beg you to note the majority. My lads," he continued, rising on a thwart, and speaking aloud, "you know the history of the ship. As to the Arabs, now they have got her they do not know how to sail her, and it is no more than a kindness to take her out of their hands. For this business I want volunteers—those who are for the reef and an attack, will rise up and cheer ; while they who like an offing have only to sit still and stay where they are.''

The words were no sooner spoken than Mr. Leach jumped up on the gunwale and waved his hat. The people rose as one man, and taking the signal from the mate, they gave three as hearty cheers as ever rung over the bottle.

"Dead against you, sir !'' observed the captain, nodding to the editor, ''and I hope you are now satisfied.''

''The ballot might have given it the other way,'' muttered Mr. Dodge ; ''there can be no freedom of election without the ballot.''

No one, however, thought any longer of Mr. Dodge or his scruples, but the whole disposition for the attack was made with promptitude and caution. It was decided that Mr. Effingham and his own servant should remain in the launch, while the captain compelled his two mates to draw lots which of them should stay behind also, a navigator being indispensable. The chance fell on the second mate, who submitted to his luck with an ill grace.

A bust of Napoleon was cut up, and the pieces of lead were beaten as nearly round as possible, so as to form a dozen leaden balls and a quantity of slugs, or langrage. The latter were put in canvas bags, while the keg of powder was opened, a flannel shirt or two were torn, and cartridges were filled. Ammunition was also distributed to the people, and Mr. Sharp examined their arms. The gun was got off the roof of the Montauk's launch, and placed on a grating forward in that of the Dane. The sails and rigging were cleared out of the boat and secured on the raft, when she was properly manned and the command of her was given to Paul.

The three other boats received their crews, with John Effingham at the head of one, the captain and his mate commanding the others. Mr. Dodge felt compelled to volunteer to go in the launch of the Dane, where Paul had now taken his station, though he did it with a reluctance that escaped the observation of no one who took the pains to observe him. Mr. Sharp and Mr. Monday were with the captain, and the false Sir George Templemore went with Mr. Leach. These arrangements completed, the whole party waited impatiently for the wind and current to set them down towards the reef, the rocks of which by this time were plainly visible, even from the thwarts of the several boats.

24

# CHAPTER XXVI.

"Hark! was it not the trumpet's voice I heard?
The soul of battle is awake within me.
The fate of ages and of empires hangs
On this dread hour."

MASSINGER.

THE two launches were still sailing side by side, and Eve now appeared at the open window next the seat of Paul. Her face was pale as when the scene of the cabin occurred, and her lip trembled.

"I do not understand these warlike proceedings," she said, "but I trust, Mr. Blunt, *we* have no concern with the present movement."

"Put your mind at ease on this head, dearest Miss Effingham, for what we now do, we do in compliance with a general law of manhood. Were your interests and the interests of those with you alone consulted, we might come to a very different decision; but I think you are in safe hands, should our adventure prove unfortunate."

"Unfortunate! It is fearful to be so near a scene like this! I cannot ask you to do anything unworthy of yourself; but, all that we owe you impels me to say, I trust you have too much wisdom, too much true courage, to incur unnecessary risks."

The young man looked volumes of gratitude, but the presence of the others kept its expression within due bounds.

"We old sea-dogs," he answered, smiling, "are rather noted for taking care of ourselves. They who are trained to a business like this usually set about it too much in a business-like manner to hazard anything for mere show."

"And very wisely; Mr. Sharp, too"— Eve's color deepened with a consciousness that Paul would have given worlds to understand—" he has a claim on us we shall never forget. My father can say all this better than I."

Mr. Effingham now expressed his thanks for all that had passed, and earnestly enjoined prudence on the young men; after which Eve withdrew her head, and was seen no more. Most of the next hour was passed in prayer by those in the launch.

By this time the boats and raft were within half a mile of the inlet, and Captain Truck ordered the kedge, which had been transferred to the launch of the Montauk, to be let go. As soon as this was done, the old seaman threw down his hat, and stood on a thwart in his gray hair.

"Gentlemen, you have your orders," he said, with dignity; for from that moment his manner rose with the occasion, and had something of the grandeur of the warrior. "You see the enemy. The reef must first be cleared, and then the ship shall be carried. God knows who will live to see the end; but that end must be success, or the bones of John Truck shall bleach on these sands! Our cry is, ' The Montauk and our own!' which is a principle Vattel will sustain us in. Give way, men! a long pull, a strong pull, and a pull all together; each boat in its station!"

He waved his hand, and the oars fell into the water at the same instant. The heavy launch was the last, for she had double-fasts to the other boat. While loosening that forward the second mate deserted his post, stepping nimbly on board the departing boat, and concealing himself behind the foremost of the two lug-sails she carried. Almost at the same instant Mr. Dodge reversed this manœuvre by pretending to be left clinging to the boat of the Montauk, in his zeal to shove off. As the sails were drawing hard, and the oars dashed the spray aside, it was too late to rectify either of these mistakes, had it been desirable.

A few minutes of stern calm succeeded, each boat keeping its place with beautiful precision. The Arabs had left the northern reef with the light; but, the tide being out, hundreds were strung along the southern range of rocks,

especially near the ship.    The wind carried the launch
ahead, as had been intended, and she soon drew near the
inlet.

"Take in the sails," said Mr. Blunt.    "See your gun
clear forward."

A fine, tall, straight, athletic young seaman stood near the
grating, with a heated iron lying in a vessel of live coals before him, in lieu of a loggerhead, the fire being covered with
a tarpauling.    As Paul spoke, this young mariner turned
towards him with the peculiar grace of a man-of-war's-man,
and touched his hat.

"Ay, ay, sir.    All ready, Mr. Powis."

Paul started, while the other smiled proudly, like one who
knew more than his companions.

"We have met before," said the first.

"That have we, sir, and in boat-duty, too.    You were the
first on board the pirate on the coast of Cuba, and I was
second."

A look of recognition and a wave of the hand passed between them, the men cheering involuntarily.    It was too
late for more, the launch being fairly in the inlet, where she
received a general but harmless fire from the Arabs.    An
order had been given to fire the first shot over the heads of
the barbarians; but this assault changed the plan.

"Depress the piece, Brooks," said Paul, "and throw in a
bag of slugs."

"All ready, sir," was uttered in another minute.

"Hold water, men—the boat is steady—let them have
it!"

Men fell at that discharge; but how many was never
known, as the bodies were hurried off the reef by those who
fled.    A few concealed themselves along the rocks, but most
scampered towards the shore.

"Bravely done!" cried Captain Truck, as his boat swept
past.    "Now for the ship, sir!"

The people cheered again, and dashed their oars into the
water.    To clear the reef was nothing; but to carry the ship
was a serious affair.    She was defended by four times the
number of those in the boats, and there was no retreat.    The

Arabs, as has already been seen, had suspended their labor during the night, having fruitlessly endeavored to haul the vessel over to the reef before the tide rose. More by accident than by calculation, they had made such arrangements, by getting a line to the rocks, as would probably have set the ship off the sands, when she floated at high water; but this line had been cut by Paul in passing, and the wind coming on shore again, during the confusion and clamor of the barbarians, or at a moment when they thought they were to be attacked, no attention was paid to the circumstance, and the Montauk was suffered to drive up still higher on the sands, where she effectually grounded at the very top of the tide. As it was now dead low water, the ship had sewed materially, and was now lying on her bilge, partly sustained by the water, and partly by the bottom.

During the short pause that succeeded, Saunders, who was seated in the captain's boat as a small-arms-man, addressed his subordinate in a low voice.

"Now, Toast," he said, "you are about to contend in battle for the first time: and I diwine, from experience, that the ewent gives you some sentiments that are werry original. My advice to you is, to shut both eyes until the word is given to fire, and then to open them suddenly, as if just awaking from sleep; after which you may present and pull the trigger. Above all, Toast, take care not to kill any of our own friends, most especially not Captain Truck, just at this werry moment."

"I shall do my endeavors, Mr. Saunders," muttered Toast, with the apathy and submissive dependence on others with which the American black usually goes into action. "If I do any harm, I hope it will be overlooked, on account of my want of experience."

"Imitate me, Toast, in coolness and propriety, and you 'll be certain not to offend. I do not mean that you are to kill the werry same *muscle*-men that I kill, but that when I kill one you are to kill another. And be werry careful not to hurt Captain Truck, who 'll be certain to run right afore the muzzle of our guns, if he sees anything to be done there."

Toast growled an assent, and then there was no other noise in the boat than that which was produced by the steady and vigorous falling of the oars. An attempt had been made to lighten the vessel by unloading her, and the bank of sand was already covered with bales and boxes, which had been brought up from the hold by means of a stage, and by sheer animal force. The raft had been extended in size, and brought round to the bank by the stern of the vessel, with the intention to load it, and to transfer the articles already landed to the rocks.

Such was the state of things about the Montauk when the boats came into the channel that ran directly up to the bank. The launch led again, her sails having been set as soon as the reef was swept, and she now made another discharge on the deck of the ship, which, inclining towards the gun, offered no shelter. The effect was to bring every Arab, in the twinkling of an eye, down upon the bank.

"Hurrah!" shouted Captain Truck; "that grist has purified the old bark! And now to see who is to own her! 'The thieves are out of the temple,' as my good father would have said."

The four boats were in a line abreast, the launch under one sail only. A good deal of confusion existed on the bank; but the Arabs sought the cover of the bales and boxes, and opened a sharp though irregular fire. Three times, as they advanced, the second mate and that gallant-looking young seaman called Brooks discharged the gun, and at each discharge the Arabs were dislodged and driven to the raft. The cheers of the seamen became animated, though they still plied the oars.

"Steadily, men," said Captain Truck, "and prepare to board."

At this moment the launch grounded, though still twenty yards from the bank, the other boats passing her with loud cheers.

"We are all ready, sir," cried Brooks.

"Let 'em have it. Take in the sail, boys."

The gun was fired, and the tall young seaman sprang upon the grating and cheered. As he looked backward, with a smile of triumph, Paul saw his eyes roll. He leaped into the air, and fell at his length dead upon the water; for such is the passage of a man in battle, from one state of existence to another.

"Where do we hang?" asked Paul, steadily; "forward or aft?"

It was forward, and deeper water lay ahead of them. The sail was set again, and the people were called aft. The boat tipped, and shot ahead towards the sands, like a courser released from a sudden pull.

All this time the others were not idle. Not a musket was fired from either boat until the whole three struck the bank, almost at the same instant, though at as many different points. Then all leaped ashore, and threw in a fire so close, that the boxes served as much for a cover to the assailants as to the assailed. It was at this critical moment, when the seamen paused to load, that Paul, just clear of the bottom, with his own hand applying the loggerhead, swept the rear of the bank with a most opportune discharge.

"Yard-arm and yard-arm!" shouted Captain Truck. "Lay 'em aboard, boys, and give 'em Jack's play!"

The whole party sprang forward, and from that moment all order ceased. Fists, handspikes, of which many were on the bank, and the butts of muskets, were freely used, and in a way that set the spears and weapons of the Arabs at defiance. The captain, Mr. Sharp, John Effingham, Mr. Monday, the *soi-disant* Sir George Templemore, and the chief mate, formed a sort of Macedonian phalanx, which penetrated the centre of the barbarians, and which kept close to the enemy, following up its advantages with a spirit that admitted no rallying. On their right and left pressed the men, an athletic, hearty, well-fed gang. The superiority of the Arabs was in their powers of endurance; for, trained to the whip-cord rigidity of racers, force was less their peculiar merit than bottom. Had they acted in concert, however, or had they been on their own desert, mounted, and with room for their subtle evolutions, the result might have been very different; but, unused to contend with an enemy who brought them within reach of the arm, their tactics were deranged, and all their habits violated. Still, their numbers were formidable, and it is probable that the accident to the launch, after all, decided the matter. From the moment the *mêlée* began not a shot was fired, but the assailants pressed upon the assailed, until a large body of the latter had collected near the raft. This was just as the launch reached the shore, and Paul perceived there was great danger that the tide might roll backward from sheer necessity. The gun was loaded, and filled nearly to the muzzle with slugs. He caused the men to raise it on their oars, and to carry it to a large box, a little apart from the confusion of the fight. All this was done in a moment, for three minutes had not yet passed since the captain landed.

Instead of firing, Paul called aloud to his friends to cease fighting. Though chafing like a vexed lion, Captain Truck complied, surprise effecting quite as much as obedience. The Arabs hardest pressed upon profited by the pause to fall back on the main body of their friends, near the raft. This was all Paul could ask, and he ordered the gun to be pointed at the centre of the group, while he advanced himself towards the enemy making a sign of peace.

" Damn 'em, lay 'em aboard ! " cried the captain ; " no quarter to the blackguards ! "

" I rather think we had better charge again," added Mr. Sharp, who was thoroughly warmed with his late employment.

" Hold, gentlemen ; you risk all needlessly. I will show these poor wretches what they have to expect, and they will probably retire. We want the ship, not their blood."

" Well, well," returned the impatient captain, " give 'em plenty of Vattel, for we have 'em now in a category."

The men of the wilderness and of the desert seem to act as much by instinct as by reason. An old sheik advanced, smiling, towards Paul, when the latter was a few yards in advance of his friends, offering his hand with as much cordiality as if they met merely to exchange courtesies. Paul led him quietly to the gun, put his hand in, and drew out a bag of slugs, replaced it, and pointed significantly at the dense crowd of exposed Arabs, and at the heated iron that was ready to discharge the piece. At all this the old Arab smiled, and seemed to express his admiration. He was then shown the strong and well-armed party, all of whom by this time had a musket or a pistol ready to use. Paul then signed to the raft and to the reef, as much as to tell the other to withdraw his party.

The sheik exhibited great coolness and sagacity, and, un-used to frays so desperate, he signified his disposition to comply. Truces, Paul knew, were common in the African combats, which are seldom bloody, and he hoped the best from the manner of the sheik, who was now permitted to return to his friends. A short conference succeeded among the Arabs, when several of them smilingly waved their hands, and most of the party crowded on the raft. Others advanced and asked permission to bear away their wounded, and the bodies of the dead, in both of which offices they were assisted by the seamen, as far as was prudent; for it was all-important to be on the guard against treachery.

In this extraordinary manner the combatants separated, the Arabs hauling themselves over to the reef by a line, their old men smiling, and making signs of amity, until they were fairly on the rocks. Here they remained but a very few minutes, for the camels and dromedaries were seen trotting off towards the Dane on the shore; a sign that the compact between the different parties of the barbarians was dissolved, and that each man was about to plunder on his own account. This movement produced great agitation among the old sheiks and their followers on the reef, and set them in mo-tion with great activity towards the land. So great was their hurry, indeed, that the bodies of all the dead, and of several of the wounded, were fairly abandoned on the rocks, at some distance from the shore.

The first step of the victors, as a matter of course, was to inquire into their own loss. This was much less than would otherwise have been, on account of their good conduct. Every man, without a solitary exception, had ostensibly behaved well; one of the most infallible means of lessening danger. Several of the party had received slight hurts, and divers bullets had passed through hats and jackets. Mr. Sharp, alone, had two through the former, besides one through his coat. Paul had blood drawn on an arm, and Captain Truck, to use his own language, resembled "a horse in fly-time," his skin having been raised in no less than five places. But all these trifling hurts and hair-breadth escapes counted for nothing, as no one was seriously injured by them, or felt sufficient inconvenience even to report himself wounded.

The felicitations were warm and general; even the seamen asking leave to shake their sturdy old commander by the hand. Paul and Mr. Sharp fairly embraced, each expressing his sincere pleasure that the other had escaped unharmed. The latter even shook hands cordially with his counterfeit, who had acted with spirit from the first to the last. John Effingham alone maintained the same cool indifference after the affair that he had shown in it, when it was seen that he had played his part with singular coolness and discretion, dropping two Arabs with his fowling-piece on landing, with a sort of sportsman-like coolness with which he was in the habit of dropping woodcock at home.

"I fear Mr. Monday is seriously hurt," this gentleman said to the captain, in the midst of his congratulations; "he sits aloof on the box yonder, and looks exhausted."

"Mr. Monday! I hope not, with all my heart and soul. He is a capital *diplomat* and a stout boarder. And Mr. Dodge, too! I miss Mr. Dodge."

"Mr. Dodge must have remained behind to console the ladies," returned Paul, "finding that your second mate had abandoned them, like a recreant that he is."

The captain shook his disobedient mate by the hand a second time, and swore he was a mutineer for violating his orders, and ended by declaring that the day was not distant when he and Mr. Leach should command two as good liners as ever sailed out of America.

"I'll have nothing to do with either of you as soon as we reach home," he concluded. "There was Leach a foot or two ahead of me the whole time: and, as for the second officer, I should be justified in logging him as having run.

Well, well ; young men will be young men ; and so would
old men too, Mr. John Effingham, if they knew how.    But
Mr. Monday does look doleful ; and I am afraid we shall
be obliged to overhaul the medicine-chest for him."

Mr. Monday, however, was beyond the aid of medicine.
A ball had passed through his shoulder-blade in landing ;
notwithstanding which he had pressed into the *mêlée*, where,
unable to parry it, a spear had been thrust into his chest.
The last wound appeared grave, and Captain Truck immediately ordered the sufferer to be carried into the ship ; John
Effingham, with a tenderness and humanity that were singularly in contrast with his ordinary sarcastic manner, volunteering to take charge of him.

" We have need of all our forces," said Captain Truck, as
Mr. Monday was borne away ; " and yet it is due to our
friends in the launch to let them know the result.  Set the
ensign, Leach : that will tell them our success, though a
verbal communication can alone acquaint them with the particulars."

" If," interrupted Paul, eagerly, " you will lend me the
launch of the Dane, Mr. Sharp and myself will beat her up
to the raft, let our friends know the result, and bring the
spars down to the inlet.  This will save the necessity of any
of the men's being absent.  We claim the privilege, too, as
belonging properly to the party that is now absent."

" Gentlemen, take any privilege you please.  You have
stood by me like heroes ; and I owe you all more than  the
heel of a worthless old life will ever permit me to pay."

The two young men did not wait for a second invitation,
but in five minutes the boat was stretching through one of
the channels that led landward ; and in five more it was
laying out of the inlet with a steady breeze.

The instant Captain Truck retrod the deck of his ship
was one of uncontrollable feeling with the weather-beaten
old seaman.  The ship had sewed too much to admit of
walking with ease, and he sat down on the coamings of the
main hatch, and fairly wept like an infant.  So high had his
feelings been wrought that this outbreaking was violent,
and the men wondered to see their gray-headed, stern old

commander so completely unmanned. He seemed at length
ashamed of the weakness himself, for, rising like a worried
tiger, he began to issue his orders as sternly and promptly
as was his wont.

"What the devil are you gaping at, men!" he growled;
"did you never see a ship on her bilge before? God
knows, and for that matter you all know, there is enough
to do, that you stand like so many marines, with their ' eyes
right!' and ' pipe-clay.'"

"Take it more kindly, Captain Truck," returned an old
sea-dog, thrusting out a hand that was all knobs, a fellow
whose tobacco had not been displaced even by the fray;
"take it kindly, and look upon these boxes and bales as
so much cargo that is to be struck in, in dock. We'll soon
stow it, and, barring a few slugs, and one four-pounder, that
has cut up a crate of crockery as if it had been a cat in a
cupboard, no great harm is done. I look upon this matter
as no more than a sudden squall, that has compelled us to
bear up for a little while, but which will answer for a winch
to spin yarns on all the rest of our days. I have fit the
French, and the English, and the Turks, in my time; and
now I can say I have had a brush with the niggers."

"D——n me, but you are right, old Tom! and I'll make
no more account of the matter. Mr. Leach, give the people
a little encouragement. There is enough left in the jug
that you'll find in the stern-sheets of the pinnace; and
then turn-to, and strike in all this dunnage, that the Arabs
have been scattering on the sands. We'll stow it when we
get the ship into an easier bed than the one in which she is
now lying."

This was the signal for commencing work; and these
straightforward tars, who had just been in the confusion and
hazards of a fight, first took their grog, and then commenced
their labor in earnest. As they had only, with their knowledge and readiness, to repair the damage done by the
ignorant and hurried Arabs, in a short time everything was
on board the ship again, when their attention was directed
to the situation of the vessel itself. Not to anticipate events,
however, we will now return to the party in the launch.

The reader will readily imagine the feelings with which
Mr. Effingham and his party listened to the report of the
first gun.   As they all remained below, they were ignorant
who the individual really was that kept pacing the roof over
their heads, though it was believed to be the second mate,
agreeably to the arrangement made by Captain Truck.

"My eyes grow dim," said Mr. Effingham, who was
looking through a glass ; "will you try to see what is passing, Eve?"

"Father, I cannot look," returned the pallid girl.   "It is
misery enough to hear these frightful guns."

"It is awful!" said Nanny, folding her arms about her
child, "and I wonder that such gentlemen as Mr. John
and Mr. Powis should go on an enterprise so wicked!"

"*Voulez-vous avoir la complaisance, Monsieur ?*"   said
Mademoiselle Viefville, taking the glass from the unresisting
hand of Mr. Effingham.   "*Ha ! le combat commence en effet !*"

"Is it the Arabs who now fire?" demanded Eve, unable,
in spite of terror, to repress her interest.

"*Non, c'est cet admirable jeune homme, Monsieur Blunt,
qui devance tous les autres !*"

"And now, Mademoiselle, *that* must surely be the barbarians?"

"*Du tout.   Les sauvages fuient.   C'est encore du bateau
de Monsieur Blunt qu'on tire.   Quel beau courage ! son
bateau est toujours des premiers !*"

"That shout is frightful!   Do they close?"

"*On crie des deux parts, je crois.   Le vieux capitaine est
en avant à présent, et Monsieur Blunt s'arrête !*"

"May Heaven avert the danger!   Do you see the gentleman at all, Mademoiselle?"

"*La fumée est trop épaisse.   Ah ! les voilà !   On tire
encore de son bateau.*"

"*Eh bien, Mademoiselle ?*" said Eve, tremulously, after a
long pause.

"*C'est déjà fini.   Les Arabes se retirent et nos amis se
sont emparés du bâtiment.   Cela a été l'affaire d'un moment,
et que le combat a été glorieux !   Ces jeunes gens sont vrai-
ment dignes d'être Français, et le vieux capitaine, aussi.*"

"Are there no tidings for us, Mademoiselle?" asked Eve, after another long pause, during which she had poured out her gratitude in trembling, but secret thanksgivings.

"*Non, pas encore. Ils se félicitent, je crois.*"

"It's time, I'm sure, ma'am," said the meek-minded Ann, "to send forth the dove, that it may find the olive-branch. War and strife are too sinful to be long indulged in."

"There is a boat making sail in this direction," said Mr. Effingham, who had left the glass with the governess, in complaisance to her wish.

"*Oui, c'est le bateau de Monsieur Blunt.*"

"And who is in it?" demanded the father, for the meed of a world could not have enabled Eve to speak.

"*Je vois Monsieur Sharp —oui, c'est bien lui.*"

"Is he alone?"

"*Non, il y en a deux—mais—oui—c'est Monsieur Blunt,— notre jeune héros!*"

Eve bowed her face, and even while her soul melted in gratitude to God, the feelings of her sex caused the tell-tale blood to suffuse her features to the brightness of crimson.

Mr. Effingham now took the glass from the spirited Frenchwoman, whose admiration of brilliant qualities had overcome her fears, and he gave a more detailed and connected account of the situation of things near the ship, as they presented themselves to a spectator at that distance.

Notwithstanding they already knew so much, it was a painful and feverish half hour to those in the launch, the time that intervened between this dialogue and the moment when the boat of the Dane came alongside of their own. Every face was at the windows, and the young men were received like deliverers, in whose safety all felt a deep concern.

"But, cousin Jack," said Eve, across whose speaking countenance apprehension and joy cast their shadows and gleams like April clouds driving athwart a brilliant sky, "my father has not been able to discover his form among those who move about on the bank."

The gentlemen explained the misfortune of Mr. Monday, and related the manner in which John Effingham had assumed the office of nurse. A few delicious minutes passed ; for nothing is more grateful than the happiness that first succeeds a victory, and the young men proceeded to lift the kedge, assisted by the servant of Mr. Effingham. The sails were set ; and in fifteen minutes the raft—the long-desired and much-coveted raft—approached the inlet.

Paul steered the larger boat, and gave to Mr. Sharp directions how to steer the other. The tide was flowing into the passage ; and, by keeping his weatherly position, the young man carried his long train of spars with so much precision into its opening, that, favored by the current, it was drawn through without touching a rock, and brought in triumph to the very margin of the bank. Here it was secured, the sails and cordage were brought ashore, and the whole party landed.

The last twenty hours seemed like a dream to all the females, as they again walked the solid sand in security and hope. They had now assembled every material of safety, and all that remained was to get the ship off the shore, and to rig her ; Mr. Leach having already reported that she was as tight as the day she left London.

## CHAPTER XXVII.

"Would I were in an ale-house in London!
I would give all my fame for a pot of ale and safety."
*Henry V.*

MADEMOISELLE VIEFVILLE, with a decision and intelligence that rendered her of great use in moments of need, hastened to offer her services to the wounded man, while Eve, attended by Ann Sidley, ascended the ship and made her way into the cabins, in the best manner the leaning position of the vessel allowed. Here they found less confusion than might have been expected, the scene being ludicrous, rather than painful, for Mr Monday was in his stateroom, excluded from sight.

In the first place, the *soi-disant* Sir George Templemore was counting over his effects, among which he had discovered a sad deficiency in coats and pantaloons. The Arabs had respected the plunder, by compact, with the intention of making a fair distribution on the reef; but, with a view to throw a sop to the more rapacious of their associates, one room had been sacked by the permission of the sheiks, This unfortunate room happened to be that of Sir George Templemore: and the patent razors, the East Indian dressing-case, the divers toys, to say nothing of innumerable vestments which the young man had left paraded in his room, for the mere pleasure of feasting his eyes on them, had disappeared.

"Do me the favor, Miss Effingham," he said, appealing to Eve, of whom he stood habitually in awe, from the pure necessity of addressing her in his distress, or of addressing no one, "do me the favor to look into my room, and see the unprincipled manner in which I have been treated. Not a comb nor a razor left ; not a garment to make myself decent in ! I 'm sure such conduct is quite a disgrace to the civilization of barbarians even, and I shall make it a point to have the affair duly represented to his majesty's minister the moment I arrive in New York. I sincerely hope you have been better treated, though I think, after this specimen of their principles, there is little hope for any one : I 'm sure we ought to be grateful they did not strip the ship. I trust we shall all make common cause against them the moment we arrive."

"We ought, indeed, sir," returned Eve, who, while she had known from the beginning of his being an imposter, was willing to ascribe his fraud to vanity, and who now felt charitable towards him on account of the spirit he had shown in the combat ; "though I trust we shall have escaped better. Our effects were principally in the baggage-room, and that, I understand from Captain Truck, has not been touched."

"Indeed you are very fortunate, and I can only wish that the same good luck had happened to myself. But then, you know, Miss Effingham, that one has need of his little comforts, and, as for myself, I confess to rather a weakness in that way."

"Monstrous prodigality and wastefulness !" cried Saunders, as Eve passed on towards her own cabin, willing to escape any more of Sir George's complaints. "Just be so kind, Miss Effingham, ma'am, to look into this here pantry, once ! Them niggers, I do believe, have had their fingers in everything, and it will take Toast and me a week to get things decorous and orderly again. Some of the shrieks" (for so the steward styled the chiefs) "have been yelling well in this place, I 'll engage, as you may see, by the manner in which they have spilt the mustard and mangled that cold duck. I 've a most mortal awersion to a man that cuts up poultry against the fibres ; and, would you think it, Miss Effingham, ma'am, that the last gun Mr. Blunt fired, dislocated, or otherwise diwerted, about half a dozen of the fowls that happened to be in the way ; for I let all the
25

poor wretches out of the coops, that they might make their
own livings should we never come back. I should think
that as polite and experienced a gentleman as Mr. Blunt
might have shot the Arabs instead of my poultry ! ''

"So it is, '' thought Eve, as she glanced into the pantry
and proceeded. " What is considered happiness to-day, gets
to be misery to-morrow ; and the rebukes of adversity are
forgotten the instant prosperity resumes its influence. Either
of these men, a few hours since, would have been most
happy to have been in this vessel, as a home, or a covering
for their heads, and now they quarrel with their good
fortune because it is wanting in some accustomed superfluity
or pampered indulgence.''

We shall leave her with this wholesome reflection uppermost, to examine into the condition of her own room, and
return to the deck.

As the hour was still early, Captain Truck, having once
quieted his feelings, went to work with zeal, to turn the late
success to the best account. The cargo that had been discharged was soon stowed again, and the next great object was
to get the ship afloat previously to hoisting in the new spars.
As the kedges still lay on the reef, and all the anchors remained in the places where they had originally been placed,
there was little to do but to get ready to heave upon the
chains as soon as the tide rose. Previously to commencing
this task, however, the intervening time was well employed
in sending down the imperfect hamper that was aloft, and
in getting up sheers to hoist out the remains of the foremast,
as well as the jury mainmast, the latter of which, it will be
remembered, was only fitted two days before. All the appliances used on that occasion being still on deck, and everybody lending a willing hand, this task was completed by
noon. The jury-mast gave little trouble, but was soon lying on the bank ; and then Captain Truck, the sheers having
been previously shifted, commenced lifting the broken foremast, and just as the cooks announced that dinner was
ready for the people the latter safely deposited the spar on
the sands.

"'Here, a sheer hulk, lies poor Tom Bowline,' '' said

Captain Truck to Mr. Blunt, as the crew came up the staging on their way to the galley, in quest of their meal. "I have not beheld the Montauk without a mast since the day she lay a new-born child at the shipyards. I see some half a dozen of these mummified scoundrels dodging about on the shore yet, though the great majority, as Mr. Dodge would say, have manifested a decided disposition to amuse themselves with a further acquaintance with the Dane. In my humble opinion, sir, that poor deserted ship will have no more inside of her by night, than one of Saunders' ducks that has been dead an hour. That hearty fellow, Mr. Monday, is hit, I fear, between wind and water, Leach."

"He is in a bad way, indeed, as I understand from Mr. John Effingham, who very properly allows no one to disturb him, keeping the state-room door closed on all but himself and his own man."

"Ay, ay, that is merciful, a man likes a little quiet when he is killed. As soon as the ship is more fit to be seen, however, it will become my duty to wait on him, in order to see that nothing is wanting. We must offer the poor man the consolations of religion, Mr. Blunt."

"They would certainly be desirable, had we one qualified for the task."

"I can't say as much in that way for myself, perhaps, as I might, seeing that my father was a priest. But then, we masters of packets have occasion to turn our hands to a good many odd jobs. As soon as the ship is snug, I shall certainly take a look at the honest fellow. Pray, sir, what became of Mr. Dodge in the skirmish?"

Paul smiled, but he prudently answered, "I believe he occupied himself in taking notes of the combat, and I make no doubt will do you full justice in the 'Active Inquirer' as soon as he gets its columns again at his command."

"Too much learning, as my good father used to say, has made him a little mad. But I have a grateful heart to-day, Mr. Blunt, and will not be critical. I did not perceive Mr. Dodge in the conflict, as Saunders calls it, but there were so

many of those rascally Arabs, that one had not an opportunity
of seeing much else.  We must get the ship outside of this
reef with as little delay as possible, for to tell you a secret''
—here the captain dropped his voice to a whisper—'' there are
but two rounds apiece left for the small-arms, and only one
cartridge for the four-pounder.  I own to you a strong desire
to be in the offing.''

'' They will hardly attempt to board us, after the specimen they have had of what we can do.''

'' No one knows, sir ; no one knows.  They keep pouring down upon the coast like crows on the scent of a carrion ;
and once done with the Dane, we shall see them in hundreds
prowling around us like wolves.  How much do we want of
high water ?''

'' An hour, possibly.  I do not think there is much time
to lose before the people get to work at the windlass.''

Captain Truck nodded, and proceeded to look into the
condition of his ground-tackle.  It was a joyous but an
anxious moment when the handspikes were first handled,
and the slack of one of the chains began to come in.  The
ship had been upright several hours, and no one could tell
how hard she would hang on the bottom.  As the chain
tightened, the gentlemen, the officers included, got upon the
bows and looked anxiously at the effect of each heave ; for
it was a nervous thing to be stranded on such a coast, even
after all that had occurred.

'' She winks, by George !'' cried the captain ; '' heave
together, men, and you will stir the sand !''

The men did heave, gaining inch by inch, until no effort
could cause the ponderous machine to turn.  The mates
and then the captain, applied their strength in succession
and but half a turn more was gained.  Everybody was now
summoned, even to the passengers, and the enormous strain
seemed to threaten to tear the fabric asunder ; and still the
ship was immovable.

'' She hangs hardest forward, sir,'' said Mr. Leach ; '' suppose we run up the stern-boat ?''

This expedient was adopted, and so nearly were the
counteracting powers balanced, that it prevailed.  A strong

heave caused the ship to start, an inch more of tide aided the effort, and then the vast hull slowly yielded to the purchase, gradually turning towards the anchor, until the quick blows of the pall announced that the vessel was fairly afloat again.

"Thank God for that, as for all his mercies!" said Captain Truck. "Heave the hussy up to her anchor, Mr. Leach, when we will cast an eye to her moorings."

All this was done, the ship being effectually secured, with due attention to a change in the wind, that now promised to be permanent. Not a moment was lost; but, the sheers being still standing, the foremast of the Dane was floated alongside, fastened to, and hove into its new berth, with as much rapidity as comported with care. When the mast was fairly stepped, Captain Truck rubbed his hands with delight, and immediately commanded his subordinate to rig it, although by this time the turn of the day had considerably passed.

"This is the way with us seamen, Mr. Effingham," he observed; "from the fall to the fight, and then again from the fight to the fall. Our work, like women's, is never done; whereas you landsmen knock off with the sun, and sleep while the corn grows. I have always owed my parents a grudge for bringing me up to a dog's life."

"I had understood it was a choice of your own, captain."

"Ay—so far as running away and shipping without their knowledge was concerned, perhaps it was; but then it was their business to begin at the bottom, and to train me up in such a manner that I would not run away. The Lord forgive me, too, for thinking amiss of the two dear old people; for, to be candid with you, they were much too good to have such a son; and I honestly believe they loved me more than I loved myself. Well, I've the consolation of knowing I comforted the old lady with many a pound of capital tea after I got into the China trade, Ma'amselle."

"She was fond of it?" observed the governess politely.

"She relished it very much, as a horse takes to oats, or a child to custard. That, and snuff and grace, composed her principal consolations."

"*Quoi?*" demanded the governess, looking towards Paul for an explanation.

"*Grace, Mademoiselle; la grace de Dieu.*"

"*Bien!*"

"It's a sad misfortune, after all, to lose a mother, Ma'amselle. It is like cutting all the headfasts, and riding altogether by the stern; for it is letting go the hold of what has gone before to grapple with the future. It is true that I ran away from my mother when a youngster, and thought little of it! but when she took her turn and ran away from me, I began to feel that I had made a wrong use of my legs. What are the tidings from poor Mr. Monday?"

"I understand he does not suffer greatly, but that he grows weaker fast," returned Paul. "I fear there is little hope of his surviving such a hurt."

The captain had got out a cigar, and had beckoned to Toast for a coal; but changing his mind suddenly, he broke the tobacco into snuff, and scattered it about the deck.

"Why the devil is not that rigging going up, Mr. Leach?" he cried, fiercely. "It is not my intention to pass the winter at these moorings, and I solicit a little more expedition."

"Ay, ay, sir," returned the mate, one of a class habitually patient and obedient; "bear a hand, my lads, and get the strings into their places."

"Leach," continued the captain, more kindly, and still working his fingers unconsciously, "come this way, my good friend. I have not expressed to you, Mr. Leach, all I wish to say of your good conduct in this late affair. You have stood by me like a gallant fellow throughout the whole business, and I shall not hesitate about saying as much when we get in. It is my intention to write a letter to the owners, which no doubt they 'll publish; for, whatever they have got to say against America, no one will deny it is easy to get anything published. Publishing is victuals and drink to the nation. You may depend on having justice done you."

"I never doubted it, Captain Truck."

"No, sir; and you never winked. The mainmast does

not stand up in a gale firmer than you stood up to the niggers."

"Mr. Effingham, sir—and Mr. Sharp—and particularly Mr. Blunt—"

"Let me alone to deal with them. Even Toast acted like a man. Well, Leach, they tell me poor Monday must slip, after all."

"I am very sorry to hear it, sir ; Mr. Monday laid about him like a soldier !"

"He did, indeed ; but Bonaparte himself has been obliged to give up the ghost, and Wellington must follow him some day ; even old Putnam is dead. Either you or I, or both of us, Leach, will have to throw in some of the consolations of religion on this mournful occasion."

"There is Mr. Effingham, sir, or Mr. John Effingham ; elderly gentlemen with more scholarship."

"That will never do. All they can offer, no doubt, will be acceptable, but we owe a duty to the ship. The officers of a packet are not graceless horse-jockeys, but sober, discreet men, and it becomes them to show that they have some education, and the right sort of stuff in them on an emergency. I expect you will stand by me, Leach, on this melancholy occasion, as stoutly as you stood by me this morning."

"I humbly hope, sir, not to disgrace the vessel, but it is likely Mr. Monday is a Church-of-England-man, and we both belong to the Saybrook Platform !"

"Ah ! the devil ! I forgot that ! But religion is religion ; old line or new line ; and I question if a man so near unmooring will be very particular. The great thing is consolation, and that we must contrive to give him, by hook or by crook, when the proper moment comes ; and now, Mr. Leach, let the people push matters, and we shall have everything up forward, and that mainmast stepped yet by ' sunset' ;" or it would be more literal to say "*sun-down* ;" Captain Truck, like a true New England man, invariably using a provincialism that has got to be so general in America.

The work proceeded with spirit, for every one was anxious to get the ship out of a berth that was so critical, as well from the constant vicinity of the Arabs as from the dangers of the weather. The wind baffled too, as it is usual on the margin of the trades, and at times it blew from the sea, though it continued light, and the changes were of short continuance. As Captain Truck hoped, when the people ceased work at night, the fore- and fore-topsail-yards were in their places, the topgallant-mast was fitted, and, with the exception of the sails, the ship was what is called a-tauto, forward. Aft, less had been done, though by the assistance of the supernumeraries, who continued to lend their aid, the two lower masts were stepped, though no rigging could be got over them. The men volunteered to work by watches through the night, but to this Captain Truck would not listen, affirming that they had earned their suppers and a good rest, both of which they should have.

The gentlemen, who merely volunteered an occasional drag, cheerfully took the lookouts, and as there were plenty of fire-arms, though not much powder, little apprehension was entertained of the Arabs. As was expected, the night passed away tranquilly, and every one arose with the dawn refreshed and strengthened.

The return of day, however, brought the Arabs down upon the shore in crowds; for the last gale, which had been unusually severe, and the tidings of the wrecks, which had been spread by means of the dromedaries far and wide, had collected a force on the coast that began to be formidable through sheer numbers. The Dane had been effectually emptied, and plunder had the same effect on these rapacious barbarians that blood is known to produce on the tiger. The taste had begotten an appetite, and from the first appearance of the light, those in the ship saw signs of a disposition to renew the attempt on their liberty.

Happily, the heaviest portion of the work was done and Captain Truck determined, rather than risk another conflict with a force that was so much augmented, to get the spars on board, and to take the ship outside of the reef, without waiting to complete her equipment. His first orders, therefore, when all hands were mustered, were for the boats to get in the kedges and the stream anchor, and otherwise to prepare to move the vessel. In the meantime other gangs were busy in getting the rigging over the mastheads and in setting it up. As the lifting of the anchors with boats was heavy work, by the time they were got on board and stowed it was noon, and all the yards were aloft, though not a sail was bent in the vessel.

Captain Truck, while the people were eating, passed through the ship, examining every stay and shroud. There were some make-shifts, it is true, but on the whole he was satisfied, though he plainly saw that the presence of the Arabs had hurried matters a little, and that a good many drags would have to be given as soon as they got beyond danger. and that some attention must be paid to seizings; still, what had been done would answer very well for moderate weather. and it was too late to stop to change.

The trade-wind had returned. and blew steadily, as if finally likely to stand : and the water outside of the reef was smooth enough to permit the required alterations, now that the heavier spars were again in their places.

The appearance of the Montauk certainly was not as stately and commanding as before the wreck, but there was an air of completeness about it that augured well. It was that of a ship of seven hundred tons, fitted with spars intended for a ship of five hundred. The packet a little resembled a man of six feet in the coat of a man of five feet nine ; and yet the discrepancy would not be apt to be noticed by any but the initiated. Everything essential was in its place, and reasonably well secured, and, as the Dane had been rigged for a stormy sea, Captain Truck felt satisfied he might, in his present plight, venture on the American coast, even in winter, without incurring unusual hazard.

As soon as the hour of work arrived, therefore, a boat was sent to drop a kedge as near the inlet as it would be safe to venture, and a little to windward of it. By making a calculation, and inspecting his buoys, which still remained where he had placed them, Captain Truck found that he could get a narrow channel of sufficient directness to permit the ship to be warped as far as this point in a straight line. Everything but the boats was now got on board, the anchor by which they rode was hove up, and the warp was brought to the capstan, when the vessel slowly began to advance towards the inlet.

This movement was a signal to the Arabs, who poured down on both reefs in hundreds, screaming and gesticulating like maniacs. It required good nerves and some self-reliance to advance in the face of such a danger, and this so much the more, as the barbarians showed themselves in the greatest force on the northern range of rocks, which offered a good shelter for their persons, completely raked the channel, and, moreover, lay so near the spot where the kedge had been dropped, that one might have jerked a stone from the one to the other. To add to the awkwardness of the affair, the Arabs began to fire with those muskets that are of so little service in close encounters, but which are notorious for sending their shot with great precision from a distance. The bullets came thick upon the ship, though the stoutness of the bulwarks forward, and their height, as yet protected the men.

In this dilemma, Captain Truck hesitated about continuing to haul ahead, and he sent for Mr. Blunt and Mr. Leach for a consultation. Both these gentlemen advised perseverance, and as the counsel of the former will succinctly show the state of things, it shall be given in his own words.

"Indecision is always discouraging to one's friends, and encouraging to one's enemies," he said, "and I recommend perseverance. The nearer we haul to the rocks, the greater will be our command of them, while the more the chances of the Arabs throwing their bullets on our decks will be diminished. Indeed, so long as we ride head to wind, they cannot fire low enough to effect their object from the northern reef, and on the southern they will not venture very near, for want of cover. It is true, it will be impossible for us to bend our sails or to send out a boat in the face of so heavy a fire, while our assailants are so effectually covered; but we may possibly dislodge them with the gun, or with our small-arms, from the decks. If not, I will head a party into the tops, from which I will undertake to drive them out of the reach of our muskets in five minutes."

"Such a step would be very hazardous to those who ventured aloft."

"It would not be without danger, and some loss must be expected ; but they who fight must expect risks."

"In which case it will be the business of Mr. Leach and myself to head the parties aloft. If we are obliged to console the dying, damn me, but we are entitled to the privilege of fighting the living."

"Ay, ay, sir," put in the mate ; "that stands to reason."

"There are three tops, gentlemen," returned Paul, mildly, "and I respect your rights too much to wish to interfere with them. We can each take one, and the effect will be in proportion to the greater means we employ—one vigorous assault being worth a dozen feints."

Captain Truck shook Paul heartily by the hand, and adopted his advice. When the young man had retired, he turned to the mate, and said,—

"After all, these men-of-war's-men are a little beyond us in the science of attack and defence, though I think I could give him a hint in the science of signs. I have had two or three touches at privateering in my time, but no regular occupation in your broadside work. Did you see how Mr. Blunt handled his boat yesterday ? As much like two double blocks and a steady drag as one belaying-pin is like another, and as coolly as a great lady in London looks at one of us in a state of nature. For my part, Leach, I was as hot as mustard, and ready to cut the throat of the best friend I had on earth ; whereas he was smiling as I rowed past him, though I could hardly see his face for the smoke of his own gun."

"Yes, sir, that's the way with your regular builts. I 'll warrant you he began young, and had kicked all the passion out of himself on old salts, by the time he was eighteen. He does n't seem, neither, like one of the true d——n-my-eye breed ; but it 's a great privilege to a man in a passion to be allowed to kick when and whom he likes."

"Not he. I say, Leach, perhaps he might lend us a hand

when it comes to the pinch with poor Monday. I have a great desire that the worthy fellow should take his departure decently.''

''Well, sir, I think you had better propose it. For my part, I 'm quite willing to go into all three of the tops alone, rather than disappoint a dying man.''

The captain promised to look to the matter, and then they turned their attention to the ship, which in a few more minutes was up as near the kedge as it was prudent to haul her.

# CHAPTER XXVIII.

" Speed, gallant bark, the tornado is past ,
    Staunch and secure thou hast weathered the blast;
    Now spread thy full sails to the wings of the morn,
    And soon the glad haven shall greet thy return."

                                                PARK.

THE Montauk now lay close to the inlet, and even a little to windward of its entrance ; but the channel was crooked, not a sail was bent, nor was it possible to bend one properly without exposing the men to the muskets of the Arabs, who, from firing loosely, had got to be more wary and deliberate, aiming at the places where a head or an arm was occasionally seen. To prolong this state of things was merely to increase the evil, and Captain Truck determined to make an effort at once to dislodge his enemies.

With this view the gun was loaded in-board, filled nearly to the muzzle with slugs, and then it was raised with care to the topgallant-forecastle, and cautiously pushed forward near the gunwale. Had the barbarians understood the construction of a vessel, they might have destroyed half the packet's crew while they were thus engaged about the forecastle, by firing through the planks ; but, ignorant of the weakness of the defences, they aimed altogether at the openings, or over the rails.

By lowering the gaff the spanker was imperfectly bent ; that is to say, it was bent upon the upper leach. The boom was got in under cover of the hurricane-house, and of the bundle of the sail ; the out-hauler was bent, the boom replaced, the sail being hoisted with a little and a hurried lacing to the luff. This was not effected without a good deal of hazard, though the nearness of the bows of the vessel to the rocks prevented most of the Arabs from perceiving what passed so far aft.   Still, others nearer to the shore caught glimpses of the actors, and several narrow escapes were the consequence.   The second mate, in particular, had a shot through his hat within an inch of his head.   By a little management, notwithstanding, the luff of the spanker was made to stand tolerably well ;  and the ship had at least the benefit of this one sail.

The Dane had been a seaman of the old school ;  and instead of the more modern spencer, his ship had been fitted with old-fashioned staysails.   Of these it was possible to bend the main and mizzen staysails in tolerable security, provided the ends of the halyards could be got down.   As this, however, would be nearly all after-sail, the captain determined to make an effort to overhaul the buntlines and leachlines of the foresail, at the same time that men were sent aloft after the ends of the halyards.   He also thought it possible to set a fore-topmast staysail flying.

No one was deceived in this matter.   The danger and the mode of operating were explained clearly, and then Captain Truck asked for volunteers.   These were instantly found ;  Mr. Leach and the second mate setting the example by stepping forward as the first two.   In order that the whole procedure may be understood, however, it shall be explained more fully.

Two men were prepared to run up on the foreyard at the word.   Both of these, one of whom was Mr. Leach, carried three small balls of marline, to the end of each of which was attached a cod-hook, the barb being filed off in order to prevent its being caught.   By means of these hooks the balls were fastened to the jackets of the adventurers.   Two others stood ready at the foot of the main and mizzen riggings.   By the gun lay Paul and three men ; while several of the passengers, and a few of the best shots among the crew, were stationed on the forecastle, armed with muskets and fowling-pieces.

"Is everybody ready ?" called out the captain from the quarter-deck.

" All ready ! " and " Ay, ay, sir ! " were answered from the different points of the ship.

" Haul out the spanker ! "

As soon as this sail was set, the stern of the ship swung round towards the inlet, so as to turn the bow on which the gun was placed towards the part of the reef where the Arabs were in greatest numbers.

" Be steady, men ! and do not hurry yourselves, though active as wild-cats ! Up, and away ! "

The two foreyard men, and the two by the after-masts sprang into the rigging like squirrels, and were running aloft before the captain had done speaking. At the the same instant one of the three by the gun leaped on the bowsprit, and ran out towards the stay. Paul and the other two rose and shoved the gun to its berth, and the small-arms men showed themselves at the rails.

So many, all in swift motion, appearing at the same moment in the rigging, distracted the attention of the Arabs for an instant, though scattering shots were fired. Paul knew that the danger would be greatest when the men aloft were stationary, and he was in no haste. Perhaps for half a minute he was busy in choosing his object, and in levelling the gun, and then it was fired. He had chosen the moment well ; for Mr. Leach and his fellow-adventurers were already on the foreyard, and the Arabs had arisen from their covers in the eagerness of taking aim. The small-arms men poured in their volley, and then little more could be done in the way of the offensive, nearly all the powder in the ship having been expended.

It remains to tell the result of this experiment. Among the Arabs a few fell, and those most exposed to the fire from the ship were staggered, losing near a minute in their confusion ; but those more remote maintained hot discharges after the first surprise. The whole time occupied in what we are going to relate was about three minutes ; the action of the several parts going on simultaneously.

The adventurer forward, though nearest to the enemy, was least exposed. Partly covered by the bowsprit, he ran nimbly out on that spar till he reached the stay. Here he cut the stop of the fore-topmast halyards, overhauled the running part, and let the block swing in. He then hooked a block that he had carried out with him, and in which the bight of a rope had been rove through the thimble, and ran in as fast as possible. This duty, which had appeared the most hazardous of all the different adventures, on account of the proximity of the bowsprit to the reef, was the first done, and with the least real risk ; the man being partly concealed by the smoke of the gun, as well as by the bowsprit. He escaped uninjured.

As the two men aft pursued exactly the same course, the movements of one will explain those of the other. On reaching the yard, the adventurer sprang on it, caught the hook of the halyard-block, and threw himself off without an instant's hesitation, overhauling the halyards by his weight. Men stood in readiness below to check the fall by easing off the other end of the rope, and the hardy fellow reached the deck in safety. This seemed a nervous undertaking to the landsmen ; but the seamen who so well understood the machinery of their vessel, made light of it.

On the foreyard, Mr. Leach passed out on one yard-arm, and his co-adventurer, a common seaman, on the other. Each left a hook in the knot of the inner buntline, as he went out, and dropped the ball of marline on deck. The same was done at the outer buntlines, and at the leachlines. Here the mate returned, according to his orders, leaped upon the rigging, and thence upon a backstay when he slid on deck with a velocity that set aim at defiance. Notwithstanding the quickness of his motions, Mr. Leach received a trifling hit on the shoulder, and several bullets whizzed near him.

The seaman on the other yard-arm succeeded equally well, escaping the smallest injury, until he had secured the leachline, when, knowing the usefulness of obtaining it, for he was on the weather side of the ship, he determined to bring in the end of the reef-tackle with him. Calling out to let go the rope on the deck, he ran out to the lift, bent over and secured the desired end, and raised himself erect, with the intention to make a run in, on the top of the yard,

Captain Truck and the second mate had both commanded him to desist in vain, for impunity from harm had rendered him foolhardy. In this perilous position he even paused to give a cheer. The cry was scarcely ended when he sprang off the yard several feet upwards and fell perpendicularly towards the sea, carrying the rope in his hand. At first, most on board believed the man had jumped into the water as the least hazardous means of getting down, depending on the rope, and on swimming, for his security; but Paul pointed out the spot of blood that stained the surface of the sea, at the point where he had fallen. The reef-tackle was rounded cautiously in, and its end rose to the surface without the hand that had so lately grasped it. The man himself never reappeared.

Captain Truck had now the means of setting three stay-sails, the spanker, and the fore-course; sails sufficient, he thought, to answer his present purposes. The end of the reef-tackle, that had been so dearly bought, was got in, by means of a light line which was thrown around it.

The order was now given to brail the spanker, and to clap on and weigh the kedge, which was done by the run. As soon as the ship was free of the bottom, the fore-topmast-staysail was set flying, like a jib-topsail, by hauling out the tack and swaying upon the halyards. The sheet was hauled to windward and the helm put down; of course the bows of the ship began to fall off, and, as soon as her head was sufficiently near her course, the sheet was drawn, and the wheel shifted.

Captain Truck now ordered the foresail, which by this time was ready, to be set. This important sail was got on the vessel, by bending the buntlines and leachlines to its head, and by hauling out the weather-head-cringle by means of the reef-tackle. As soon as this broad spread of canvas was on the ship, her motion was accelerated, and she began to move away from the spot, followed by the furious cries and menaces of the Arabs. To the latter no one paid any heed, but they were audible until drowned in distance. Although aided by all her spars, and the force of the wind on her hull, a body as large as the Montauk required some little time to overcome the *vis inertiæ*, and several anxious minutes passed before she was so far from the cover of the Arabs as to prevent their clamor from seeming to be in the very ears of those on board. When this did occur, it brought inexpressible relief, though it perhaps increased the danger, by increasing the chances of the bullets hitting objects on deck.

The course at first was nearly before the wind, when the flat rock, so often named, being reached, the ship was compelled to haul up on an easy bowline, in order to pass to windward of it. Here the staysails aft and the spanker were set, which aided in bringing the vessel to the wind, and the fore-tack was brought down. By laying straight out of the pass, a distance of only a hundred yards, the vessel would be again clear of everything, and beyond all the dangers of the coast, so long as the present breeze stood. But the tide set the vessel bodily towards the rock, and her condition did not admit of pressing hard upon a bowline. Captain Truck was getting to be uneasy, for he soon perceived that they were nearing the danger, though very gradually, and he began to tremble for his copper. Still the vessel drew steadily ahead, and he had hopes of passing the outer edge of the rocks in safety. This outer edge was a broken, ragged, and pointed fragment, that would break in the planks should the vessel rest upon it an instant, while falling in that constant heaving and setting of the ocean, which now began to be very sensibly felt. After all his jeopardy, the old mariner saw that his safety was at a serious hazard, by one of those unforeseen but common risks that environ the seaman's life.

"Luff! luff! you can," cried Captain Truck, glancing his eye from the rock to the sails, and from the sails to the rock. "Luff, sir—you are at the pinch!"

"Luff it is, sir!" answered the man at the wheel, who stood abaft the hurricane-house, covered by its roof, over which he was compelled to look, to get a view of the sails. "Luff I may, and luff it is, sir."

Paul stood at the captain's side, the crew being ordered to keep themselves as much covered as possible, on account

of the bullets of the Arabs, which were at this time patter-
ing against the vessel, like hail at the close of a storm.

"We shall not weather that point of ragged rock," exclaimed the young man, quickly; "and if we touch it the
ship will be lost."

"Let her claw off," returned the old man sternly. "Her
cutwater is up with it already. Let her claw off."

The bows of the ship were certainly up with the danger,
and the vessel was slowly drawing ahead; but every moment
its broadside was set nearer to the rock, which was now
within fifty feet of them. The fore-chains were past the
point, though little hope remained of clearing it abaft. A
ship turns on her centre of gravity as on a pivot, the two
ends inclining in opposite directions; and Captain Truck
hoped that as the bows were past the danger, it might be
possible to throw the after part of the vessel up to the wind,
by keeping away, and thus clear the spot entirely.

"Hard up with your helm!" he shouted; "hard up!
Haul down the mizzen staysail, and give her sheet!"

The sails were attended to, but no answer came from the
wheel, nor did the vessel change her course.

"Hard up, I tell you, sir—hard up—hard up, and be
d——d to you!"

The usual reply was not made. Paul sprang through the
narrow gangway that led to the wheel. All that passed
took but a minute, and yet it was the most critical minute
that had yet befallen the Montauk; for had she touched
that rock but for an instant, human art could hardly have
kept her above water an hour.

"Hard up, and be d——d to you!" repeated Captain
Truck, in a voice of thunder, as Paul darted round the
corner of the hurricane-house.

The seaman stood at the wheel, grasping its spokes firmly,
his eyes aloft as usual, but the turns of the tiller rope
showed that the order was not obeyed.

"Hard up, man, hard up! are you mad?" Paul uttered
these words as he sprang to the wheel, which he made whirl
with his own hands in the required direction. As for the
seaman, he yielded his hold without resistance, and fell like

a log as the wheel flew round. A ball had entered his back, and passed through his heart, and yet he had stood steadily to the spokes, as the true mariner always clings to the helm while life lasts.

The bows of the ship fell heavily off, and her stern pressed up towards the wind ; but the trifling delay so much augmented the risk, that nothing saved the vessel but the formation of the run and counter, which, by receding as usual, allowed room to escape the dangerous point, as the Montauk hove by on a swell.

Paul could not see the nearness of the escape, but the purity of the water permitted Captain Truck and his mates to observe it with a distinctness that almost rendered them breathless. Indeed there was an instant when the sharp rock was hid beneath the counter, and each momentarily expected to hear the grating of the fragment, as it penetrated the vessel's bottom.

"Relieve that man at the wheel, and send him hither this moment," said Captain Truck, in a calm, stern voice, that was more ominous than an oath.

The mate called a seaman, and passed aft himself to execute the order. In a minute he and Paul returned, bearing the body of the dead mariner, when all was explained.

"Lord, thy ways are unsearchable!" muttered the old master, uncovering himself, as the corpse was carried past, "and we are but as grains of seed, and as the vain butterflies in thy hand!"

The rock once cleared, an open ocean lay to leeward of the packet, and bringing the wind a little abaft the beam, she moved steadily away from those rocks that had been the witnesses of all her recent dangers. It was not long before she was so distant that all danger from the Arabs ceased. The barbarians, notwithstanding, continued a dropping fire and furious gesticulations, long after their bullets and menaces became matters of indifference to those on board.

The body of the dead man was laid between the masts, and the order was passed to bend the sails. As all was ready,

in half an hour the Montauk was standing off the land
under her three topsails, the reef now distant nearly a
league.  The courses came next, when the topgallant-yards
were crossed and the sails set; the lighter canvas followed,
and some time before the sun disappeared, the ship was
under studding-sails, standing to the westward, before the
trades.

For the first time since he received the intelligence that
the Arabs were the masters of the ship, Captain Truck now
felt real relief.  He was momentarily happy after the combat, but new cares had pressed upon him so soon, that he
could scarcely be said to be tranquil.  Matters were now
changed.  His vessel was in good order, if not equipped
for racing, and, as he was in a low latitude, had the trade-
winds to befriend him, and no longer entertained any apprehension of his old enemy the Foam, he felt as if a
mountain had been removed from his breast.

"Thank God," he observed to Paul, "I shall sleep to-
night without dreaming of Arabs or rocks, or scowling faces
at New York.  They may say that another man might
have shown more skill in keeping clear of such a scrape,
but they will hardly say that another man could have got
out of it better.  All this handsome outfit, too, will cost the
owners nothing—literally nothing; and I question if the
poor Dane will ever appear to claim the sails and spars.  I
do not know that we are in possession of them exactly
according to the law of Africa, for of that code I know
little; or according to the law of nations, for Vattel, I believe, has nothing on the subject; but we are in possession
so effectually, that, barring the nor'westers on the American
coast, I feel pretty certain of keeping them until we make
the East River."

"It might be better to bury the dead," said Paul; for he
knew Eve would scarcely appear on deck as long as the
body remained in sight.  "Seamen, you know, are superstitious on the subject of corpses."

"I have thought of this, but hoped to cheat those two
rascals of sharks that are following in our wake, as if they
scented their food.  It is an extraordinary thing, Mr. Blunt,

that these fish should know when there is a body in a ship, and that they will follow it a hundred leagues to make sure of their prey."

"It would be extraordinary, if true; but in what manner has the fact been ascertained?"

"You see the two rascally pirates astern?" observed Mr. Leach.

"Very true; but we might also see them were there no dead body about the ship. Sharks abound in this latitude, and I have seen several about the reef since we went in."

"They'll be disappointed as to poor Tom Smith," said the mate, "unless they dive deep for him. I have lashed one of Napoleon's busts to the fine fellow's feet, and he'll not fetch up until he's snugly anchored on the bottom."

"This is a fitting hour for solemn feelings," said the captain, gazing about him at the heavens and the gathering gloom of twilight. "Call all hands to bury the dead, Mr. Leach. I confess I should feel easier myself as to the weather, were the body fairly out of the ship."

While the mate went forward to muster the people, the captain took Paul aside with a request that he would perform the last offices for the deceased.

"I will read a chapter in the Bible myself," he said; "for I should not like the people to see one of the crew go overboard, and the officers have no word to say in the ceremonies; it might beget disrespect, and throw a slur on our knowledge; but you man-of-war's-men are generally more regularly brought up to prayers than us liners, and if you have a proper book by you, I should feel infinitely obliged if you would give us a lift on this melancholy occasion."

Paul proposed that Mr. Effingham should be asked to officiate, as he knew that gentleman read prayers in his cabin, to his own party, night and morning.

"Does he?" said the captain; "then he is my man, for he must have his hand in, and there will be no stammering or boggling. Ay, ay; he will fetch through on one tack. Toast, go below, and present my compliments to Mr. Effingham, and say I should like to speak to him; and, harkee,

Toast, desire him to put a prayer-book in his pocket, and then step into my state-room, and bring up the Bible you will find under the pillow. The Arabs had a full chance at the plunder; but there is something about the Book that always takes care of it. Few rogues, I've often remarked, care about a Bible. They would sooner steal ten novels than one copy of the sacred writ. This of mine was my mother's, Mr. Blunt, and I should have been a better man had I overhauled it oftener."

We pass over most of the arrangements, and come at once to the service, and to the state of the ship, just as her inmates were assembled on an occasion which no want of formality can render anything but solemn and admonitory. The courses were hauled up, and the main-topsail had been laid to the mast, a position in which a ship has always an air of stately repose. The body was stretched on a plank that lay across a rail, the leaden bust being inclosed in the hammock that enveloped it. A spot of blood on the cloth alone betrayed the nature of the death. Around the body were grouped the crew, while Captain Truck and his mates stood at the gangway. The passengers were collected on the quarter-deck, with Mr. Effingham, holding a prayer-book, a little in advance.

The sun had just dipped into the ocean, and the whole western horizon was glorious with those soft, pearly, rainbow hues that adorn the evening and the morning of a low latitude, during the soft weather of the autumnal months. To the eastward, the low line of coast was just discernible by the hillocks of sand, leaving the imagination to portray its solitude and wastes. The sea in all other directions was dark and gloomy, and the entire character of the sunset was that of a grand picture of ocean magnificence and extent, relieved by a sky in which the tints came and went like the well-known colors of the dolphin: to this must be added the gathering gloom of twilight.

Eve pressed the arm of John Effingham, and gazed with admiration and awe at the imposing scene.

"This is the seaman's grave!" she whispered.

"And worthy it is to be the tomb of so gallant a fellow.

The man died clinging to his post; and Powis tells me that his hand was loosened from the wheel with difficulty."

They were silent, for Captain Truck uncovered himself, as did all around him, placed his spectacles, and opened the sacred volume. The old mariner was far from critical in his selections of readings, and he usually chose some subject that he thought would most interest his hearers, which were ordinarily those that most interested himself. To him Bible was Bible, and he now turned to the passage in the Acts of the Apostles in which the voyage of St. Paul from Judea to Rome is related. This he read with steadiness, some quaintness of pronunciation, and with a sort of breathing elasticity, whenever he came to those verses that touched particularly on the navigation.

Paul maintained his perfect self-command during this extraordinary exhibition, but an unbidden smile lingered around the handsome and chiselled mouth of Mr. Sharp. John Effingham's curved face was sedate and composed, while the females were too much impressed to exhibit any levity. As to the crew, they listened in profound attention, occasionally exchanging glances whenever any of the nautical expedients struck them as being out of rule.

As soon as this edifying chapter was ended, Mr. Effingham commenced the solemn rites for the dead. At the first sound of his voice, a calm fell on the vessel as if the Spirit of God had alighted from the clouds, and a thrill passed through the frames of the listeners. Those solemn words of the Apostle commencing with, "I am the resurrection and the life, saith the Lord: he that believeth in me, though he were dead, yet shall he live: and whosoever liveth and believeth in me, shall never die," could not have been better delivered. The voice, intonation, utterance, and manner of Mr. Effingham were eminently those of a gentleman; without pretension, quiet, simple, and mellow, while, on the other hand, they were feeling, dignified, distinct, and measured.

When he pronounced the words, "I know that my Redeemer liveth, and that He shall stand at the latter day upon the earth: and though, after my skin, worms destroy my body, yet in my flesh shall I see God," etc., etc., the men stared about them as if a real voice from heaven had made the declaration, and Captain Truck looked aloft like one expecting a trumpet-blast. The tears of Eve began to flow as she listened to the much-loved tones; and the stoutest heart in the much-tried ship quailed. John Effingham made the responses of the psalm steadily, and Mr. Sharp and Paul soon joined him. But the profoundest effect was produced when the office reached those consoling but startling words from the Revelation, commencing with, "I heard a voice from heaven saying unto me, Write, From henceforth blessed are the dead who die in the Lord," etc. Captain Truck afterwards confessed that he thought he heard the very voice, and the men actually pressed together in their alarm. The plunge of the body was also a solemn instant. It went off the end of the plank feet foremost, and, carried rapidly down by the great weight of the lead, the water closed above it, obliterating every trace of the seaman's grave. Eve thought that its exit resembled the few brief hours that draw the veil of oblivion around the mass of mortals when they disappear from earth.

Instead of asking for the benediction at the close of the ceremony, Mr. Effingham devoutly and calmly commenced the psalm of thanksgiving for victory, "If the Lord had not been on our side, now may we say, if the Lord himself had not been on our side, when men rose up against us, they would have swallowed us up quick, when they were so wrathfully displeased with us." Most of the gentlemen joined in the responses, and the silvery voice of Eve sounded sweet and holy amid the breathings of the ocean. Te Deum Laudamus, "We praise Thee, O God! we acknowledge Thee to be the Lord!" "All the earth doth worship Thee, the Father everlasting;" closed the offices, when Mr. Effingham dismissed his congregation with the usual layman's request for the benediction.

Captain Truck had never before been so deeply impressed with any religious ceremony, and when it ceased he looked wistfully over the side at the spot where the body had fallen, or where it might be supposed to have fallen—for the ship had drifted some distance—as one takes a last look at the grave of a friend.

"Shall we fill the main-topsail, sir?" demanded Mr. Leach, after waiting a minute or two in deference to his commander's feelings; "or shall we hook on the yard-tackles, and stow the launch?"

"Not yet, Leach, not yet; it will be unkind to poor Jack to hurry away from his grave so indecently. I have observed that the people about the river always keep in sight till the last sod is stowed and the rubbish is cleared away. The fine fellow stood to those spokes as a close-reefed topsail in a gale stands the surges of the wind, and we owe him this little respect."

"The boats, sir?"

"Let them tow awhile longer. It will seem like deserting him to be rattling the yard-tackles and stowing boats directly over his head. Your gran'ther was a priest, Leach, and I wonder you don't see the impropriety of hurrying away from a grave. A little reflection will hurt none of us."

The mate admired at a mood so novel for his commander, but he was fain to submit. The day was fast closing notwithstanding, and the skies were losing their brilliancy in hues that were still softer and more melancholy, as if nature delighted, too, in sympathizing with the feelings of these lone mariners.

## CHAPTER XXIX.

*" Sir, 't is my occupation to be plain."*

*Lear.*

THE barbarians had done much less injury to the ship and her contents than under the circumstances could have been reasonably hoped. The fact that nothing could be effectually landed where she lay was probably the cause, the bales that had actually been got out of the ship having been put upon the bank with a view to lighten her, more than for any other reason. The compact, too, between the chiefs had its influence probably, though it could not have lasted long with so strong temptations to violate it constantly before the eyes of men habitually rapacious.

Of course, one of the first things after each individual had ascertained his own losses, was to inquire into those of his neighbors, and the usual party in the ladies' cabin was seated around the sofa of Eve, about nine in the evening, conversing on this topic, after having held a short but serious discourse on their recent escape.

"You tell me, John, that Mr. Monday has a desire to sleep?" observed Mr. Effingham, in the manner in which one puts an interrogation.

"He is easier, and dozes. I have left my man with him with orders to summon me the instant he awakes."

A melancholy pause succeeded, and then the discourse took the channel from which it had been diverted.

"Is the extent of our losses in effects known?" asked Mr. Sharp. "My man reports some trifling deficit, but nothing of any value."

" Your counterfeit," returned Eve, smiling, " has been the principal sufferer. One would think, by his plaints, that not a toy is left in Christendom."

" So long as they have not stolen from him his good name I shall not complain, as I may have some use for it when we reach America, of which now, God be praised ! there are some flattering prospects."

" I understand from my connections that the person who is known in the main cabin as Sir George Templemore, is not the person who is known as such in this," observed John Effingham, bowing to Mr. Sharp, who returned his salute as one acknowledges an informal introduction. " There are certainly weak men to be found in high stations all over the world, but you will probably think I am doing honor to my own sagacity, when I say that I suspected, from the first, that he was not a true Amphitryon. I had heard of Sir George Templemore, and had been taught to expect more in him than even a man of fashion—a man of the world —while this poor substitute can scarcely lay claim to be either."

John Effingham so seldom complimented that his kind words usually told, and Mr. Sharp acknowledged the politeness, more gratified than he was probably willing to acknowledge to himself. The other could have heard of him only from Eve and her father, and it was doubly grateful to be spoken of favorably in such a quarter. He thought there was a consciousness in the slight confusion that appeared on the face of the daughter, which led him to hope that even the latter had not considered him unworthy of recollection ; for he cared but little for the remembrances of Mr. Effingham, if they could all be transferred to his child.

" This person, who does me the honor to relieve me from the trouble of bearing my own name," he resumed, " cannot be of very lofty pretensions, or he would have aspired higher. I suspect him of being merely one of those silly young countrymen of mine, of whom so many crowd stage-coaches and packets, to swagger over their less ambitious fellow-mortals with the strut and exactions of the hour."

"And yet, apart from his folly in 'sailing under false colors,' as our worthy captain would call it, the man seems well enough."

"A folly, cousin Jack," said Eve, with laughing eyes, though she maintained a perfect demureness with her beautiful features, "that he shares in common with so many others!"

"Very true, though I suspect he has climbed to commit it, while others have been content to descend. The man himself behaved well yesterday, showing steadiness as well as spirit in the fray."

"I forgive him his usurpation for his conduct on that occasion," returned Mr. Sharp, "and wish with all my heart the Arabs had discovered less affection for his curiosities. I should think that they must find themselves embarrassed to ascertain the uses of some of their prizes—such, for instance, as the button-hooks, the shoe-horn, knives with twenty blades, and other objects that denote a profound civilization."

"You have not spoken of your luck, Mr. Powis," added Mr. Effingham; "I trust you have fared as well as most of us, though, had they visited their enemies according to the injury received from them, you would be among the heaviest of the sufferers."

"My loss," replied Paul, mournfully, "is not much in pecuniary value, though irreparable to me."

A look of concern betrayed the general interest, for, as he really seemed sad, there was a secret apprehension that his loss even exceeded that which his words would give them reason to suppose. Perceiving the curiosity that was awakened, and which was only suppressed by politeness, the young man added,—

"I miss a miniature, that to me is of inestimable value."

Eve's heart throbbed, while her eyes sunk to the carpet. The others seemed amazed, and after a brief pause, Mr. Sharp observed,—

"A painting on its own account would hardly possess much value with such barbarians. Was the setting valuable?"

"It was of gold, of course, and had some merit in the way of workmanship. It has probably been taken as curious, rather than for its specific value; though to me, as I have just said, the ship itself could scarcely be of more account—certainly not as much prized."

"Many light articles have been merely mislaid; taken away through curiosity or idleness, and left where the individual happened to be at the moment of changing his mind," said John Effingham; "several things of mine have been scattered through the cabins in this manner, and I understand that divers vestments of the ladies have found their way into the state-rooms of the other cabin; particularly a night-cap of Mademoiselle Viefville's, that has been discovered in Captain Truck's room, and which that gallant seaman has forthwith condemned as a lawful waif. As he never uses such a device on his head, he will be compelled to wear it next his heart. He will be compelled to convert it into a *liberty*-cap."

"*Ciel!* if the excellent captain will carry us safe to New York," coolly returned the governess, "he shall have the prize, *de tout mon cœur; c'est un homme brave, et c'est aussi un brave homme, à sa façon.*"

"Here are two hearts concerned in the affair already, and no one can foresee the consequence; but," turning to Paul, "describe this miniature, if you please, for there are many in the vessel, and yours is not the only one that has been mislaid."

"It was a miniature of a female, and one too, I think, that would be remarked for her beauty."

Eve felt a chill at her heart.

"If, sir, it is the miniature of an elderly lady," said Ann Sidley, "perhaps it is this which I found in Miss Eve's room, and which I intended to give to Captain Truck in order that it might reach the hands of its right owner."

Paul took the miniature, which he regarded coldly for a moment, and then returned to the nurse.

"Mine is the miniature of a female under twenty," he said, coloring as he spoke; "and is every way different from this."

This was the painful and humiliating moment when Eve Effingham was made to feel the extent and the nature of the interest she took in Paul Powis. On all the previous occasions in which her feelings had been strongly awakened on his account, she had succeeded in deceiving herself as to the motive, but now the truth was felt in that overwhelming form that no sensitive heart can distrust.

No one had seen the miniature, though all observed the emotion with which Paul spoke of it, and all secretly wondered of whom it could be.

" The Arabs appear to have some such taste for the fine arts as distinguishes the population of a mushroom American city," said John Effingham ; " or one that runs to portraits, which are admired while the novelty lasts, and then are consigned to the first spot that offers to receive them."

" Are your miniatures all safe. Eve ? " Mr. Effingham inquired with interest ; for among them was one of her mother that he had yielded to her only through strong parental affection, but which it would have given him deep pain to discover was lost, though John Effingham, unknown to him, possessed a copy.

" It is with the jewelry in the baggage-room, dearest father, and untouched of course. We are fortunate that our passing wants did not extend beyond our comforts, and luckily they are not of a nature to be much prized by barbarians. Coquetry and a ship have little in common, and Mademoiselle Viefville and myself had not much out to tempt the marauders."

As Eve uttered this, both the young men involuntarily turned their eyes towards her, each thinking that a being so fair stood less in need than common of the factitious aid of ornaments. She was dressed in a dark French chintz, that her maid had fitted to her person in a manner that it would seem none but a French assistant can accomplish, setting off her falling shoulders, finely-moulded bust, and slender-rounded waist, in a way to present a modest outline of their perfection. The dress had that polished medium between fashion and its exaggeration, that always denotes a high association, and perhaps a cultivated mind—certainly a culti-

vated taste—offending neither usage on the one hand, nor
self-respect and a chaste appreciation of beauty on the other.
Indeed, Eve was distinguished for that important acquisition
to a gentlewoman, an intellectual or refined toilette ; not intellect and refinement in extravagance and caricature, but as
they are displayed in fitness, simplicity, elegance, and the
proportions.  This much, perhaps, she owed to native taste,
as the slight air of fashion, and the high air of a gentlewoman, that were thrown about her person and attire, were
the fruits of an intimate connection with the best society of
half the capitals of the European continent.  As an unmarried female, modesty, the habits of the part of the world in
which she had so long dwelt, and her own sense of propriety,
caused her to respect simplicity of appearance ; but through
this, as it might be in spite of herself, shone qualities of a
superior order.  The little hand and foot, so beautiful and
delicate, the latter just peeping from the dress under which
it was usually concealed, appeared as if formed expressly to
adorn a taste that was every way feminine and alluring.

"It is one of the mysteries of the grand designs of Providence, that men should exist in conditions so widely distant
from each other," said John Effingham, abruptly, "with a
common nature that can be so much varied by circumstances.  It is almost humiliating to find one's self a man,
when beings like these Arabs are to be classed as fellows."

"The most instructed and refined, cousin Jack, may get a
useful lesson, notwithstanding your disrelish for the con-
sanguinity, from this very identity of nature," said Eve,
who made a rally to overcome feelings that she deemed girlish and weak.  "By showing us what we might be ourselves, we get an admonition of humility ; or by reflecting
on the difference that is made by education, does it not strike
you that there is an encouragement to persevere until better
things are attained ?"

"The globe is but a ball, and a ball, too, insignificant,
even when compared with the powers of man," continued
the other.  "How many navigators now circle it ! even you,
sir, may have done this, young as you still are," turning to
Paul, who made a bow of assent : "and yet, within these

narrow limits, what wonderful varieties of physical appearance, civilization, laws, and even of color, do we find, all mixed up with points of startling affinity."

"So far as a limited experience has enabled me to judge," observed Paul, "I have everywhere found, not only the same nature, but a common innate sentiment of justice that seems universal; for even amidst the wildest scenes of violence, or of the most ungovernable outrages, this sentiment glimmers through the more brutal features of the being. The rights of property, for instance, are everywhere acknowledged; the very wretch who steals whenever he can, appearing conscious of his crime, by doing it clandestinely, and as a deed that shuns observation. All seem to have the same general notions of natural justice, and they are forgotten, only through the policy of systems, irresistible temptation, the pressure of want, or the result of contention."

"Yet, as a rule, man everywhere oppresses his weaker fellow."

"True; but he betrays consciousness of his error, directly or indirectly. One can show his sense of the magnitude of his crime even by the manner of defending it. As respects our late enemies, I cannot say I felt any emotion of animosity while the hottest engaged against them, for their usages have rendered their proceedings lawful."

"They tell me," interrupted Mr. Effingham, "that it is owing to your presence of mind and steadiness that more blood was not shed unnecessarily."

"It may be questioned," continued Paul, noticing this compliment merely by an inclination of the head, "if civilized people have not reasoned themselves, under the influence of interest, into the commission of deeds quite as much opposed to natural justice as anything done by these barbarians. Perhaps no nation is perfectly free from the just imputation of having adopted some policy quite as unjustifiable in itself as the system of plunder maintained among the Arabs."

"Do you count the rights of hospitality as nothing?"

"Look at France, a nation distinguished for refinement, among its rulers at least. It was but the other day that the effects of the stranger who died in her territory were appropriated to the uses of a monarch wallowing in luxury. Compare this law with the treaties that invited strangers to repair to the country, and the wants of the monarch who exhibited the rapacity, to the situation of the barbarians from whom we have escaped, and the magnitude of the temptation we offered, and it does not appear that the advantage is much with Christians. But the fate of shipwrecked mariners all over the world is notorious. In countries the most advanced in civilization they are plundered, if there is an opportunity, and, at need, frequently murdered."

"This is a frightful picture of humanity," said Eve, shuddering. "I do not think that this charge can be justly brought against America."

"That is far from certain. America has many advantages to weaken the temptation to crime, but she is very far from perfect. The people on some of her coasts have been accused of resorting to the old English practice of showing false lights, with a view to mislead vessels, and of committing cruel depredations on the wrecked. In all things I believe there is a disposition in man to make misfortune weigh heaviest on the unfortunate. Even the coffin in which we inter a friend costs more than any other piece of work of the same amount of labor and materials."

"This is a gloomy picture of humanity, to be drawn by one so young," Mr. Effingham mildly rejoined.

"I think it true. All men do not exhibit their selfishness and ferocity in the same way; but there are few who do not exhibit both. As for America, Miss Effingham, she is fast getting vices peculiar to herself and her system, and, I think, vices which bid fair to bring her down, ere long, to the common level, although I do not go quite so far in describing her demerits as some of the countrymen of Mademoiselle Viefville have gone."

"And what may that have been?" asked the governess eagerly, in English.

"*Pourrie avant d'être mûre. Mûre*; America is certainly far from being; but I am not disposed to accuse her yet of being quite *pourrie*."

"We had flattered ourselves," said Eve, a little reproach-fully, "with having at last found a countryman in Mr. Powis."

"And how would that change the question? Or, do you admit that an American can be no American, unless blind to the faults of the country, however great?"

"Would it be generous for a child to turn upon a parent that all others assail?"

"You put the case ingeniously, but scarcely with fairness. It is the duty of the parent to educate and correct the child, but it is the duty of the citizen to reform and improve the character of his country. How can the latter be done, if nothing but eulogies are dealt in? With foreigners, one should not deal too freely with the faults of his country, though even with the liberal among them one would wish to be liberal, for foreigners cannot repair the evil; but with one's countrymen I see little use and much danger, in ob-serving a silence as to faults. The American, of all others, it appears to me, should be the boldest in denouncing the common and national vices, since he is one of those who, by the institutions themselves, has the power to apply the remedy."

"But America is an exception, I think, or perhaps it would be better to say I *feel*, since all other people deride at, mock her, and dislike her. You will admit this yourself, Sir George Templemore?"

"By no means: in England, now, I consider America to be particularly well esteemed."

Eve held up her pretty hands, and even Mademoiselle Viefville, usually so well-toned and self-restrained, gave a visible shrug.

"Sir George means in his country," dryly observed John Effingham.

"Perhaps the parties would better understand each other," said Paul, coolly, "were Sir George Templemore to descend to particulars. He belongs himself to the liberal school, and may be considered a safe witness."

"I shall be compelled to protest against a cross-examina-tion on such a subject," returned the baronet laughing.

"You will be satisfied, I am certain, with my simple declaration. Perhaps we still regard the Americans as *tant soit peu* rebels; but that is a feeling that will soon cease."

"That is precisely the point on which I think liberal Englishmen usually do great justice to America, while it is on other points that they betray a national dislike."

"England believes America hostile to herself; and if love creates love, dislike creates dislike."

"This is at least something like admitting the truth of the charge, Miss Effingham," said John Effingham, smiling, "and we may dismiss the accused. It is odd enough that England should consider America as rebellious, as is the case with many Englishmen, I acknowledge, while, in truth, England herself was the rebel, and this, too, in connection with the very questions that produced the American Revolution."

"This is quite new," said Sir George, "and I confess some curiosity to see how it can be made out."

John Effingham did not hesitate about stating his case.

"In the first place you are to forget professions and names," he said, "and to look only at facts and things. When America was settled, a compact was made, either in the way of charters or of organic laws, by which all the colonies had distinct rights, while, on the other hand, they confessed allegiance to the king. But in that age the English monarch was a king. He used his veto on the laws, for instance, and otherwise exercised his prerogatives. Of the two, he influenced parliament more than parliament influenced him. In such a state of things, countries separated by an ocean might be supposed to be governed equitably, the common monarch feeling a common parental regard for all his subjects. Perhaps distance might render him even more tender of the interest of those who were not present to protect themselves."

"This is putting the case loyally, at least," said Sir George, as the other paused for a moment.

"It is precisely in that light that I wish to present it. The degree of power that parliament possessed over the colonies was a disputed point; but I am willing to allow that parliament had all power."

"In doing which, I fear, you will concede all the merits," said Mr. Effingham.

"I think not. Parliament then ruled the colonies absolutely and legally, if you please, under the Stuarts ; but the English rebelled against these Stuarts, dethroned them, and gave the crown to an entirely new family,—one with only a remote alliance with the reigning branch. Not satisfied with this, the king was curtailed in his authority ; the prince, who might with justice be supposed to feel a common interest in all his subjects, became a mere machine in the hands of a body who represented little more than themselves, in fact, or a mere fragment of the empire, even in theory ; transferring the control of the colonial interest from the sovereign himself to a portion of his people, and that, too, a small portion. This was no longer a government of a prince who felt a parental concern for all his subjects, but a government of a *dique* of his subjects, who felt a selfish concern only for their own interests."

"And did the Americans urge this reason for the revolt?" asked Sir George. "It sounds new to me."

"They quarrelled with the results, rather than with the cause. When they found that legislation was to be chiefly in the interests of England, they took the alarm, and seized their arms, without stopping to analyze causes. They probably were mystified too much with names and professions to see the real truth, though they got some noble glimpses of it."

"I have never before heard this case put so strongly," cried Paul Powis, "and yet I think it contains the whole merit of the controversy as a principle."

"It is extraordinary how nationality blinds us," observed Sir George, laughing. "I confess, Powis,"—the late events had produced a close intimacy and a sincere regard between these two fine young men,—"that I stand in need of an explanation."

"You can conceive of a monarch," continued John Effingham, "who possesses an extensive and efficient power?"

"Beyond doubt ; nothing can be plainer than that."

"Fancy this monarch to fall into the hands of a fragment

of his subjects, who reduce his authority to a mere profession, and begin to wield it for their own especial benefit, no longer leaving him a free agent, though always using the authority in his name."

"Even that is easily imagined."

"History is full of such instances. A part of the subjects, unwilling to be the dupes of such a fraud, revolt against the monarch in name, against the cabal in fact. Now who are the real rebels? Profession is nothing. Hyder-Ali never seated himself in the presence of the prince he had deposed, though he held him captive during life."

"But did not America acquiesce in the dethronement of the Stuarts?" asked Eve, in whom the love of the right was stronger even than the love of country.

"Beyond a doubt, though America neither foresaw nor acquiesced in all the results. The English themselves, probably, did not foresee the consequences of their own revolution; for we now find England almost in arms against the consequences of the very subversion of the kingly power of which I have spoken. In England it placed a portion of the higher classes in possession of authority, at the expense of all the rest of the nation; whereas, as respects America, it set a remote people to rule over her, instead of a prince who had the same connection with his colonies as with all the rest of his subjects. The late English reform is a peaceable revolution; and America would very gladly have done the same thing, could she have extricated herself from the consequences, by mere acts of congress. The whole difference is, that America, pressed upon by peculiar circumstances, preceded England in the revolt about sixty years, and that this revolt was against an usurper, and not against the legitimate monarch, or against the sovereign himself."

"I confess all this is novel to me," exclaimed Sir George.

"I have told you, Sir George Templemore, that, if you stay long enough in America, many novel ideas will suggest themselves. You have too much sense to travel through the country seeking for petty exceptions that may sustain your aristocratical prejudices, or opinions, if you like that better ; but will be disposed to judge a nation, not according to preconceived notions, but according to visible facts."

"They tell me there is a strong bias to aristocracy in America ; at least such is the report of most European travellers."

"The report of men who do not reflect closely on the meaning of words. That there are real aristocrats in opinion in America is very true ; there are also a few monarchists, or those who fancy themselves monarchists."

"Can a man be deceived on such a point ? "

"Nothing is more easy. He who would set up a king merely in name, for instance, is not a monarchist, but a visionary, who confounds names with things."

"I see you will not admit of a balance in the state."

"I shall contend that there must be a preponderating authority in every government, from which it derives its character ; and if this be not the king, that government is not a real monarchy, let the laws be administered in whose name they may. Calling an idol Jupiter does not convert it into a god. I question if there be a real monarchist left in the English empire at this very moment. They who make the loudest professions that way strike me as being the rankest aristocrats, and a real political aristocrat is, and always has been, the most efficient enemy of kings."

"But we consider loyalty to the prince as attachment to the system."

"That is another matter ; for in that you may be right enough, though it is ambiguous as to terms."

"Sir—gentlemen—Mr. John Effingham, sir," interrupted Saunders, "Mr. Monday is awake, and so werry conwalescent—I fear he will not live long. The ship herself is not so much conwerted by these new spars as poor Mr. Monday is conwerted since he went to sleep."

"I feared this," observed John Effingham, rising. "Acquaint Captain Truck with the fact, steward ; he desired to be sent for at any crisis."

He then quitted the cabin, leaving the rest of the party wondering that they could have been already so lost to the

situation of one of their late companions, however different
from themselves he might be in opinions and character.
But in this they merely showed their common connection
with all the rest of the great family of man, who uniformly
forget sorrows that do not press too hard on self, in the reaction of their feelings.

## CHAPTER XXX.

"Watchman, what of the night?  Watchman, what of the night?"
ISAIAH.

THE principal hurt of Mr. Monday was one of those wounds that usually produce death within eight-and-forty hours. He had borne the pain with resolution ; and, as yet, had discovered no consciousness of the imminent danger that was so apparent to all around him. But a film had suddenly passed from before his senses ; and, a man of mere habits, prejudices, and animal enjoyments, he had awakened at the very termination of his brief existence to something like a consciousness of his true position in the moral world, as well as of his real physical condition. Under the first impulse of such an alarm, John Effingham had been sent for ; and he, as has been seen, ordered Captain Truck to be summoned. In consequence of the previous understanding, these two gentlemen and Mr. Leach appeared at the state-room door at the same instant. The apartment being small, it was arranged between them that the former should enter first, having been expressly sent for ; and that the others should be introduced at the pleasure of the wounded man.

"I have brought my Bible, Mr. Leach," said the captain, when he and the mate were left alone, "for a chapter is the very least we can give a cabin-passenger, though I am a little at a loss to know what particular passage will be the most suitable for the occasion. Something from the Book of Kings would be likely to suit Mr. Monday, as he is a thorough-going king's man."

"It is so long since I read that particular book, sir," returned the mate, diligently thumbing his watch-key, "that I should be diffident about expressing an opinion. I think, however, a little Bible might do him good."

"It is not an easy matter to hit a conscience exactly between wind and water. I once thought of producing an impression on the ship's company by reading the account of Jonah and the whale as a subject likely to attract their attention, and to show them the hazards we seamen run ; but, in the end, I discovered that the narration struck them all aback as a thing not likely to be true. Jack can stand anything but a fish story, you know, Leach."

"It is always better to keep clear of miracles at sea, I believe, sir, when the people are to be spoken to : I saw some of the men this evening wince about that ship of St. Paul's carrying out anchors in a gale."

"The graceless rascals ought to be thankful they are not at this very moment trotting through the Great Desert lashed to dromedaries' tails ! Had I known that, Leach, I would have read the verse twice. But Mr. Monday is altogether a different man, and will listen to reason. There is the story of Absalom, which is quite interesting ; and perhaps the account of the battle might be suitable for one who dies in consequence of a battle ; but, on the whole, I remember my worthy old father used to say that a sinner ought to be well shaken up at such a moment."

"I fancy, sir, Mr. Monday has been a reasonably steady man as the world goes. Seeing that he is a passenger, I should try and ease him off handsomely, and without any of these Methodist surges."

"You may be right, Leach, you may be right ; do as you would be done by, is the golden rule, after all. But, here comes Mr. John Effingham ; so I fancy we may enter."

The captain was not mistaken, for Mr. Monday had just taken a restorative, and had expressed a desire to see the two officers. The state-room was a small, neat, and even beautifully finished apartment, about seven feet square. It had originally been fitted with two berths ; but previously to taking possession of the place, John Effingham had caused the carpenter to remove the upper, and Mr. Monday now lay in what had been the lower bed. This situation placed him below his attendant, and in a position where he might be the more easily assisted. A shaded lamp lighted the room, by means of which the captain caught the anxious expression of the dying man's eye, as he took a seat himself.

"I am grieved to see you in this state, Mr. Monday," said the master, "and this all the more since it has happened in consequence of your bravery in fighting to regain my ship. By rights this accident ought to have befallen one of the Montauk's people, or Mr. Leach, here, or even myself, before it befell you."

Mr. Monday looked at the speaker as if the intended consolation had failed of its effect, and the captain began to suspect that he should find a different subject for his new ministrations. By way of gaining time, he thrust an elbow into the mate's side as a hint that it was now his turn to offer something.

"It might have been worse, Mr. Monday," observed Leach, shifting his attitude like a man whose moral and physical action moved *pari passu:* "it might have been much worse. I once saw a man shot in the under jaw, and he lived a fortnight without any sort of nourishment!"

Still Mr. Monday gazed at the mate as if he thought matters could not be much worse.

"That *was* a hard case," put in the captain; "why, the poor fellow had no opportunity to recover without victuals."

"No, sir, nor any drink. He never swallowed a mouthful of liquor of any sort from the time he was hit, until he took the plunge when we threw him overboard.

Perhaps there is truth in the saying that "Misery loves company," for the eye of Mr. Monday turned towards the table on which the bottle of cordial still stood, and from which John Effingham had just before helped him to a swallow, under the impression that it was of no moment what he took. The captain understood the appeal, and influenced by the same opinion concerning the hopelessness of the patient's condition, besides being kindly anxious to console him, he poured out a small glass, all of which he permitted the other to drink. The effect was instantaneous, for it would seem this treacherous friend is ever ready to produce a momentary pleasure as a poor compensation for its lasting pains.

"I don't feel so bad, gentlemen," returned the wounded man, with a force of voice that startled his visitors. "I feel better—much better, and am very glad to see you. Captain Truck, I have the honor to drink your health."

The captain looked at the mate as if he thought their visit was twenty-four hours too soon, for live, all felt sure, Mr. Monday could not. But Leach, better placed to observe the countenance of the patient, whispered his commander that it was merely "a catspaw, and will not stand."

"I am very glad to see you both, gentlemen," continued Mr. Monday, "and beg you to help yourselves."

The captain changed his tactics. Finding his patient so strong and cheerful, he thought consolation would be more easily received just at that moment, than it might be even half an hour later.

"We are all mortal, Mr. Monday—"

"Yes, sir; all very mortal."

"And even the strongest and boldest ought occasionally to think of their end."

"Quite true, sir; quite true. The strongest and boldest. When do you think we shall get in, gentlemen?"

Captain Truck afterwards affirmed that he was "never before taken so flat aback by a question as by this." Still he extricated himself from the dilemma with dexterity, the spirit of proselytism apparently rising within him in proportion as the other manifested indifference to his offices.

"There is a port to which we are all steering, my dear sir," he said; "and of which we ought always to bear in mind the landmarks and beacons, and that port is heaven."

"Yes," added Mr. Leach, "a port that, sooner or later, will fetch us all up."

Mr. Monday gazed from one to the other, and something like the state of feelings from which he had been aroused by the cordial, began to return.

"Do you think me so bad, gentlemen?" he inquired, with a little of the eagerness of a startled man.

"As bad as one bound direct to so good a place as I hope and trust is the case with you, can be," returned the captain, determined to follow up the advantage he had gained. "Your wound, we fear, is mortal, and people seldom remain long in this wicked world with such sort of hurts."

"If he stands that," thought the captain, "I shall turn him over, at once, to Mr. Effingham."

Mr. Monday did not stand it. The illusion produced by the liquor, although the latter still sustained his pulses, had begun to evaporate, and the melancholy truth resumed its power.

"I believe, indeed, that I am near my end, gentlemen," he said faintly; "and am thankful—for—for this consolation."

"Now will be a good time to throw in the chapter," whispered Leach; "he seems quite conscious, and very contrite."

Captain Truck, in pure despair, and conscious of his own want of judgment, had determined to leave the question of the selection of this chapter to be decided by chance. Perhaps a little of that mysterious dependence on Providence, which renders all men more or less superstitious, influenced him; and that he hoped a wisdom surpassing his own might direct him to a choice. Fortunately, the Book of Psalms is near the middle of the sacred volume, and a better disposition of this sublime repository of pious praise and spiritual wisdom could not have been made; for the chance-directed peruser of the Bible will perhaps oftener open among its pages than at any other place.

If we should say that Mr. Monday felt any very profound spiritual relief from the reading of Captain Truck, we should both overrate the manner of the honest sailor, and the intelligence of the dying man. Still the solemn language of praise and admonition had an effect, and, for the first time since childhood, the soul of the latter was moved. God and judgment passed before his imagination, and he gasped for breath in a way that induced the two seamen to suppose the fatal moment had come, even sooner than they expected. The cold sweat stood before the forehead of the patient, and his eyes glared wildly from one to the other. The paroxysm, however, was transient, and he soon settled down into a state of comparative calmness, pushing away the glass that Captain Truck offered, in mistaken kindness, with a manner of loathing.

" We must comfort him, Leach," whispered the captain ; "for I see he is fetching up in the old way, as was duly laid down by our ancestors in the platform. First, groanings and views of the devil, and then consolation and hope. We have got him into the first category, and we ought now, in justice, to bring-to, and heave a strain to help him through it."

" They generally give 'em prayer, in the river, in this stage of the attack," said Leach. " If you can remember a short prayer, sir, it might ease him off."

Captain Truck and his mate, notwithstanding the quaintness of their thoughts and language, were themselves solemnly impressed with the scene, and actuated by the kindest motives. Nothing of levity mingled with their notions, but they felt the responsibility of officers of a packet, besides entertaining a generous interest in the fate of a stranger who had fallen, fighting manfully at their side. The old man looked awkwardly about him, turned the key of the door, wiped his eyes, gazed wistfully at the patient, gave his mate a nudge with his elbow to follow his example, and knelt down with a heart momentarily as devout as is often the case with those who minister at the altar. He retained the words of the Lord's Prayer, and these he repeated aloud, distinctly, and with fervor, though not with a literal conformity to the text. Once Mr. Leach had to help him to the word. When he rose, the perspiration stood on his forehead, as if he had been engaged in severe toil.

Perhaps nothing could have occurred more likely to strike the imagination of Mr. Monday, than to see one, of the known character and habits of Captain Truck, thus wrestling with the Lord in his own behalf. Always obtuse and dull of thought, the first impression was that of wonder ; awe and contrition followed. Even the mate was touched, and he afterwards told his companion on deck, that " the

hardest day's work he had ever done, was lending a hand
to rouse the captain through that prayer."

"I thank you, sir," gasped Mr. Monday, "I thank you
--Mr. John Effingham- -now, let me see Mr. John Effingham. I have no time to lose, and wish to see *him*."

The captain rose to comply, with the feelings of a man
who had done his duty, and, from that moment, he had a
secret satisfaction at having so manfully acquitted himself.
Indeed, it has been remarked by those who have listened
to his whole narrative of the passage, that he invariably
lays more stress on the scene in the state-room, than on the
readiness and skill with which he repaired the damages
sustained by his own ship, through the means obtained from
the Dane, or the spirit with which he retook her from the
Arabs.

John Effingham appeared in the state-room, where the
captain and Mr. Leach left him alone with the patient.
Like all strong-minded men, who are conscious of their
superiority over the rest of their fellow-creatures, this gentleman felt disposed to concede most to those who were the
least able to contend with him. Habitually sarcastic and
stern, and sometimes forbidding, he was now mild and discreet. He saw, at a glance, that Mr. Monday's mind was
alive to novel feelings; and aware that the approach of
death frequently removes moral clouds that have concealed
the powers of the spirit while the animal part of the being was
in full vigor, he was surprised at observing the sudden change
that was so apparent in the countenance of the dying man.

"I believe, sir, I have been a great sinner," commenced
Mr. Monday, who spoke more feebly as the influence of the
cordial evaporated, and in short and broken sentences.

"In that you share the lot of all," returned John Effingham. "We are taught that no man of himself, no unaided
soul, is competent to its own salvation. Christians look to
the Redeemer for succor."

"I believe I understand you, but I am a business man,
sir, and have been taught that reparation is the best atone-
ment for a wrong."

"It certainly should be the *first*."

"Yes, indeed it should, sir. I am but the son of poor parents, and may have been tempted to some things that are improper. My mother, too—I was her only support. Well, the Lord will pardon it, if it were wrong, as I dare say it might have been. I think I should have drunk less and thought more, but for this affair—perhaps it is not yet too late."

John Effingham listened with surprise, but with the coolness and sagacity that marked his character. He saw the necessity, or at least the prudence, of there being another witness present. Taking advantage of the exhaustion of the speaker, he stepped to the door of Eve's cabin, and signed Paul to follow him. They entered the state-room together, when John Effingham took Mr. Monday soothingly by the hand, offering him a nourishment less exciting than the cordial, but which had the effect to revive him.

"I understand you, sir," continued Mr. Monday, looking at Paul; "it is all very proper; but I have little to say— the papers will explain it all. Those keys, sir—the upper drawer of the bureau, and the red morocco case—take it all —this is the key. I have kept everything together, from a misgiving that an hour would come. In New York you will have time—it is not yet too late."

As the wounded man spoke at intervals, and with difficulty, John Effingham had complied with his directions before he ceased. He found the red morocco case, took the key from the ring, and showed both to Mr. Monday, who smiled and nodded approbation. The bureau contained paper, wax, and all the other appliances of writing. John Effingham inclosed the case in a strong envelope, and affixed to it three seals, which he impressed with his own arms; he then asked Paul for his watch, that the same might be done with the seal of his companion. After this precaution, he wrote a brief declaration that the contents had been delivered to the two, for the purpose of examination, and for the benefit of the parties concerned, whoever they might be, and signed it. Paul did the same, and the paper was handed to Mr. Monday, who had still strength to add his own signature.

"Men do not usually trifle at such moments," said John Effingham, "and this case may contain matter of moment to wronged and innocent persons. The world little knows the extent of the enormities that are thus committed. Take the case, Mr. Powis, and lock it up with your effects, until the moment for the examination shall come."

Mr. Monday was certainly much relieved after this consignment of the case into safe hands, trifles satisfying the compunctions of the obtuse. For more than an hour he slumbered. During this interval of rest, Captain Truck appeared at the door of the state-room to inquire into the condition of the patient, and, hearing a report so favorable, in common with all whose duty did not require them to watch, he retired to rest. Paul had also returned, and offered his services, as indeed did most of the gentlemen; but John Effingham dismissed his own servant even, and declared it was his intention not to quit the place that night. Mr. Monday had reposed confidence in him, appeared to be gratified by his attentions and presence, and he felt it to be a sort of duty, under such circumstances, not to desert a fellow-creature in his extremity. Anything beyond some slight alleviation of the sufferer's pains was hopeless; but this, he rightly believed, he was as capable of administering as another.

Death is appalling to those of the most iron nerves, when it comes quietly and in the stillness and solitude of night. John Effingham was such a man; but he felt all the peculiarity of his situation as he sat alone in the state-room by the side of Mr. Monday, listening to the washing of the waters that the ship shoved aside, and to the unquiet breathing of his patient. Several times he felt a disposition to steal away for a few minutes, and to refresh himself by exercise in the pure air of the ocean; but as often was the inclination checked by jealous glances from the glazed eye of the dying man, who appeared to cherish his presence as his own last hope of life. When John Effingham wetted his feverish lips, the look he received spoke of gratitude and thanks, and once or twice these feelings were audible in whispers. He could not desert a being so helpless, so

28

dependent; and, although conscious that he was of no material service beyond sustaining his patient by his presence, he felt that this was sufficient to exact much heavier sacrifices.

During one of the troubled slumbers of the dying man, his attendant sat watching the struggles of his countenance, which seemed to betray the workings of the soul that was about to quit its tenement, and he mused on the character and fate of the being whose departure for the world of spirits he himself was so singularly called on to witness.

"Of his origin I know nothing," thought John Effingham, "except by his own passing declarations, and the evident fact, that, as regards station, it can scarcely have reached mediocrity. He is one of those who appear to live for the most vulgar motives that are admissible among men of any culture, and whose refinement, such as it is, is purely of the conventional class of habits. Ignorant, beyond the current opinions of a set; prejudiced in all that relates to nations, religions, and characters; wily, with an air of blustering honesty; credulous and intolerant; bold in denunciations and critical remarks, without a spark of discrimination, or any knowledge but that which has been acquired under a designing dictation; as incapable of generalizing as he is obstinate in trifles; good-humored by nature, and yet querulous from imitation—for what purposes was such a creature brought into existence to be hurried out of it in this eventful manner?" The conversation of the evening recurred to John Effingham, and he inwardly said, "If there exist such varieties of the human race among nations, there are certainly as many species, in a moral sense, in civilized life itself. This man has his counterpart in a particular feature in the every-day American absorbed in the pursuit of gain; and yet how widely different are the two in the minor points of character! While the other allows himself no rest, no relaxation, no mitigation of the eternal gnawing of the vulture rapacity, this man has made self-indulgence the constant companion of his toil; while the other has centred all his pleasures in gain, this Englishman, with the same object in view, but

obedient to national usages, has fancied he has been allevi-
ating his labors by sensual enjoyments. In what will their
ends differ? From the eyes of the American the veil will
be torn aside when it is too late, perhaps, and the object of
his earthly pursuit will be made the instrument of his punishment, as he sees himself compelled to quit it all for the
dark uncertainty of the grave; while the blusterer and the
bottle-companion sinks into a forced and appalled repent-
ance, as the animal that has hitherto upheld him loses its
ascendency.''

A groan from Mr. Monday, who now opened his glassy
eyes, interrupted these musings. The patient signed for the
nourishment, and he revived a little.

"What is the day of the week?" he asked, with an
anxiety that surprised his kind attendant.

"It is, or rather it *was*, Monday; for we are now past
midnight."

"I am glad of it, sir—very glad of it."

"Why should the day of the week be of consequence to
you now?"

"There is a saying, sir—I have faith in sayings—they
told me I was born of a Monday, and should die of a
Monday."

The other was shocked at this evidence of a lingering and
abject superstition in one who could not probably survive
many hours, and he spoke to him of the Saviour, and of his
mediation for man. All this could John Effingham do at
need; and he could do it well, too, for few had clearer per-
ceptions of this state of probation than himself. His weak
point was in the pride and strength of his character; qualities that indisposed him in his own practice to rely on any
but himself, under the very circumstances which would
impress on others the necessity of relying solely on God.
The dying man heard him attentively, and the words made
a momentary impression.

"I do not wish to die, sir," Mr. Monday said suddenly,
after a long pause.

"It is the general fate; when the moment arrives, we
ought to prepare ourselves to meet it."

"I am no coward, Mr. Effingham."

"In one sense I know you are not, for I have seen you proved. I hope you will not be one in any sense. You are now in a situation in which manhood will avail you nothing: your dependence should be placed altogether on God."

"I know it, sir—I try to feel thus; but I do not wish to die."

"The love of Christ is illimitable," said John Effingham, powerfully affected by the other's hopeless misery.

"I know it—I hope it—I wish to believe it. Have *you* a mother, Mr. Effingham?"

"She has been dead many years."

"A wife?"

John Effingham gasped for breath, and one might have mistaken him, at the moment, for the sufferer.

"None: I am without parent, brother, sister, wife, or child. My nearest relatives are in this ship."

"I am of little value; but such as I am, my mother will miss me. We can have but one mother, sir."

"This is very true. If you have any commission or message for your mother, Mr. Monday, I shall have great satisfaction in attending to your wishes."

"I thank you, sir; I know of none. She has her notions on religion, and—I think it would lessen her sorrow to hear that I had a Christian burial."

"Set your heart at rest on that subject: all that our situation will allow, shall be done."

"Of what account will it all be, Mr. Effingham? I wish I had drunk less, and thought more."

John Effingham could say nothing to a compunction that was so necessary, though so tardy.

"I fear we think too little of this moment in our health and strength, sir."

"The greater the necessity, Mr. Monday, of turning our thoughts towards the divine mediation which alone can avail us, while there is yet opportunity."

But Mr. Monday was startled by the near approach of death, rather than repentant. He had indurated his feelings

by the long-continued practice of a deafening self-indulgence, and he was now like a man who unexpectedly finds
himself in the presence of an imminent and overwhelming
danger, without any visible means of mitigation or escape.
He groaned and looked around him, as if he sought something to cling to, the spirit he had shown in the pride of his
strength availing nothing. All these, however, were but
passing emotions, and the natural obtusity of the man
returned.

"I do not think, sir," he said, gazing intently at John
Effingham, "that I have been a very great sinner."

"I hope not, my good friend; yet none of us are so free
from spot as not to require the aid of God to fit us for his
holy presence."

"Very true, sir—very true, sir. I was duly baptized and
properly confirmed."

"Offices which are but pledges that we are expected to
redeem."

"By a regular priest and bishop, sir—orthodox and dignified clergymen!"

"No doubt: England wants none of the forms of religion.
But the contrite heart, Mr. Monday, will be sure to meet
with mercy."

"I feel contrite, sir, very contrite."

A pause of half an hour succeeded, and John Effingham
thought at first that his patient had again slumbered; but,
looking more closely at his situation, he perceived that his
eyes often opened and wandered over objects near him.
Unwilling to disturb this apparent tranquillity, the minutes were permitted to pass away uninterrupted, until Mr.
Monday spoke again of his own accord.

"Mr. Effingham—sir—Mr. Effingham," said the dying
man.

"I am near you, Mr. Monday, and will not leave the
room."

"Bless you, bless you, do not *you* desert me!"

"I shall remain: set your heart at rest, and let me know
your wants."

"I want life, sir."

"That is the gift of God, and its possession depends solely on his pleasure. Ask pardon for your sins, and remember the mercy and love of the blessed Redeemer."

"I try, sir. I do not think I have been a *very* great sinner."

"I hope not : but God can pardon the penitent, however great their offences."

"Yes, sir, I know it—I know it. This affair has been so unexpected. I have even been at the communion-table, sir ; yes, my mother made me commune. Nothing was neglected, sir."

John Effingham was often proud and self-willed in his communications with men, the inferiority of most of his fellow-creatures to himself, in principles as well as mind, being too plainly apparent not to influence the opinions of one who did not too closely study his own failings ; but, as respects God, he was habitually reverent and meek. Spiritual pride formed no part of his character, for he felt his own deficiency in the Christian qualities, the main defect arising more from a habit of regarding the infirmities of others, than from dwelling too much on his own merits. In comparing himself with perfection, no one could be more humble, but in limiting the comparison to those around him, few were prouder, or few more justly so, were it permitted to make such a comparison at all. Prayer with him was not habitual, or always well ordered, but he was not ashamed to pray ; and when he did bow down his spirit in this manner, it was with the force, comprehensiveness, and energy of his character. He was now moved by the feeble and commonplace consolations that Mr. Monday endeavored to extract from his situation. He saw the peculiarly deluding and cruel substitution of forms for the substance of piety that distinguishes the policy of all established churches, though, unlike many of his own countrymen, his mind was superior to those narrow exaggerations that, on the other hand, too often convert innocence into sin, and puff up the votary with the conceit of a sectarian and his self-righteousness.

"I will pray with you, Mr Monday," he said, kneeling

at the side of the dying man's bed : " we will ask mercy of God together, and he may lessen these doubts."

Mr. Monday made a sign of eager assent, and John Effingham prayed in a voice that was distinctly audible to the other. The petition was short, beautiful, and even lofty in language, without a particle of Scripture jargon, or of the cant of professed devotees ; but it was a fervent, direct, comprehensive, and humble appeal to the Deity for mercy on the being who now found himself in extremity. A child might have understood it, while the heart of a man would have melted with its affecting and meek sincerity. It is to be hoped that the Great Being, whose Spirit pervades the universe, and whose clemency is commensurate with his power, also admitted the force of the petition, for Mr. Monday smiled with pleasure when John Effingham arose.

"Thank you, sir- a thousand thanks," muttered the dying man, pressing the hand of the other. "This is better than all."

After this Mr. Monday was easier, and hours passed away in nearly a continued silence. John Effingham was now convinced that his patient slumbered, and he allowed himself to fall into a doze. It was after the morning watch was called, that he was aroused by a movement in the berth. Believing his patient required nourishment, or some fluid to moisten his lips, John Effingham offered both, but they were declined. Mr. Monday had clasped his hands on his breast, with the fingers uppermost, as painters and sculptors are apt to delineate them when they represent saints in the act of addressing the Deity, and his lips moved, though the words were whispered. John Effingham kneeled, and placed his ear so close as to catch the sounds. His patient was uttering the simple but beautiful petition transmitted by Christ himself to man, as the model of all prayer.

As soon as the other had done, John Effingham repeated the same prayer fervently and aloud himself, and when he opened his eyes, after this solemn homage to God, Mr. Monday was dead.

## CHAPTER XXXI.

"Let me alone : dost thou use to write
Thy name? or hast thou a mark to thyself, like an
Honest, plain-dealing man ? "

*Jack Cade.*

AT a later hour, the body of the deceased was consigned to the ocean with the forms that had been observed the previous night at the burial of the seaman. These two ceremonies were sad remembrancers of the scene the travellers had passed through; and, for many days, the melancholy that they naturally excited pervaded the ship. But, as no one connected by blood with any of the living had fallen, and it is not the disposition of men to mourn always, this feeling gradually subsided, and at the end of three weeks the deaths had lost most of their influence, or were recalled only at moments by those who thought it wise to dwell on such solemn subjects.

Captain Truck had regained his spirits; for, if he felt mortified at the extraordinary difficulties and dangers that had befallen his ship, he also felt proud of the manner in which he had extricated himself from them. As for the mates and crew, they had already returned to their ordinary habits of toil and fun, the accidents of life making but brief and superficial impressions on natures accustomed to vicissitudes and losses.

Mr. Dodge appeared to be nearly forgotten during the first week after the ship succeeded in effecting her escape; for he had the sagacity to keep himself in the background, in the hope that all connected with himself might be overlooked in the hurry and excitement of events. At the end of that period, however, he resumed his intrigues, and was soon actively engaged in endeavoring to get up a "public opinion," by means of which he proposed to himself to obtain some reputation for spirit and courage. With what success this deeply-laid scheme was likely to meet, as well as the more familiar condition of the cabins, may be gathered by a conversation that took place in the pantry, where Saunders and Toast were preparing the hot punch for the last of the Saturday nights that Captain Truck expected to be at sea. This discourse was held while the few who chose to join in jollification that peculiarly recalled the recollection of Mr. Monday, were slowly assembling round the great table at the urgent request of the master.

"Well, I must say, Mr. Toast," the steward commenced, as he kept stirring the punch, "that I am werry much rejoiced Captain Truck has resuscertated his old nature, and remembers the festivals and fasts, as is becoming the master of a liner. I can see no good reason because a ship is under jury-masts, that the passengers should forego their natural rest and diet. Mr. Monday made a good end, they say, and he had as handsome a burial as I ever laid eyes on at sea. I don't think his own friends could have interred him more efficaciously, or more piously, had he been on shore."

"It is something, Mr. Saunders, to be able to reflect beforehand on the respectable funeral that your friends have just given you. There is a great gratification to contemplate on such an event."

"You improve in language, Toast, that I will allow; but you sometimes get the words a little wrong. We suspect before a thing recurs, and reflect on it after it has ewentuated. You might have suspected the death of poor Mr. Monday after he was wounded, and reflected on it after he was interred in the water. I agree with you that it is consoling to know we have our funeral rights properly delineated. Talking of the battle, Mr. Toast, I shall take this occasion to express to you the high opinion I entertain of your own good conduct. I was a little afraid you might injure Captain 'Truck in the conflict; but, so far as I have ascertained, on close inwestigation, you hurt nobody. We colored people have some prejudices against us, and I always rejoice when I meet with one who assists to put them down by his own conduck."

"They say Mr. Dodge did n't do much harm, either," returned Toast. "For my part, I saw nothing of him after I opened my eyes; though I don't think I ever stared about me so much in my life."

Saunders laid a finger on his nose, and shook his head significantly.

"You may speak to me with confidence and mistrust, Toast," he said, "for we are friends of the same color, besides being officers in the same pantry. Has Mr. Dodge conwersed with you concerning the ewents of those two or three werry ewentful days?"

"He has insinevated considerable, Mr. Saunders; though I do not think Mr. Dodge is ever a werry free talker."

"Has he surgested the propriety of having an account of the whole affair made out by the people, and sustained by affidavits?"

"Well, sir, I imagine he has. At all ewents, he has been much on the forecastle lately, endeavoring to persuade the people that *they* retook the ship, and that the passengers were so many encumbrancers in the affair."

"And are the people such *non composses* as to believe him, Toast?"

"Why, sir, it is agreeable to humanity to think well of ourselves. I do not say that anybody actually believes this; but, in my poor judgment, Mr. Saunders, there are men in the ship that would find it pleasant to believe it, if they could."

"Werry true; for that is natural. Your hint, Toast, has enlightened my mind on a little obscurity that has lately prewailed over my conceptions. There are Johnson, and Briggs, and Hewson, three of the greatest skulks in the ship, the only men who prewaricated in the least, so much as by a cold look, in the fight; and these three men have told me that Mr. Dodge was the person who had the gun

put on the box ; and that he druv the Arabs upon the raft.
Now, I say, no men with their eyes open could have made
such a mistake, except they made it on purpose.   Do you
corroborate or contrawerse this statement, Toast ? "

" I contrawerse it, sir ; for in my poor judgment it was
Mr. Blunt."

" I am glad we are of the same opinion.   I shall say
nothing till the proper moment arrives, and then I shall exhibit my sentiments, Mr. Toast, without recrimination or
anxiety, for truth is truth."

" I am happy to observe that the ladies are quite relaxed
from their melancholy, and that they now seem to enjoy
themselves ostensibly."

Saunders threw a look of envy at his subordinate, whose
progress in refinement really alarmed his own sense of superiority ; but, suppressing the jealous feeling, he replied with
dignity,—

" The remark is quite just, Mr. Toast, and denotes penetration.   I am always rejoiced when I perceive you ele-
wating your thoughts to superior objects, for the honor of
the color."

" Mister Saunders ! " called out the captain from his seat
in the arm-chair, at the head of the table.

" Captain Truck, sir."

" Let us taste your liquors."

This was the signal that the Saturday night was about to
commence, and the officers of the pantry presented their
compounds in good earnest.   On this occasion the ladies
had quietly but firmly declined being present, but the
earnest appeals of the well-meaning captain had overcome
the scruples of the gentlemen, all of whom, to avoid the
appearance of disrespect to his wishes, had consented to
appear.

" This is the last Saturday night, gentlemen, that I shall
probably ever have the honor of passing in your good company," said Captain Truck, as he disposed of the pitchers
and glasses before him, so that he had a perfect command
of the appliances of the occasion, " and I feel it to be a
gratification with which I would not willingly dispense.

We are now to the westward of the Gulf, and, according to
my observations and calculations, within a hundred miles of
Sandy Hook, which, with this mild southwest wind, and our
weatherly position, I hope to be able to show you some
time about eight o'clock to-morrow morning. Quicker passages have been made certainly, but forty days, after all, is
no great matter for the westerly run, considering that we
have had a look at Africa, and are walking on crutches."

"We owe a great deal to the trades," observed Mr.
Effingham, "which have treated us as kindly towards the
end of the passage, as they seemed reluctant to join us in
the commencement. It has been a momentous month, and
I hope we shall all retain healthful recollections of it as
long as we live."

"No one will retain as *grateful* recollections of it as
myself, gentlemen," resumed the captain. "You had no
agency in getting us into the scrape, but the greatest possible agency in getting us out of it. Without the knowledge,
prudence, and courage that you have all displayed, God
knows what would have become of the poor Montauk, and
from the bottom of my heart I thank you, each and all,
while I have the heartfelt satisfaction of seeing you around
me, and of drinking to your future health, happiness, and
prosperity."

The passengers acknowledged their thanks in return, by
bows, among which that of Mr. Dodge was the most elaborate and conspicuous. The honest captain was too much
touched, to observe this little piece of audacity, but, at that
moment, he could have taken even Mr. Dodge in his arms
and pressed him to his heart.

"Come, gentlemen," he continued; "let us fill, and do
honor to the night. God has us all in his holy keeping,
and we drift about in the squalls of life, pretty much as he
orders the wind to blow. 'Sweethearts and wives!' and,
Mr. Effingham, we will not forget beautiful, spirited, sensible, and charming daughters."

After this piece of nautical gallantry, the glass began to
circulate. The captain, Sir George Templemore—as the
false baronet was still called in the cabin, and believed to

be by all but those who belonged to the *coterie* of Eve—
and Mr. Dodge, indulged freely, though the first was too
careful of the reputation of his ship, to forget that he was
on the American coast in November. The others partook
more sparingly, though even they submitted in a slight degree to the influence of good cheer, and for the first time
since their escape, the laugh was heard in the cabin as was
wont before to be the case. An hour of such indulgence
produced again some of the freedom and ease which mark
the associations of a ship, after the ice is fairly broken, and
even Mr. Dodge began to be tolerated. This person, notwithstanding his conduct on the occasion of the battle, had
contrived to maintain his ground with the spurious baronet,
by dint of assiduity and flattery, while the others had
rather felt pity than aversion, on account of his abject cow-
ardice. The gentlemen did not mention his desertion at
the critical moment (though Mr. Dodge never forgave those
who witnessed it), for they looked upon his conduct as the
result of a natural and unconquerable infirmity, that rendered him as much the subject of compassion as of reproach.
Encouraged by this forbearance, and mistaking its motives,
he had begun to hope his absence had not been detected in
the confusion of the fight, and he had even carried his
audacity so far, as to make an attempt to persuade Mr.
Sharp that he had actually been one of those who went in
the launch of the Dane, to bring down the other boat and
raft to the reef, after the ship had been recaptured. It is
true, in this attempt, he had met with a cold repulse, but it
was so gentlemanlike and distant, that he had still hopes of
succeeding in persuading the other to believe what he affirmed ; by way of doing which, he endeavored all he could
to believe it himself. So much confusion existed in his own
faculties during the fray, that Mr. Dodge was fain to fancy
others also might not have been able to distinguish things
very accurately.

Under the influence of these feelings, Captain Truck,
when the glass had circulated a little freely, called on the
editor of the " Active Inquirer " to favor the company with
some more extracts from his journal. Little persuasion was

necessary, and Mr. Dodge went into his state-room to bring forth the valuable records of his observations and opinions, with a conviction that all was forgotten, and that he was once more about to resume his proper place in the social relations of the ship. As for the four gentlemen who had been over the ground the other pretended to describe, they prepared to listen, as men of the world would be apt to listen to the superficial and valueless comments of a tyro, though not without some expectations of amusement.

"I propose that we shift the scene to London," said Captain Truck, "in order that a plain seaman, like myself, may judge of the merits of the writer—which, I make no doubt, are very great; though I cannot now swear to it with as free a conscience as I could wish."

"If I knew the pleasure of the majority," returned Mr. Dodge, dropping the journal, and looking about him inquiringly, "I would cheerfully comply with it; for I think the majority should always rule. Paris, or London, or the Rhine, are the same to me; I have seen them all, and am just as well qualified to describe the one as to describe the other."

"No one doubts it, my dear sir; but I am not as well qualified to understand one of your descriptions as I am to understand another. Perhaps, even you, sir, may express yourself more readily, and have better understood what was said to you, in English, than in a foreign tongue."

"As for that, I do not think the value of my remarks is lessened by the one circumstance, or enhanced by the other, sir. I make it a rule always to be right, if possible; and that, I fancy, is as much as the natives of the countries themselves can very well effect. You have only to decide, gentlemen, whether it shall be England, or France, or the Continent."

"I confess an inclination to the *Continent*," said John Effingham; "for one could scarcely wish to limit a comprehensiveness like that of Mr. Dodge's to an island, or even to France."

"I see how it is," exclaimed the captain; "we must put the traveller through all his paces, and have a little of both;

so Mr. Dodge will have the kindness to touch on all things in heaven and earth, London and Paris inclusive."

On this hint the journalist turned over a few pages carelessly, and then commenced : —

"'Reached *Bruxelles*'" (Mr. Dodge pronounced this word Brucksills) "'at seven in the evening, and put up at the best house in the place, called the Silver Lamb, which is quite near the celebrated town-house, and, of course, in the very centre of the *beau* quarter. As we did not leave until after breakfast next morning, the reader may expect a description of this ancient capital. It lies altogether on a bit of low, level land—'"

"Nay, Mr. Dodge," interrupted the *soi-disant* Sir George, "I think that must be an error. I have been at Brussels, and I declare, now, it struck me as lying a good deal on the side of a very steep hill !"

"All a mistake, sir, I do assure you. There is no more hill at *Brucksills* than on the deck of this ship. You have been in too great a hurry, my dear Sir George ; that is the way with most travellers ; they do not give themselves time to note particulars. You English especially, my dear Sir George, are a little apt to be precipitate ; and I dare say, you travelled post, with four horses, a mode of getting on by which a man may very well transfer a hill, in his imagination, from one town to another. I travelled chiefly in a *voitury*, which afforded leisure for remarks."

Here Mr. Dodge laughed ; for he felt that he had got the best of it.

"I think you are bound to submit, *Sir George Templemore*," said John Effingham, with an emphasis on the name that raised a smile among his friends ; "Brussels certainly lies on a flat ; and the hill you saw has, doubtless, been brought up with you from Holland in your haste. Mr. Dodge enjoyed a great advantage in his mode of travelling ; for, by entering a town in the evening, and quitting it only in the morning, he had the whole night to look about him."

"That was just my mode of proceeding, Mr. John Effingham : I made it a rule to pass an entire night in every large town I came to."

" A circumstance that will give a double value to your opinions with our countrymen, Mr. Dodge, since they very seldom
give themselves half that leisure when once in motion. I
trust you have not passed over the institutions of Belgium,
sir ; and most particularly the state of society in the capital,
of which you saw so much ? "

" By no means ; here are my remarks on these subjects :
'Belgium, or *The Belges*, as the country is now called, is
one of the upstart kingdoms that have risen in our times ;
and which, from signs that cannot be mistaken, is fated soon
to be overturned by the glorious principles of freedom.
The people are ground down, as usual, by the oppression
of hard task-masters, and bloody-minded priests. The monarch, who is a bigoted Catholic of the House of Saxony,
being a son of a king of that country, and a presumptive heir
to the throne of Great Britain, in right of his first wife,
devoting all his thoughts to miracles and saints. The nobles
form a class by themselves, indulging in all sorts of vices'—
I beg pardon, Sir George, but the truth must be told in our
country, or one had better never speak—' all sorts of vices,
and otherwise betraying the monstrous tendencies of the
system.' "

" Pray, Mr. Dodge," interrupted John Effingham, "have
you said nothing as to the manner in which the inhabitants
relieve the eternal *ennui* of always walking on a level surface ? "

" I am afraid not, sir. My attention was chiefly given to
the institutions, and to the state of society, although I can
readily imagine they must get to be heartily tired of a dead
flat."

" Why, sir, they have contrived to run a street up and
down the roof of the cathedral ; and up and down this street
they trot all hours of the day."

Mr. Dodge looked distrustful ; but John Effingham
maintained his gravity. After a pause the former continued :—

" 'The usages of *Brucksills* are a mixture of Low Dutch
and High Dutch habits, as is the language. The king
being a Polander, and a grandson of Augustus, King of

Poland, is anxious to introduce the customs of the Russians into his court ; while his amiable young queen, who was born in New Jersey when her illustrious father kept the school at Haddonfield, early imbibed those notions of republicanism which so eminently distinguish his Grace the Honorable Louis Philippe Orleans, the present King of the French.' ''

"Nay, Mr. Dodge," said Mr. Sharp, "you will have all the historians ready to cut your throat with envy ! ''

"Why, sir, I feel it a duty not to throw away the great opportunities I have enjoyed ; and America is a country in which an editor may never hope to mystify his readers. We deal with them in facts, Mr. Sharp ; and although this may not be your English practice, we think that the truth is powerful and will prevail. To continue : ' The kingdom of *The Belges* is about as large as the northeast corner of Connecticut, including one town in Rhode Island ; and the whole population may be about equal to that of our tribe of Creek Indians, who dwell in the wilder parts of our State of Georgia.' ''

"This particularity is very convincing," observed Paul ; "and then it has the merit, too, of coming from an eye-witness."

"I will now, gentlemen, return with you to Paris, where I stayed all of three weeks, and of the society of which my knowledge of the language will, of course, enable me to give a still more valuable account."

"You mean to publish these hints, I trust, sir ?" inquired the captain.

"I shall probably collect them, and enlarge them in the way of a book ; but they have already been laid before the American public in the columns of the ' Active Inquirer.' I can assure you, gentlemen, that my colleagues of the press have spoken quite favorably of the letters as they appeared. Perhaps you would like to hear some of their opinions?''

Hereupon Mr. Dodge opened a pocket-book, out of which he took six or eight slips of printed paper, that had been preserved with care, though obviously well thumbed. Opening one, he read as follows ;—

29

"'Our friend Dodge, of the "Active Inquirer," is instructing his readers, and edifying mankind in general, with some
very excellent and pungent remarks on the state of Europe,
which part of the world he is now exploring with some such
enterprise and perseverance as Columbus discovered when
he entered on the unknown waste of the Atlantic. His
opinions meet with our unqualified approbation, being sound,
American, and discriminating. We fancy these Europeans
will begin to think in time that Jonathan has some pretty
shrewd notions concerning themselves, the critturs!' This
was extracted from the 'People's Advocate' a journal edited
with great ability, by Peleg Pond, Esquire, a thorough-
going republican, and a profound observer of mankind."

"In his own parish in particular," quaintly added John
Effingham. "Pray, sir, have you any more of these critical
*morceaux* ?"

"At least a dozen," beginning to read again: "'Steadfast Dodge, Esquire, the editor of the "Active Inquirer," is
now travelling in Europe, and is illuminating the public mind
at home, by letters that are Johnsonian in style, Chester-
fieldian in taste and in knowledge of the world, with the
redeeming qualities of nationality and republicanism and
truth. We rejoice to perceive by these valuable contributions to American literature, that Steadfast Dodge, Esquire,
finds no reason to envy the inhabitants of the Old World
any of their boasted civilization ; but that, on the contrary,
he is impressed with the superiority of our condition over
all countries, every post that he progresses. America has
produced but few men like Dodge ; and even Walter Scott
might not be ashamed to own some of his descriptions. We
hope he may long continue to travel.'"

"*Voitury*," added John Effingham, gravely. "You perceive, gentlemen, how modestly these editors set forth their
intimacy with the traveller—'our friend Dodge, of the
"Active Inquirer,"' and 'Steadfast Dodge, Esquire!'—a
mode of expression that speaks volumes for their own taste,
and their profound deference for their readers."

"We always speak of each other in this manner, Mr.
John Effingham—that is our *esprit du corps*."

" And I should think that there would be an *esprit de corps*
in the public to resist it," observed Paul Blunt.

The distinction was lost on Mr. Dodge, who turned over
to one of his most elaborate strictures on the state of society
in France, with all the self-complacency of besotted ignorance and provincial superciliousness.  Searching out a place
to his mind, this profound observer of men and manners, who
had studied a foreign people, whose language when spoken
was gibberish to him, by travelling five days in a public
coach, and living four weeks in taverns and eating-houses,
besides visiting three theatres, in which he did not understand a single word that was uttered, proceeded to lay before
his auditors the results of his observations.

" ' The state of female society in France is truly awful,' "
he resumed ; " ' the French Revolution, as is universally
known, having left neither decorum, modesty, nor beauty
in the nation.  I walk nightly in the galleries of the Palais
Royal, where I locate myself, and get every opportunity of
observing the peculiarities of ladies of the first taste and
fashion in the metropolis of Europe.  There is one duchess
in particular, whose grace and *embonpoint* have, I confess,
attracted my admiration.  This lady, as my *lacquais de place*
informs me, is sometimes termed *la mère du peuple*, from
her popularity and affability.  The young ladies of France,
judging from the specimens I have seen here—which must
be of the highest class in the capital, as the spot is under
the windows of one of the royal palaces—are by no means
observable for that quiet reserve and modest diffidence that
distinguish the fair among our own young countrywomen ;
but it must be admitted they are remarkable for the manner
in which they walk alone, in my judgment a most masculine
and unbecoming practice.  Woman was not made to live
alone, and I shall contend that she was not made to walk
alone.  At the same time, I confess there is a certain charm
in the manner in which these ladies place a hand in each
pocket of their aprons, and balance their bodies, as they
move like duchesses through the galleries.  If I might humbly suggest, the American fair might do worse than imitate
this Parisian step ; for, as a traveller, I feel it a duty to

exhibit any superior quality that other nations possess. I would also remark on the general suavity of manners that the ladies of quality'" (this word Mr. Dodge pronounced *qua-a-lity*) "'observe in their promenades in and about this genteel quarter of Paris.'"

"The French ladies ought to be much flattered with this notice of them," cried the captain, filling Mr. Dodge's glass. "In the name of truth and penetration, sir, proceed."

"'I have lately been invited to attend a ball in one of the first families of France, which resides in the Rue St. Jacques, or the St. James' of Paris. The company was select, and composed of many of the first persons in the kingdom of *des Français*. The best possible manners were to be seen here, and the dancing was remarkable for its grace and beauty. The air with which the ladies turned their heads on one side, and inclined their bodies in advancing and retiring, was in the first style of the court of Terpsichore. They were all of the very first families of France. I heard one excuse herself for going away so early, as Madame la Duchesse expected her ; and another observed that she was to leave town in the morning with Madame la Vicomtesse. The gentlemen, with few exceptions, were in fancy dresses, appearing in coats, some of sky-blue, some green, some scarlet, and some navy-blue, as fancy dictated, and all more or less laced on the seams ; much in the manner as was the case with the Honorable the King the morning I saw him leave for *Nully*. This entertainment was altogether the best conducted of any I ever attended, the gentlemen being condescending, and without the least pride, and the ladies all grace.'"

"Graces would be more expressive, if you will excuse my suggesting a word, sir," observed John Effingham, as the other paused to take breath.

"'I have observed that the people in most monarchies are abject and low-minded in their deportment. Thus the men take off their hats when they enter churches, although the minister be not present ; and even the boys take off their hats when they enter private houses. This is commencing servility young. I have even seen men kneeling on the cold

pavements of the churches in the most abject manner, and
otherwise betraying the feeling naturally created by slavish
institutions.'"

"Lord help 'em!" exclaimed the captain; "if they
begin so young, what a bowing and kneeling set of blackguards they will get to be in time!"

"It is to be presumed that Mr. Dodge has pointed out the
consequences in the instance of the abject old men mentioned, who probably commenced their servility by entering
houses with their hats off," said John Effingham.

"Just so, sir," rejoined the editor. "I throw in these
little popular traits because I think they show the differ-
ences between nations."

"From which I infer," said Mr. Sharp, "that in your
part of America boys do not take off their hats when they
enter houses, nor men kneel in churches?"

"Certainly not, sir. Our people get their ideas of manliness early; and as for kneeling in churches, we have some
superstitious sects---I do not mention them; but, on the
whole, no nation can treat the house of God more rationally
than we do in America."

"That I will vouch for," rejoined John Effingham; "for
the last time I was at home I attended a concert in one of
them, where an *artiste* of singular nasal merit favored the
company with that admirable piece of conjoined sentiment
and music entitled 'Four-and-twenty fiddlers all in a row!'"

"I'll engage for it," cried Mr. Dodge, swelling with
national pride, "and felt all the time as independent and
easy as if he was in a tavern. O! superstition is quite ex-
tinct in *Ameriky!* But I have a few remarks on the Church
in my notes upon England—perhaps you would like to hear
them?"

"Let me entreat you to read them," said the true Sir
George Templemore, a little eagerly.

"Now, I protest against any illiberality," added the false
Sir George, shaking his finger.

Mr. Dodge disregarded both; but, turning to the place,
he read aloud, with his usual self-complacency and unction :—

"'To-day I attended public worship in St.——Church, Minories. The congregation was composed of many of the first people of England, among whom were present Sir Solomon Snore, formerly HIGH Sheriff of London, a gentleman of the first consideration in the empire, and the celebrated Mr. Shilling, of the firm of Pound, Shilling, and Pence. There was certainly a fine air of polite life in the congregation, but a little too much idolatry. Sir Solomon and Mr. Shilling were both received with distinction, which was very proper, when we remember their elevated rank; but the genuflexions and chanting met with my very unqualified disapprobation.'"

"Sir Solomon and the other personage you mention were a little *pursy*, perhaps," observed Mr. Sharp, "which destroyed their grace."

"I disapprove of all kneeling, on general principles, sir. If we kneel to one, we shall get to kneel to another, and no one can tell where it will end. 'The exclusive manner in which the congregation were seated in pews with sides so high that it was difficult to see your nearest neighbor—and these pews'" (Mr. Dodge pronounced this word *poohs*) "'have often curtains that completely inclose their owners—is a system of selfishness that would not be long tolerated in *Ameriky*.'"

"Do individuals own their pews in America?" inquired Mr. Sharp.

"Often," returned John Effingham; "always, except in those particular portions of the country where it is deemed invidious, and contrary to the public rights, to be better off than one's neighbor, by owning anything that all the community has not a better claim to than its proprietor."

"And cannot the owner of the pew curtain it, with a view to withdraw into himself at public worship?"

"America and England are the antipodes of each other in all these things. I dare say, now, that you have come among us with an idea that our liberty is so very licentious, that a man may read a newspaper by himself?"

"I confess, certainly, to that much," returned Mr. Sharp, smiling.

"We shall teach him better than this, Mr. Dodge, before we let him depart. No, sir; you have very contracted ideas of liberty, I perceive. With us everything is settled by majorities. We eat when the majority eats; drink when the majority drinks; sleep when the majority sleeps; pray when the majority prays. So far from burying ourselves in deep wells of pews, with curtains around their edges, we have raised the floors, amphitheatre fashion, so that everybody can see everybody; have taken away the sides of the pews, which we have converted into free and equal seats, and have cut down the side of the pulpit, so that we can look at the clergyman; but I understand there is actually a project on foot to put the congregation into the pulpit, and the parson into the aisle, by way of letting the latter see that he is no better than he should be. This would be a capital arrangement, Mr. Dodge, for the 'Four-and-twenty fiddlers all in a row.'"

The editor of the "Active Inquirer" was a little distrustful of John Effingham, and he was not sorry to continue his extracts, although he was obliged to bring himself still further under the fire of his assailant.

"'This morning,'" Mr. Dodge resumed, "'I stepped into the coffee-room of the Shovel and Tongs public-house, to read the morning paper, and, taking a seat by the side of a gentleman who was reading the "Times," and, drawing to me the leaves of the journal, so that it would be more convenient to peruse, the man insolently and arrogantly demanded of me, What the devil I meant? This intolerance in the English character is owing to the narrowness of the institutions, under which men come to fancy liberty applies to persons instead of majorities.'"

"You perceive, Mr. Sharp," said John Effingham, "how much more able a stranger is to point out the defects of national character than a native. I dare say, that in indulging your individuality hitherto, you have imagined you were enjoying liberty."

"I fear I have committed some such weakness—but Mr. Dodge will have the goodness to proceed."

The editor complied as follows: "'Nothing has surprised me more than the grovelling propensities of the English on the subject of names. Thus, this very inn, which in America would be styled the Eagle Tavern, or the Oriental or Occidental Hotel, or the Anglo-Saxon Democratical Coffee-House, or some other equally noble and dignified appellation, is called the Shovel and Tongs. One tavern, which might very appropriately be termed The Saloon of Peace, is very vulgarly called Dolly's Chop-House.' "

All the gentlemen, not excepting Mr. Sharp, murmured their disgust at so coarse a taste. But most of the party began now to tire of this pretending ignorance and provincial vulgarity, and, one by one, most of them soon after left the table. Captain Truck, however, sent for Mr. Leach, and these two worthies, with Mr. Dodge and the spurious baronet, sat an hour longer, when all retired to their berths.

# CHAPTER XXXII.

"I'll meet thee at Philippi."

SHAKESPEARE.

HAPPY is the man who arrives on the coast of New York, with the wind at the southward, in the month of November. There are two particular conditions of the weather, in which the stranger receives the most unfavorable impressions of the climate that has been much and unjustly abused, but which two particular conditions warrant all the evil that has been said of it. One is a sweltering day in summer, and the other an autumnal day, in which the dry north wind scarce seems to leave any marrow in the bones.

The passengers of the Montauk escaped both these evils, and now approached the coast with a bland southwest breeze and a soft sky. The ship had been busy in the night, and when the party assembled on deck in the morning, Captain Truck told them that in an hour they should have a sight of the long-desired western continent. As the packet was running in at the rate of nine knots, under topmast and top-gallant studding-sails, being to windward of her port, this was a promise that the gallant vessel seemed likely enough to redeem.

"Toast!" called out the captain, who had dropped into his old habits as naturally as if nothing had occurred, "bring me a coal; and you, Master Steward, look well to the breakfast this morning. If the wind stands six hours longer, I shall have the grief of parting with this good company, and you the grief of knowing you will never set another meal before them. These are moments to awaken sentiment, and yet I never knew an officer of the pantry that did not begin to grin as he drew near his port."

"It is usually a cheerful moment with every one, I believe, Captain Truck," said Eve, "and most of all, should it be one of heartfelt gratitude with us."

"Ay, ay, my dear young lady ; and yet I fancy Mr. Saunders will explain it rather differently. Has no one sung out 'Land,' yet, from aloft, Mr. Leach? The sands of New Jersey ought to be visible before this."

"We have seen the haze of the land since daylight, but not land itself."

"Then, like old Columbus, the flowered doublet is mine —Land, ho !"

The mates and the people laughed, and, looking ahead, they nodded to each other, and the word "Land" passed from mouth to mouth, with the indifference with which mariners first see it in short passages. Not so with the rest. They crowded together, and endeavored to catch a glimpse of the coveted shore, though, with the exception of Paul none could perceive it.

"We must call on you for assistance," said Eve, who now seldom addressed the handsome young seaman without a flush on her own beautiful face ; "for we are all so lubberly that none of us can see that which we so earnestly desire."

"Have the kindness to look over the stock of that anchor," said Paul, glad of an excuse to place himself nearer to Eve, "and you will discover an object on the water."

"I do," said Eve, "but is it not a vessel ?"

"It is ; but a little to the right of that vessel, do you not perceive a hazy object at some elevation above the sea ?"

"The cloud, you mean—a dim, ill-defined, dark body of vapor ?"

"So it may seem to you, but to me it appears to be the land. That is the bluff-like termination of the celebrated highlands of Navesink. By watching it for half an hour, you will perceive its form and surface grow gradually more distinct."

Eve eagerly pointed out the place to Mademoiselle Viefville and her father, and from that moment, for near an hour,

most of the passengers kept it steadily in view.  As Paul
had said, the blue of this hazy object deepened ; then its base
became connected with the water, and it ceased to resemble
a cloud at all.   In twenty more minutes the faces and angles
of the hills became visible, and trees started out of their sides.
In the end a pair of twin lights were seen perched on the
summit.

But the Montauk edged away from these highlands, and
shaped her course towards a long, low spit of sand, that lay
several miles to the northward of them.   In this direction
fifty small sail were gathering into, or diverging from the
pass, their high, gaunt-looking canvas resembling so many
church towers on the plains of Lombardy.   These were
coasters, steering towards their several havens.   Two or
three outward-bound ships were among them, holding their
way in the direction of China, the Pacific Ocean, or Europe.

About nine, the Montauk met a large ship standing on a
bowline, with everything set that would draw, and heaping
the water under her bows.   A few minutes after, Captain
Truck, whose attention had been much diverted from the
surrounding objects by the care of his ship, came near the
group of passengers, and once more entered into conversation.

"Here we are, my dear young lady !" he cried, "within
five leagues of Sandy Hook, which lies hereaway, under our
lee bow ; as pretty a position as heart could wish.   This
lank, hungry-looking schooner in-shore of us, is a news-ves-
sel, and, as soon as she is done with the brig near her, we
shall have her in chase, when there will be a good opportunity to get rid of all our spare lies.   This little fellow to
leeward, who is clawing up towards us, is the pilot ; after
whose arrival my functions cease, and I shall have little to
do but to rattle off Saunders and Toast, and to feed the pigs."

"And who is this gentleman ahead of us, with his main-
topsail to the mast, his courses in the brails, and his helm
a-lee?" asked Paul.

"Some chap who has forgotten his knee-buckles, and has
been obliged to send a boat up to town to hunt for them,"
coolly rejoined the captain, while he sought the focus of the

glass, and levelled it at the vessel in question. The look
was long and steady, and twice Captain Truck lowered the
instrument to wipe the moisture from his own eye. At
length he called out, to the amazement of everybody,—

"Stand by to in all studding-sails, and to wear to the
eastward. Be lively, men, be lively! The eternal Foam,
as I am a miserable sinner!"

Paul laid a hand on the arm of Captain Truck, and
stopped him, as the other was about to spring towards the
forecastle, with a view to aid and encourage his people.

"You forget that we have neither spars nor sails suited
to a chase," said the young man. "If we haul off to seaward on any tack we can try, the corvette will be too much
for us now, and excuse me if I say that a different course
will be advisable."

The captain had learned to respect the opinion of Paul,
and he took the interference kindly.

"What choice remains, but to run down into the very
jaws of the lion," he asked, "or to wear round, and stand
to the eastward?"

"We have two alternatives. We may pass unnoticed, the
ship being so much altered ; or we may haul up on the tack
we are on, and get into shallow water."

"He draws as little as this ship, sir, and would follow.
There is no port short of Egg Harbor, and into that I
should be bashful about entering with a vessel of this size ;
whereas, by running to the eastward, and doubling Montauk,
which would owe us shelter on account of our name, I might
get into the Sound, or New London, at need, and then claim
the sweepstakes, as having won the race."

"This would be impossible, Captain Truck, allow me to
say. Dead before the wind, we cannot escape, for the land
would fetch us up in a couple of hours ; to enter by Sandy
Hook, if known, is impossible, on account of the corvette
and, in a chase of a hundred and twenty miles, we should be
certain to be overtaken."

"I fear you are right, my dear sir, I fear you are right.
The studding-sails are now in, and I will haul up for the
highlands, and anchor under them, should it be necessary.

We can then give this fellow Vattel in large quantities, for I hardly think he will venture to seize us while we have an anchor fast to good American ground."

"How near dare you stand to the shore?"

"Within a mile ahead of us; but to enter the Hook, the bar must be crossed a league or two off."

"The latter is unlucky; but, by all means, get the vessel in with the land; so near as to leave no doubt as to our being in American waters."

"We'll try him, sir, we'll try him. After having escaped the Arabs, the deuce is in it, if we cannot weather upon John Bull! I beg your pardon, Mr. Sharp; but this is a question that must be settled by some of the niceties of the great authorities."

The yards were now braced forward, and the ship was brought to the wind, so as to head in a little to the northward of the bathing-houses on Long Branch. But for this sudden change of course, the Montauk would have run down dead upon the corvette, and possibly might have passed her undetected, owing to the change made in her appearance by the spars of the Dane. So long as she continued "bows on," standing towards them, not a soul on board the Foam suspected her real character, though, now that she acted so strangely, and offered her broadside to view, the truth became known in an instant. The mainyard of the corvette was swung, and her sails were filled on the same course as that on which the packet was steering. The two vessels were about ten miles from the land, the Foam a little ahead, but fully a league to leeward. The latter, however, soon tacked and stood in-shore. This brought the vessels nearly abreast of each other, the corvette a mile or more dead to leeward, and distant now some six miles from the coast. The great superiority of the corvette's sailing was soon apparent to all on board both vessels, for she apparently went two feet to the packet's one.

The history of this meeting, so unexpected to Captain Truck, was very simple. When the gale had abated, the corvette, which had received no damage, hauled up along the African coast, keeping as near as possible to the supposed track of the packet, and failing to fall in with her chase, she had filled away for New York. On making the Hook she took a pilot, and inquired if the Montauk had arrived. From the pilot she learned that the vessel of which she was in quest had not yet made its appearance, and she sent an officer up to the town to communicate with the British consul. On the return of this officer, the corvette stood away from the land, and commenced cruising in the offing. For a week she had now been thus occupied, it being her practice to run close in, in the morning, and to remain hovering about the bar until near night, when she made sail for an offing. When first seen from the Montauk, she had been lying-to, to take in stores sent from the town, and to communicate with a news-boat.

The passengers of the Montauk had just finished their breakfast, when the mate reported that the ship was fast shoaling her water, and that it would be necessary to alter the course in a few minutes, or to anchor. On repairing to the deck, Captain Truck and his companions perceived the land less than a mile ahead of them, and the corvette about half that distance to the leeward, and nearly abeam.

"That is a bold fellow," exclaimed the captain, "or he has got a Sandy Hook pilot on board him."

"Most probably the latter," said Paul: "it is not likely he would be here on this duty, and neglect so simple a precaution."

"I think this would satisfy Mr. Vattel, sir," returned Captain Truck, as the man in the chains sung out, "And a half three!" "Hard up with the helm, and lay the yards square, Mr. Leach."

"Now we shall soon know the virtue of Vattel," said John Effingham, "as ten minutes will suffice to raise the question very fairly."

The Foam put her helm down, and tacked beautifully to the southeast. As soon as the Montauk—which vessel was now running along-shore, keeping in about four fathoms water, the sea being as smooth as a pond—was abeam, the corvette wore round, and began to close with her chase, keeping on her eastern, or outer board.

"Were we an enemy, and a match for that sloop," said Paul, "this smooth water and yard-arm attitude would make quick work."

"Her captain is in the gangway, taking our measure," observed Mr. Truck : "here is the glass; I wish you to examine his face, and tell me if you think him a man with whom the law of nations will avail anything. See the anchor clear, Mr. Leach, for I 'm determined to bring up all standing, if the gentleman intends to renew the old tricks of John Bull on our coast. What do you make of him, Mr. Blunt ? "

Paul did not answer, but laying down the glass, he paced the deck rapidly with the manner of one much disturbed. All observed this sudden change, though no one presumed to comment on it. In the meantime the sloop-of-war came up fast, and in a few minutes her larboard fore-yard-arm was within twenty feet of the starboard main-yard-arm of the Montauk, the two vessels running on parallel lines. The corvette now hauled up her forecourse, and let her topgallant-sails settle on the caps, though a dead silence reigned in her.

" Give me the trumpet," said Captain Truck, stepping to the rail ; " the gentleman is about to give us a piece of his mind."

The English captain, who was easily known by his two epaulettes, also held a trumpet ; but neither of the two commanders used his instrument, the distance being sufficiently near for the natural voice.

"I believe, sir," commenced the man-of-war's-man, "that I have the pleasure to see Captain Truck, of the Montauk, London packet ? "

"Ay, ay ; I 'll warrant you he has my name alongside of John Doe and Richard Roe," muttered Mr. Truck, "spelt as carefully as it could be in a primer. I am Captain Truck, and this is the Montauk. May I ask the name of your vessel, and your own, sir ? "

" This is his Britannic majesty's ship, the Foam, Captain Ducie."

" The Honorable Captain Ducie ! " exclaimed Mr. Sharp.

"I thought I recognized the voice; I know him intimately well."

"Will he stand Vattel?" anxiously demanded Mr. Truck.

"Nay, as for that, I must refer you to himself."

"You appear to have suffered in the gale," resumed Captain Ducie, whose smile was very visible, as he thus addressed them like an old acquaintance. "We fared better ourselves, for I believe we did not part a rope-yarn."

"The ship pitched every stick out of her," returned Captain Truck, "and has given us the trouble of a new outfit."

"In which you appear to have succeeded admirably. Your spars and sails are a size or two too small; but everything stands like a church."

"Ay, ay, now we have got on our new clothes, we are not ashamed to be seen."

"May I ask if you have been in port to do all this?"

"No, sir; picked them up along-shore."

The Honorable Captain Ducie thought he was quizzed, and his manner became a little more cold, though it still retained its gentlemanlike tone.

"I wish much to see you in private, sir, on an affair of some magnitude, and I greatly regret it was not in my power to speak you the night you left Portsmouth. I am quite aware you are in your own waters, and I feel a strong reluctance to detain your passengers when so near their port; but I shall feel it as a particular favor if you will permit me to repair on board for a few minutes."

"With all my heart," cried Captain Truck: "if you will give me room, I will back my main-topsail, but I wish to lay my head off-shore. This gentleman understands Vattel, and we shall have no trouble with him. Keep the anchor clear, Mr. Leach, for 'Fair words butter no parsnips.' Still, he is a gentleman; and, Saunders, put a bottle of the old madeira on the cabin table."

Captain Ducie now left the rigging in which he had stood, and the corvette luffed off to the eastward, to give room to the packet, where she hove-to with her fore-topsail aback. The Montauk followed, taking a position under her lee. A quarter boat was lowered, and in five minutes its oars were tossed at the packet's lee-gangway, when the commander of the corvette ascended the ship's side, followed by a middle-aged man in the dress of a civilian, and a chubby-faced midshipman.

No one could mistake Captain Ducie for anything but a gentleman. He was handsome, well-formed, and about five-and-twenty. The bow he made to Eve, with whose beauty and air he seemed instantly struck, would have become a drawing-room; but he was too much of an officer to permit any further attention to escape him until he had paid his respects to, and received the compliments of, Captain Truck. He then turned to the ladies and Mr. Effingham, and repeated his salutations.

"I fear," he said, "my duty has made me the unwilling instrument of prolonging your passage, for I believe few ladies love the ocean sufficiently, easily to forgive those who lengthen its disagreeables."

"We are old travellers, and know how to allow for the obligations of duty," Mr. Effingham civilly answered.

"That they do, sir," put in Captain Truck; "and it was never my good fortune to have a more agreeable set of passengers. Mr. Effingham, the Honorable Captain Ducie; the Honorable Captain Ducie, Mr. Effingham; Mr. John Effingham, Mam'selle V. A. V." (endeavoring always to imitate Eve's pronunciation of the name); "Mr. Dodge, the Honorable Captain Ducie; the Honorable Captain Ducie, Mr. Dodge."

The Honorable Captain Ducie and all the others, the editor of the "Active Inquirer" excepted, smiled slightly, though they respectively bowed and courtesied; but Mr. Dodge, who conceived himself entitled to be formally introduced to every one he met, and to know all he saw, whether introduced or not, stepped forward promptly, and shook Mr. Ducie very cordially by the hand.

Captain Truck now turned in quest of some one else to introduce; Mr. Sharp stood near the capstan, and Paul had retired as far aft as the hurricane-house.

"I am happy to see you in the Montauk," added Captain

Truck, insensibly leading the other towards the capstan, "and am sorry I had not the satisfaction of meeting you in England. The Honorable Captain Ducie, Mr. Sharp; Mr. Sharp, the Honorable Captain—"

"George Templemore!" exclaimed the commander of the corvette, looking from one to the other.

"Charles Ducie!" exclaimed the *soi-disant* Mr. Sharp.

"Here then is an end of part of my hopes, and we have been on a wrong scent the whole time."

"Perhaps not, Ducie: explain yourself."

"You must have perceived my endeavors to speak you, from the moment you sailed?"

"To speak us!" cried Captain Truck. "Yes, sir, we did observe your endeavors to speak us."

"It was because I was given to understand that one calling himself Sir George Templemore, an impostor, however, had taken passage in this ship; and here I find that we have been misled, by the real Sir George Templemore's having chosen to come this way instead of coming by the Liverpool ship. So much for your confounded fashionable caprice, Templemore, which never lets you know in the morning whether you are to shoot yourself or to get married before night."

"And is this gentleman Sir George Templemore?" pithily demanded Captain Truck.

"For that I can vouch, on the knowledge of my whole life."

"And we know this to be true, and have known it since the day we sailed," observed Mr. Effingham.

Captain Truck was accustomed to passengers under false names, but never before had he been so completely mystified.

"And pray, sir," he inquired of the baronet, "are you a member of Parliament?"

"I have that honor."

"And Templemore Hall is your residence, and you have come out to look at the Canadas?"

"I am the owner of Templemore Hall, and hope to look at the Canadas before I return."

"And," turning to Captain Ducie, "you sailed in quest of another Sir George Templemore—a false one?"

"That is a part of my errand," returned Captain Ducie, smiling.

"Nothing else?—you are certain, sir, that this is the whole of your errand?"

"I confess to another motive," rejoined the other, scarce knowing how to take Captain Truck's question; "but this one will suffice for the present, I hope."

"This business requires frankness. I mean nothing disrespectful; but I am in American waters, and should be sorry, after all, to be obliged to throw myself on Vattel."

"Let me act as mediator," interrupted Sir George Templemore. "Some one has been a defaulter, Ducie; is it not so?"

"This is the simple truth; an unfortunate, but silly young man, of the name of Sandon. He was intrusted with a large sum of the public money, and has absconded with quite forty thousand pounds."

"And this person, you fancy, did me the honor to travel under my name?"

"Of that we are certain. Mr. Green here," motioning to the civilian, "comes from the same office, and traced the delinquent, under your name, some distance on the Portsmouth road. When we heard that a Sir George Templemore had actually embarked in the Montauk, the admiral made no scruple in sending me after the packet. This has been an unlucky mistake for me, as it would have been a feather in the cap of so young a commander to catch the rogue."

"You may choose your feather, sir," returned Captain Truck, "for you will have a right to wear it. The unfortunate young man you seek is, out of question, in this ship."

Captain Truck now explained that there was a person below who had been known to him as Sir George Templemore, and who, doubtless, was the unhappy delinquent sought. But Captain Ducie did not betray the attention or satisfaction that one would have expected from this information, his eye being riveted on Paul, who stood beneath the hurricane-house. When the latter saw that he attracted attention, he advanced slowly, even reluctantly, upon the quarter-deck. The meeting between these two gentlemen was embarrassed, though each maintained his self-possession.

"Mr. Powis, I believe?" said the officer, bowing haughtily.

"Captain Ducie, if I am not mistaken?" returned the other, lifting his hat steadily, though his face became flushed.

The manner of the two, however, was but little noticed at the moment, though all heard the words. Captain Truck drew a long "Whe-e-e-w!" for this was rather more than even he was accustomed to, in the way of masquerades. His eye was on the two gentlemen as they walked aft together, and alone, when he felt a touch upon his arm. It was the little hand of Eve, between whom and the old seaman there existed a good deal of trifling, blended with the most entire good-will. The young lady laughed with her sweet eyes, shook her fair curls, and said mockingly,—

"Mr. Sharp, Mr. Blunt; Mr. Blunt, Mr. Sharp!"

"And were you in the secret all this time, my dear young lady?"

"Every minute of it; from the buoys of Portsmouth to this very spot."

"I shall be obliged to introduce my passengers all over again!"

"Certainly; and I would recommend that each should show a certificate of baptism, or a passport, before you announce his or her name."

"*You* are, at least, the beautiful Miss Effingham, my dear young lady?"

"I 'll not vouch for that, even," said Eve, blushing and laughing.

"That is Mr. John Effingham, I hope!"

"For that I *can* vouch. There are not *two* cousin Jacks on earth."

"I wish I knew what the other business of this gentleman is! He seems amicably disposed, except as regards Mr. Blunt. They looked coldly and suspiciously at each other."

Eve thought so too, and she lost all her desire for pleasantry. Just at this moment Captain Ducie quitted his companion, both touching their hats distantly, and returned to the group he had so unceremoniously left a few minutes before.

"I believe, Captain Truck, you now know my errand," he said, "and can say whether you will consent to my examining the person whom you have mentioned?"

"I know *one* of your errands, sir; you spoke of having *two*."

"Both will find their completion in this ship, with your permission."

"Permission! That sounds well, at least, my dear young lady. Permit me to inquire, Captain Ducie, has either of your errands the flavor of tobacco about it?"

The young man looked surprised, and he began to suspect another mystification.

"The question is so singular, that it is not very intelligible."

"I wish to know, Captain Ducie, if you have anything to say to this ship in the way of smuggling?"

"Certainly not. I am not a custom-house officer, sir, nor on the revenue duty; and I had supposed this vessel a regular packet, whose interest is too plain to enter into such a pursuit."

"You have supposed nothing but the truth, sir; though we cannot always answer for the honesty or discretion of our people. A single pound of tobacco might forfeit this noble ship; and, observing the perseverance with which you have chased me, I was afraid all was not right with the excise."

"You have had a needless alarm then, for my two objects in coming to America are completely answered by meeting with Mr. Powis and the Mr. Sandon, who, I have been given to understand, is in his state-room below."

The party looked at each other, but nothing was said.

" Such being the facts, Captain Ducie, I beg to offer you
every facility, so far as the hospitality of my ship is concerned."

" You will permit us to have an interview with Mr. Sandon ?"

" Beyond a doubt.  I see, sir, you have read Vattel, and
understand the rights of neutrals, or of independent nations.
As this interview most probably will be interesting, you
may desire to have it held in private, and a state-room will
be too small for the purpose.  My dear young lady, will
you have the complaisance to lend us your cabin for half an
hour?"

Eve bowed assent, and Captain Truck then invited the
two Englishmen below.

" My presence at this interview is of little moment," observed Captain Ducie ; " Mr. Green is master of the whole
affair, and I have a matter of importance to arrange with
Mr. Powis.  If one or two of you gentlemen will have the
kindness to be present, and witnesses of what passes between
Mr. Sandon and Mr. Green, it would be a great favor.
Templemore, I may claim this of you ?"

" With all my heart, though it is an unpleasant office to
see guilt exposed.  Should I presume too much by asking
Mr. John Effingham to be of our party ?"

" I was about to make the same request," put in the captain.  " We shall then be two Englishmen and two Yankees,—if Mr. John Effingham will allow me so to style
him ?"

" Until we get within the Hook, Captain Truck, I am a
Yankee ; once in the country, I belong to the Middle States,
if you will allow me the favor to choose."

The last speaker was stopped by a nudge from Captain
Truck, who seized an opportunity to whisper,—

" Make no such distinction between outside and inside, I
beg of you, my dear sir.  I hold that the ship is, at this
identical moment, in the United States of America in a positive sense, as well as by a legal fiction ; and I think Vattel
will bear me out in it."

" Let it pass for that, then.  I will be present at your interview with the fugitive. If the case is not clear against him, he shall be protected."

Things were now soon arranged ; it being decided that Mr. Green, who belonged to one of the English offices, accompanied by the gentlemen just named, should descend to the cabin of Miss Effingham, in order to receive the delinquent ; while Captain Ducie should have his interview with Paul Powis in the state-room of the latter.

The first party went below immediately ; but Captain Ducie remained on deck a minute or two to give an order to the midshipman of his boat, who immediately quitted the Montauk, and pulled to the corvette. During this brief delay Paul approached the ladies, to whom he spoke with a forced indifference, though it was not possible to avoid seeing his concern.

His servant, too, was observed watching his movements with great interest ; and when the two gentlemen went below in company, the man shrugged his shoulders, and actually held up his hands, as one is wont to do at the occurrence of any surprising or distressing circumstance.

## CHAPTER XXXIII.

" Norfolk, for thee remains a heavy doom,
Which I with some unwillingness pron :nce. "
                                        S:AKESPEARE.

THE history of the unfortunate young man, who, after escaping all the hazards and adventures of the passage, was now so unexpectedly overtaken as he was about to reach what he fancied an asylum, was no more than one of those commonplace tissue of events that lead, through vanity and weakness, to crime. His father had held an office under the British government. Marrying late, and leaving a son and daughter just issuing into life at the time of his decease, the situation he had himself filled had been given to the first, out of respect to the unwearied toil of a faithful servant.

The young man was one of those who, without principles or high motives, live only for vanity. Of prominent vices he had none, for there were no salient points in his character on which to hang any quality of sufficient boldness to encourage crime of that nature. Perhaps he owed his ruin to the circumstance that he had a tolerable person, and was six feet high, as much as to any one other thing. His father had been a short, solid, square-built little man, whose ambition never towered above his stature, and who, having entered fairly on the path of industry and integrity early in life, had sedulously persevered in it to the end. Not so with the son. He read so much about aristocratic stature, aristocratic ears, aristocratic hands, aristocratic feet, and aristocratic air, that he was delighted to find that in all these high qualities he was not easily to be distinguished from most of the young men of rank he occasionally saw

riding in the parks or met in the streets; and, though he
very well knew he was not a lord, he began to fancy it a
happiness to be thought one by strangers, for an hour or
two in a week.

His passion for trifles and toys was inherent, and it had
been increased by reading two or three caricatures of fashionable men in the novels of the day, until his happiness
was chiefly centred in its indulgence. This was an ex-
pensive foible; and its gratification ere long exhausted his
legitimate means. One or two trifling and undetected
peculations favored his folly, until a large sum happening
to lie at his sole mercy for a week or two, he made such
an inroad on it as compelled a flight. Having made up his
mind to quit England, he thought it would be as easy to
escape with forty thousand pounds as with the few hundreds he had already appropriated to himself. This capital
mistake was the cause of his destruction; for the magnitude of the sum induced the government to take unusual
steps to recover it, and was the true cause of its having
despatched the cruiser in chase of the Montauk.

The Mr. Green who had been sent to identify the fugitive, was a cold, methodical man, every way resembling the
delinquent's father, whose office-companion he had been,
and in whose track of undeviating attention to business and
negative honesty he had faithfully followed. He felt the
peculation, or robbery, for it scarce deserved a milder term,
to be a reproach on the corps to which he belonged, besides
leaving a stigma on the name of one to whom he had himself looked up as to a model for his own imitation and government. It will readily be supposed, therefore, that this
person was not prepared to meet the delinquent in a very
forgiving mood.

"Saunders," said Captain Truck, in the stern tone with
which he often hailed a top, and which implied that instant
obedience was a condition of his forbearance, "go to the
state-room of the person who has called himself Sir George
Templemore—give him my compliments—be very particular, Mr. Saunders—and say Captain Truck's compliments, and then tell him I expect the honor of his company

in this cabin—the honor of his company, remember, in this cabin. If that don't bring him out of his state-room, I 'll contrive something that shall."

The steward turned up the white of his eyes, shrugged his shoulders, and proceeded forthwith on the errand. He found time, however, to stop in the pantry, and to inform Toast that their suspicions were at least in part true.

"This elucidates the circumstance of his having no attendant with him, like other gentlemen on board, and a wariety of other incidents, that much needed dewelopment. Mr. Blunt, I do collect from a few hints on deck, turns out to be a Mr. Powis, a much genteeler name; and as they spoke to some one in the ladies' cabin as 'Sir George,' I should not be overcome with astonishment should Mr. Sharp actually ewentuate as the real baronite."

There was time for no more, and Saunders proceeded to summon the delinquent.

"This is the most unpleasant part of the duty of a packet-master between England and America," continued Captain Truck, as soon as Saunders was out of sight. "Scarce a ship sails that has not some runaway or other, either in the steerage or in the cabins, and we are often called on to aid the civil authorities on both sides of the water."

"America seems to be a favorite country with our English rogues," observed the office-man, dryly. "This is the third that has gone from our own department within as many years."

"Your department appears to be fruitful of such characters, sir," returned Captain Truck pretty much in the spirit in which the first remark had been given.

Mr. Green was as thorough-going an Englishman as any of his class in the island. Methodical, plodding, industrious, and regular in all his habits, he was honest by rule, and had no leisure or inclination for any other opinions than those which were obtained with the smallest effort. In consequence of the limited sphere in which he dwelt, in a moral sense at least, he was a mass of the prejudices that were most prevalent at the period when he first obtained his notions. His hatred of France was unconquerable, for he

had early learned to consider her as the fast enemy of England ; and as to America, he deemed her to be the general
asylum of all the rogues of his own country—the possession
of a people who had rebelled against their king, because the
restraints of law were inherently disagreeable to them.  This
opinion he had no more wish to proclaim than he felt a
desire to go up and down declaring that Satan was the
father of sin ; but the fact in the one case was just as well
established in his mind as in the other.  If he occasionally
betrayed the existence of these sentiments, it was as a man
coughs ; not because he particularly wishes to cough, but
because he cannot help it.  Finding the subject so naturally
introduced, therefore, it is no wonder if some of his peculiar
notions escaped him in the short dialogue that followed.

"We have our share of bad men, I presume, sir," he
rejoined to the thrust of Captain Truck ; "but the thing
that has most attracted comment with us, is the fact that
they all go to America."

"And we receive our share of rogues, I presume, sir ;
and it is the subject of animadversion with *us* that they all
come from England."

Mr. Green did not feel the force of this retort ; but he
wiped his spectacles as he quietly composed his features
into a look of dignified gravity.

"Some of your most considerable men in America, I believe, sir," he continued, "have been Englishmen who preferred a residence in the colonies to a residence at home."

"I never heard of them," returned the captain ; "will
you have the goodness to name just one?"

"Why, to begin, there was your Washington.  I have
often heard my father say he went to school with him in
Warwickshire, and that he was thought anything but very
clever, too, while he lived in England."

"You perceive, then, that we made something of him
when we got him over on this side ; for he turned out in
the end to be a very decent and respectable sort of person.
Judging from the language of some of your prints, sir, I
should suppose that King William enjoyed the reputation
of being a respectable man in your country?"

Although startled to hear his sovereign spoken of in this irreverent manner, Mr. Green answered promptly,—

"He is a king, sir, and comports himself as a king."

"And all the better, I dare say, for the thrashing he got when a youngster, from the Vermont tailor."

Now Captain Truck quite as religiously believed in this vulgar tale concerning the prince in question, as Mr. Green believed that Washington had commenced his career as one no better than he should be, or as implicitly as Mr. Steadfast Dodge gave credit to the ridiculous history of the schoolmaster of Haddonfield ; all three of the legends belonging to the same high class of historical truths.

Sir George Templemore looked with surprise at John Effingham, who gravely remarked,—

"Elegant extracts, sir, from the vulgar rumors of two great nations. We deal largely in these legends, and you are not quite guiltless of them. I dare say, now, if you would be frank, that you yourself have not always been deaf to the reports against America."

"You surely do not imagine that I am so ignorant of the career of Washington ? "

"Of that I fully acquit you ; nor do I exactly suppose that your present monarch was flogged by a tailor in Vermont, or that Louis Philippe kept school in New Jersey. Our position in the world raises us beyond these elegances ; but do you not fancy some hard things of America, more especially concerning her disposition to harbor rogues, if they come with full pockets ? "

The baronet laughed, but he colored. He wished to be liberal, for he well knew that liberality distinguishes the man of the world, and was an indispensable requisite for a gentleman ; but it is very hard for an Englishman to manifest true liberality towards the *ci-devant* colonies, and this he felt in the whole of his moral system, notwithstanding every effort to the contrary.

"I will confess that case of Stephenson made an unfavorable impression in England," he said with some reluctance.

"You mean the absconding member of Parliament,"

returned John Effingham, with emphasis on the four last words. "You cannot mean to reproach us with his selection of a place of refuge; for he was picked up at sea by a foreign ship that was accidentally bound to America."

"Certainly not with that circumstance, which as you say, was purely an accident. But was there not something extraordinary in his liberation from arrest?"

"Sir George Templemore, there are few Englishmen with whom I would dwell an instant on this subject," said John Effingham gravely; "but you are one of those who have taught me to respect you, and I feel a strong regret whenever I trace any of these mistaken notions in a man of your really generous disposition. A moment's reflection will show you that no civilized society could exist with the disposition you hint at; and as for the particular case you have mentioned, the man did not bring money of any moment with him, and was liberated from arrest on a principle common to all law, where law is stronger than political power, and which principle we derive directly from Great Britain. Depend on it, so far from there being a desire to receive rich rogues in America from other countries, there is a growing indisposition to receive emigrants at all; for their number is getting to be inconvenient to the native population."

"Why does not America pass reciprocal laws with us, then, for the mutual delivery of criminals."

"One insuperable objection to such a reciprocity arises from the nature of our government, as a confederation, since there is no identity in our own criminal jurisprudence; but a chief reason is the exceedingly artificial condition of your society, which is the very opposite of our own, and indisposes the American to visit trifling crimes with so heavy punishment. The American, who has a voice in this matter, you will remember, is not prepared to hang a half-starved wretch for a theft, or to send a man to Botany Bay for poaching. The facility with which men obtain a livelihood in America has hitherto converted most rogues into comparatively honest men when they get there; though I think the day is near, now your own policy is so much improved, when we shall find it necessary in self-defence to change our policy. The common language, as I am told, induces many knaves, who now find England too hot to hold them, to migrate to America."

"Captain Ducie is anxious to know whether Mr. Truck will quietly permit this criminal to be transferred to the Foam."

"I do not think he will permit it at all without being overpowered, if the request be urged in any manner as a right. In that case, he will very properly think that the maintenance of his national character is of more importance than the escape of a dozen rogues. You may put a harsh construction on his course; but I shall think him right in resisting an unjust and an illegal invasion of his rights. I had thought Captain Ducie, however, more peaceably disposed, from what has passed."

"Perhaps I have expressed myself too strongly. I know he would wish to take back the criminal; but I scarce think that he meditates more than persuasion. Ducie is a fine fellow, and every way a gentleman."

"He appears to have found an acquaintance in our young friend, Powis."

"The meeting between these two gentlemen has surprised me, for it can scarcely be termed amicable: and yet it seems to occupy more of Ducie's thoughts just now than the affair of the runaway."

Both now became silent and thoughtful, for John Effingham had too many unpleasant suspicions to wish to speak, and the baronet was too generous to suggest a doubt concerning one whom he felt to be his rival, and whom, in truth, he had begun sincerely to respect, as well as to like. In the meantime, a discussion, which had gradually been growing more dogged and sullen on the part of Mr. Green, and more biting and caustic on that of Captain Truck, was suddenly terminated by the reluctant and tardy appearance of Mr. Sandon.

Guilt, that powerful vindicator of the justice of Providence, as it proves the existence of the inward monitor, conscience was painfully impressed on a countenance that, in general, expressed little beyond a vacant vanity. Although

of a tall and athletic person, his limbs trembled in a way to
refuse to support him, and when he saw the well-known face
of Mr. Green, the unhappy young man sank into a seat,
from a real inability to stand. The other regarded him
sternly through his spectacles, for more than a minute.

"This is a melancholy picture, Henry Sandon," he at
length said. "I am, at least, glad that you do not affect to
brazen out your crime, but that you show a proper sense of
its enormity. What would your upright and painstaking
father have said, had he lived to see his only son in this
situation?"

"He is dead!" returned the young man, hoarsely. "He
is dead, and never can know anything about it."

The unhappy delinquent experienced a sense of frightful
pleasure as he uttered these words.

"It is true, he is dead; but there are others to suffer by
your misconduct. Your innocent sister is living, and feels
all your disgrace."

"She will marry Jones, and forget it all. I gave her a
thousand pounds, and she is married before this."

"In that you are mistaken. She has returned the money,
for she is, indeed, John Sandon's daughter, and Mr. Jones
refuses to marry the sister of a thief."

The delinquent was vain and unreflecting, rather than
selfish, and he had a natural attachment to his sister, the
only other child of his parents. The blow, therefore, fell on
his conscience with double force, coming from this quarter.

"Julia can compel him to marry her," said the startled
brother; "he is bound by a solemn engagement, and the
law will protect her."

"No law can make a man marry against his will, and
your poor, unfortunate sister is too tender of your feelings,
whatever you may have been of hers, to wish to give Mr.
Jones an opportunity of defending himself by exposing your
crime. But this is wasting words, Mr. Sandon, for I am
wanted in the office, where I have left things in the hands
of an inexperienced substitute. Of course you are not prepared to defend an act that your conscience must tell you is
inexcusable."

"I am afraid, Mr. Green, I have been a little thoughtless; or, perhaps, it would be better to say, unlucky."

Mr. Sandon had fallen into the general and delusive mistake of those who err, in supposing himself unfortunate rather than criminal. With an ingenuity that, exercised in a better cause, would have made him a respectable man, he had been endeavoring to excuse his crime to himself, on various pleas of necessity, and he had even got at last to justify his act, by fancying that some trifling wrong he had received, or which he fancied he had received, in the settlement of his own private account, in some measure excused his fraud, although his own denied claim amounted merely to the sum of twenty pounds, and that which he had taken was so large. It was under the influence of such feelings that he made the answer just given.

"A little thoughtless! unlucky! And is this the way, Henry Sandon, that you name a crime that might almost raise your upright father from his grave? But I will speak no more of feelings that you do not seem to understand. You confess to have taken forty thousand pounds of the public money, to which you have no right or claim?"

"I certainly have in my hands some money, which I do not deny belongs to government."

"It is well; and here is my authority to receive it from you. Gentlemen, will you have the kindness to see that my powers are regular and authentic?"

John Effingham and the others cast their eyes over the papers, which seemed to be in rule, and they said as much.

"Now, sir," resumed Mr. Green, "in the first place, I demand the bills you received in London for this money, and your regular indorsement in my favor."

The culprit appeared to have made up his mind to this demand, and, with the same recklessness with which he had appropriated the money to his own use, he was now ready to restore it, without proposing a condition for his own safety. The bills were in his pocket, and seating himself at a table, he made the required indorsement, and handed them to Mr. Green.

"Here are bills for thirty-eight thousand pounds," said

that methodical person, after he had examined the drafts, one by one, and counted their amount; "and you are known to have taken forty thousand. I demand the remainder."

"Would you leave me in a strange country, penniless?" exclaimed the culprit, in a tone of reproach.

"Strange country! penniless!" repeated Mr. Green, looking over his spectacles, first at Mr. Truck, and then at Mr. Sandon. "That to which you have no claim must be restored, though it strip you to the skin. Every pound you have belongs to the public, and to no one else."

"Your pardon, Mr. Green, and green enough you are, if you lay down that doctrine," interrupted Captain Truck, "in which neither Vattel, nor the revised statutes, will bear you out. A passenger cannot remove his effects from a ship, until his passage be first paid."

"That, sir, I dispute, in a question affecting the king's revenues. The claims of government precede all others, and the money that has once belonged to the crown, and which has not been regularly paid away by the crown, is the crown's still."

"Crowns and coronations! Perhaps, Master Green, you think you are in Somerset House at this present speaking?"

Now Mr. Green was so completely a star of a confined orbit, that his ideas seldom described a tangent to their ordinary revolutions. He was so much accustomed to hear of England ruling colonies, the East and the West, Canada, the Cape, and New South Wales, that it was not an easy matter for him to conceive himself to be without the influence of the British laws. Had he quitted home with the intention to emigrate, or even to travel, it is probable that his mind would have kept a more equal pace with his body; but summoned in haste from his desk, and with the office spectacles on his nose, it is not so much a matter of wonder that he hardly realized the truths of his present situation. The man-of-war, in which everything was his majesty's, sustained this feeling, and it was too sudden a change to expect such a man to abandon all his most cherished notions at a moment's warning. The irreverent ex-

31

clamation of Captain Truck shocked him, and he did not
fail to show as much by the disgust pictured in his countenance.

"I am in one of his majesty's packets, sir, I presume,
where, you will permit me to say, a greater deference for the
high ceremonies of the kingdom ought to be found."

"This would make even old Joe Bunk laugh. You are
in a New York liner, sir, over which no majesty has any
control, but their majesties John Griswold & Co. Why, my
good sir, the sea has unsettled your brain!"

Now Mr. Green did know that the United States of
America had obtained their independence, but the whole
proceeding was so mixed up with rebellion, and a French
alliance, in his mind, that he always doubted whether the
new republic had a legal existence at all, and he had been
heard to express his surprise that the twelve judges had not
long since decided this state of things to be unconstitutional,
and overturned the American government by *mandamus*.
His disgust increased, accordingly, as Captain Truck's irrev-
erence manifested itself in stronger terms, and there was
great danger that the harmony, which had hitherto prevailed
between the parties, would be brought to a violent termination.

"The respect for the crown in a truly loyal subject, sir,"
Mr. Green returned, sharply, "is not to be unsettled by the
sea; not in my case, at least, whatever it might have been
in your own."

"My own! why, the devil, sir, do you take me for a
subject?"

"A truant one, I fear, though you may have been born
in London itself."

"Why, my dear sir," said Captain Truck, taking the
other by a button, as if he pitied his hallucination, "you
don't breed such men in London. I came from the river,
which never had a subject in it, or any other majesty than
that of the Saybrook Platform. I begin to understand you,
at least; you are one of those well-meaning men who fancy
the earth but a casing to the island of Great Britain.
Well, I suppose it is more the fault of your education

than of your nature, and one must overlook the mistake. May I ask what is your further wish, in reference to this unhappy young man?"

"He must refund every pound of the public money that remains in his possession."

"That is just, and I say, yea."

"And all who have received from him any portion of this money, under whatever pretences, must restore it to the crown."

"My good sir, you can have no notion of the quantity of champagne and other good things this unfortunate young man has consumed in this ship. Although but a sham baronet, he has fared like a real lord; and you cannot have the heart to exact from the owners the keeping of your rogues."

"Government makes no distinction, sir, and always claims its own."

"Nay, Mr. Green," interrupted Sir George Templemore, "I much question if government would assert a right to money that a peculator or a defaulter fairly spends, even in England; much less does it seem to me it can pretend to the few pounds that Captain Truck has lawfully earned."

"The money has not been lawfully earned, sir. It is contrary to law to assist a felon to quit the kingdom, and I am not certain there are no penalties for that act alone; and as for the public money, it can never legally quit the treasury without the proper office forms."

"My dear Sir George," put in the captain, "leave me to settle this with Mr. Green, who, no doubt, is authorized to give a receipt in full. What is to be done with the delinquent, sir, now that you are in possession of his money?"

"Of course he will be carried back in the Foam, and I mourn to be compelled to say, that he must be left in the hands of the law."

"What, with or without my permission?"

Mr. Green stared, for his mind was precisely one of those which would conceive it to be a high act of audacity in a *ci-devant* colonist to claim the rights of an old country, even did he really understand the legality and completeness of the separation.

" He has committed forgery, sir, to conceal his peculation. It is an awful crime ; but they that commit it cannot
hope to escape the consequences."

" Miserable imposter ! is this true?" Captain Truck
sternly demanded of the trembling culprit.

" He calls an oversight forgery, sir," returned the latter,
huskily. " I have done nothing to affect my life or liberty."

At this moment Captain Ducie, accompanied by Paul
Powis, entered the cabin, their faces flushed, and their manner to each other a little disturbed, though it was formally
courteous. At the same instant, Mr. Dodge, who had been
dying to be present at the secret conference, watched his
opportunity to slip in also.

" I am glad you have come, sir," said Mr. Green, " for
here may be occasion for the services of his majesty's
officers. Mr. Sandon has given up these bills, but two
thousand pounds remain unaccounted for, and I have traced
thirty-five, quite clearly, to the master of this ship, who has
received it in the way of passage money."

" Yes, sir, the fact is as plain as the highlands of Navesink from the deck," dryly added Captain Truck.

" One thousand of this money has been returned by the
defaulter's sister," observed Captain Ducie.

" Very true, sir ; I had forgotten to give him credit for
that."

" The remainder has probably been wasted in those silly
trifles of which you have told me the unhappy man was so
fond, and for which he has bartered respectability and peace
of mind. As for the money paid this ship for the passage,
it has been fairly earned, nor do I know that government
has any power to reclaim it."

Mr. Green heard this opinion with still greater disgust
than he had felt towards the language of Captain Truck,
nor could he very well prevent his feelings escaping him in
words.

" We truly live in perilous times," he muttered, speaking
more particularly to John Effingham, out of respect to his
appearance, " when the scions of the nobility entertain notions
so loose. We have vainly fancied in England that the enor-

mities of the French revolution were neutralized by Billy Pitt ; but, sir, we still live in perilous times, for the disease has fairly reached the higher classes. I hear that designs are seriously entertained against the wigs of the judges and bishops, and the next thing will be the throne ! All our venerable institutions are in danger."

" I should think the throne might indeed be in danger, sir," returned John Effingham, gravely, " if it reposes on wigs."

" It is my duty, Captain Truck," continued Captain Ducie, who was a man so very different from his associate that he scarcely seemed to belong to the same species, " to request you will deliver to us the person of the culprit, with his effects, when we can relieve you and your passengers from the pain of witnessing any more of this unpleasant scene."

At the sound of the delivery of his person, all the danger of his situation rushed forcibly before the imagination of the culprit. His face flushed and became pale, and his legs refused to support him, though he made a desperate effort to rise.

After an instant of silence, he turned to the commander of the corvette, and, in piteous accents, appealed to him for mercy.

" I have been punished severely already," he continued, as his voice returned, " for the savage Arabs robbed me of everything I had of any value. These gentlemen know that they took my dressing-case, several other curious and valuable articles for the toilet, and nearly all my clothes."

" This man is scarcely a responsible being," said John Effingham, " for a childish vanity supplies the place of principles, self-respect, and duty. With a sister scorned on account of his crimes, conviction beyond denial, and a dread punishment staring him in the face, his thoughts still run on trifles."

Captain Ducie gave a look of pity at the miserable young man, and, by his countenance, it was plain to see that he felt no relish for his duty. Still, he felt himself bound to urge on Captain Truck a compliance with his request. The

master of the packet was a good deal divided by an inherent
dislike of seeming to yield anything to a British naval
officer, a class of men whom he learned in early life most
heartily to dislike; his kind feelings towards this particular
specimen of the class; a reluctance to give a man up to a
probable death, or some other severe punishment; and a
distaste to being thought desirous of harboring a rogue. In
this dilemma, therefore, he addressed himself to John Effingham for counsel.

"I should be pleased to hear your opinion, sir, on this
matter," he said, looking at the gentleman just named, "for
I own myself to be in a category. Ought we, or not, to
deliver up the culprit?"

"*Fiat justitia ruat cœlum*," answered John Effingham,
who never fancied any one could be ignorant of the meaning of these familiar words.

"That I believe indeed to be Vattel," said Captain
Truck; "but exceptions alter rules. This young man has
some claims on us on account of his conduct when in front
of the Arabs."

"He fought for himself, sir, and has the merit of preferring liberty in a ship to slavery in a desert."

"I think with Mr. John Effingham," observed Mr.
Dodge, "and can see no redeeming quality in his conduct
on that occasion. He did what we all did; or, as Mr.
John Effingham has so pithily expressed it, he preferred
liberty in our company to being an Arab's slave."

"You will not deliver me up, Captain Truck!" exclaimed
the delinquent. "They will hang me, if once in their power.
O! you will not have the heart to let them hang me!"

Captain Truck was startled at this appeal, but he sternly
reminded the culprit that it was too late to remember the
punishment when the crime was committed.

"Never fear, Mr. Sandon," said the office-man with a
sneer; "these gentlemen will take you to New York, for
the sake of the thousand pounds, if they can. A rogue is
pretty certain of a kind reception in America, I hear."

"Then, sir," exclaimed Captain Truck, "you had better
go in with us."

"Mr. Green, Mr. Green, this is indiscreet, to call it by
no worse a term," interposed Captain Ducie, who, while he
was not free from a good deal of the prejudices of his companion, was infinitely better bred, and more in the habit of
commanding himself.

"Mr. John Effingham, you have heard this wanton insult,"
continued Captain Truck, suppressing his wrath as well as
he could : " in what manner ought it to be resented?"

"Command the offender to quit your ship instantly,"
said John Effingham firmly.

Captain Ducie started, and his face flushed; but disre-
garding him altogether, Captain Truck walked deliberately
up to Mr. Green, and ordered him to go into the corvette's
boat.

" I shall allow of neither parley nor delay," added the
exasperated old seaman, struggling to appear cool and dignified, though his vocation was little for the latter.   "Do
me the favor, sir, to permit me to see you into your boat,
sir.   Saunders, go on deck, and tell Mr. Leach to have the
side manned—with *three* side-boys, Saunders; and now I
ask it as the greatest possible favor, that you will walk on
deck with me, or—or—damn me, but I'll drag you there,
neck and heels ! "

It was too much for Captain Truck to seem calm when
he was in a towering passion, and the outbreak at the close
of this speech was accompanied by a gesture with a hand
which was open, it is true, but from which none of the arts
of his more polite days could erase the knobs and hue that
had been acquired in early life.

"This is strong language, sir, to use to a British officer,
under the guns of a British cruiser," exclaimed the commander of the corvette.

" And his was strong language to use to a man in his
own country and in his own ship.   To you, Captain Ducie,
I have nothing to say, unless it be to say you are welcome.
But your companion has indulged in a coarse insult on my
country, and damn me if I submit to it, if I never see
St. Catherine's Docks again.   I had too much of this when
a young man, to wish to find it repeated while an old one."

Captain Ducie bit his lip, and he looked exceedingly vexed. Although he had himself blindly imbibed the notion that America would gladly receive the devil himself if he came with a full pocket, he was shocked with the coarseness that would throw such an innuendo into the very faces of the people of the country. On the other hand, his pride as an officer was hurt at the menace of Captain Truck, and all the former harmony of the scene was threatened with a sudden termination. Captain Ducie had been struck with the gentlemanlike appearance of both the Effinghams, to say nothing of Eve, the instant his foot touched the deck of the Montauk, and he now turned with a manner of reproach to John Effingham, and said,—

"Surely, sir, *you* cannot sustain Mr. Truck in his extraordinary conduct!"

"You will pardon me if I say I do. The man has been permitted to remain longer in the ship than I would have suffered."

"And, Mr. Powis, what is your opinion?"

"I fear," said Paul, smiling coldly, "that I should have knocked him down on the spot."

"Templemore, are you, too, of this way of thinking?"

"I fear the speech of Mr. Green has been without sufficient thought. On reflection he will recall it."

But Mr. Green would sooner part with life than part with a prejudice, and he shook his head in the negative in a way to show that his mind was made up.

"This is trifling," added Captain Truck. "Saunders, go on deck, and tell Mr. Leach to send down through the skylight a single whip, that we may whip this polite personage on deck; and, harkee, Saunders, let there be another on the yard, that we may send him into his boat like an anker of gin!"

"This is proceeding too far," said Captain Ducie. "Mr. Green, you will oblige me by retiring; there can be no suspicion cast on a vessel-of-war for conceding a little to an unarmed ship."

"A vessel of war should not insult an unarmed ship, sir!" rejoined Captain Truck, pithily.

Captain Ducie again colored; but as he had decided on his course, he had the prudence to remain silent. In the meantime Mr. Green sullenly took his hat and papers, and withdrew into the boat; though, on his return to London, he did not fail to give such a version of the affair as went altogether to corroborate all his own and his friends' previous notions of America; and, what is equally singular, he religiously believed all he had said on the occasion.

"What is now to be done with this unhappy man?" inquired Captain Ducie when order was a little restored.

The misunderstanding was an unfortunate affair for the culprit. Captain Truck felt a strong reluctance to deliver him up to justice after all they had gone through together; but the gentlemanlike conduct of the English commander, the consciousness of having triumphed in the late conflict, and a deep regard for the law, united on the other hand to urge him to yield the unfortunate and weak-minded offender to his own authorities.

"You do not claim a right to take him out of an American ship by violence, if I understand you, Captain Ducie?"

"I do not. My instructions are merely to demand him."

"That is according to Vattel. By demand you mean, to request, to ask for him?"

"I mean to request, to ask for him," returned the Englishman, smiling.

"Then take him, of God's name; and may your laws be more merciful to the wretch than he has been to himself, or to his kin."

Mr. Sandon shrieked, and he threw himself abjectly on his knees between the two captains, grasping the legs of both.

"O! hear me! hear me!" he exclaimed in a tone of anguish. "I have given up the money, I will give it all up! all to the last shilling, if you will let me go! You, Captain Truck, by whose side I have fought and toiled, you will not have the heart to abandon me to these murderers!"

"It's d——d hard!" muttered the captain, actually wiping his eyes; "but it is what you have drawn upon yourself, I fear. Get a good lawyer, my poor fellow, as soon as you arrive; and it's an even chance, after all, that you go free !"

"Miserable wretch !" said Mr. Dodge, confronting the still kneeling and agonized delinquent. "Wretch ! these are the penalties of guilt. You have forged and stolen, acts that meet with my most unqualified disapprobation, and you are unfit for respectable society. I saw from the very first what you truly were, and I permitted myself to associate with you, merely to detect and expose you, in order that you might not bring disgrace on our beloved country. An imposter has no chance in America ; and you are fortunate in being taken back to your own hemisphere."

Mr. Dodge belonged to a tolerably numerous class, that is quaintly described as being "law honest " ; that is to say, he neither committed murder nor petty larceny. When he was guilty of moral slander, he took great care that it should not be legal slander ; and, although his whole life was a tissue of mean and baneful vices, he was quite innocent of all those enormities that usually occupy the attention of a panel of twelve men. This, in his eyes, raised him so far above less prudent sinners as to give him a right to address his quondam associate as has been just related. But the agony of the culprit was past receiving an increase from this brutal attack ; he merely motioned the coarse-minded sycophant and demagogue away, and continued his appeals to the two captains for mercy. At this moment Paul Powis stepped up to the editor, and in a low but firm voice ordered him to quit the cabin.

"I will pray for you—be your slave—do all you ask if you will not give me up !" continued the culprit, fairly writhing in his agony. "O ! Captain Ducie, as an English nobleman, have mercy on me."

"I must transfer the duty to subordinates," said the English commander, a tear actually standing in his eye. "Will you permit a party of armed marines to take this unhappy being from your ship, sir ? "

"Perhaps this will be the best course, as he will yield

only to a show of force. I see no objection to this, Mr.
John Effingham?''

"None in the world, sir. It is your object to clear your
ship of a delinquent, and let those among whom he committed the fault be the agents.''

"Ay, ay, this is what Vattel calls the comity of nations.
Captain Ducie, I beg you will issue your orders.''

The English commander had foreseen some difficulty, and,
in sending away his boat when he came below, he had sent
for a corporal's guard. These men were now in a cutter,
near the ship, lying off on their oars, in a rigid respect to
the rights of a stranger, however,—as Captain Truck was
glad to see, the whole party having gone on deck as soon
as the arrangement was settled. At an order from their
commander, the marines boarded the Montauk, and proceeded below in quest of their prisoner.

Mr. Sandon had been left alone in Eve's cabin; but as
soon as he found himself at liberty, he hurried into his own
state-room. Captain Truck went below, while the marines
were entering the ship; and, having passed a minute in his
own room, he stepped across the cabin, to that of the culprit.
Opening the door without knocking, he found the unhappy
man in the very act of applying a pistol to his head, his own
hand being just in time to prevent the catastrophe. The
despair portrayed in the face of the criminal prevented reproach or remonstrance, for Captain Truck was a man of
few words when it was necessary to act. Disarming the
intended suicide, he coolly counted out to him thirty-five
pounds, the money paid for his passage, and told him to
pocket it.

"I received this on condition of landing you safe in New
York," he said; "and as I shall fail in the bargain, I
think it no more than just to return you the money. It
may help you on the trial.''

"Will they hang me?" asked Mr. Sandon hoarsely, and
with an imbecility like that of an infant.

The appearance of the marines prevented reply, the prisoner was secured, his effects were pointed out, and his person

was transferred to the boat with the usual military promptitude. As soon as this was done the cutter pulled away from the packet, and was soon hoisted in again on the corvette's deck. That day month the unfortunate victim of a passion for trifles committed suicide in London, just as they were about to transfer him to Newgate ; and six months later his unhappy sister died of a broken heart.

# CHAPTER XXXIV.

"We'll attend you there.
Where, if you bring not Marcius, we'll proceed
In our first way."

*Coriolanus.*

EVE and Mademoiselle Viefville had been unwilling spectators of a portion of the foregoing scene, and Captain Ducie felt a desire to apologize for the part he had been obliged to act in it. For this purpose he had begged his friend the baronet to solicit a more regular introduction than that received through Captain Truck.

"My friend Ducie is solicitous to be introduced, Miss Effingham, that he may urge something in his own behalf, concerning the commotion he has raised among us."

A graceful assent brought the young commander forward, and as soon as he was named he made a very suitable expression of his regret to the ladies, who received it, as a matter of course, favorably.

"This is a new duty to me, the arrest of criminals," added Captain Ducie.

The word *criminals* sounded harsh to the ear of Eve, and she felt her cheek becoming pale.

"Much as we regret the cause." observed the father, "we can spare the person you are about to take from us without much pain; for *we* have known him for an impostor from the moment he appeared. Is there not some mistake? That is the third trunk that I have seen passed into the boat marked P. P."

Captain Ducie smiled, and answered,—

"You will call it a bad pun if I say P. P. see," pointing to Paul, who was coming from the cabin attended by Captain Truck. The latter was conversing warmly, gesticulating towards the corvette, and squeezing his companion's hand.

"Am I to understand," said Mr. Effingham earnestly, "that Mr. Powis, too, is to quit us?"

"He does me the favor, also,"—Captain Ducie's lip curled a little at the word *favor*,—"to accompany me to England."

Good breeding and intense feeling caused a profound silence, until the young man himself approached the party. Paul endeavored to be calm, and he even forced a smile as he addressed his friends.

"Although I escape the honors of a marine guard," he said, and Eve thought he said it bitterly, "I am also to be taken out of the ship. Chance has several times thrown me into your society, Mr. Effingham—Miss Effingham—and, should the same good fortune ever again occur, I hope I may be permitted to address you at once as an old acquaintance."

"We shall always entertain a most grateful recollection of your important services, Mr. Powis," returned the father; "and I shall not cease to wish that the day may soon arrive when I can have the pleasure of receiving you under my own roof."

Paul now offered to take the hand of Mademoiselle Viefville, which he kissed gallantly. He did the same with Eve's, though she felt him tremble in the attempt. As these ladies had lived much in countries in which this graceful mode of salutation prevails among intimates, the act passed as a matter of course.

With Sir George Templemore, Paul parted with every sign of good-will. The people, to whom he had caused a liberal donation to be made, gave him three cheers, for they understood his professional merits at least; and Saunders, who had not been forgotten, attended him assiduously to the side of the ship. Here Mr. Leach called, "The Foams away!" and Captain Ducie's gig was manned. At the

gangway Captain Truck again shook Paul cordially by the
hand, and whispered something in his ear.

Everything being now ready, the two gentlemen prepared
to go into the boat.   As Eve watched all that passed with
an almost breathless anxiety, a little ceremonial that now
took place caused her much pain.   Hitherto the manner of
Captain Ducie, as respected his companion, had struck her
as equivocal.   At times it was haughty and distant, while
at others it had appeared more conciliatory and kind.   All
these little changes she had noted with a jealous interest,
and the slightest appearance of respect or of disrespect was
remarked, as if it could furnish a clue to the mystery of
the whole procedure.

"Your boat is ready, sir," said Mr. Leach, stepping out
of the gangway to give way to Paul, who stood nearest to
the ladder.

The latter was about to proceed, when he was touched
lightly on the shoulder by Captain Ducie, who smiled, Eve
thought haughtily, and intimated a desire to precede him.
Paul colored, bowed, and falling back, permitted the English
officer to enter his own boat first.

"*Apparemment le capitaine. Inglais est un peu sans façon
— Voilà qui est poli!*" whispered Mademoiselle Viefville.

"These commanders of vessels of war are little kings,"
quietly observed Mr. Effingham, who had unavoidably
noticed the whole procedure.

The gig was soon clear of the ship, and both the gentlemen repeated their adieus to those on deck.   To reach the
corvette, to enter her, and to have the gig swinging on her
quarter occupied but five minutes.

Both ships now filled away, and the corvette began to
throw out one sheet of cloth after another until she was
under a cloud of canvas, again standing to the eastward
with studding-sails alow and aloft.   On the other hand the
Montauk laid her yards square, and ran down to the Hook.
The pilot from the corvette had been sent on board the
packet, and, the wind standing, by eleven o'clock the latter
had crossed the bar.   At this moment the low, dark stern

of the Foam resembled a small black spot on the sea sustaining a pyramid of cloud.

"You were not on deck, John, to take leave of our young friend Powis," said Mr. Effingham, reproachfully.

"I do not wish to witness a ceremony of this extraordinary nature. And yet it might have been better if I had."

"Better, cousin Jack!"

"Better. Poor Monday committed to my care certain papers that, I fancy, are of moment to some one, and these I intrusted to Mr. Powis, with a view to examine them together when we should get in. In the hurry of parting, he has carried them off."

"They may be reclaimed by writing to London," said Mr. Effingham quietly. "Have you his address?"

"I asked him for it, but the question appeared to embarrass him."

"Embarrass, cousin Jack!"

"Embarrass, Miss Effingham."

The subject was now dropped by common consent. A few moments of awkward silence succeeded, when the interest inseparable from a return home, after an absence of years, began to resume its influence, and objects on the land were noticed. The sudden departure of Paul was not forgotten, however, for it continued the subject of wonder with all for weeks, though little more was said on the subject.

The ship was soon abreast of the Hook, which Eve compared, to the disadvantage of the celebrated American haven, with the rocky promontories and picturesque towers of the Mediterranean.

"This portion of our bay, at least, is not very admirable," she said, "though there is a promise of something better above."

"Some New York cockney, who has wandered from the crackling heat of his Nott stove, has taken it into his poetical imagination to liken this bay to that of Naples," said John Effingham; and his fellow-citizens greedily swallow the absurdity, although there is scarcely a single feature in common to give the foolish opinion value."

"But the bay above *is* beautiful!"

"Barely pretty; when one has seen it alone, for many years, and has forgotten the features of other bays, it does not appear amiss; but *you*, fresh from the bolder landscapes of Southern Europe, will be disappointed."

Eve, an ardent admirer of nature, heard this with regret, for she had as much confidence in the taste of her kinsman as in his love of truth. She knew he was superior to the vulgar vanity of giving an undue merit to a thing because he had a right of property in it; was a man of the world, and knew what he uttered on all such matters; had not a particle of provincial admiration or of provincial weakness in his composition; and, although as ready as another, and far more able than most, to defend his country and her institutions from the rude assault of her revilers, that he seldom made the capital mistake of attempting to defend a weak point.

The scenery greatly improved, in fact, however, as the ship advanced; and while she went through the pass called the Narrows, Eve expressed her delight. Mademoiselle Viefville was in ecstasies, not so much with the beauties of the place as with the change from the monotony of the ocean to the movement and liveliness of the shore.

"You think this noble scenery?" said John Effingham.

"As far from it as possible, cousin Jack. I see much meanness and poverty in the view, but at the same time it has fine parts. The islands are not Italian, certainly; nor these hills, nor yet that line of distant rocks; but, together, they form a pretty bay, and a noble one in extent and uses, at least."

"All this is true. Perhaps the earth does not contain another port with so many advantages for commerce. In this respect I think it positively unequalled; but I know a hundred bays that surpass it in beauty. Indeed, in the Mediterranean it is not easy to find a natural haven that does not."

Eve was too fresh from the gorgeous coast of Italy to be in ecstasies with the meagre villages and villas that more or less lined the bay of New York; but when they reached a point where the view of the two rivers, separated by the

town, came before them, with the heights of Brooklyn—
heights comparatively if not positively—on one side, and the
receding wall of the palisadoes on the other, Eve insisted
that the scene was positively fine.

"You have well chosen your spot," said John Effingham ;
"but even this is barely good. There is nothing surpassing
about it."

"But it is home, cousin Jack."

"It is *home*, Miss Effingham," he answered, gaping ;
"and as you have no cargo to sell, I fear you will find it an
exceedingly dull one."

"We shall see—we shall see," returned Eve, laughing.
Then, looking about her for a few minutes, she added, with
a manner in which real and affected vexation were prettily
blended, "In one thing I do confess myself disappointed."

"You will be happy, my dear, if it be in only one."

"These smaller vessels are less picturesque than those I
have been accustomed to see."

"You have hit upon a very sound criticism, and, by going
a little deeper into the subject, you will discover a singular
deficiency in this part of an American landscape. The
great height of the spars of all the smaller vessels of these
waters, when compared with the tame and level coast, river
banks, and the formation of the country in general, has the
effect to diminish still more the outlines of any particular
scene. Beautiful as it is, beyond all competition, the Hud-
son would seem still more so, were it not for these high and
ungainly spars."

The pilot now began to shorten sail, and the ship drew
into that arm of the sea which, by a misnomer peculiarly
American, it is the fashion to call the East River. Here our
heroine candidly expressed her disappointment, the town
seeming mean and insignificant. The Battery, of which she
remembered a little, and had heard so much, although beautifully placed, disappointed her, for it had neither the extent
and magnificence of a park nor the embellishments and luxurious shades of a garden. As she had been told that her
countrymen were almost ignorant of the art of landscape
gardening, she was not so much disappointed with this spot,

however, as with the air of the town, and the extreme filth
and poverty of the quays. Unwilling to encourage John
Effingham in his disposition to censure, she concealed her
opinions for a time.

" There is less improvement here than even I expected "
said Mr. Effingham, as they got into a coach on the wharf.
" They had taught me, John, to expect great improvements."

" And great, very great improvements have been made in
your absence. If you could see this place as you knew it in
youth, the alterations would seem marvellous."

" I cannot admit this. With Eve, I think the place mean
in appearance, rather than imposing, and so decidedly provincial as not to possess a single feature of a capital."

" The two things are not irreconcilable, Ned, if you will
take the trouble to tax your memory. The place *is* mean
and provincial, but thirty years since it was still meaner and
more provincial than it is to-day. A century hence it will
begin to resemble a large European town."

" What odious objects these posts are ! " cried Eve.

" They give the streets the air of a village, and I do not
see their uses."

" These posts are for awnings, and of themselves they
prove the peculiar country character of the place. If you
will reflect, however, you will see it could not well be otherwise. This town to-day contains near three hundred thousand souls, two thirds of whom are in truth emigrants from
the interior of our own or of some foreign country ; and
such a collection of people cannot in a day give a town any
other character than that which belongs to themselves. It
is not a crime to be provincial and rustic ; it is only ridiculous to fancy yourselves otherwise, when the fact is apparent."

" The streets seem deserted. I had thought New York a
crowded town."

" And yet this is Broadway—a street that every American will tell you is so crowded as to render respiration
impossible."

" John Effingham excepted," said Mr. Effingham, smiling.

" Is *this* Broadway ? " cried Eve, fairly appalled.

" Beyond a question. Are you not smothered ? "

Eve continued silent until the carriage reached the door of her father's house. On the other hand, Mademoiselle Viefville expressed herself delighted with all she saw—a circumstance that might have deceived a native of the country, who did not know how to explain her raptures. In the first place she was a Frenchwoman, and accustomed to say pleasant things ; then she was just relieved from an element she detested, and the land was pleasant in her eyes. But the principal reason is still in reserve : Mademoiselle Viefville, like most Europeans, had regarded America not merely as a provincial country, and this without a high standard of civilization for a province, as the truth would have shown, but as a semi-barbarous quarter of the world ; and the things she saw so much surpassed her expectations that she was delighted, as it might be, by contrast.

As we shall have a future occasion to speak of the dwelling of Mr. Effingham, and to accompany the reader much further in the histories of our several characters, we shall pass over the feelings of Eve when fairly established that night under her own roof. The next morning, however, when she descended to breakfast, she was met by John Effingham, who gravely pointed to the following paragraph in one of the daily journals :—

"The Montauk, London packet, which has been a little out of time, arrived yesterday, as reported in our marine news. This ship has met with various interesting adventures, that, we are happy to hear, will shortly be laid before the world by one of her passengers, a gentleman every way qualified for the task. Among the distinguished persons arrived in this ship is our contemporary, Steadfast Dodge, Esquire, whose amusing and instructing letters from Europe are already before the world. We are glad to hear that Mr. Dodge returns home better satisfied than ever with his own country, which he declares to be quite good enough for him. It is whispered that our literary friend has played a conspicuous part in some recent events on the coast of

Africa, though his extreme and well-known modesty renders him indisposed to speak of the affair ; but we forbear ourselves, out of respect to a sensibility that we know how to esteem !

" His Britannic majesty's ship Foam, whose arrival we noticed a day or two since, boarded the Montauk off the Hook, and took out of her two criminals, one of whom, we are told, was a defaulter for one hundred and forty thousand pounds, and the other a deserter from the king's service, though a scion of a noble house. More of this to-morrow."

The morrow never came, for some new incident took the place of the promised narration ; a people who do not give themselves time to eat, and with whom " go ahead " has got to be the substitute of even religion, little troubling themselves to go back twenty-four hours in search of a fact.

" This must be a base falsehood, cousin Jack," said Eve, as she laid down the paper, her brow flushed with an indignation that, for the moment, proved too strong for even apprehension.

" I hope it may turn out to be so, and yet I consider the affair sufficiently singular to render suspicion at least natural."

How Eve both thought and acted in the matter, will appear hereafter.

THE END.

CPSIA information can be obtained at www.ICGtesting.com
Printed in the USA
LVOW051955070313

323223LV00001B/50/P

9 781443 702096